THE BEAM SERIES

MOONBEAM

A DRAGONIAN SERIES NOVEL

ADRIENNE WOODS

Fire Quill Publishing
www.firequillpublishing.com

Formatting done by FQP Design

Manufactured in South Africa and the USA
First Fire Quill Publishing edition November 2016

ISBN: 0-9969748-4-9
ISBN-13: 978-0-9969748-4-4

EDICATION

TO JORDAN, JAYDEN, MADDISON AND JAMIE-
LEIGH.
OUR FUTURE.

.

OTHER NOVELS

FIREBOLT
THUNDERLIGHT
FROSTBITE
MOONBEAM
STARLIGHT

NOVELLAS

VENOM
POISON

BEAM SERIES
MOONBEAM
STARBEAM (COMING 2017)
DARKBEAM PART I (COMING 2017)
DARKBEAM PART II (COMING 2018)

ACKNOWLEGEMENT

I would just like to say thank you to the number one in my life. The big guy Upstairs. Thank you for choosing me to write this story, for helping me find new ways of making this series last a teeny bit longer, for guiding me when I hit dead ends, for truly loving me like nobody else ever would. I'm nothing without YOU. NOTHING.

Second, my family. Heinrich my husband, who went many times to bed without me as I write and craft my work. To my two beautiful daughters, still too little to enjoy mommy's dragons. Without you, my life would be dull and meaningless.

To Fire Quill Publishing: Anika, the best assistant I know. I ever had. You are more than just an assistant.

To Hillery, still a true Paegeian. Sorry that I made your eyes almost feel as if they were going to pop out.

To Jessie, I'm so honored to have you join the Dragonian Team. I can't wait to see what you are going to do with the other novels. I've learned as a writer so much from you already.

To Joemel, again for truly capturing my imagination and what I had in my mind for Moonbeams' cover. Truly breathtaking.

To all my fans. Without you, this series would not have been anywhere. I can't express enough how blessed I am to have you as fans of this series.

I hope you are going to enjoy Moonbeam, which is a story I always wondered about, but then we wouldn't have the Dragonian series. So hope you love this as much as I enjoyed writing this story.

ONE

4 Millennia later

THEO

It's been said that the greatest love that ever existed is God's love. He sent his only son to die for our sins. A son who did no evil and never acted with evil intent. A son who rose from death and lived for eternity. They say that everyone who believes in him will earn that same eternal life.

My great-great-great-great-Nanna and her beloved Rubicon shared the second-deepest love ever known, a love that lasted thousands of years. They would've died for one another without a second thought. You don't find a love like that anymore.

The saddest part was that she had to say goodbye to him 1,022 years ago. It was his time, but because he had imparted his essence to her, she couldn't go with him.

She was in some ways stronger than him.

Everyone thought that she would die of a broken heart. But her family, a tree with many snaking branches, loved her so much—and she them—that they brought a spark back into her. She found a way to make peace with the departure of her Rubicon. She was content to wait for the day when he would come and fetch her.

I never knew the Rubicon my Nanna spoke of personally, but I'd heard many stories about him.

I was born only twenty-eight years ago, but I knew what he looked like because her face lit up every time I entered her room. I was always begging her to tell me stories about the "Big Guy." That was what she always called him.

Her eyes sparkled as she wove her stories. I knew she loved him truly, even after all this time. I wanted to have a love like that one day. I wished for someone to love me the way she still loved the Rubicon.

When I was six, a very special egg hatched.

Nanna could hear the thoughts of the dragon inside that egg before the shell even cracked. It was the new Rubicon entering this world. She still had a connection with it, even after the previous one died.

The new Rubicon's name was Morgan. She was the ugliest baby dragon I'd ever seen. But Nanna had stared at her with so much love and admiration.

She'd helped Morgan into this world, guided her to the light. She treasured her always. Soon she saw that I was the lucky one who would claim her when her sixteenth birthday came.

Even the Viden couldn't see that. So many of them had come and gone, all of them Moon-Bolts. Their Foretellings had guided many to do great things. Some

Foretellings magically appeared in a book. These books were housed inside the library. Nanna had her own special book. The words didn't appear magically, but what she said always came true. She always spoke clearly, never in tongues and never in riddles.

She had guided our family through all of our Foretellings. The Viden's mind couldn't glimpse of our bloodline's futures. Only Nanna and a Moon-Bolt named George, who had died thousands of years ago, could do that.

George had been one of their greatest friends. When he died, his Dragonian left this world a few days later. They too shared a special bond, the kind that was so rare, just like Nanna and her Rubicon.

When Morgan finally got her human form, it was the opposite of her dragon form. She was a darling blond-haired little girl, with the most beautiful red brown eyes.

She had a sweet soul—smart as hell and as naughty as they come. Although we never went to Dragonia Academy together, I'd been one of her friends from birth. I claimed her six years ago when the darkness inside her started to claw its way into her soul.

She's known that I would become her rider—her Dent—as Rubicons would never be good without their Light.

The pain in my heart grew sharper as I watched Nanna's fragile body lying on the bed. She still had her spark, but her body was finally giving up. Her mind rambled about things that I didn't know had passed or were yet to come. She'd spoken about an evil so strong that it ripped her entire family apart. It scared me. I couldn't find anything in the library about what she could be talking about. She was so old. It would cost me my essence to discover what she'd been talking about for the past week.

She was close to her time. She was going home. Back to him.

I couldn't imagine life without her. She was the only constant in our family tree, yet even that was coming to an end. Soon she would be no more.

A knock came at the door. Morgan appeared. No longer a little girl, Morgan was stunning. "How is she?" she whispered as she came over for a kiss.

She sat on the sofa next to me. I wrapped my arms around her. Although I couldn't hear her heartbeat, I knew it was beating at the same pace as mine.

"In and out. She thought I was him a couple times today."

Tears welled up in Morgan's eyes. She walked over to Nanna's bed.

Nanna was awake. "My sweet, sweet Morganna."

Morgan smiled. "Don't leave me, please."

"Shush, child. You know you are not the only Rubicon who needs me."

Morgan fluffed Nanna's pillow. "What am I going to do without you?"

"You have Theo. Just think, when I'm gone, the two of you will drive one another insane."

I chuckled. I knew I would start hearing Morgan's thoughts when Nanna passed. There was that twinkle in her eyes once more.

"You will be fine. I've taught you everything you need to know. The rest you must discover together."

She nodded.

"Do me a favor?" Nanna asked.

"Anything," Morgan said.

"Go see if his star is still gone."

Morgan rushed to the windowsill. For the past week the Southern Star had been missing from the night sky. It had been written that the day the Rubicon died, a star would appear in the South. It was the brightest star, even brighter than the North Star. Books spoke about the North Star that guided everyone; even the Bible spoke about the North Star, never the Southern Star.

It hadn't left the sky for the past thousand years.

They all believed it was his star. His soul watching over her. It was so far-fetched, so silly. But seven days ago, that star had just vanished. Did it fall? I didn't know. But Nanna truly believed that it was him coming to fetch her. The myth didn't seem so silly anymore.

Since that star disappeared, Nanna had grown weaker and weaker. It was as if she was giving up. She'd made peace with it. We hadn't. I wasn't ready to say goodbye. Who would keep the peace? Who would they go to if they couldn't make a decision? Nanna was that person. Sure there were other old Dragonians, but Nanna was the wisest of them all.

I couldn't say goodbye to her yet. Not with a world looming over my shoulder. I was the next in line; she'd given the crown to me and not my father. I had no idea if I could do it the way she had with her Rubicon.

She said that was the reason she'd given it to me: a great king never knew he was a great king.

I wasn't so sure.

ELENA

It was late. I faded in and out of different timelines. I'd said goodbye to loved ones so many times. Watched them return to the ground, become the dust they were made of. So many had died before my eyes. First my father, then his wife.

Then my friends, their faces forgotten, the memories weak.

Blake had always been at my side, making it easier…and then he'd gone, too. I thought I was going to die myself, but I found love again through so many things.

Especially the new ones who came into this world.

New ones for me to love, to hold, to guide, and to say goodbye to again.

One might say it was cruel. That it must be too tiring to open your heart again to love another. But for me, it was natural. It was my life. It felt full.

I'd helped many. I'd guided plenty. I'd loved many. But had I ever truly loved the way my father had?

I didn't know anymore what had truly happened and what hadn't. Trying to recall where they fit together was impossible.

Morgan came tonight again. She'd confirmed it. His star was still gone. He was finally coming for me.

I heard a sniff and opened my eyes.

Theo leaned back on his haunches near my closet. The sweet boy was a spitting image of my Blake. He laughed it off every time I told him that.

What is he doing here? Why doesn't he go to bed and sleep? I'd taught him the most. He was ready even if he didn't believe it himself. He was ready.

He finally looked up. It felt as if my soul was on fire. A new kind of life filled me. My stomach fluttered.

His eyes were soft with compassion. I hadn't been looked at like that for almost a thousand years.

Not Theo.

Blake.

"What took you so long?"

"I told you before. Time works differently on the other side," he said softly.

He was so handsome, always had been, right up until the day he'd left my side.

"I've missed you so much," my old voice said. *Lucky bastard. He'd gotten his young body back.*

"I missed you more," he whispered.

"How long do I have?"

"One more day, Elena."

I smiled. One more day. Then I was going to go home.

"Your mother is quite the organizer up there," he joked. "I had to keep on helping her get things ready for you."

I smiled. "Our first shopping spree?" His face fell, so I asked, "Why the long face, my love?"

He touched my rumpled cheek. "You need to remember what truly happened, Elena."

I swallowed. I knew what he was talking about. I'd struggled with that for the past week.

"You need to tell Theo what he has to do. Otherwise they will be stuck with the wrong future."

"What do you mean?" I spoke softly.

The timelines, the different stages of my life, all jumped back into place as his finger brushed my temple. The one that had truly happened, but only the two of us remembered…and another one that everyone else believed was the truth.

"They can't be stuck with that past. You need to tell him what he must do."

It didn't make sense. But then it came back to me. The

night Blake had run into our room and uttered a horrible truth.

"That was…Theo?" I asked.

He nodded.

A tear welled up. "But you said it was you?"

"I was wrong. I wish I wasn't." His expression held immeasurable compassion.

"So I did…" My lip started to tremble. I couldn't even finish my sentence.

He nodded again.

"She was an innocent baby, wasn't she?"

"Shh. She understands, Elena. She knows why we had to do it. Silho is waiting for you, too. She cannot wait to finally meet her mom."

I sniffed hard.

"Will I remember this tomorrow?"

"It will hold." He smiled.

I returned his smile, although it didn't reach my eyes. "Still a master. I hope I don't have to kill other women up there."

He laughed. "It's a kill-free environment. And I only have eyes for you. You know that. Sleep, my sweet love." His lips brushed across my forehead. "I'll be back tomorrow."

I closed my eyes and waited for the last day of my life.

What was I going to choose tomorrow…my daughter or my entire family tree?

WO

4 millennia ago

ELENA

It had been eight years since my father was freed from Etan, and four years since I became Mrs. Blake Leaf. It had been the most amazing four years. He was my soul mate. He treated me not just like the princess of Paegeia but the queen of his heart.

And he was one hell of a romantic! The night he'd asked me to marry him had been magical.

He'd written me daily poems—I was a sucker for them. We had a date planned and he'd taken me on a special trip on my father's yacht.

We spoke aloud a lot that night; he'd been guarded with his mind. A whole ten and a half months after I could read his mind, it happened for Blake. We'd spent almost an entire year in silence, using only our minds to communicate with one another. We did it so long that it actually started to worry our parents.

But whenever he had surprises planned for me, I couldn't get a peep out of him. He was highly skilled at hiding things he didn't want me to know.

I struggled to such a degree that it left me with headaches, yet I still had no idea what he had planned.

But on that night, I forgot about everything.

Dessert was set. The chef who had gone with us gave Blake a basket. He started to strip down. I yearned for him; he still refused to break the promise of chastity he'd made my mother. For a moment, I got lost in my mind, searching for the delicious memory of the only night he'd slept with me.

"Where are we going?"

"Wait and see." He unbuttoned his shirt. I stared at him and reluctantly turned around.

"Stop thinking about that," he said, making me laugh. "It's not that easy for me either."

I shook my head. *I can't help it.*

When I turned around, I grunted. He was buck naked with only the basket in his hand.

"Stop," he warned and I laughed again.

I tried to think of anything else, but it was hard not to think of his perfectly sculpted body and with me lying...

"Elena!" he roared.

"Sorry!"

He shook his head as he helped me up onto the ledge of the yacht.

"Seriously, woman." His lopsided smile and smoldering eyes made my knees go weak.

He wrapped his arm around my waist and leaped into the air.

I couldn't help but shout out, "Woohoo!" It was an awesome feeling.

He morphed into his dragon form and held me in his paw because of the tiny excuse for a dress I had on.

I was always trying to get him to forget about my mother's promise, but Blake had turned into such a good boy that sometimes I ached for the bad boy he used to be.

I felt the landing. It was gracious, but I still felt it.

He opened his palm. We were on a mountaintop. The stars shone brilliantly. The huge, full moon illuminated the landscape below.

The trees were behind us. A blanket was spread out in the clearing. A lantern shed warm light over the pillows stacked on the blanket.

He'd come here before our date. I saw it from him, and then he closed off his mind.

"How do you do that?" I muttered.

"Easy," he said. He pulled on his pants and picked up his shirt, pulling his arms into the sleeves. He didn't button up his shirt. He grabbed me and kissed me fiercely.

My hormones raged.

He laughed. "You are driving me insane with your thoughts."

I grunted; I got nothing from him whatsoever. I hated this.

"Oh, it's payback time," he whispered.

I hated it. Ten months were hardly worth payback. And what happened when he start hearing my thoughts? He'd gone and found a way to block me out.

We settled on the blanket. He popped a bottle of champagne. Nothing special about that. I had secretly hoped he would just ask me, but I had always been disappointed on date nights when champagne was popped and no question came. I knew my father was behind this. How many times he'd asked him for my hand already, I didn't know. A lot. But my dad just kept telling him, "It's not time yet."

The champagne meant absolutely nothing.

He read Shakespeare aloud as I listened. The faint light didn't affect his eyes. He was stirring up things again that shouldn't be stirred up.

I was lying with my head on his stomach while he lay on his back, reading from *A Midsummer Night's Dream*.

We shared dragon kisses. They were almost the same as Italian kisses, but instead of the chocolate, it was covered with an orange-flavored caramel topping and filled with a dark chili-chocolate ice cream. He would use his frost to keep them cold.

It was to die for.

"The end," Blake said, finished with the book.

"Beautiful. Now where is my poem?" I asked and he smiled.

"What if I tell you there is no poem tonight?"

"Four years of daily poems and tonight you don't have one? Nah. I don't buy it."

He laughed, shifted, and slid a rumpled piece of paper from his back pocket.

He hated it when I read his poems while he was watching me, but I didn't care.

He handed it over and held it tight so I couldn't get it.

"Seriously," I complained. "You're going to tear it."

He laughed and let go.

I pushed myself up and kneeled, unfolding it.

It was a long one.

I have dreamed of the light
Since the dark crawled at my soul.
It felt as if I would break,
Then you came and made me whole.

"Aww."
He just smiled and shook his head.

Finally, I can breathe,
as you drove my demons away.
And no matter what may happen,
I know with you I'm meant to stay.
So I thank the heavens each day
that you are by my side.
Never losing faith in me,
you'll always be my guide.

Okay this was going to be one of those poems that made me cry. I could just feel it.

And if the world crashes down,
my life would be complete.
With you by my side,
never missing a beat.
There's only one thing left
that will change our life.
What I want to know is…
will you be my wife?

My heart fluttered as I read the last sentence. Tears welled up in my eyes. My dad had finally said yes.
"You're serious?"

He beamed. I flung my arms around his neck and kissed him.

"Yes, yes. A million times yes," I cried. "When did you ask him?"

"Last week, but he told me he had to think. I think Constance actually put her foot down this time."

I squealed gleefully and planted my lips on his.

His thoughts streamed into my head and I chuckled with my lips still pressed against his.

"This was why…"

"Yes, that was why I had to shield you off. I didn't want to spoil anything." He got up and took out a small jewelry box from inside the basket. He gave it to me.

I opened the box and gasped. A large stone glittered, nestled in black velvet.

"The gem's called a dragon stone," he said. "It belonged to your grandmother. The band is brand-new, though. It took about three days to make this beauty."

"It's dazzling."

He took the ring out of its box and put it on my finger, kissing my knuckles softly. He looked up at me through his thick lashes. "You are beautiful."

I sighed and smiled like an idiot. Could I be any happier? I grabbed and kissed him again.

All sorts of feelings awoke, and for once he didn't stop. He lowered me to the ground.

My legs twirled around his waist. His body pressed hard on mine.

I was going to lose it.

When my breathing became heavier he stopped, grunted and pushed himself off me.

"Seriously?!" I huffed.

"I made a promise, Elena."

"To a ghost, Blake. She's not here." Anger laced my tone.

"Don't be like that. Please." He pulled me into his arms. His lips touched my earlobe. "You have no idea how hard this is for me."

"It doesn't look hard," I whined.

"Well," he said, and I could tell that he was grinning. "It is."

The magical night ended.

I never thought I could dislike my mom. *Why did she have to threaten him like that?* Still, forgiving him was easy. He was trying his best to keep his promise. And nothing I was going to say would break his will.

He took me straight to the castle after the mountain. I hated that I had to say goodbye to him again. Why couldn't we just go to his place instead?

He had a beautiful apartment on the coast. I loved that place so much. My father never let me sleep over.

"Soon they can't say anything." Blake didn't change back from his dragon form and I knew why. The temptation was always strongest during goodbyes.

"Yes, you'd better hope my dad sets the date soon and not three years from now."

His dragon face fell. *Yep.* I saw the cussing in his mind.

"Sleep tight." I laughed.

He growled. "Sleep tight, princess."

"Fly safe."

"I will."

"Sweet dreams," I said.

"My dreams can't possibly be sweeter than what my life is right now." He was still flapping his wings, hovering in the air. "I will go on my knees tonight and pray that it won't be three years from today."

I laughed and went into my room.

I hated saying goodbye.

I went to my father and Constance's room and knocked on their door.

"Enter," Constance said. I opened the door, ran inside, and jumped onto their bed. My dad was already asleep.

"Look!" I yelled.

She squealed, sharing my excitement. "It is gorgeous, Elena! Tell me everything. How did he ask you?"

I showed her the poem. My father opened his one eye.

"Thank you, Daddy," I fell on him and kissed him on the burnt side of his face.

"Uh-huh. Where is he?"

"Not here." I sighed. "Don't." I was so not having this conversation with him.

"It's gorgeous, Elena," Constance gushed. "He sure knows how to write a poem."

"He sure does." I took it from her and hugged her.

"Thank you," I whispered in her ear. "I know the Silver Annex foot came out."

She laughed.

"It was time. I couldn't handle his disappointment any longer," she whispered back.

I said goodnight and left.

My phone rang. It was Blake.

"You show them?" he asked.

"Yes, I did," I said and put the phone on my bed as I walked into my closet.

"Elena, I swear if you undress in front of me again,

I'm going to switch off my phone."

I laughed. "I'll get undressed in my closet."

I put my sexy nighties on.

He grunted appreciatively and then started to laugh.

"What, I can't wear this now?" I said when he refused to look at me.

"This is so unfair," he said and then his face disappeared.

I ran to my Cammy and phoned him again. It just rang.

I tried a few more times, but he didn't answer.

He hadn't just put the phone down on me, had he?

I phoned him again. He didn't answer. It went to voicemail.

Pick up. Pick up. Pick up!

I wanted to cry. So that attempt was a big no. I shouldn't have done that.

I chucked my phone in the drawer, climbed into bed, and pulled the covers over my head.

I hated this so much. So, so much. All because of a stupid promise. My engagement ring's gem glowed under the covers. It was gorgeous. Unique.

I heard something outside my door. I pulled the covers from my face and stared at the door.

Was someone here? I called Blake a few times in my thoughts, but he was too far out of reach.

I immediately went into Dragonian mode. I climbed out of bed and grabbed the ornament that stood on my nightstand.

Looking down at my nighties, I sighed and rolled my eyes. I shouldn't have worn these stupid nighties. If I had to fight…the image in my head was comical.

I wrapped my duvet around my torso. Gripping the

ornament like a weapon underneath the duvet, I walked to the door.

I reached out slowly and cracked open the door.

Blake. He leaned against the wall, wearing only his jeans. He didn't seem impressed, not one bit. With arms folded, his entire demeanor screamed bad boy.

The door swung open and I pulled him inside.

Our lips touched. We didn't speak. We just kissed as if Paegeia's survival depended on it. He shouldn't have come.

He pushed me against the wall. Hard. He pulled the blanket off me, revealing my nighties and the ornament I'd hidden underneath the blanket.

He chuckled. "Love, you can wield fire and lightning, and you grabbed a nightstand knickknack?"

"Shut up." I pulled him closer to me.

He groaned as our bodies slammed together. His hands roved over me.

When his lips brushed the skin on my neck softly, goosebumps skittered all over my body. "If your mother shows up to haunt my ass, you are going to do the explaining," he spoke fast.

"It will be my pleasure," I said. We both laughed.

Fiercely, he kissed me. His hands grabbed my thighs, lifting me up from the floor. My legs curled around his waist as he pushed his body against mine.

He was built to last. Everything about him was driving me crazy. His kisses became faster as he shredded my nighties off with one tug.

His hands fiddled with his jeans. A tearing sound filled the room.

He pressed his lips against mine. Our tongues danced. It was a dance only we knew.

He pressed hard into me again. His thrusts were vigorous, achingly urgent, and powerful. In less than two minutes I had to suppress moans.

I was rushed to euphoria.

THREE

The wedding took place three months later. Constance had hired the best event coordinators for our special day.

It was something Paegeia had never seen: a blend of a traditional dragon wedding and a royal one.

The tabloids couldn't stop talking about the big event.

Everyone who was anyone was going to be there. Oh, and one more thing…it was going to be held in the sky.

A heavenly wedding.

Most people only dreamed of something like that, but once everyone started exploring ways to make it happen, I realized it was really possible.

Blake loved the sky. He was made for the sky. Apparently that was how all dragons got married.

It was just going to be a little bit trickier.

A month before the wedding, my father called for

Blake. He moved in, taking a temporary room in the castle until the wedding. He spent as much time with Dad as he could, learning about being a ruler. Dad took him under his wing. He taught him everything he knew about how to be a great king. Which was a lot.

At night, Blake sneaked into my room, dodging all the booby traps my father had laid out.

The magical day had finally come.

I couldn't stop staring at myself in the mirror.

My dress was white with purplish-black lace trim that matched the color of Blake's dragon skin. The back was netted with a thin, translucent layer of lace woven into the shape of a dragon. My shoulders were bare and the sleeves caught on my forearms, fanning out to my wrists in folds of purple lace.

I'd never seen such a puffy dress in my entire life. The skirt threatened to drown my legs. But the dress tapered at my waist into a corset that was a mixture of faux purple leather and white satin.

When I first saw it and felt its softness in my hands, I'd thought Blake had offered some of his skin, but he hadn't. It was all a reproduction.

I couldn't believe that such a beautiful gown had been created just for me. In that moment, I felt like a fairy-tale princess.

Blake planned on wearing traditional dragon attire. At first I thought he was going to show up naked, but I was assured that wouldn't be the case. Dragon and human weddings were usually done in human form, thank goodness.

There had just never been one in which the bride was of royal blood.

His outfit reminded me of a Scottish kilt. Blake was

going to get married in a dress, too. I teased him about it, but he just stared at me. He didn't think I was very funny.

His kilt didn't have plaid; it had scales. It was his color—deep purple. It came with a piece that reminded me of the Samurai 3000 vest, just softer around the edges and much more elaborately decorated with raven-black satin and gold trimmings. A cape draped over his shoulders. Boots laced up to his knees. He would look like some sort of Greek god. I could already imagine what was waiting for me at the altar. A hot wave washed over me. Dizziness and doubt clouded my mind.

I was going to become someone's wife. Not just any someone—the Rubicon's. What if I didn't make him happy? What if everything was going to change?

Was this too early? Was this the reason why my father kept telling him no—because he knew I wasn't ready?

I backed away from the mirror to the fan. I spread my arms wide like a bird's wings and waited for the air to cool my head.

That was how Becky and Sammy found me. They both looked pretty in their gold-and-purple dresses.

"Okay, what is up with you?" Becky asked.

"I don't know. I'm so hot." My voice sounded strangled.

She walked over. Her cropped black hair bobbed with each perky step. "You are the most gorgeous bride I've ever seen, Elena."

Half my lip rose.

Her big brown eyes narrowed. "No, you are *not* having cold feet!"

"I don't know," I whined. "It's the Rubicon, for crying out loud, Becky."

"And he is marrying the freakin' Princess of Paegeia,

Elena. You don't think that is intimidating for him, too?"

I took a deep breath. She had a point.

"It's Blake. Your knight in shining armor. Your Dent. The guy who would literally give you the moon and the stars if he could. He will love you forever, Elena." She took a strand of my hair and fixed it.

"When did you become so wise?" I asked.

"The day I became Mrs. George Mills."

We both laughed.

"Please don't break my brother's heart," Sammy said. I'd forgotten she was here, too. She had become like a shadow the past few years. Becky and I had tried everything to pull her out of it, but after a while, we just stopped. She clearly didn't want to be saved from torturing herself over Dean's death. I hadn't seen her famous dimples in forever.

I went over to her and gave her a hug, careful not to mess up her coiffed auburn hair. "I would never break his heart. I love him too much."

"Good," she whispered. "Now go and marry him."

The door opened and my father walked in with Constance. Dad was downright dapper in his leather suit and delicate, yet manly crown. A cape cascaded from his back.

Tears welled up in his eyes as he stared at me.

"Say something. Please."

He shook his head and wiped his tears away. "May I have a moment with my daughter alone, ladies?" They left the room.

He took my hands gently in his. "You look so much like your mother today." His voice broke.

"Dad."

"No, Elena." He took my hands and kissed them.

"I've been wrong these past four years, trying to keep you all to myself. Forgive me."

Tears pricked my eyes, reflecting his. "There is nothing to forgive," I said. He handed me a tissue before a tear rolled down my cheek. "Constance will kill me if I ruin your makeup."

I laughed ruefully. "I'm sure if they can create a wedding hovering in the sky, they can fix ruined makeup."

He laughed. "It looks stunning out there. You know if you're not ready, Elena, he will understand. We can still slip out the back."

"You forgot one thing," I joked.

"What?"

"We'll tumble to our deaths."

He threw back his head and laughed.

I joined in. When our chuckles subsided, he sighed. "No, I'm serious. We won't fall to our deaths." He touched my face gently with his palm.

"I'm ready, Dad. I want to marry him."

"Okay, sweet pea." He kissed me on my head. "I'll let everyone know it's time to begin."

A soaring melody of violins floated to us. My bridesmaids included Sammy, my best friend and Blake's sister; Becky, my other best friend and old roommate from Dragonia; and Annie, Blake's fantastic cousin and my step-sister who happens to be one of my favorite people.

They all walked out, stately and serene, to the rhythm of the music. I couldn't recall if I'd ever heard this melody, but it was beautiful.

"Ready?" my father asked.

I smiled. "Ready."

He pulled my veil over my face and we stepped out the door.

Earlier this morning when Constance brought me here with Becky and everyone else, it hadn't looked anything like this. It had just been a room hovering in the sky by loads and loads of enchantments.

Now, it was as if heaven had come down to us to make this wedding possible.

Rows and rows of chairs were lined up on both sides. A flouncy bow adorned each chair back. There was even a red carpet. A soft mist covered the ground. Clouds mixed with rose veins lined the walls. Dragons flapped their wings, hovering in the air.

At the front, my gorgeous groom stood in his Adonis attire. Waiting for me to marry him.

Everyone stared at me, but I couldn't keep my eyes away from my prize. It was as if I'd won him somehow.

He was standing underneath an arch made of clouds threaded with soft colors and flowers.

As I came closer, I could see tears shining in his eyes.

My father leaned slightly toward me. "See, I'm not the only one bedazzled by how beautiful you look today, Elena."

My heart warmed.

When we finally reached the front, my father turned to me and lifted my veil. He kissed me on both cheeks.

The priest spoke loudly. "Who is giving this woman away?"

"I do," my father said. He turned to look at Blake. He just stared at him until everyone watching started to laugh.

"Make her happy, Blake."

"You know I will," Blake answered.

He took my hand and put it in Blake's, before stepping off the altar.

The ceremony started, but to be honest, I didn't hear much of it. I couldn't stop staring at Blake, and he couldn't stop staring at me.

"You may now speak your vows," the priest said.

Blake went first. He took the ring out of his pocket. Very romantic.

"Sorry, I have many trust issues," he said to the crowd, who laughed.

He put the ring on my finger. "With this ring, I promise to give you my soul and my undying love.

I place this ring upon your hand.
You have made me a better man.
With your sweet love and gentle kiss,
The darkness from my soul you forever dismiss.
With this circle of gold, I solemnly vow
To love you until my life takes its final bow."

Tears filled my eyes as he spoke the words. I felt each syllable imprint on my soul. *Rhyming. It just had to be rhyming...*

As I felt the cool circle of gold nestle onto my finger, I turned to Becky, who had been holding Blake's ring for me.

The ring felt heavy in my hand as I turned back and stared into his peacock-blue eyes. The same eyes I wanted to look into for the rest of my life.

Taking a deep breath, I began my vows. I hadn't planned them in advance. I let my heart speak the truth.

"While our challenges have been many, there has

really only been one constant for me, and that is my soul-deep love for you. Even when you pushed me away, deep down I knew we were meant to be together and destined to face the challenges of this world together, hand-in-hand, forever. You are more than my dragon. You are my heart, my soul, and the very life force that flows in my veins. I promise to keep you, love you, and care for you, until my dying breath."

I could feel the emotions flow out of me. Light sparkled in his eyes as I slipped his ring onto his finger. I could feel the moment our lives became one.

"I now pronounce you husband and wife. You may kiss your bride."

Blake stepped forward, his hand curled around my waist and he kissed me softly.

I didn't dare open my eyes, since this kiss was our first as husband and wife. When we finally broke away it was dark, and I looked around me.

I realized he'd covered this private moment with his wings, partially transformed. Then he lowered his wings and the crowd came back into view.

Everyone cheered.

The reception took place in the sky as well. It all went by so quickly. Toward the end, Blake took me for a flight.

The stars were like diamonds tonight. He took me to our special spot by the river.

It still took my breath away, with the fireflies lighting the way.

I slid off his wing, and when I turned around my husband was naked, and I was in his arms.

What followed next was a blur.

We made love right there under our tree without

tearing my dress.

Like I'd always said, he was a jack-of-all-trades.

We stayed there until the sun came up, and then we returned to the castle.

That was our wedding. Beautiful. Impossible to forget.

My dad gave us our own wing in the castle—the west wing that had once been my mother's. They'd rebuilt it. We would never be able to fill all those rooms. Every night we made love. For hours. I thought I was going to die of happiness.

Getting pregnant wasn't as easy as I'd thought it would be. Several times I'd thought I was, but then it turned out that I was just late.

But when the day came, it was even more magical than I could have dreamed. Now it was my turn to try and block out my thoughts. I was going to break the news to Blake at dinner.

Blake had been away for a few days, helping my father with some of the threats the Wyverns posed again. I didn't like it when he was gone for so long.

My dad didn't even know yet, but Constance said she would tell him before dinner when he came back, so it could only be Blake's surprise.

I spent the entire day waiting for him by the window of our room, praying to see his outline.

"Constance!" I yelled and run out of the room. "They are here."

Sure, he was the Rubicon, but Wyverns, they would always be Wyverns. I was glad to have him back safe and sound.

He landed hard. The ground rumbled; his dragon form was bigger than ever.

He morphed back to his human form and I was in his arms, kissing him everywhere.

"I was only gone for three days, Elena."

"Three days too long."

He laughed. "So how is my favorite person?" He squinted at me.

"I'm perfect."

"What are you trying to hide from me?" he asked in a serious tone.

"Nothing! I'm not hiding anything."

"Why can't I reach your mind, Elena?"

"You can't?" I tried to sound surprised. "Guess I finally found a way to block you."

He shook his head. "Fine, whatever," he mumbled. He took the robe that Jeeves held toward him.

"Thank you, Jeeves."

"Welcome back, my prince," he said.

Blake huffed. "Still need to get used to that one," he said as he pulled the robe over his body. He flung his arm around me and we walked side-by-side to the castle. "Seriously, Elena. You are starting to freak me out, just a little."

"Nothing? You can't see anything?" I was smiling ear-to-ear.

"Nothing. It's scary." He took a huge breath, which made me laugh.

"It's not funny! I feel off balance."

"Soon. Just be patient."

We got ready for dinner and went down around seven o'clock. It was nice to have a full table for tonight.

Isabel had come over for dinner. Sir Robert had been away with my father, so he didn't know about anything either.

My father caught me in the kitchen right before we sat down.

"Sweet pea," he whispered with tears in his eyes, hugging me tightly.

"I don't want to say anything. You've been trying so hard to keep this a secret."

"Shh, Dad."

"Sorry," he said and mouthed, *Congratulations*.

We sat down and dinner started.

They talked about the Wyverns and everything that had happened the past three days.

Blake was quiet, very quiet. I tried to peer into his mind to see what was bothering him, but I was scared that would open the gateway for him to see my thoughts too and ruin the surprise.

Finally, it was time for dessert.

The staff all exited the kitchen. A plate covered with a silver bowl was placed in front of each of us.

They all took off the silver lids with a flourish to reveal dessert on every plate—except Blake's. On his plate was a pair of booties.

I looked at him sitting next to me as he stared at his plate. For a very, very long time.

The silence stretched around the table as everyone looked at him, waiting in anticipation for his reaction. Nobody expected this.

I looked at my father, who still had excitement on his face. I begged him with my eyes to do something, but he shrugged.

Blake still stared at the stupid plate.

Then finally he moved his head and met my eyes. "You serious?"

I nodded.

"I'm going to be a dad?"

He was scaring me. "Yes, you are going to be a father."

A sloppy grin spilled over his face. He grabbed me and hugged me tight as I unleashed the lock on my mind and my thoughts streamed into his.

He laughed.

"Good surprise?" I asked.

"The best," he said, touching my belly and kissing my lips.

The pregnancy was a blast. It went slow, but eventually the big day arrived.

I didn't know who was more nervous—my father or Blake.

Constance told them both to go wait in the living room. I'd planned a royal home birth.

A beautiful little girl made her grand entrance four hours later. We called her Silho.

She had dark fuzz down to the nape of her neck and the most angelic face. A perfect mixture of Blake and me.

Life was beautiful. A princess couldn't ask for more.

EIGHTEEN MONTHS LATER...

We were preparing for the Royal Chastniss tournament.

It wasn't Warbel. Chastniss was much more fun. It reminded me a lot of lacrosse but with dragons. Like all dragon games, this one was dangerous.

As I suited up under a glittering night sky and watched Blake transform into his dragon form, I reminded myself of the rules. We were allowed to use our abilities—except for Blake and me, who were only allowed to use one, no swapping. The pink kiss was forbidden, as that one was a killer. Literally. That ability inflicted a gruesome death at its mere touch. So, we usually went with lightning or frost.

I climbed up on Blake's back and he leapt into the sky gracefully. My heart lurched with the thrill; I'd never get tired of flying.

The riders played with an old sheepskin ball astride a dragon. A huge racket was used to hit the ball, then the players chased it and hit it again. Teams were three against three. A dragon took up the position of keeper and stood guard in front of a net close to the ground or way up in the sky.

Our goal was the sky since Blake loved to fly, and our opposing team was on the ground. We had plenty of hard flying to do and plenty of defending, making sure that the ball stayed close to our opponents' net.

In between all this, we had to duck and dive the other abilities. Blake cheated in the beginning, swapping and changing abilities to use on the others, but we would get suspended for ten minutes and usually ended up losing the game.

Love, stop daydreaming and hold on tight. Blake's voice popped into my head and brought me back to earth—or more accurately back to reality where I was sitting on his back.

I rolled a few of his catfish-like whiskers slightly around my hand. I mentally sent the message: *I'm ready.*

My father disliked that we wouldn't speak a single word to one another, but when we told him that we did speak, just silently, he relaxed. He was downright impressed with what we could do. Admiration often shone in his eyes when he realized we were speaking to each other in our special way. He was really in awe of us.

"GO!" Becky yelled. She and George were always on our side.

Since George got that first vision of Blake being stuck in what we now call The Nether, he had seen so many things about the two of us. Beautiful things and scary things he didn't want to share. Those frightened me. He wouldn't even tell Becky.

I yelled out of excitement as I wound up to hit the ball with the racket.

Sir Robert dashed past us. My father hit the ball first and it careened back down.

Blake grunted and swooped around, and my father laughed gleefully. We chased after the ball.

Becky served it cleanly back to me. I smacked it before my father could reach me.

"Slow down, Elena, before your hurt yourself!" my father yelled.

"I can take care of myself, old man," I joked. After all, he was about two hundred and seventy now, give or take a couple years. But he still resembled a man in his late forties. His dragon, Sir Robert—my father-in-law—had given him his essence a very long time ago.

The game was fun. Laughter soared all around us. A couple of bystanders watched from below, crying out excitedly at our antics.

Sir Robert and Blake chased the ball. He'd gotten faster since my father's return. Blake increased his velocity as his father was on his tail. The wind tore at my blonde hair, adorning it with microscopic pearls of moisture.

We streaked toward our goal post. *Not far now*.

"Let them go!" my father yelled at last. Sir Robert would kill himself if he tried to keep up with Blake at these speeds.

I felt as if I was on an insane rollercoaster with no brakes.

My enthusiasm ripped a scream from my lungs, clawing its way out of my throat. It echoed through the night sky as we climbed higher and higher, hitting the ball each time I passed it.

Emanual was my father's goalkeeper. He lurked high up in the darkness—how high, we didn't know. It was one thing to get the ball, but another thing altogether to get past him.

A bright light appeared right in front of us out of nowhere. Blake didn't have time to stop.

We flew right through the dazzling light. He slowed down.

"What the hell was that?" I spoke out loud for the first time. I craned my neck to look behind us. The light was gone. When Blake turned around, it reappeared. But then I realized it hadn't reappeared; I was seeing it through his mind.

I don't know. It came out of nowhere.

The sky was crystal clear. A million stars were strewn across the black velvet blanket of night.

There were no signs of our game. The world was deathly quiet, all sounds of our onlookers and the other players simply vanished. I didn't like this. Not one bit.

A string of thoughts zigzagged through Blake's head. The stars in this sky weren't part of our galaxy. In Blake's mind, I could see that some of these constellations didn't exist.

This made no sense.

Threads of worry curled around Blake's mind like clinging ivy. His fear became my own. My heart fluttered anxiously. I didn't know what any of this meant.

Blake, where are we? What was that bright light? And what do you mean these aren't our constellations?

I have no idea. I don't like this. This place feels wrong, Elena.

I know, I feel it, too. What is it with the stars? I asked him again.

Some of them shouldn't be in the sky. They fell a long time ago.

What does this mean? Just get us back, please.

Okay, hold on.

He veered off course. The hair on my neck stood on end as the wind brushed against my face. We weren't even close to the palace, but a few miles away, we saw the palace standing tall in the horizon.

I loved flying. I lived for it. But his fear, his thoughts, had become mine. I shared his mounting unease.

Fire light caught my eye. I peered down toward Mount Likwa, a hulking mountain nearby the castle.

Atop the mountain a battle was being waged. *War.*

The whiz of fire arrows. Steel breaking against steel. Humans screaming in agony as they perished. These sounds pierced my eardrums.

I sensed Blake watching the images in my mind. He fanned his wings to slow down to make sense of what we were seeing.

It was a battle to the death.

What is that? Who is it? Why don't we know about

this? Alarm ratcheted through my tone.

We need to get back, Elena. We need to warn your father and the others!

Just get us the hell out of here, I ordered.

He sped up.

Sharp pain seared through my waist. But it wasn't me who had been hit. It was him.

"Blake!" I yelled. *Are you okay?*

His wingbeats faltered, barely noticeable. *Yes, I'm fine.*

I prayed for the castle. He was always saying stuff like this—that he was fine, not to worry—but I always knew the truth. This thing hurt like hell. Another thing our connection let us experience: each other's pain.

Drowsiness rose through me, sudden and unexpected. I glanced at my waist and realized it wasn't Blake's pain I was experiencing after all. It was my own. The feathers of a blazing owl placed in a beautiful formation at the tip of an arrow jutted halfway from the side of my torso.

I'd been hit, not Blake, it was me...*From that distance? How?*

Elena! Blake must have sensed the turmoil inside my head. A soft keening sound left his core. My eyes felt heavy, so heavy. The last thing I was aware of before I blacked out, before I lost complete control of my sight, was slipping off his back. Into nothingness.

BLAKE

Elena was losing consciousness. I had to tune her out in order to fly straight. I saw her figure plummeting through empty air past my paw.

I darted after her and grabbed her with my claw. She was so tiny.

Got you. Just hold on, I begged. I flew like I'd never flown before. I raced back toward the castle, or at least back to where the stars made some sense. How bad was her injury? Where were we? What had happened?

The bright light was up ahead. I didn't even try to stop this time. I picked up speed and zoomed straight through it.

A voice in the darkness. King Albert. "What do you mean they never came this way?"

"They never reached the goal post, my king," Emanual said.

"Help!" I roared. I could hear from the rhythm of their heartbeats that they knew I was desperate.

"Blake!" King Albert yelled.

"Son!" my father shouted.

"Here," I called. *Is she okay?* Miles melted before me. Within five breaths I saw two dragon silhouettes against the smudge of a cloud. The King's figure perched atop my father.

"Something is wrong!" my father said as he picked up the deranged tone in my voice.

Elena! I tried to connect with her mind, but she was as vacant as a stone-cold wall. Either that or the connection had been broken again. I couldn't go through that. Not again.

"Stay with me!" I said.

"Blake!" Her father's voice was confused and worried tone. "Where is Elena?"

"In my paw. I think an arrow hit her. There is war on Mount Likwa."

George and Becky came into view.

"War?" my father said.

"Get Elena back to Constance. Now," King Albert ordered. "Blake, stay with her. The rest—" he nodded at George and Emanual "—Mount Likwa. Now."

"Is Elena going to be okay?" Becky sounded deranged, but nevertheless followed King Albert and the rest. I nodded. What else could I do?

"George, be safe. It's full-on war."

He nodded as I opened up my speed again and zoomed to the west wing.

I tried to connect with Elena's mind as our landing came into sight.

I landed. In three steps I turned back into my human form and carried her into our room.

"Constance!" I yelled. She had been looking after Silho, but I was sure Annie or someone would've told her that something had happened to us. They had to know something was wrong.

Elena's body lay lifeless inside my arms. Her mind was one gaping pit of darkness.

My heart clenched as I looked at the arrow. I'd once made the mistake of pulling one out. Constance wouldn't be able to heal her and neither could I, but Constance would know how to make her more comfortable.

Her heart was still beating, and she was still breathing. A beautiful sign of life. I didn't like the blackout or the fact that her eyes were closed.

"Elena," I slapped her face softly. "Stay with me!" I didn't sound like me anymore. My sight blurred. Tears spurred on by my worst fear welled up in my eyes.

"C'mon, baby, wake up." Begging harder, trying to tune in. She was gone. A pool of darkness had replaced the space where her thoughts used to be.

The door flew open and hit the wall hard. Constance ran toward us.

"What the hell?" she gasped as she took in Elena's lifeless body covered with blood in my arms.

"She got hit."

"Blake, how the hell did that happen?"

"I don't know." My voice shook.

Silho was still in her arms. My daughter started to cry. Constance handed her to a shocked Annie, who took her out of the room without a word.

"One minute we were okay, and the next..." I trailed off. *The bright light.*

"What? What came next, Blake?" Constance asked.

My gaze shifted to meet hers. "The bright light."

"What bright light?" Constance asked, attending to Elena and the arrow that bristled from her hip. "We need to get this thing out of her." She spoke more to herself than to me.

"There was a bright light, we flew into it, and then everything was just...wrong."

"What do you mean?" She took out the arrow as Simone, Elena's personal lady, came in with bandages and towels. Tears lingered in her eyes She loved Elena like a sister.

"She got hit?" Simone asked.

I ignored her.

Constance handed her the arrow she'd managed to take out of Elena without breaking it. She barked orders for warm water and more towels. "Make sure you don't get your prints on the shaft. We can wipe it for fingerprints later." She looked at Simone.

By now the commotion had alarmed more of the night staff. Soon everyone was bringing Constance what she needed.

"We saw a full-on battle on Mount Likwa. Nothing made sense," I continued explaining. I knew I should go help fight, but I couldn't tear myself from my love's side.

"Mom?" Annie came back without Silho. Tears streamed down her face. "Plucky, what happened?" she asked.

I didn't want to retell the story. *The bright light? What was that?*

"I'm sure it will be okay. Dad probably went to have a look." Constance answered on my behalf, reassuring Annie's worry. If only she could alleviate mine. But the fact that I couldn't connect with her drove me insane.

"Will she be okay?"

"She has to be," Constance said. "She has no choice."

I looked at my torso and arms. My chest was smeared with Elena's blood. *Don't die. Please. I can't do this without you.* I begged inside my mind. Hers was still dark.

"Where is she now, Blake?" Annie wiped at her eyes.

I shook my head.

"Nothing?"

Constance looked at Annie as she tried to cover Elena's wound. "She is going to be fine, sweetheart."

Annie nodded as Constance worked to stabilize Elena. "She's lost a lot of blood, Blake. Why isn't she healing yet?"

"She is out, Constance. It works slower when you lose consciousness," I barked back. Tonight's events had taken a toll on all of us. I was still in shock. I tried to help when Constance told me to press hard. She was screaming for the phone and Jeeves told her that they'd already called the hospital.

"We need to make sure that there wasn't poison on that tip."

My heart felt as if it wasn't beating. *Poison?* It had never even crossed my mind.

"Jeeves!" I yelled again, and the old man entered the room a few seconds later. "Phone Ralph. He needs to come and look at the arrow."

Jeeves nodded and left.

The more we knew, the better we could treat her.

"Good call, Blake."

"I wasn't the one who thought about the poison."

I bent down over Elena and brushed my lips on her head. *Don't leave me.*

FOUR

BLAKE

Elena had been unconscious for almost two days. Ralph had come the night Elena was shot and taken the arrow in a container so they could do as many tests on it as they could think of. There was no war, or even a sign of a war taking place on Mount Likwa. My father was worried. So was king Albert, but I know what I saw. The arrow that shot Elena was proof too.

Two days and we hadn't heard anything yet.

How difficult could it be? Unless there wasn't an antidote.

Please, please don't let that be the case.

I'd never prayed as much as I had the past two days.

I didn't have my orbs anymore. I could...*no, don't think like that, Blake. She is still alive.* That was all I wanted.

My mom had taken Silho to the manor. The vibe

inside the castle upset her, and she didn't understand why her mother wasn't around. Why she didn't want to wake up.

This reminded me of the time she'd been in her two-month coma. I felt lost without hearing her thoughts. So disoriented.

Her thoughts were dark. She wasn't even dreaming. I couldn't reach her.

We still had no idea what kind of poison was on the tip of the arrow. If there even was any poison.

If not, why wasn't she waking?

They'd had it now for more than forty hours and we still had no idea what was in her system.

I tried to sleep, but couldn't, so I just sat in a chair next to our bed all day and all night.

Her father came in regularly. So did Constance and Annie.

Becky and George slept in the guest room. Even Sammy came.

She'd accepted the position my father had offered her three years ago, but she hadn't taken another rider yet.

Dean had been a great guy. It was clear Sammy would never trust another the way she'd trusted him. He'd died during the freeing of Etan. I doubted my sister would ever be the same again. That haunted sadness never really left her face.

She'd seemed fine right after his death. I guess she'd had to make sure I was fine for Elena's sake before she had her meltdown. A part of her had shattered so badly that nobody could heal it. I couldn't heal it, and neither could my father or any of her friends.

Elena, on the other hand, had healed. The scar was almost gone. It'd taken twenty-four hours for the gash to close.

By tomorrow the mark would be completely gone, but something told me that she would still be asleep. Trapped.

It had to be poison. Why else would she still be knocked out like that, unreachable?

Her heartbeat was steady, yet soft. More proof of my theory that poison flowed through her veins. It was as if she was slipping into hibernation, her body shutting down softly.

She needed to wake up soon.

The door opened and Ralph walked in. We'd finally gotten the phone call that he needed to see us as soon as possible.

King Albert, Constance, my father, Emanual, and Annie waited for him in the library.

Ralph nodded toward us. He greeted all of us. Another scientist followed him in. Both faces were grave.

"No, no, no, no…There has to be an antidote!" I was strangely shrill. Constance placed her hand on my shoulder.

King Albert looked as if he were going to collapse. But my father stood ramrod straight beside him.

"It's not that, Blake. Sorry, my king. Here." He took a small vial out of his pocket. We all exhaled in unison.

"The poison in her blood and on this tip, was none other than Louie's berries."

"Louie's berries?" I said.

"A slow death awaits Elena."

A gaping maw opened in my chest, unbearable and

achingly empty. I closed my eyes and hugged my aunt and mother-in-law. It had been her call. She'd mentioned the poison.

She stroked my torso and pressed her head into my chest as she took the vial from Ralph.

"There is more."

We all looked at Ralph.

"Find out. I'll stay with Elena." Constance looked up at me. I nodded.

I watched her leave. Elena *had* to wake up.

We'd given him Louie so he could take the poison from his berries to use it on the Saadedine. Nothing had worked as it should.

"What news do you have? That expression on your face... You almost gave us a heart attack."

"Sorry, my king. We are struggling to accept it ourselves." Ralph glanced at the scientist next to him. "It's the arrow."

The gaping maw in my chest threatened to consume me.

King Albert spoke first. "What about it?"

The scientist behind Ralph wiggled toward the table. On it lay with a solitary envelope and a crate stuffed with documents.

We all went over to the table and watched him open the envelope. The heavy parchment crinkled audibly in his hands. Inside was the weapon that had almost killed my reason for living. Well, the most important one, anyway.

"My name is Kingston," he said, sounding slightly out of breath. His hands, though, were steady. Excitement sparkled in his bright blue eyes. "I work in the historical department at KU Labs."

"Historical?" I repeated.

He reached out his hand with a slight bow at the waist to King Albert.

"Wait, what the hell has this got to do with the arrow?" Confusion clouded my mind.

"Blake, you need to sit down. All of you," Ralph said. I looked at my father, standing like always, a few inches from King Albert.

"Proceed." King Albert looked at Kingston, ignoring Ralph's gesture.

Kingston removed the arrow as if it were a great treasure. A snarl curled my lip. They should've burned that thing. "We have performed every kind of test we could think of on this arrow. I promise you, the data we collected…" He shook his head, a smile tugging at the corners of his lips. Then he seemed to realize how inappropriate his enthusiasm was. "Sorry, let me proceed."

"What about the arrow?"

"The arrow is more than two hundred years old."

The room fell silent as everyone considered those impossible words.

"What?" We all looked at him, mouths agape.

"How is that possible? It should have disintegrated by now." My father raised his eyebrows, staring at what looked like a new, yet delicately crafted arrow, not a two-hundred-year-old artifact.

"Exactly our point," Ralph said. "No chemicals could preserve this arrow, and we found no trace of any charms. Whoever shot Elena at that distance must have been one of the best wielders in the entire world."

"So," Kingston said, "we researched this type of arrow, and we've got a fingerprint off it." He looked at

Albert. "Believe me when I tell you that none of it makes sense."

"I agree," King Albert said. "Who's the culprit? Who almost killed my daughter?" he asked through clenched teeth.

Ralph paused.

"*Who*, Ralph?" King Albert insisted. His anger was palpable.

I didn't like this side of him.

"It was...Queen Catherine."

The entire room fell into a deadly silence. We all stared at the arrow, not one of us had the nerve to say what was on everyone's mind. A million thoughts zipped through my head.

How could this belong to Queen Catherine? It hit Elena in the stomach, and...

"Wait, someone kept Catherine's arrow and hit Elena with it?" King Albert was thinking in the same direction as me.

"No, my king," Ralph said. He took a deep breath. "If they'd kept it this long, it wouldn't have been in this sort of condition."

"Spit it out, man. What are you trying to say?" I asked.

Ralph looked at me. "I'm saying that somehow, you and Elena went back two hundred years. Queen Catherine shot Elena."

If shock was what we'd felt a few minutes ago, then I didn't know what to call this feeling that rushed through me. Something heavy and hot trickled through my limbs.

The ache in my chest expanded. *Elena.*

King Albert took the arrow. It looked brand new. It couldn't have been two hundred years old.

His eyes traveled down the long shaft, seeking something. Then they widened in surprise. He dropped the arrow and it clattered to the floor. He fell into his chair. His face was slack.

"Al!" My father was at his side at once.

"Look," King Albert said, pointing at the arrow.

It was as if my father knew what he was looking for. He found it immediately.

"Katie's markings?" he said. He looked at me.

"Blake, the battle you saw," he started. "You said it was on Mount Likwa?"

I nodded. "The stars were all wrong."

"What do you mean?"

"They were wrong, Dad!" I yelled. "Some fell. A long time ago."

"Two hundred years ago?" Ralph said.

I didn't want to nod, but I had no choice. How could this be?

"Then it's a miracle," Kingston said with a smile lingering on his lips. "You found a way to jump back in time."

ELENA

Life started to return. I felt many things at once: the pain in my side where...my eyes popped open. Blake was the first one I saw, worry etched on his face.

"Shh," he said. My bed shifted as he climbed up

beside me. "Easy." He lay his head near mine, cupping the back of my head softly. I could count his black eyelashes. I could stay here forever. Except for the pain.

Alarm crept in. "What happened? Where am I?" I trailed off. Taking in my surroundings, I realized I knew this place. It was our room. I relaxed marginally.

Blake just hugged me tighter. *I thought you were dead! I felt so helpless.*

"I'm okay," I said aloud, my voice hoarse. I breathed in his scent. His closeness, his unique scent calmed me down. I was safe, I was alive, and he was here. It was all that mattered.

His thoughts invaded. A flash of the events I'd missed, all his worries, my family's worries, and frightening images of blood and war kept me occupied for a few minutes. They were fast, but the emotion and the clarity made them so real. He'd been completely beyond himself.

Two days?

How scared he'd been when I'd blacked out, the connection broken again. How they'd waited for the scientists. My heart beating softer. The sensation of his unending terror was suffocating.

Where is Silho?

He showed me that Isabel had taken her and she was at the manor, safe and sound.

Then the scientists came. Ralph. The revelation. The antidote. I gasped.

Louie's berries?

He nodded.

I met Kingston through him, a history scholar, which didn't make sense at all. They spoke about the peculiar arrow. He said it was two hundred years old and that it belonged…to my mother. My mother had shot me…

We'd jumped back in time.

"What?" It came out louder than I wanted it to. Shock rippled through my entire being. *We'd jumped back in time. My mother…*

I didn't care that my mother had shot me. She'd thought…whatever she'd thought…It was war. We'd jumped back two hundred years.

"What is going on in that mind of yours?" Blake asked. He couldn't connect the pictures of my jumbled thoughts.

Save my mother? Goran! We can warn them.

Blake squinted and then he got what I was thinking.

He jumped up. "No!"

For the first time I realized we weren't alone. Across the room, Constance and my father jumped at his seemingly sudden reaction.

"What is going on?" my father asked.

Blake got up from the bed and started to pace.

I noticed Annie sitting on a chair in the corner. She looked relieved. All of them did. But more worry lines appeared.

"Elena, I'm *not* going to do that." Blake's voice broke my gaze from Annie.

Just like that, he'd said no. "Blake, if what you showed me is the truth…" I thought back to that time underneath the tree when I couldn't remember anything. When I'd thought he was saying goodbye. He had jumped back. It was *his* ability, not the Dent.

That time he'd been gone, just vanished. What if it hadn't been caused by breaking his oath? What if it was linked to this? This might be the beginning of the bright light, all those bright lights he and George had been speaking about for years.

My eyes found Blake. He squinted at me.

He shook his head. *You don't know that.*

I spoke aloud. "I do, Blake. It explains everything."

My father cleared his throat. "What is going on?" Our silent conversations frustrated all of them

Blake's eyes flashed. Was it condescension or embarrassment? "Elena thinks I own a new ability."

"Own?" Constance asked, looking from Blake to me still sitting in my bed. "But only Dragonians have abilities, not their dragons."

"It's the only thing that makes sense," I said out loud. Silently I added, *With the dent. You know it is. You were there, Blake. It explains why you didn't remember me the first time you met me. Because you weren't there. But you were there the next time.*

Blake closed his eyes, rested his hands on his head. The way he did when he felt frustrated. I had to get through to him.

We can go back twenty-seven years and warn my parents. We can tell them that Goran is the one who is going to betray them.

"Elena, I'm not going to do it!" he said, pulling me out of my blithe thoughts. The feeling of meeting my mother for real, and being able to grow up, have a different life, disappeared instantly with his words.

Why?

I'm not going to mess with the past. You never know what it is you are going to change.

I stared at him in disbelief. He hadn't even given this a second thought. It was no from the beginning.

"What is going on? You are scaring us," my father said in a gentle tone.

Blake knew how badly I wanted my mother, how badly I wanted to have grown up this side, to not have the past I had. He knew.

We'd always tried not to talk about what-ifs, because they didn't exist. But here in front of us was a real what-if. We truly did have the ability to change things.

And he didn't want to fix what had happened.

"It's final, Elena!" he roared. He stomped out of the room.

"What the hell is going on?" Annie sounded freaked out.

I sighed as tears welled up in my eyes.

"Elena." My father spoke softly and stroked my back with his one hand.

I shook my head. "He doesn't want to go back and warn you about Goran. He doesn't want us to change that past."

My father listened with concern etched across his features as I told him everything.

"Blake does have a point, sweetheart. You can't tamper with the past."

"Dad, if we could warn you that this was going to happen, that Goran was behind all of this…Wouldn't you try to save Mom?"

"Save Mom? What about Constance and Annie, Elena?" My father sounded disappointed.

I realized how ungrateful I must sound.

"Don't, Albert. I'm with Elena. It means that the Creepers would've never come, and Katie would still be alive, caring for her daughter the way she always wanted. Lee would still be here. Annie wouldn't…" She couldn't finish. "All your men, nobody would have experienced the darkness that came with Goran."

I just stared at both of them. I felt terrible, wanting my mother back, changing this life that was already good and sweet.

"I appreciate it, but Blake made up his mind," I said.

She looked at me with eyes filled with compassion. She came over to my bed and sat down next to me, rubbing my shoulder.

My father spoke. "Some things are meant to stay in the past, Elena." He sat down in the spot Blake had occupied a few minutes earlier, near Constance. The thought of being able to correct his mistakes was a hard pill to swallow. Something sweet yet unknown. Fear, danger, all of it was reflected on my father's face. He almost never carried that look anymore.

"Then why did he get this ability, Dad? Why? Don't you want to be able to do things differently? Save Mom?"

"Don't *ask* me that, Elena!" He got up and paced.

Constance, Annie, and I just stared at him. Then Constance smiled. "I would love to go back and save Lee if I had the ability."

He stopped. He leveled a stare at her as if what she said was blasphemy. "And give up your place as my queen?"

She went over to my father and laid her hands on his cheek. "My dearest Albert. You seem to be forgetting something. If Elena and Blake go back, we wouldn't even know we were married. If it means all the people in Paegeia can be alive and well, without living in constant fear of what happened so many years ago, then yes. I would give up everything."

FIVE

ELENA

That was two weeks ago.

I hadn't spoken with Blake more than five sentences since then.

He'd tried to make things right, but I could still see his intent in his mind. He wanted me to get over it, to forget about it. He'd refused to give in, to give me what I didn't just want but desperately needed. To save my mom.

Constance got it. Even Annie did. The possibility of saving her father was something she would do in a heartbeat, to erase her horrible past. She would if she owned that ability.

Blake, well…he became more and more like my father.

A great power like that comes with a price. What price, we didn't know, but Blake didn't even want to give it a thought or find out.

He loved his abilities, but not this one.

I was standing with Silho sleeping in my arms. She didn't feel heavy as toddlers should. I was rocking her absentmindedly and gazing out the window over the castle grounds when Blake came in.

"Elena."

I filled my mind with a lullaby Constance used to sing. I didn't dare think about anything else. He wouldn't get anything from my mind.

Ignoring him, I carried Silho to her crib and laid her down gently. Without waking, she popped her thumb in her mouth as I tucked the blanket under her chin. Her dark eyelashes flickered against her chubby cheek as her eyes followed innocent dreams.

I could tell he didn't like the silence from me.

"You are just as stubborn as your mother," he grunted. That got my attention.

"Oh really, *really*? Just as stubborn as her? Well, I wouldn't know as I *never had the chance to meet her*, Blake." Venom dripped from my voice. "And now that we have the chance to save her..." My hands were all over the place. I looked at the ceiling. "You are too shit-scared to take it. To help me go and warn them about what is going to happen."

"Yes, I'm scared, Elena," he whispered loudly, not wanting to wake Silho. "All you care about is going back to save her. What about the people in your life? You ever think about them? What about Becky and Sammy? What if they are never in your life? Worse, what if you don't make it to your sixteenth birthday?"

"Why wouldn't I make it to my sixteenth birthday?" I frowned. "I made it with evil dragons trying to kill me,

Blake."

"Fine, then what about Silho?" His face drained of color.

I saw it flashing through his mind before he said it aloud. She might not be in our lives. That terrified him more than anything else. That was his deepest fear. Losing our daughter.

My eyes welled up. Fondness for him wormed its way into my heart despite how angry I felt.

"You don't know that. She is a part of us. She will be there." I was stubborn.

"No, you don't know that," he said through gritted teeth. Tears filled his eyes. "Changing the past has a price, Elena. Consequences."

I didn't care. I was that selfish and that dead-set on going back to warn them. "Fine. What about Lucian?" I didn't want to bring that up. Heaven knew how guilty he felt over Lucian's death. He was worried about who I would have chosen if Lucian had survived. "What about Brian, Desi, King Helmut, and Queen Margerite? All of them who died for nothing! All of them could live. If you just…"

No! he roared. Silent or not, his message was loud and clear. He rushed out of the room. The door slammed behind him. Silho whimpered at the noise. I wanted to cuss as I rushed to her and stroked her tiny body, encouraging her to go back to sleep.

I sighed as I watched her close her eyes again.

She was the spitting image of her father. She had his raven hair, his beautiful peacock eyes—mixed with my green ones—even his cheekbones.

The only thing she had from me was my chin and my nose. Or at least it seemed that way for now; one could never really tell with babies.

I sighed. Was I a bad mother? What if Blake was right? What if we went back in time and changed things, and she was never born? I'd seen the terror he felt at this possibility. It loomed so clear in his mind.

Tears lingered in my eyes as I continued stroking her precious face.

What was my mother going through when she had to give me up? I didn't know if I would be able to do that. And yet here I was, contemplating going back and saving her. Ready to risk Silho's very existence.

Constance was an amazing substitute mother. But even so, there would always be that emptiness inside me, of wanting my real mother by my side.

Ever since the night Blake had given me that chance to meet her, it had only grown stronger, the hole she'd left in my chest when I had to say goodbye.

Sure, it had diminished after a while. I was one of the happiest women in this world. But then when I'd gotten pregnant with Silho, the hole had appeared again. I wanted my baby to have her grandmother.

I would always imagine her somewhere close, enjoying this special time with all of us. But she wasn't really there.

It had hit me even harder the minute they put Silho in my arms. She'd cried her heart out with her first few breaths. My tears were happy ones...until the worry arose. How were we going to raise her? What my mother had gone through with me flooded my thoughts. It had suffocated me. It turned me into a paranoid mother for the first few months, scared that someone was going to take her away from me, or that I was going to be forced to give Silho up for her own safety, like my mother had

with me. I had been a mess

Blake would find me crying. Sometimes I locked myself in the bathroom to weep. Sometimes he caught my tears early in the mornings.

My mother gave me up to save my life. I would never be able to do what she'd had to do. Could I, even if Silho's life was in danger?

I could relate to why she'd transformed into a living corpse the last year of her life.

Life couldn't have been easy on her.

Yet my husband had the ability to change all of this. And he didn't even give it a second thought.

That was the hardest pill to swallow.

Becky and George arrived.

George went fishing with Blake. Becky and little Dean visited me and Silho. Dean was about four months older than Silho. He was the spitting image of his mom but sported his dad's dimples.

We took iced beverages out to the garden and watched the two little ones play on a blanket spread under the trees. My father stopped by to greet Becky and tousle Dean's hair, but he faded away without saying anything further.

Nobody wanted to talk about it.

Becky waited till my father left. Then she opened her mouth. "Blake has a point, Elena. If there's any chance that Silho wouldn't be born…"

I scowled. "I know, Becky. I feel like a bad mom."

"You are not a bad mom. I understand why you want to do this, why it's so hard to resist. Since that night we found out what Blake could do…" She sighed with such force, her short black hair flopped off her forehead. "Just thinking about what life would be like with my father at our side, watching me grow up…" I could see it in her brown eyes as she stared at nothing in front of her. "But he is right. You don't know what price you'll have to pay to fix the past."

I shook my head. "Sammy?" I said. One word.

"What about Sammy?"

"Don't tell me you didn't think about her, Becky. If we could go back and save Dean…"

"It's in the past, Elena. Sammy is fine."

"Sammy isn't fine, Becky," I retorted. "She hasn't been fine for a long time. She carries guilt around with her every day. She can't forgive herself for not protecting him. She throws herself into work all the time. She won't visit for more than ten minutes at a time, then concocts excuses to fly off. She *isn't* fine. She's never going to be fine without him."

"He wasn't her Dent."

"And neither is Sir Robert my father's. It doesn't mean she didn't love him. Dragons love differently."

I couldn't believe that we were fighting over this.

"What about Lucian?" Becky insisted. "Have you thought about what any of this will do to him? You and Blake?"

I started to laugh. "There will be no Lucian and me if we go back, Becky. Still, he will be alive and not killed like a fucking animal."

She looked pensive. "So if you go back and change the past, how do you think it will affect you, Elena?"

"I don't care. I just want to save the people I loved, the people who deserve to be alive."

59

She nodded. "You think George and I…"

I threw up my hands. "Oh come on! He is your Dent. That will never change."

Her mouth quirked in response to my temper. "I'm just weighing everything up before I put myself in your corner, Elena."

She was beginning to see my point. Finally, someone other than Constance and Annie stood in my corner.

A smile sprawled over my face. "He is going to hate me for this. He already hates me for just thinking about this. For making his life a living hell at the moment."

"Well, you did turn into a spoiled brat." Classic Becky with her two cents.

I giggled. "I miss Sammy. I want her to be happy. If we go back and change everything, she might get her chance. Dean might not even be her Dragonian. She might eventually find her Dent. Who knows, maybe he died."

"Or she," Becky chirped.

"Fine," I allowed grudgingly. "Or she. When the Creepers consumed everything."

She lapsed into silence for a long time. We both watched the kiddos tussling under the tree. "You know how big this change is going to be, Elena?"

I nodded.

"No, I don't think you really do."

"I do, Becky. I've had two weeks to think about why I shouldn't do this, and the reasons I should always outweigh the reasons I shouldn't."

"What if Dean isn't going to be in our lives? What if Silho isn't going to be in yours?"

"I don't know. I can't answer that. But something tells me they will be there." Though there was no evidence of this, I felt in my bones it was true.

Her lips vibrated as she blew out some air. "Okay, fine. If this is what you want to do. You know me. Always in your corner no matter how crazy it sounds."

I grabbed her around her neck and pulled her into a fierce hug. "Thanks, Becks."

Becky and Dean left the minute George and Blake came back from their fishing.

Blake looked even more pissed off. I could see that the two of them had spoken about this today. He'd blocked me out, but not before I'd gotten most of what George had to say.

His visions, the ones he didn't want to share, were of a different life. A better life.

George was trying to persuade him to go for it. That news hit me harder than I'd thought. I smiled at George as he walked past me. I now understood why Becky was so adamant. She was on Blake's side—well, she had been, but she wasn't anymore.

Blake picked Silho up from the blanket and walked with her into the castle. I packed up the drinks and blanket and followed him in.

We didn't speak about it that night. Constance tried to get conversation around the dinner table going, but the minute Blake's plate was cleared, he stood up, collected Silho into his arms, and left again.

I threw my fork on the plate with a loud clatter. *Was this how it was going to be from now on? Neither of us compromising?* I yelled after him in my mind, but he didn't answer.

"Elena, give him some time," Constance spoke softly.

"Don't," my father said. "It's in the past, Constance. Nothing happens without a reason. We don't know what the future—I mean, our present—would be like if the Creepers didn't exist."

"It can't be worse, Albert. It could only be better. All those families. The McKenzies. Your men. Devoted men who died, who should never have died. Have you even considered how many dragons and Dragonians will never team up because some of them don't exist anymore?"

"Please," I interrupted. "Don't argue. It's not your fight. This is between Blake and me."

My father's expression was filled with kindness. "Elena, I know why you want to go back."

"No, Dad. You don't. You had her for more than two hundred years. It's not that I'm not happy. I am. But if there is a shred of a chance to save her...To be able to grow up with a mother, to grow up in this world...Then yes. I would give up my happiness and take that chance to find out. I would do it in a heartbeat. And that is something none of you will understand. None of you grew up the way I did."

I looked at Annie, who studied her plate, face pink. "Well, Annie knows what I feel," I amended. "She's probably the only one."

Constance touched Annie's hand. A small smile tugged at the corners of Annie's mouth.

"May I be excused?" I asked.

My father nodded.

I got up and walked past Jeeves and a couple of the dining staff. "Thanks, Jeeves, the dinner was amazing."

"I'll tell the chef, Princess."

They were never going to budge. Not my father, and not Blake. My mother was going to stay where she was: a memory buried in a grave that held no bones. That was something I had to get over.

SIX

ELENA

I stood at the threshold of our bedroom. Though I was tired, our big bed held no appeal. I'd been sleeping alone the last few days. Blake had this thing about not sleeping in the same bed if either one of us was angry. It wasn't anger in me; it was sadness. Okay there was a little anger, but mostly sadness for my mother, sadness for the fact that my daughter wasn't enough. Guilt, too.

I was adamant. I didn't want to believe that she wouldn't be there. She was a part of us. Of course she would be there. Everything would work out the exact same way, just with a happier ending. If only he could see it.

I felt so alone. It was nothing to do with sleeping in that huge bed by myself. My husband wasn't on the same page as me. This had almost never happened in eight years.

I went over to Silho's crib and said goodnight to Simone, who was reading her a story softly. She set aside the book and gave me a small curtsy before she exited the room.

She had been my maid for a long time. She knew a dark cloud stalked me. I kissed Silho softly on her cheek and tucked her in. She made me sad. Sad that my mother never had the opportunity to see me when I was this age. Sad that she might be the price we would have to pay if we went back to change the past. Still, I would do anything for her. Anything. She was my precious little girl. I understood why Blake didn't want to do this. If I knew for certain she wouldn't be in our lives, I wouldn't do this. But I knew she would be. *A mother always knows.* She was meant to be our princess. If only her father could see it.

BLAKE

Three weeks. We had been going on like this for three weeks. Elena wasn't going to budge. She would never give up. I wouldn't either. Not with Silho's life at stake. I loved her too much. Without her, I wouldn't be the man I was today.

Yes, Elena had changed me, but Silho had taken me to another level. Silho had injected a whole new meaning into my life. I could fuck up everything around me except being her father.

If only her mother could see it. But she wasn't interested in my thoughts lately.

I tuned out all the sounds around me. The past few weeks I'd tried. I'd tried to see a way to give Elena what she needed, but it always boiled down to one thing: one road, and a life without Silho. George had confirmed it today; he'd seen it. He'd gotten really good at seeing into the future. That had made my mind up. My answer would never change. Why had he seen a different outcome? He'd seen a different world, a different future.

We couldn't, we wouldn't go back. Still, George had seen it.

My door opened. At first I thought it was Elena sneaking in. She always gave up when she knew I wouldn't change my mind. *Ha!* George's vision had been wrong. But the minute I tried to read her mind, see her intentions, I couldn't.

My arm swung to my lamp. I gasped at what the light revealed.

A familiar form stood before me, hands in the air as if to say he meant me no harm.

Why would he? He was…me? I was staring at myself.

I shut my eyes. *You are dreaming, Blake.* But when I opened my eyes again, he was still there.

"I mean you no harm. I just come with a message."

His voice was my voice. He looked exactly like me. A bit older, but he was me.

My heartbeat rose. "Why are you here?"

"You know why."

"No, I don't." I pushed myself off my bed, not breaking eye contact.

"May I sit down?"

Unnerved, I nodded. I followed him to the chair, watching him like a hawk.

"You need to go back."

I scowled. "Don't ask me that. Silho won't be …"

"She is going to destroy Paegeia if you don't. She'll

bring you more sorrow than you can handle."

My breath constricted. My legs became liquid and I sank into the chair opposite the man who looked so much like me. "What?" *No, she would never.* "Who are you?"

"I'm you. You know that." His peacock-blue eyes challenged me, and I nodded. I'd seen a lot of crazy things, and there was no other explanation. Especially now that I owned the ability to travel in time. I was meeting with my future self.

"What I said about her, it's the truth," he insisted. He sounded so hollow. So tired. "Silho will destroy everything."

Silho...impossible! "No, she wouldn't. Never. Not how we've been raising her."

He sighed. "You mean the way *you've* been raising her."

I squinted. A new fear tried to strangle me. "What do you mean, I?"

"She is going to kill Elena. We all thought it was an accident, but it wasn't. Silho is dark. Always has been. If you don't listen to me, you will lose everything." He looked so lost. "So please, I'm begging you, go back. Give your people a different future, one without heartache."

"When?" I asked.

Mutely, he shook his head.

"When is she going to kill Elena?"

"I tried too many times to save her. It still always happens later or earlier, no matter what I do to change the timeline. I could never kill my own daughter...and the ones who tried met my wrath. I'm tired," he said through clenched teeth. "Please."

I just sat there, numb.

"Change the past, I'm begging you. Give our people a different future. Please."

He got up slowly and I snapped out of it. "Where are you going?"

"Back to my time. Hopefully back to a better future where the love of my life still exists."

I looked at him again. He did look exhausted. Even angry. Angry at whom? Me. Himself.

It was me.

He paused at the door.

"Wait," I stalled. "Are you sure there is nothing we can do for Silho?"

"We tried everything…There is nothing. You will always protect her with your life, even though you know the truth. You can't help it. You love her too much. But she was never supposed to be born."

He left.

My daughter, my adorable, sweet little girl…was going to kill her mother.

Pain stabbed through my heart as I tried to imagine the type of sorrow he spoke of. How much pain my child had unleashed on me. Murdering her mother. Those delicate hands raised against her mother. She couldn't. She wouldn't be able to.

I fell to my knees as the pain expanded, stronger and stronger. Waves of grief crashed on the shore of my being. I wouldn't be able to live without Elena. I wasn't as strong as her father. I would never find another love. I was a dragon. She was my Dent.

I got up from the floor and rushed to my wife.

ELENA

I sat at the windowsill, looking at the moon. It was so bright tonight.

A knock on the door made me jump. I climbed down. "Enter," I said. An older, blonde woman opened the door.

She gasped as she saw me. I'd never seen this woman in my entire life. Yet she knew me. She was wearing a staff uniform.

"Can I help you?"

"Sorry to bother you, Princess," she said and closed the door behind her. My heart beat harder as she came over to me. Who was she?

She came to a halt and bestowed upon me a beautiful smile. Her dark eyes shone.

"I never thought I would see you again." She threw her arms around my neck.

I hadn't expected that, not one bit.

"Okay," I said as I tapped her back awkwardly. "Do I know you?" Was this some escaped patient from an asylum?

"Not yet," she whispered.

I frowned. "What did you say?"

"Morgan," Blake's voice called from outside. I looked at my closed door and back to this woman.

"How do..."

"I've got to go. Everything will work out the way it's meant to be. I promise."

She ran to the door and left.

Dumbfounded, I just stood there blinking at where she'd disappeared. Who the hell was this Morgan? How did she know me? Then whatever glued me to the floor let go and I rushed after her, opening the door. I found nothing.

My heart raced. Anger boiled inside of me.

A bright flash lit up the evening sky, then it disappeared.

Not yet… I thought about her words. I looked at the sky again. It was filled with stars and a beautiful moon. *It couldn't be…?*

My door opened again and Blake ran in. He didn't say anything. He was deranged. He cried. I got a dose of images from his thoughts. He was in a full-blown panic. *Silho.* Sobbing, he flung his arms around me.

"You're scaring me! What about Silho?" I asked.

He didn't respond. Pain and darkness emanated from him. His body shook in my embrace.

"Blake, please," I begged. "What about Silho?"

Then I saw it. Someone had visited him. Another Blake. He had a conversation with his older self. A self that was weary, broken. He'd begged. He'd revealed a horrible truth to Blake about Silho. She was going to destroy the world one day. She was going to kill…me.

I gasped and pushed him away.

"You weren't supposed to see that," he cried. "I didn't want to believe him, but he said she was never supposed to be born."

She killed—will kill—me. Why?

"We need to go back. If that is what it takes for the future to be brighter, we must go back. We need to set this right, Elena."

Hot tears flowed over my cheeks. Silho was going to be the price we were going to have to pay.

My baby girl was destined to become evil. *How? Why?* In all my what-ifs, I'd never considered this possibility.

"Was it really you?" I asked.

He nodded.

I believed him. Somehow. Crazy as this all was. I sniffled. "So…Morgan?"

He cocked his head, awkward in my arms. "Who?"

"There was a woman earlier. Just now. She didn't make any sense, just hugged me and then told me she never thought it was possible that she would ever see me…" I gasped. "She never did, because Silho killed me."

"Shh, you weren't supposed to see that, Elena. I tried so hard to hide it, but my emotions…I'm sorry." He hugged me tighter. "It will never happen. I promise. We will change it. You are *not* going to die."

SEVEN

ELENA

We spoke to everyone close to us.

My father didn't understand our reasoning at first. He was scared. But the minute Blake told him about the visit from his future self, he understood. Sadness pervaded him. Sadness, but not resistance.

We had to make things right. Not just for the people, but for Silho, too. She would have peace in the afterlife.

We were going to change the past.

Nobody had ever gotten that opportunity before. We were going to try.

"What if you don't listen to us?" I asked my father. Déjà vu crept into my gut.

"Then *make* us listen, Elena. Goran had a militia stationed on the northern side of the castle behind the forest. Tell me they will be there."

"Dad." I sighed.

"Make me believe you."

"What about Mom?"

"Your mother is out of the question, Elena. She was lost. She wouldn't even see you. I'm sorry, sweet pea. I doubt you will see your mother on this trip."

Disappointment filled my chest, but I nodded.

He looked worried. His eyes shone with tears.

"Dad?"

"It's Goran, Elena. Just try to be as gentle as possible."

I got what he was saying. Goran's betrayal had been a hard blow back when it had happened. Hearing it from someone's mouth before it even came to pass would be even harder.

"I will try my best. Promise."

A layout of the old castle before my mother's wing burned down lay open on the table between us. He was showing me all the hidden passages. If anything went wrong, we would at least be able to get away safely.

I said goodnight and returned to my room.

Blake was playing with Silho on the bed. He hadn't attended any of the evening meetings with my father. He knew what would happen when we got back to our own timeline.

Silho wouldn't be here.

I climbed on the bed. She turned her face toward me and smiled. She was so damn beautiful. It was hard to imagine that her future was so dark.

I bent and kissed her temple. My lips lingered as tears welled up in my eyes.

She clutched one of Blake's wristbands in her tiny fist. Her chubby arms swung wildly. Joyous cackles spilled her mouth. She crawled over to Blake and fell on him as she kissed him.

Blake rubbed her back and my leg with his other free hand.

It was so unreal to think she would become someone evil. Someone who would destroy our world.

We spent the entire night with her. When Simone arrived to give her a bath, I sent her away. I wanted to do it myself.

Blake and I wanted to spend every minute we could with her. Every last, precious millisecond.

When we returned, everything would be changed. Whether my mother would be here or not, this present moment would be different. My father would be different. Sammy and Becky, everyone.

I just hoped it would be for the best.

Silho slept with us the evening before our departure.

I sobbed in the bathroom. My breath came in gulping waves, salty with crocodile tears that wouldn't stop. I couldn't imagine life without my baby girl. Even if she was destined to be evil, she was my *daughter*. She would *always* be my daughter. But she couldn't have this life. I couldn't allow her to have a dark future. I could change it. Her mother and father had the ability to change it. I believed with my entire heart that we would see her one day again in the afterlife. Surely timelines converged there. She would understand.

She would have to understand. I hoped.

My cries echoed throughout the night.

The next morning, I packed a bag with some essentials—water bottles, bandages—just in case we ran into trouble. We all had breakfast together. Everyone came, even Sammy. Displaying the most emotion I'd seen in her for years, Sammy begged us not to go.

Silho was going to stay with my father until everything changed. I wondered what it would be like for them.

I hoped it would be easy, that they'd be waking up with no knowledge of what they had lost. If they were all going to remember this past, this world, it would be hard. But Ralph had said it would be impossible for them to remember our version of things. So it would only be Blake and me who would remember this life, this truth…and Silho.

Saying goodbye was the hardest. Especially when it came to Constance and Annie.

"You know you will always be my sister, no matter what happens," I said, hugging Annie.

"I know."

I looked at Constance. "It's not that you weren't a wonderful mother. You are the best…"

"Shh, Elena. You don't need to explain. I know. A mother always knows. And it's time that you meet your own. Make them see. Make them believe." She hugged me tight. "I know you can do it."

Blake carried Silho in his arms. She was happy. This was how I wanted to remember her. A happy baby.

My dad was next. I kissed him and he swept me into an embrace. "I will try my best to be as gentle as possible, Dad."

He smiled. "Be careful, Elena. Goran was extremely powerful, even back then. Don't let him get suspicious."

"I won't."

Then it was Silho. My daughter. My heart. I took her from Blake and just held her tight. Tears poured down my cheeks. Her bright eyes went round with childlike wonder at the wetness on my face.

Blake rubbed my shoulder as he bent over to kiss her on her raven-black curls.

"I love you, baby girl. So much. I will always love you, forever and ever."

She toyed with my necklace, not understanding a single word. I pressed my lips on her head. My heart felt too heavy to move on. *She will be happy, Elena. George saw it.*

He showed me the vision that George explained to him. She was happy. So happy. Playing in a beautiful garden surrounded by loving people, Cara among them. I knew it was heaven.

That gave my soul a modicum of peace.

I gave her to Constance. Blake disrobed and changed into his dragon form. I bundled his clothes up for later.

I could barely speak past the stranglehold of grief. "See you soon."

"You bet on it, sweet pea. Now go save your mom, and good luck." My father gave me one last hug. "I know you can do it," he whispered into my ear.

Shouldering my backpack, I nodded and climbed onto Blake's wing. I didn't look at my family again. It was just too hard.

So where to, Elena?

I don't know. Something tells me jumping back in time is a Rubicon thing.

He laughed. It wasn't an out-of-his-belly type of laugh, and it wasn't a chuckle either. It was something in between.

Okay, so let's try this. He started to calculate everything. The speed he'd flown that night we'd gone back in time, the distance, what he'd been thinking... No, that one wasn't really necessary; he'd been having fun. It wasn't connected to anything. He hadn't been thinking about the past.

Hold on!

I wrapped his tendrils—which I sometimes teased him by saying they looked like catfish whiskers—gently around my palms. When I gave him the go ahead, he darted up into the sky and flew up into the air. His speed took my breath away. The whipping wind stole the tears from my eyes.

He zipped back down and up again. We carried on like that for at least twenty minutes. Nothing happened.

There was no bright light, no passing back in time.

I don't know what happened, Elena. I don't know how to do this.

It's okay. We will get there. Just be patient.

Frustration colored his thoughts. *Maybe it was a night thing. I think we should camp until nighttime and see what happens.*

I hoped he was right about this and it wasn't some sort of a mental thing.

It's not a mental connection, Elena.

I sometimes hated that he was so married to my thoughts.

I love it.

I chuckled. He broke the wall of my grief for just a moment. But it settled back on my shoulders, heavy and implacable.

We landed on Mount Likwa and waited underneath one of the trees until night came.

"So," he spoke out loud as I was resting with my back against his chest. He was still naked, but we were both too grief-stricken to be stricken with lust at the moment. Our fingers were intertwined. The sound of buzzing insects were as loud as a sledge hammer on a busy road.

"I think we should not introduce ourselves to your father as ourselves."

"You mean pretend to be other people?" I asked, confused.

"Yes. It's the only way for Goran not to suspect anything."

I sighed. My father had warned me not to let him suspect anything, that he'd been powerful, even back then.

Silence shrouded us. How were we going to get my father, Sir Robert, and Goran to trust us?

I advocated for keeping our true forms, me a Dragonian and Blake the Rubicon.

He didn't think it was a good idea, since no two Rubicons existed at the same time and his father might get worried.

I argued that my father, in his curiosity to know me— a rider of a Rubicon—would keep Sir Robert at ease. We would come in peace, even if I had to say it a thousand times for Sir Robert to not get paranoid and do something stupid.

Blake didn't like this at all, but it was the only way to

pique their interest. We hoped to get an invitation to stay over at the castle, even just for a night.

I would do anything to meet my mother, anything.

My father had made it clear that my mother would be out of the question. That we couldn't get to her. That she didn't want to see anybody. She didn't even want to see my father. Not to mention two strangers.

Blake rubbed my arm. "We will make them believe, Elena. I promise."

I had a bad feeling about this. What if they didn't believe us? "How are we going to do this, Blake. Jump back to the right time, the exact time that both of us were already born?"

He grunted. "I don't know how this ability works, Elena. We'll figure it out."

When darkness fell and the stars started to shine, I could see a bright light forming in Blake's mind up in the sky. My head jerked up but I only saw stars, no light.

Still Blake saw it.

"You can't see it?"

"Unless I'm looking through your eyes, no."

"You are right, then. It is only a Rubicon thing." He got up and gave me a hand. His hand didn't leave mine as he guided it around his neck. I climbed on his back, and then he ran, jumped off the cliff and morphed midair.

I still couldn't see the bright light, but through Blake's mind, I could see it as clear as he did.

It came closer and closer. Both our hearts beat at the same pace. We were excited, yet terrified of what we would find behind that light.

Screaming, I shut my eyes against the brilliance. The light engulfed us. All I could think about was that night we'd done this the first time. The night my mother had shot me with one of her arrows.

I didn't want that again.

Daylight seeped through my eyelids.

We did it?

I opened my eyes and saw open lands. Here and there were a few homes.

Where are we?

Your guess is as good as mine. Blake flew toward the trees. *I have no idea what I'm doing, remember?*

I heard people shouting below. A male voice bellowed, "Ready the dragon catcher!"

I couldn't see who it was, but I knew it wasn't good. We had to be in Quitto's time, back when they used nasty contraptions to capture dragons.

Two Rubicons couldn't exist in the same time. If we found him, we couldn't kill him. My great-great-grandfather needed to kill him. Otherwise our bloodline would never become royalty.

Trepidation grew larger than grief. Changing the past came at a steep price.

EIGHT

ELENA

We landed in the woods. Blake changed back into his human form and hurriedly pulled his clothes on. We figured if we could pass over Quitto, it might not be so terrible. We knew about this era. The Dragonians of this time were like Vikings. Stubborn as hell. Impossible to negotiate with.

And they killed all dragons. They didn't even know dragons had a human form yet.

Under no circumstances could Blake reveal his dragon form.

"We need to find out the exact year, Elena."

"Don't do this. I don't want to be stuck here, Blake."

"You won't, but I need to know if this is the timeline we think it is."

"Okay, then change our appearance and I'll come with you."

"No, you stay here." He was adamant.

"I'm not splitting up." My voice was shrill. "Haven't you learned through all these years, shit happens when the two of us split up?"

His jaw was set. He reminded me of Herbert.

"I'm coming with. Otherwise we are staying here until nightfall."

"Okay, fine. Let's go."

He muttered an incantation that only changed our wardrobe so we could blend into the era of my great-great-great-grandfather. His jeans and black V-neck transformed to a loose white tunic and brown leather pants. I found myself wearing a thin brown dress, more a potato sack, instead of my sweater and jeans. *Ugh, Blake. You couldn't make it a little less hideous?*

He chuckled.

It really was a bummer that we could only jump back at night. We were stuck here, for better or worse, for at least a few hours. Then we'd have to try time-jumping again to land in the right era.

Where are we?

I think we are somewhere in Tith.

Tith?

I looked down at the mountain. It didn't look anything like Tith.

They lived differently in this time, Elena. You won't find cities or modern plumbing, so I suggest you hold it in.

I laughed nervously. I didn't want to think about trying to take a wee, not in this era. As we walked, I wondered how they took care of their business in this era.

A shovel and a couple minutes of digging, Blake chirped.

Don't roll your eyes at me. I'm serious. We don't have a shovel, Elena.

Shut up, then.

Blake laughed. I shouldered my backpack, which resembled a potato sack even more than my dress, and followed him. He found a wide dirt path through the woods, well-worn by travelers. No doubt it led to a village, where we could find out exactly which time period we had blasted into.

The village wasn't big. It was mostly comprised of rows of houses made from stones and straw-thatched roofs. It smelled like garbage, mildew, and urine. I covered my nose with my sleeve.

Smoke curled from their chimneys, but we saw no one in the muddy street. We approached a small tavern with a wine barrel burned into the wooden bark attached to the doorway. As we passed, a drunk man was tossed out of the door. His filthy arms pin-wheeled wildly as he stumbled a few feet from me.

Blake dropped into battle stance that years of training had drilled into his instinct. He reached out his hand for me protectively. I ran toward him. We left the drunkard behind; no doubt he wouldn't be coherent.

The streets were caked with churned mud. Dust lay thick in the air. *How did people live in this era?* I coughed as the stench seeped through my sleeve to my nostrils.

A door opened and a woman threw a bucket of dirty water right in front of my feet.

I paused and watched it spread across the street, inches from my toes.

It wasn't water at all; it was their sewage!

"Ugh," I groaned, disgusted. I almost lost it. Blake,

with a huge grin plastered on his face, helped me over it so that it didn't touch my shoes or the horrible excuse for a dress.

You are such a snob. He was enjoying this.

I huffed. *I'm not a snob. I just dislike everything about this era. Can you please find out in which era we are so we can get out of here, please?*

And how do you suppose I do that, Princess? Go into the bar and say, "Can you please tell me what day it is?"

I couldn't help but laugh. The way he'd said it was so hilarious, using his mother's high English accent.

A bigger house stood at the end of the street.

What was burned above the door gave me the shivers. It carried the symbol that was still used today. A skull of a dragon. It was the symbol of the black market. The place where the body parts of slaughtered dragons were hawked by murderers.

Blake held my hand tighter. This was a terrible time, indeed.

Can we please not go in there?

He wanted to see what was going on in there. He wanted to try to change this. Maybe end the black market. It was something nobody could put a stop to in our future.

I hated this so much, but I relented. We opened the door and went in.

Wooden buckets littered the floor. Dragon scales—white, blue, green, red, copper—all types of dragons were killed like soulless animals. Dragon intestines were strewn about. Dried blood caked the edges of the room. Tears welled up in my eyes.

Don't cry, Elena. They won't understand.

I already hated my great-great-great-grandfather. I

remembered the wax doll they had of him inside the museum in Etan. *I'm so sorry.*

But Blake was right. They didn't know better.

Then someone needs to tell them.

They need to kill Quitto. Otherwise your great-great-great-grandfather will never become king.

Something sprang into my mind. A scrap I'd read somewhere. Great men slew dragons, it had said. But only the brave ones tamed them.

I could see my face staring at everything through Blake's eyes. I looked at him. He squinted.

What is it?

I think you just found a way for us to change this era, Elena.

What? Are you insane?

We need to find your great-great-great grandfather.

I didn't like this idea, but Blake went around asking villagers where William Malone could be found. They all directed him to a farm two miles from the village.

We headed there as quickly as we could. Forty minutes later we stood at the edge of the property. It wasn't a farm. Sure, it looked like one, but as we approached, all the hair on my body stood on end.

Blake didn't look anything like the other men. He was big, but he was fine and neat. I ruffled his black hair anxiously.

It's not going to work. Change your appearance.

He was about to when one of the men, who was sharpening a knife on a whetstone, looked up.

"May I help you?" the guy asked. I gasped. It was him. My great-great-great-grandfather.

"Good day." Blake tried to imitate their stilted accent. "My name is Blake."

Shit! I yelled.

"That's a bit of an unusual name you have there."

"It's just a name," he said, trying to charm a creature that couldn't be charmed.

"I am William Malone. I'm the keeper of this fine establishment. You looking for some weapons? You have a dragon problem?"

He was already in the dragon business.

"No," Blake said.

"Then what do you want?"

"I come with a plan."

William frowned suspiciously. "What plan?"

"To make all your Quitto problems disappear."

"Who is Quitto?" He asked.

"The dragon haunting your world."

William ground his teeth. "Didn't your mother ever tell you not to give anything you don't like a name?"

"That she did," Blake lied easily.

William pulled his sword. I stepped in front of Blake.

Don't do anything stupid. Without him, your family line will never come to exist.

William laughed scornfully. "And who is this young lass?"

"My name is Eleanore," I said. It sounded like a name that would fit with his time.

His lip curled. "You dare speak to a man?"

I sighed and rolled my eyes. "You're seriously kidding me, right?"

Elena, your language.

William squinted. "She is a brave lass. That I can give her. But you should control your woman."

Lowering his sword, he gestured for us to follow him. As we stepped over the threshold of his house, he asked us if we were hungry.

Blake nodded. *Accept. They hate it when people decline.*

Sitting and hugging my disguised backpack between my knees, I turned up my nose at the white slop he put in front of us. Blake ate it as if there was no tomorrow. I smiled when I found William's eyes on me and put my hand into the slop. *No fucking spoons. When were spoons invented?*

As I tried to stomach the gelatinous muck, my eyes snagged on a birthmark on William's arm. It was dark just like mine.

Blake looked up when he saw it in my mind.

William Malone was Quitto's Dent.

He had covered it up. Marks like that were considered signs a person would become evil. How had my pops hidden it all these years?

He pulled a sword. "I don't know what you think you saw, but it's not what you think." He thrust his blade at Blake.

"Calm down," Blake said. "We mean you no harm." He nodded toward me. "She has that same mark."

William's eyes narrowed. He turned his gaze from Blake to me.

"Show me."

Show him, Elena, if you don't want to be stuck in this era. I do not want to die by this man's hand.

My limbs shaking, I got up, gave William a glare and lifted up the hemline of my dress, revealing my mark above my knee. "Now put your sword down, sir."

William laughed and sheathed his sword. "I might be many things, lass, but I'm no sir."

The day progressed quickly. Blake told William where to find the Rubicon. William listened eagerly. It was the foundation of our entire world. What if all those wars had needed to happen? What if we shouldn't change anything?

"Give me your service and we can rid the world of all the rodents in the sky," William begged Blake.

"That's not why I'm here. I have a different proposal, one I need you to be open-minded about."

William nodded, wiping his filthy hands on his pants leg.

"You could slay the dragon," Blake said, his voice low and intense. "But have you ever considered taming it?"

William froze on Blake. "Are you possessed? Nobody could tame that thing."

"You can. That mark is not what you think it is. It's the mark of the Dragon Riders."

"Dragon Riders?" William roared.

Blake, he can't be reasoned with. He's killed too many of them already.

"It's blasphemy!" His eyes twitched. "How do you even know this?"

Shit. Fuck. We need to get out of here, Blake. The sun is almost down.

"Speak, slayer!" William demanded. "How?"

"He's not a slayer!" I yelled. I'd had it with his short temper and his vileness.

"Lass, I told you before, shut your trap."

"Don't you dare tell me what I can and can't do."

William got it. I could see it in his eyes. He whipped out his weapon. Incredibly fast for a hulking giant.

I voiced an incantation just as the sword was in his

hand. The blade had already been flung into the air, turning end over end straight for my beloved's head. At my words it took a different course and hit the wall.

Blake and I darted out of the house.

An alarm went off. It wasn't going to be long before we were surrounded by slayers.

What are we going to do?

Sorry, you were right, Blake admitted. *He can't be reasoned with.*

He was Quitto's rider, wasn't he?

Elena, it's a different time. He's killed way too many already to even consider that possibility. Your great-great-great-grandfather was an important man, but he wasn't a brave one.

We just need to get out of here. Just morph, Blake.

An arrow whizzed overhead. William was shooting at us! We missed another arrow thanks to our enhanced hearing. A third arrow scratched Blake's arm.

He grabbed me and leaped into the sky, morphing into his dragon form.

"It's the devil!" I heard William scream below.

Get me on your back, and fly faster.

He flipped me onto his back and zoomed up in the sky. I clutched my backpack to my chest, unwilling to drop it. Men screamed in terror below; they'd never seen a dragon as massive as Blake.

I could hear the alarm in William's voice, the chase, the hunger. He was vile. *How could my bloodline be descendants from that?*

It felt like we were never going to escape this era. It was the golden hour now, the sun's rays lengthening, but not fast enough. Blake flew higher, past the clouds. He hovered in the air to wait until it was over. We had reached an altitude where no arrows or man-made spikes could reach us. They arced upward in vain attempts, fell in anti-climactic parabolas, and clattered harmlessly among the villagers who shouted futilely at us.

Sorry, Elena.

It's okay. This is safe for now.

Then we heard a screech. I looked toward the horizon. A hulking beast hurtled toward us, dark purple with eyes that glittered with hatred. It was Quitto.

Blake.

Fuck, he said as the Rubicon of this time came in fast.

Blake descended. The sun was ready to set, but it was moving slow.

Blake couldn't kill Quitto; that was William's duty.

My heart galloped in my chest. Danger threatened all around us. In the sky, Quitto. Down below, slayers. All united, in this moment, against us.

I don't want to die here!

We won't. Blake roared and flew up into the sky again. *Just hold on.* He connected hard with Quitto's body. A message: he was bigger and stronger, so back off. But it only angered the ancient dragon all the more. Unlike Blake, Quitto was a dark Rubicon, dark and evil.

They chased one another. Quitto breathed his fire, and I blocked it.

He knocked into Blake. I lost my grip and tumbled through the sky like a ragdoll.

Blake darted back down and caught me, but we were almost in range of the slayers.

Then the bright flash finally appeared.

We both saw it. Blake flew fast toward it.

Quitto saw it, too. He sensed that the light represented some kind of escape. Blake readied to try and knock him unconscious until we were safely out of this era.

He connected hard with him.

My mind become disoriented. He collided so hard with Quitto that he almost lost consciousness himself.

The other Rubicon crashed down onto one of the mountains. An easy kill for William now. Even as I struggled, guilt racked me. What had we done?

Stay with me, I cried in my mind. Blake shook it off as the light brightened.

The swooshing sound came near and I turned to see what was following us. It was one of those spears attached to a net.

A sharp pain pierced through my leg.

Blake growled and I screamed.

Breathe through it, Elena. Just breathe.

Then I realized it wasn't my pain. I looked down at Blake's back paw and saw the spear sticking out of his thigh.

The bright light was right in front of us. I saw it through Blake's mind.

Bite down on your teeth. I'm going to remove the spear.

Blake ground his fangs so hard, I could hear it. I uttered a spell.

The spear shattered in two as Blake pushed harder to get to the light.

The swooshing sound came near again and I erected my magical shield around us. The rest of the spear broke away and fell back down to the ground.

Your quarrel is with Quitto, not us.

The bright light engulfed us and we were free.

NINE

ELENA

Blake hurtled toward the ground. His mind was blank as he struggled to hold on.

Blake! Wake up.

Our speed increased as he tumbled down to the treetops below. They were coming nearer. I kept yelling his name inside my mind.

He finally opened his eyes, but he was still disoriented.

Close your eyes, I said, calmer than I felt. *Trust mine.*

He did, and he righted his position just as we were about to hit. We skidded through the trees and came to a crash-landing.

Dust lay heavy around us. My body ached. I'd never felt so tired.

When I opened my eyes, Blake's hulking figure lay paces from mine.

I had no idea where we were, in which era we were, and whether we were in danger.

I grunted from the twinge of an array of scrapes. My face, my elbow, my torso…everything was sore. My clothes had changed back to the sweater and jeans I'd been wearing in the future, but the material was now torn and grubby from our fall. I thanked the heavens that my ability to heal would kick in soon.

I sucked air through my teeth against the pain and crawled toward Blake.

He was so huge that it took me a few minutes just to reach his face.

I tried to connect with his mind. He was stone cold. Nothing penetrated. He was just a big, dark, black space.

I stroked his face, touching his scales.

The tip of the spear was still lodged in his thigh. *Better get that out now, before he wakes up.* I climbed onto the injured leg and all the way up to his thigh.

He didn't even move.

I stood over the end of the spear, which was the size of a medium tree trunk, and wrapped both my hands around the end that protruded from his body.

I closed my eyes and gathered the strength I needed to yank it out.

He was already healing, and I knew he couldn't with half a tree sticking out his leg.

This is going to hurt like hell. Sorry, baby.

I waited a few seconds, took a huge breath, and pulled as hard as I could.

A sickening tearing sound signified flesh that had healed ripping open again.

Blake growled pitifully.

The spear was much bigger than I'd thought. I threw my weight into it and yanked as hard as I could, trying not to hurt him. After a few minutes, the end finally appeared. Bits of flesh and one shiny purple scale clung to it. I grimaced and tossed the spear to the ground.

Motherfucker! Blake's voice screamed inside my mind.

"You'll be okay. It's merely a flesh wound now. Just go back to sleep," I said, sliding down his tail. Twigs crunched underfoot as I walked back to his face.

I laid a hand against his jowl. He felt hot—but in dragon form, he was always hot. I couldn't tell if it was a fever or just his normal temperature, especially in the sunlight that streamed down through the trees.

"Can you change back?"

His labored panting made him look like a breathing house. "I'll try." The words barely came out.

If anything happened to him…*No, I can't think like that. We've been through worse. He's fine.*

He grunted. The huge heap of dragon in front of me turned back into the man I loved with every inch of my body.

He looked tired. His leg was soaked with crimson liquid. His skin was warm. Too warm for my taste.

The shredded wound dominated his thigh. I took off my sweater and cinched it around his thigh to staunch the flow of his precious blood.

At least the trees covered us. I prayed that we'd made it out of that horrible era.

My great-great-great-grandfather wasn't the nicest

person I'd ever met. We couldn't have possibly gotten anything through that thick skull of his. What had we been thinking? They were so stupid back then.

After overcoming my pride and doing my business in the forest—no toilet! —I stayed with Blake until the break of dawn. Then I went in search of water. Anything to bring his temperature down.

The fact that this ability of ours only worked at night was a huge obstacle. We should have practiced more. Found a way to do this right from the start. We should never have tried to jump around through time, not knowing where we would end up.

Even as I pondered how foolhardy we'd been, my surroundings enchanted me. This verdant forest and unpolluted air felt like its own brand of magic. I had to admit, the untouched nature of the past, this uncorrupted earth, was surely worthy of losing a couple breaths over.

As I walked, I heard rushing water, but I had no idea how far it was.

Birdcalls formed a joyous cacophony around me as mates called each other. They were so loud I almost didn't hear the footfalls of another human.

I hid behind a tree to hide from whoever walked past. A teenage girl, around fourteen, maybe sixteen. She had dark hair and walked with a bow and arrow and a sack made of what appeared to be deer skin. Her shoes were hand-sewn, tanned leather. Okay, so we hadn't yet reached our target era, but at least we weren't in King William's time anymore.

I waited for the girl to pass, but the sole of my foot crushed a few twigs. Though the sound was subtle, my entire body froze. Had she heard that?

I couldn't hear her footfalls anymore. I listened

harder. I heard her heartbeat rise steadily.

"Who is there?" she asked.

Shit. Fuck.

I made myself go even quieter. My breathing diminished to almost nothing. My own heartbeat turned softer. Something Blake and I shared when he'd given me a piece of his heart was the ability to exert my will over my heartbeat. His piece could regulate the tempo.

She walked closer to my hiding spot. Just as I contemplated showing myself, hands up in the air to indicate I was no threat, a squirrel skittered past me, and darted into a nearby tree.

"You scared me!" she spoke to the squirrel. Now I prayed that she couldn't actually speak to animals. It wouldn't be completely crazy in Paegeia.

Her footsteps moved away from my hiding spot, deeper into the forest.

"Thank you," I whispered to the squirrel. I could still see him, his bushy tail twitching as he regarded me from his perch. He just looked at me, blinking, before turning and scurrying into his nest.

I waited for twenty minutes to be sure the girl was truly gone. Then I continued my search for the river, stopping occasionally to scratch tree trunks with rocks to make sure I could find my way back. The roar of water was deceptive; it took me an hour to find it. The water glinted with early morning sunlight, surprisingly bright, as I filled the empty water bottled from my backpack with the clear water that gurgled over the rocks.

Finding my way back to Blake wasn't the easiest thing in the world—even with all the markings I'd left in the tree trunks.

He was still fast asleep when I reached him. The sun

filtered through the thick leaves of the forest, turning the scene into a fairy tale.

I bent and touched his head. He was still warm.

I poured some water over my spare shirt from my pack and gently placed it on his head.

You're going to be okay. Nobody is going to die in the past. Nobody.

Fear thrilled through me. If he died, I'd be stuck here forever.

I kissed his temple and investigated the wound on his leg.

It was closing now. The blood wasn't oozing out anymore, but the sweater I'd tied around his wound was soaked with blood.

Some of his muscle showed, but it looked ten times better than it had a few hours ago.

Time inched by. Periodically, I wrung out the sweater and refreshed it with cool water.

You will be okay. You will pull through. Your healing ability is starting to kick in. But other thoughts crowded in. *Why isn't he waking up? Give him time, Elena. He was just shot down with a freakin' spear meant for Quitto.* I wondered what the history books would say now. That he'd had a wildling, a wild girl for a rider. I looked like one, and the way I'd spoken to William supported that.

Ugh, William. He was such an arrogant bastard. How had he ever become king? They were all like that in those days, though. Hard, cold, soulless. How many dragons had they killed?

Was there still a chance that maybe, just maybe, things might turn out differently? If William would take some of the things Blake had said into consideration…

Would he try to trust some dragon species?

I sighed.

I was starting to get nervous about the price we were going to pay for the things we'd done. Perhaps we had interfered too much. My father's words jumped into my head. *You don't know what price you must pay to fix the past.* I was starting to understand why neither of them had wanted to do this at all. Meddling with the past was a dangerous thing.

By now the sun was at its highest. I'd drifted asleep with Blake's head on my lap. When he finally stirred, the sun started to set. His movement woke me from my slumber. I opened my eyes and looked down.

Sweat droplets no longer stood on his brow. His hair was dry. The fever had finally broken.

I lifted his head softly from my lap and helped resettle him on the soft grass. I moved to check his leg. I peeked beneath his trousers, sticky now from Blake's blood.

The wound, now closed, resembled a big, ugly red scar. His healing abilities were amazing, but always took longer when he was stone-cold unconscious.

I removed the sweater from around his leg and let the scar breathe. I leaned against the tree with his head on my lap again.

He is going to be fine, I said to myself again.

Of course I'm fine. Blake's voice invaded my brain. My eyes shot open as I looked down at him.

I showered his gorgeous face with kisses. I'd been so scared. Terrified that I wouldn't hear his voice again.

His hand brushed my back as his laughter filled my

mind.

Told you before. I am the Rubicon, Elena.

I kept kissing him as my words slipped out. "I'm sorry. This was stupid, Blake."

"No, it wasn't." He touched my face and wiped away tears I hadn't noticed were there. "We need to do this not just for Silho, Elena, but for our people, too."

I nodded and a small smile tugged at the corner of my lips. I wasn't so sure about this anymore.

I am.

What a one-eighty.

We had no idea what era we were in. I told him about the girl from earlier, but that she hadn't seen me. "From the look of her clothes, I'd guess, give or take a few decades, that we're somewhere in the nineteenth century," I concluded.

"Wait until nightfall. Then we can leave. If we are in the nineteenth century, it means our parents might not be born yet. And if they are...I do not want to run into a teenage Robert Leaf. He won't understand any of this. Not yet."

Agree with you on that one.

The forest was safe. For now. We decided to wait until nightfall and try to jump in time to the place we needed to be.

We started to configure all our time jump experiences into a plan. We tried to figure out what Blake thought about when he went through. He insisted, though, that he was never thinking about anything specific—just trying to get away.

We had. Away from King William, all the way to one of his descendants' timelines, whether it was my grandfather—he was the ruler in the nineteenth century—or my father.

We wanted to land closer to the twenty-first century, in the time we existed.

When hunger gnawed at our bellies, we each had a granola bar from my pack. We munched in silence. We didn't want to think about the Creepers. The possibility that we might jump into that time horrified us both. By then, it would be too late.

The only solution was the early twenty-first century, or maybe the late twentieth century.

When the stars twinkled overhead, we waited in anticipation for the bright light to show itself. I tried to come up with names to call it. "White light" didn't sound correct.

Beam? Blake's voice popped into my head.

He'd nailed it perfectly, just like he always did.

Not long after, the Beam finally revealed itself. I saw it through Blake's mind. We were ready for it.

I put on my pack and climbed onto Blake's back. He leaped into the air with me, transforming midway and darting toward the Beam.

Be careful with your thoughts, Elena.

Late twentieth century, I thought. It was all I thought about. Well, that and my mother.

Blake's thoughts synchronized with mine. We both focused on the late twentieth century. The bright light swallowed us.

We opened our eyes and we saw lights like a nest of fireflies below.

We were somewhere in the twentieth century, past the invention of electricity, past primitive plumbing systems and whatnot.

This era was more breathable.

There were not as many forests as the two previous places we'd found. We were really close to our target timeline.

A bonus was we'd arrived here at nighttime.

Blake seemed tired. Going through this Beam had taken a lot of his energy. We needed to find a spot and camp out for the night. We waited for daylight so we could find out which time this was with less chance of being detected.

We found a spot in a small patch of trees.

Blake was restless. He wanted to take precautions. I agreed. He transformed us both into two completely different-looking people. He had blonde hair and reminded me of Lucian's guard—the one who had protected us at Dragonia Academy all those years ago. I had shoulder-length red hair and a face dusted with freckles. It was the girl from the Never-Breath's song. His imaginary friend. I laughed at my resemblance through his mind.

"Now I can finally say you wrote that song for me."

He chuckled. We lay on the ground and went to sleep, his arms wrapped securely around my chest.

"Woohoo!" Emanual's voice said.

What the hell is he doing here?

It took me a second to realize that I wasn't in my own time anymore. My eyes flew open.

I found his bulky, shaven-headed figure looking down on us. Golf clubs were slung over his shoulder. A happy grin plastered his face. I wished that I could go and hug him, but he wouldn't understand. He didn't know me yet, and he didn't know this girl I looked like.

More laughter floated toward us. I looked past him and saw my father, Sir Robert, and King Helmut. Tears wanted to well up, but I pushed them back. Behind him, speaking over a Cammy, was Goran. The traitor was pretending to be their friend.

I smacked Blake with the back of my hand; he still looked like Cooper. He woke up instantly.

We are in a different timeline. Don't say their names. We made it, I think. My voice rambled in his head.

Your name, Elena?

Merica. It was all I could think of.

"You know that this is a private golf course, right?" Emanual said to us.

"Sorry, it was late last night. We came from afar and didn't realize," Blake said. He sounded different.

"What is your name?" Emanual handed him his hand and Blake took it.

"Cooper," we both said, me in his head, Blake out loud.

"And this is my rider, Merica."

"Merica?" Emanual smiled. "Nice to meet you two."

My father came forward, still smiling. I returned a grin. We pretended not to be royalty. "Your Majesty," I said with a curtsey. Blake bowed.

"Get up." My father still carried humor in his voice. "Where did you come from?"

Let me talk, Elena.

I nodded once and watched my father staring at me until Blake spoke.

"We came from the North side of Elm, a small village right by the border of the Wall."

"Wow, that is far," King Helmut chirped.

"What business do you have here in Etan?" My father asked.

Tell him what we are?

Blake hesitated. *How do you tell someone that you are the Rubicon?*

"Running away from our village," Blake said and I could see the plan forming in his head. He was a genius.

"Running away? Why?"

"Because of what we are."

My father was intrigued. "What are you?"

"I'm a Rubicon dragon."

Everyone gasped. We had their attention. Silence lingered in the air. My father's lips curved. It looked like hope. I couldn't help but think the timeline we'd reached was perfect.

Sir Robert didn't share my father's curiosity. He immediately drew a golf club. His posture suggested that he was going to use it to protect his son, also a Rubicon.

He started to go for Blake.

Blake covered me. His shield was around us. To their eyes, we vanished, blending in with our surroundings.

I think we've got the right timeline.

Yep, I'm already born. Otherwise my father wouldn't have done what he just did. He's afraid.

All of them were in shock, trying to figure out where the two of us had gone.

They looked around. Their lips were moving. My father's hand touched Sir Robert's chest. He wanted to know more. Goran disconnected his phone call and stood at my father's side.

That smile lingered on my dad's mouth as he stared at us, or where we'd been a few moments ago.

I don't like the look on Goran's face, I muttered.

I told him I am a Rubicon. He doesn't have to wait anymore. This mission just got more dangerous.

We've been in plenty of those before, Blake.

He snorted. *That we have. By the look on your father's face, I guess you've been born, too. Your father wants to know more.*

The question is, how long do we have before the Creepers come?

We will find out soon enough.

My father spoke to Sir Robert. What they said, I didn't know; we couldn't hear through the shield. But he lowered the golf club. When the danger had passed, my father walked slowly toward us, his lips were moving.

Lower your shield.

He did.

"...mean you no harm," were the last words my father spoke. When we reappeared, he touched Blake's shoulder. All their eyes were on us. Shock laced with admiration was written all over their faces. Even Goran's.

I didn't like this. Not one bit.

Stop staring at him, Elena. I can take care of myself. He wants his match. He will get it soon enough.

I liked that.

"How did you do that?" my father asked, looking at Blake, then at me.

"It's a technique I picked up," Blake said evasively.

"What else can you do?" My father was curious about us.

Great call, Elena. Scary call, but this might just work. Don't tell them about our connection.

I won't.

"I'm fully developed. I have all my abilities. And

Merica is my rider. My true rider. I mean no harm."

"Have you turned dark?" Sir Robert wanted to know.

"As dark as Quitto. But like I said, Merica showed me the light. I'm not that dragon anymore."

"Al," Sir Robert said.

"He seems like he's telling the truth, Bob."

"Two Rubicons can't live in the same time," he growled through clenched teeth.

The words popped out of my mouth before I could consider them. "We mean your son no harm."

Sir Robert's eyes flashed at me. "How do you know about my son?" he barked.

"We heard about him," I said quickly. "And Cooper felt something when his egg hatched."

Nice comeback.

"It's one of the reasons we left our village. They were scared if you knew about his existence, you would try to slay him. It's why we are here: to show you that's not necessary."

Every one of them kept quiet for a while.

Please buy it, please, please.

They are contemplating, Elena. Just give them time.

"What do you think, Goran?" my father asked.

Not him, please.

He stepped forward and looked Blake straight in the eye. *Don't see the enchantment. Don't see it.*

He smiled. "I think they are telling the truth. Might as well see where this leads."

I hated the tone he used. He wanted to claim Blake. I knew it.

"Perfect!" My father clapped his hands again as more danger threw a sudden weight on my shoulders.

I can handle him, Elena. We know what he is.

"Would you like to come over to the castle?"

TEN

ELENA

So, we'd gotten an invitation. We followed them all the way back to the castle. Sir Robert asked me questions about how I'd tamed the Rubicon. I answered as best I could with Blake's help. He was busy speaking to my father about the two of us. Just as I'd thought he would.

He wanted to learn more, to know what my future would involve.

I gasped as I reached the back of the castle. It looked so different. The waterfall was still there, but there were many more things going on in our backyard. For one, there was a maze, similar to the maze Lucian had taken me through in Tith. Our new castle didn't have one; instead there were large oak trees shading tall windows.

This castle was so much bigger, so much more majestic, than the one I now called home. My eyes landed on the west wing. I knew she was in there, somewhere.

Just looking at it was causing me to push back the tears.

We followed them through a back door. In our castle this entire area had been turned into a porch, the same porch where I'd found my father and Constance dancing.

My gaze caught on one room at the top of the west wing that had an opening. *Is that my mother's room?*

When we entered, Goran excused himself from the group and my eyes found Blake. I had no idea how long we had. For all we knew he could be going to get his militia now, to command the attack.

Calm down, Elena. I will find out. Just calm down.

I know you will. I took a deep, steadying breath. *I'm just on edge.*

"Abby, would you be so kind as to show our visitors to the guest room, please?"

She bowed, smiled, and told us to follow her.

She led us to the east wing. It was just as I remembered it that night Lucian had brought me here through a memory to let me see how much both my parents wanted me. It was perfect with the royal blue carpets, not the cherry wood Dad had put in after the renovation.

We walked down a hall that had many of my ancestors' pictures lining the walls. For some funny reason, I felt like I was finally home. The paintings had been destroyed during the battle. William's mug smirked down from one.

Blake squeezed my shoulder.

I told you it was beautiful.

Yes, you did.

"You two don't say much, do you?" Abby was rather

bold for a maid.

"We are souls with not a lot to say," I said, smiling.

She opened the guestroom door. "Fresh towels are in the bathroom."

"Thank you so much." Blake sounded as charming as he could and she closed the door.

Okay so both of us are born, my mind rambled. *I need to know how much time…*

His peacock eyes were filled with compassion. *Calm down, love. We will. Just be patient.*

What if it is tonight?

Then I will scorch his ass while you go free your mom. As simple as that.

I nodded.

We defeated him once, Elena. He brushed my cheek. *We can do it again. Your blood is the key. Your parents might not know it, so this night might have a different outcome, if…* He lingered on the "if." *If this is the night.*

I sighed. *Okay.*

We had a feast of a breakfast. Over the past forty-eight hours, we had eaten nothing but William's slop and granola bars. We were ravenous.

All my father's men and his dragon were sitting around a table with Goran at the other end.

How easy it would be just to wring his neck…

Don't, Elena. I know you want him to die. But we can't leave this era if we can't get to the Beam. We can't go home, Blake warned me.

The hardest part was walking past Goran from the coffee station. I would've loved to know what was going on in his mind at this moment. How great was his hatred for my father, smiling at him, pretending to be his friend, when in fact he was far from it?

We got seated close to my father and the first thing Blake grabbed was the newspaper in front of my dad.

He only looked at the date. It was reflected in his mind for me to see. We'd landed perfectly this time, at the cusp of the twenty-first century. In fact, we had three days before the betrayal.

Not a lot of time to get my dad to trust us. *How are we going to tell him?*

My father asked Blake a question. He answered it through a joke. Everyone laughed. Then he gave me his silent answer. *Through our Moon-Bolt gift.*

Perfect.

I had a croissant with eggs. Blake ate like a demon. It had been two days since we'd had a decent meal.

"That trip must have been really long," Goran noted in a tone that made my skin crawl. As if he knew we were from the future, as if he knew exactly who we were.

Easy, Elena. It's just a comment.

"Two days' flight. Without rest or a meal."

"Then have another plate," my father said. They laughed again.

The door creaked open. We were about five paces away from the hallway. One of the older maids appeared. Everyone looked up—my father, Goran, and Sir Robert.

I squinted at them and looked at the maid.

Another woman followed her. I gasped when I saw who it was: my mother.

"Katie!" My father's entire face lit up, but she was a shell of a woman.

She stopped and stared at him. Blake stroked my leg

underneath the table to calm the emotions that were jumping all over the place in my heart.

"What, Albert?" she said without any rhythm. Like a zombie.

"Join us for breakfast, please. We have extraordinary guests this morning."

"I'm not in the mood for your hosting games," she said as she walked on without giving us the time of day.

The dining area fell into an awkward silence. Everyone looked down. My father's face fell and he sighed. His lips curved into a smile.

"Forgive my queen. She lost her dragon a year ago."

You sure it's just her dragon, Dad?

Easy, love, Blake warned again.

I kept thinking about my mother. Blake's memories didn't portray her in the best light.

"She was part of a Dent, right?" I asked, and my father nodded.

"I can just imagine what she must be going through. If I lost…"

Cooper, Blake reminded me.

"Cooper, I wouldn't know how to go on," I laid it on thick.

"Well, I'm sure it would be something like that." My father gave a kind smile.

I didn't want to look at Goran anymore. He was going to go down. I didn't care how. He would not be in our future. He wasn't going to be the reason my mom died. She was going to live, and she would be reunited with me. Soon.

We told them as much as we could over the next few hours. All the abilities we had—well, not the mind reading one, but the others.

Goran listened with big ears. My father, too. Both men were really intrigued, and Sir Robert as well, but all of them did it for different reasons.

"That vanishing thing you do?" Goran asked Blake.

"I call it my blending technique. I don't really vanish."

"It's remarkable," he said.

"We are one of a kind." Blake sounded so friendly but in his mind, he wanted to wring Goran's neck.

"And your shield?"

I knew what he was doing. He wanted to see if Blake was really that powerful.

"One of the best there is," he boasted.

"How good?" My father wanted to know.

Blake told them only half of it. He didn't mention that ours had turned solid a few years ago. It wasn't easy to do.

They all listened to him with admiration.

I missed his real face. He shot me a picture of himself shaving in the mirror.

I smiled a secret little smile. But I caught Goran's eyes on me. Watching. Calculating.

That night I struggled to fall asleep. *I could go and kill Goran. Right now.*

Blake touched my breast. *Don't. Just don't. I'm already on edge and I just want something to take my mind off today.*

Images of the two of us on the bed flashed through his mind. Heat flooded my cheeks. I turned around.

Let's see what tomorrow brings.

He didn't look like Blake.

Close your eyes, Elena.

I did. He changed into my Blake.

He kissed me. His lips were light as feathers. Hot. It still felt like him. It was him, just in disguise. He pulled me in closer, pushing me beneath his powerful body and nestling in between my legs. I gasped in ecstasy.

With each thrust, each kiss, it progressed into something much more than making love.

He was literally inside my head. It felt as if a dragon possessed me, and Blake, Blake was the whisperer who calmed my soul.

Only one day remained.

When we walked downstairs, we found my father and Goran at the table. Sir Robert hadn't come in yet.

They were talking about something that was going to happen in the next few weeks. A meeting with the Wyverns.

I looked at Blake as we approached them.

Soon, Elena. We will tell him soon.

I nodded.

Just don't say anything about the Wyverns. He is their king.

"Have you seen the Rogue yourself?"

Rogue? I thought.

"No, not yet. Soon, Al," Goran said, lying to my father's face. "I saw his second-in-command and he said he would speak to him. He's interested in an alliance. Your dream of freeing all dragons will come true."

I hated his tone. He'd manipulated my father so much. Preyed on his dreams. Making it sound like a reality that was, in fact, fiction.

You think the bastard is this Rogue they are talking about?

Goran? Yeah, he is. Rogue was another name for the Wyvern King.

I despised him even more.

We walked into the dining area and my father's face lit up.

"Oh good. The lovebirds are finally awake," Goran said as if he knew what we'd done last night.

"Sorry if we kept you awake," Blake said and my father laughed.

"Goran has enhanced hearing, and some of the rooms are not soundproof. Sorry about that," my father apologized. I flushed crimson and giggled, embarrassed.

"Oh, please don't. This castle hasn't had much love lately. You are a breath of fresh air."

I gaped. Was my father flirting with me?

Blake laughed in my head.

"Easy there, King Albert. I'm still a very possessive dragon," Blake teased.

My father and Goran roared with laughter.

A little while later, my father took us on a tour of the castle. He spoke about all our ancestors. Blake stopped in front of William.

"King William and his bravery," he said.

"He wasn't brave," my father spoke. "He never wanted to find a way to tame them."

"Well, I'm sure if someone told him that dragons

could actually be changed, then maybe he would've listened."

"Nah, I don't believe that. He wasn't a man they could reasoned with."

"How did the name Quitto come into existence?" Blake asked.

"He gave it to him, actually. Or so the tale goes."

"The tale?"

"I'm sure they told you about the previous Rubicon. Funny." My father looked pensive as he ambled further down the hall.

He walked into the library and took an old book of the shelf. It was a book about the Rubicon.

I've never seen that book before.

It was destroyed, Elena.

He plopped it on the table and started paging through it rapidly.

"What is it?" Blake asked.

"On his deathbed, he revealed that there was a time when there appeared to be two Rubicons soaring the sky at the same time." My father read with his finger tracing the paragraphs. He showed it to Blake.

"I always thought it was symbolic, but now I realize there really must have been two."

I read it, too. There was nothing written about a wildling. Blake carried on reading, dying to know if we'd made a difference in that timeline, but it seemed we hadn't. William still slayed dragons and ended up killing the Rubicon. Slaughter was his addiction.

Fucking asshole.

Blake put the book down. He wielded his shield around us and looked at my father.

My father squinted. "You can hardly hear it."

"Advanced, my king."

"Albert, please."

Blake smiled and let down his shield.

Why didn't you tell him? We might never get another chance.

It's too early in the day, love. If it goes wrong, we won't be able to leave.

I got what he was saying. If my father didn't believe him, we would be stuck in this time, maybe even killed.

We left the library and the tour progressed.

The lobby was gorgeous. Most of it had been destroyed and rebuilt in my time. These stairs were different. My mother's painting hung way above.

She was so beautiful, vivacious and young—twenty, maybe twenty-one.

He needed to believe us.

We ate lunch outside on a porch that was also destroyed in our time. Small dogs cavorted at our feet.

Goran was nowhere to be found.

"I'm sorry to intrude," Blake said. "Enhanced hearing. I couldn't help but overhear your conversation this morning."

My father sipped coffee and put it back on the saucer.

"You want to know what it is I love about Wyverns?"

He nodded.

"Dragon is dragon, whether they have four legs or two. They have human forms, too, you know, and we do know of one or two with a few abilities," my father spoke.

"*All* of them have abilities," I spoke up.

My father's gaze found mine. "You know the Wyverns?"

"My king, they can't be reasoned with. You need to

let this dream go."

"Goran can speak fluent Wyvic, and he told me differently."

I hated that. I just wished that I could tell him that he was the one that Irene warned them about, the one that was going to betray them, shake him until he listened.

"Then I wish you luck. We trusted a Wyvern once, in our village. We thought he wanted to change, but we lost a dear friend. He only wanted to kill Merica."

My father stared at me.

"Sorry that we don't share your beliefs," I spoke.

"He told you what they can do?"

I nodded. "But it's best to leave it there." He was going to tell Goran this. I knew he would.

"Please," he insisted. "I'm intrigued by them. Tell me."

Tell him, Elena. It won't matter if he shares this with Goran or not, Blake encouraged me.

I told him what Paul told me. What they could do. "All the Wyverns are fire-breathers. The Raven-Snout can influence minds, read it, put thoughts into it, and make them see things that aren't there. The Hammer-Head is a trickster, their form can appear and re-appear in different spots. They say the older they get the more copies of themselves they can generate. The Brown-Horn's scales are like flying stars. They can release them and new ones can grow in their place. The same for some of the horns on their back. Their horns are dangerous and carries a poison, that ages you extremely fast until you die.

The Spike and Spear-Tail look so much alike. But one has the ability to see through animal eyes' and the other one can suck out souls.

"The more they have, the longer they can live. With each soul they have a life. So they can die ten times over."

My father was hanging onto my every word.

But he had admiration for them still, not fear. He needed fear.

My heart beat faster as Queen Margerite and King Helmut made their appearance.

Lucian was holding her hand. He was only four.

"You must be the special guests," Queen Margerite said. I couldn't stop looking at Lucian. He was hiding behind his mother.

Blake answered on my behalf.

She found me staring at him.

"Oh, he is a bit shy around strangers."

I laughed. "He's gorgeous! How old is he?"

"Four," she said. "You have any children?"

Oh, Silho. With just those words, I was rendered mute with fresh grief. I shook my head. I didn't anymore.

"It's really nice meeting you, but excuse me." She smiled at me, then my father. "Is she in her room?"

His nod turned into a sigh.

"Don't. I'll never give up on her." She walked to where I assumed was my mother's chamber.

We left them in peace to discuss their meeting next week with this Rogue—whom we knew to be Goran.

We went to the courtyard. It was larger than what I was used to.

Everything was so different.

I know. Blake hugged me.

Queen Margerite left with Lucian. She wasn't even gone half an hour before she returned with tears in her eyes.

"Is everything okay?" I asked her.

"Yes. Don't mind me."

I pretended to see something in the distance. I broke everything down to Blake in my mind. If we couldn't get through to my father, then at least we could get through to her: never trust Wyverns. Blake rushed to my side.

"Is she okay?"

"It's our Moon-Bolt gift," he explained.

"Oh my." She sounded worried.

I pretended to snap out of it. I looked at Lucian with grave eyes.

"What did you see?" she demanded as she pulled Lucian closer to her.

"Please tell me." She was on the verge of tears. I was scaring her.

"Don't trust Wyverns. Ever. Otherwise you will lose…" I just stared at Lucian. She gasped, getting my meaning.

"They can't be trusted," I whispered. She needed to protect her children with her life.

"Excuse me," I said. "I have to go lie down."

Blake followed me. *That was fucking brilliant, Elena. No, it wasn't. I hated that look on her face.*

He squeezed my hand. *She needs to be scared.*

Why doesn't my dad just fucking listen?

He has many dreams, he said reasonably. *He believes in good more than he does in evil, love. It's why he got that name. The Greatest King.*

I hated that name. He was too good, and everyone would pay for it.

At five we found my father inside the library.

"May we join you?" Blake asked, and my father nodded.

It was time.

"Where is Goran?"

"Oh, he left for the day to visit the Wyverns. He will be back around nine this evening."

Plotting your murder. Rage rose in me.

"What is it?" My father caught the look on my face.

Blake wielded his shield and the two of us moved closer to him and took the seats in front of him.

"I'm sorry to do this to you. Our intentions in coming weren't a hundred percent honest."

My father narrowed his eyes.

"One of our other gifts is seeing into the future, Albert," Blake said.

Let me. I looked at Blake and then back at my father.

"We have no limits in whose future we see."

My father looked at me.

"We know about her. We've seen her."

My father was so good at protecting my existence. "Who are you talking about?"

"You know who. Your daughter."

My father closed his eyes and took a huge breath.

You're doing a great job, love, Blake said.

"We've also seen who will betray you, Albert. It's someone very close."

He opened his eyes. "I know it's someone close. We've always known that. But who?"

I shook my head. "You are not going to like this, but

I promise you, tomorrow he will destroy everything you love."

"Tell me who," he grunted.

The words that would crush my father dried up in my throat.

"You know who," Blake said. "You said it yourself. He can speak Wyvic."

My father's eyes widened. "No! He would never do that. He's like my brother." His entire demeanor changed.

"Okay, calm down. We are just the messengers. We can't control what we see. We thought it was best to tell you," Blake said. "What you do with it is up to you. We will go now."

Get up, Elena.

"Please," I begged. "Let us tell you how—"

Elena, Blake's voice said again, sharp.

"Leave me." My father's tone was stern.

I nodded.

Blake and I got up and we went to our room. *I really thought we had him, Elena. What happened?*

I don't know. We were gentle.

Not gentle enough. Three days wasn't nearly long enough to win his trust. Not even to mention doing it in two.

It wasn't enough.

We planted the seed. What he does with it is up to him.

I didn't like that. We didn't even tell him how, nothing. He just didn't give us the chance.

We found the room. We grabbed our backpack and packed as fast as we could. If my father didn't decide to kill us for treason, Goran definitely would when he found out we had exposed him.

As we were about to exit the room, the command came. My father wanted to arrest us, to throw us in the dungeon. Something about a hearing.

I didn't like this. In Blake's mind I saw images of Goran and him. If Goran discovered who we really were, this could end in a catastrophe. If we were placed in the dungeon we would certainly die there.

They will execute us.

Does this room have a secret entrance, Elena?

I closed my eyes, remembering the layout of the castle my father showed us.

It didn't.

But I knew the nearest one.

We slipped out the door as they stomped up the stairs. I found the statue my father told me about. I pressed its nose and a hidden panel opened. We slipped through and it closed.

We waited.

I could hear my father in our room.

"They are here. He's protecting them. Feel every inch of this room. They are hiding somewhere." He sounded furious as he stormed out.

He walked our way. *Please don't open this panel, please,* I prayed.

Blake blended us in just in case.

"Al, what is it?" Sir Robert asked. "What happened?"

"Treason. You were right, Bob. Two Rubicons can't exist at the same time." My father's words riled up his dragon.

I gasped as I remembered something. *I dreamed*

about this!

Blake sucked air through his teeth with the shock if the memory. *What were their names?*

I think it was Cooper and Merica.

It hadn't been just a dream. It was me, getting a glimpse of the future through a dream, eight years ago.

So it hadn't happened exactly the way I'd dreamt about it, but it was the same concept. My father didn't believe us.

The seed is planted, love. We have to get out of here.

ELEVEN

ELENA

Elena, we have to leave. Blake's urgent tone thrilled through my mind. *You heard what your father is going to do if he finds us.*

I dragged my feet. I didn't want to go. Planting the seed wasn't good enough. *No, I won't leave without knowing for sure that Goran will die.*

Then how? he asked as we hid in our confined space inside the wall.

My mother flashed through my mind. The enchantment was wearing off.

Are you insane?

She is our last hope, Blake. I could plead, tell her the truth. You saw her. This is what she wants.

No, your father gave us a direct order not to go to your mother. Seeing her was a plus. You can forget about speaking to her. Elena, you don't know the state your mother is in.

She is my last hope now, I retorted.

My mind was set. Blake didn't like it, but he had no choice. He wouldn't leave my side.

We rushed as swiftly as we could through the walls to the west wing. Cobwebs tickled my face in the darkness. I knew more or less how to get there. My father had shown me the levers that released hidden walls from inside. I found one underneath a huge letter W. At last, the west wing.

I pushed the lever and the door opened. It was a section in a castle we'd never been in.

Blake rushed to the nearest door. He blended us in. We walked down a long cobblestone path that led to my mother's wing, past a guard who was looking out into the late afternoon sky, and once we were safe, he let the blending technique disappear.

I was standing in front of my mother's doors.

She was my last hope.

My hands balled into fists. I knocked three times on her door.

It opened a few seconds later. Her lady's face appeared, looking harried.

"Can I help you?" she asked.

"We need to speak to Queen Catherine, please. It is urgent."

"The queen doesn't wish to be disturbed," she said bluntly and closed the door.

I pressed my foot in the jamb before it shut.

"We have news about Elena." It just came out of my

mouth.

The door opened again and her face appeared, this time looking suspicious. "Who?" she asked.

"Just tell the queen that."

She closed the door. Seconds dragged by. Was this going to get her attention? Blake was on edge.

Then the lady reappeared and showed us in.

We walked into my mother's chambers. It was warm, beautiful, and soft, just like her. It had two huge doors—one where only her bedroom could be, and another door hiding who knew what.

We stood in a sort of living room with the most beautiful fireplace.

An arm grabbed me and shoved me against the wall, hard.

Blake moved to protect me, but I flicked my hand up to block him. A knife lay cold against the tender flesh under my chin. My face was inches away from my mother's.

"How do you know that name?" she demanded.

My hand was still raised towards Blake, holding him back with my ability.

"We came to warn you," I grunted. Her blade was sharp and I could feel it cutting through my soft skin.

Twice now, Mom? I couldn't help the thought. "Your husband doesn't want to listen. But you might."

Her eye twitched. She pulled away the knife from my throat.

I touched my neck. Blood smeared my fingers. Blake rushed to my side and placed his warm hand on my wound. My mother watched as she saw him erase the scrape on my neck and a thin line appeared on his neck. She gasped.

Anger still flared in her eyes. The lioness she used to be, protecting me—well, baby me who was thousands of miles away from her.

"That doesn't explain how you know that name." She pointed at me with a second dagger still lodged in her fist.

"My dragon is a Rubicon. We can see into the future."

She gasped, her eyes were huge and she stared at both of us.

"There can't be two living Rubicons at the same time."

"We don't mean you any harm." I sighed. We'd just had this conversation. I moved in front of Blake. My mother wasn't thinking clearly. She wasn't thinking at all. "We only came to tell you what we saw. We know who will betray you. We know that he is doing it tomorrow with a Wyvern army."

"What?" Her mouth grew into a thin line. "Who?"

"You know who! He is the only one who can speak their language," I said.

"Who?" she barked, angry tears in her eyes. I realized I'd gotten that trait from her. Both of us had our emotions connected to our tear ducts.

"Goran."

Saying his name, it was as if all the life left her. Fat tears rolled over her cheeks as she contemplated this. *He's evil, seriously!* I shouted in my head. She shook her head. "No, he would never do that."

"You are going to be tied to that bed." I pointed at one of the doors, hoping it was her bedroom. My voice grew shrill though I kept my volume low. "And you will die on that bed. You will be burned to death."

She looked at her the intricately carved door to her

sleeping chamber. No doubt she was visualizing my harsh prediction. Grabbing her dark hair with the palm of her hand, she paced a few steps toward us and a few paces back to her fireplace.

Be gentle, Elena, Blake cautioned in my head.

I ignored him. She wasn't my father. She was my mother. She needed to hear it. She needed to believe me.

She paced in front of her fireplace. I decided to go to her. "Please, you have to believe me. If you don't kill him, you will never see Elena again. She will grow up without you."

My mother stopped immediately and looked at once at me.

I was the key to getting through to her. Dammit, I was the key to my father as well, but I'd gotten too eager.

Elena, we need to hurry. They are coming.

"Five more minutes," I said over my shoulder, out loud.

My mother's head shot toward him. "You can hear his thoughts?"

I nodded. "He is much more powerful than you think."

She frowned thoughtfully. It was the way I'd said it. As if I was talking about Blake and not the guy he pretended to be at this very moment.

Elena, Blake growled.

I don't care anymore. She needs to believe me. I looked at him.

"Elena will not even know who you are, or who she is. Tanya will break her promise. She will leave your child with Jako."

"Jako found them?"

I nodded.

My mother stared at nothing. Worry lines deepened around her eyes. She looked so vulnerable.

She retreated and plummeted into a chair. "No," she finally said. "She promised. She can't come back."

"She can. After you are dead, the vow will vanish and she will leave him and her on the other side of that wall, and she will come straight back."

My mother's glistening gaze sought mine. "But…she promised."

"She is Chromatic. It's not her fault. Elena will grow up on the run. She'll have to move every three months because dragons will find out about her and hunt her down. Dragons working with Goran, who will order her killed. It will never be over if you don't fix it before it begins."

"Goran? Goran loves me, he would never…"

I wanted to take her in my arms. "It's why he'll do it. Because he loves you too much. He would kill for you. He is not sane."

She kept on shaking her head. This wasn't my mother. This wasn't the strong and intelligent woman I had hoped to meet. Disappointment rolled through me, followed by the threat of tears.

"Elena will only find Paegeia when she is sixteen. Jako will never speak to her about this world. He will die before telling her who she truly is." This wasn't exactly true, but it was close enough, and I didn't have enough time for the long version. "She will never know that dragons even exist. Will never know who she is. Won't even know that you are her mother," I said through clenched teeth.

Her head shot up at me.

"She will grow up with no place to call home." I

forced gentleness back into my tone. "Is that the life you want for her?"

"No." She shook her head. Her voice broke. Her lower jaw trembled slightly. I didn't know if she was answering my question, or if she still didn't believe me, but she was breaking. She wanted to be reunited with me. I could see it in her eyes.

"How do you know this? And don't tell me you saw it."

"Fine," I said. My mother was smarter than that.

Elena, are you insane? I'd almost forgotten Blake was by my side in the intensity of my connection with my mother.

"I know this, because it was my life, Mom."

She stared at me, mouth agape.

Elena!

I ignored Blake. "Blake developed his newest ability at the age of thirty. He can jump back in time. I chose to save you. Goran will kill you. I will grow up without a mother." My emotions had taken a toll on me. I swiped at a tear that rolled down my cheek. "Daddy doesn't believe us and won't hear anything about it. He didn't even let us finish, and now, now he is hunting us like animals."

Her entire face changed. She looked at me with disgust. I didn't understand this.

"You are not my daughter. Get out!"

She knows what I look like? How?

"Just wait," I said quickly as I put it together. It was as if I could read her mind like I did with Blake. "We had to use an enchantment because of my resemblance to you and Daddy, and because of Blake's," I said, her arm still pointing at the door.

Blake was a ball of nervous energy, practically bouncing on the balls of his feet. *Elena, we don't have time.*

"Please, just wait." I spoke to both of them.

Then the top of Blake's head started to turn darker.

"Look for yourself," I said to my mother. She turned around and looked at him.

She watched as the blonde guy changed drastically into a second Sir Robert, but with soft peacock eyes that could look straight into one's soul.

She stared at him, the hinge of her jaw hanging open. I could feel the enchantment wearing off me, too. She walked slowly toward Blake and cupped his face with both her hands, looking up at him. "This cannot be…"

Blake smiled. "The last time you saw me, I was almost five years old. Playing with my cousin in your garden. You remember the bench. I finally understand your stares."

She started to cry in earnest.

In my peripheral vision I saw my hair getting thicker and lighter. My true appearance had returned. She would see it for herself.

"Mom," I whispered.

She looked at me. Her eyebrows shot up into the stratosphere. She gasped. Her hands cupped her mouth as she stared at me with wild eyes.

And then she stopped staring and ran toward me, flinging her arms around my neck. She pulled me into the embrace I'd only felt once, that night Blake helped me to say goodbye.

She sobbed. She finally believed me.

"We can't stay. Goran has a militia waiting on the North side. If you don't do this, he will ruin my life. End yours. Destroy the people of Etan's lives. Torture Daddy for years. They will believe you when you give them the location where they are stationed."

"Look at you. You look so much like your father." She smiled, tugging on my hair slightly. Clearly she hadn't heard a word I'd said. This was too much for her to take in.

I laughed. "Yeah, I get that a lot. But you have to listen. The North side of Etan, Mom."

"How old are you?"

I sighed. "Twenty-six. I can't stay, Mom. Dad is looking for us as we speak. He thinks we're traitors. We need to get back to our time."

She nodded and looked back at Blake. "You are a second Robert Leaf, but Isabel's soul is staring straight at me through those blue peacock eyes."

"*Please*, Mom. Just do it. For me. I need you."

"Okay, baby." She stroked my cheek softly. Her hands were so warm. I closed my eyes "The pond didn't lie when it showed me your face."

"The pond?" Then I remembered her name in the book. That was why she'd entered the Sacred Cavern. This was what she'd needed the pond for. To look into her future, to see if she was going to ever have children. She must've seen me.

I grabbed her again and pulled her into my chest. She smelled of vanilla.

Another thought invaded my mind. "In ten years, Wyverns are going to come to find a truce. They can't be trusted. Ever. You hear?" Desi couldn't die. Not this time.

She nodded.

"Don't forget that. No matter what Dad says, they can

never be trusted."

"I promise I won't forget." She held me at arm's length and looked me over as if storing up the memory of me. A twinkle glinted in her eyes.

"North side, Mom. Tomorrow. Maybe they're already there."

She nodded, clutched my arm, and pulled me to her chest.

"Elena, we need to go," Blake said through gritted teeth. I could see in his thoughts his burning need to get me out of harm's way.

"Love you," I said to my mother. She nodded in my arms. I felt the movement in the nape of my neck.

She didn't say it back. But I knew there was a chance I would now grow up hearing it. She just need to kill him.

When Blake opened the door, we could hear the guards running toward Queen Catherine's wing.

She reached past him and closed the door. "Follow me," she said. "There's a secret access." She led us to her room. I barely took in the unmade bed and air of loneliness as she took us to a wall panel. This hidden passage wasn't even on the layout of the plans that my father had shown us.

She opened it. Blake stepped in first.

"Be safe. I promise I will see you again." A beautiful smile transformed her face.

"I trust you." I hugged her one last time. I didn't want to break the hug, but I had no choice. "Will you be okay?"

She gave me a sideways glance. "I'm the Queen of Paegeia. I'll be fine."

I let out a startled laugh.

She pushed us through the opening in the panel and

shut it behind me slowly. Neither of us wanted to say goodbye. "Just go straight." Her voice was muffled through the wood. "The tunnel will lead you outside."

I nodded. I rushed after Blake down a pitch-black hall, relying on his senses not to run into things. His relief at finally being able to move flooded my senses.

Once we were outside, we searched through his mind for the Beam that would take us back to the present. That Beam would either take me to a new future or the same one. I just hoped that my mom was going to make it this time.

TWELVE

CATHERINE

I saw them lift off. My baby girl and her dragon. Extraordinary visitors indeed. Al hadn't realized how extraordinary they were when he'd said it.

The dragon darted into the air. A gasp left my mouth as he vanished into thin air and then a bright light engulfed the sky.

A familiarity of that light entered my mind. About two hundred years ago during the war. There had been the outline of a huge dragon. I gasped. I'd shot at them with my arrow.

Oh my gosh. I could've hurt her.

I looked back at the sky. The light vanished, leaving not a speck in the sky.

They were gone, just like that.

Was that them? Is she safe? What will she find? Will I be there? I have to be there. I just have to.

I didn't care that it was Goran anymore. She'd called him insane. His father was right, and we were wrong. Wyverns. It was a hard pill to swallow, but they'd had all the evidence, she'd lived through it. I would ask her one day what her life was, one day when Elena would meet the future Elena. One day.

The knock on my door came.

I reached it before Sophie could.

I grabbed my lady. She hadn't expected the roughness of my touch. I yanked her back. My shield sparkled around us.

"You will remember nothing. I was whimpering inside my room, just like every night. Nobody was inside my chambers. The name Elena means nothing. You don't know an Elena." I looked into a pair of wide eyes turning a lovely, but vacant, green as I erased tonight's memory. She stood there, dazed by what I'd done to her. Satisfied, I slowly walked back to my room. I reached my room and softly closed the door behind me.

Insistent knocks on the door filled the chamber.

Sophie must have shaken off her daze, remembering nothing. The gift of persuasion. A gift from my sister. A gift I could use no matter how many miles or magical walls were between us. The sister who, according to Elena from the future, would eventually break her promise. That saddened me the most. Knowing that she wasn't strong enough in the end.

But she would be. Everything was going to change. Everything. My little girl would come home. She would grow up with me by her side. *She will know who she is.*

I just had to take care of this problem.

"Has anybody come to see the queen?" Albert's voice boomed in my outer chamber.

I huffed and laid back on my bed.

"No, Your Majesty. Nobody was here. Is everything all right?" she asked.

Should I go to him, ask what is the matter? No, I'm not going to. He didn't want to even listen to them. No matter that he didn't know who she was. He'd promised me that if he found out who was going to betray us, he would kill him or her on the spot.

He'd lied.

"Is she..." His tone went softer, barely audible, but I could hear him loud and clear. Something he never remembered.

"She is asleep, Your Majesty. Crawled in around seven."

"How is she doing?"

"I fear the queen will never recover from her sister's disappearance," she said. In my newly revived mental state, I felt a sharp twinge of guilt at the dejection in my lady's voice. She deserved better.

"Don't say that. There is always hope."

"Sorry, my king. I didn't mean it in an ill way."

"Albert, they spotted them." Helmut or Goran's voice. I could never tell their voices apart, but telling their faces apart was easy because of Helmut's mustache.

"Thank you, Sophie." His voice was kind. How did it all go so wrong, so fast? He hadn't searched hard enough. And now that he knew...It was like he was betraying me. Choosing Goran over me. Over his queen and his daughter.

"It's my pleasure, Your Majesty."

She closed the door and that was it. My mind whirred as I tried to come up with a plan of how to get close to Goran. Then I realized I already had one. Elena had given it to me. He'd betrayed Albert for me. He loved me. That was how I was going to get close to him. And then I would cut his heart out of his chest with my dagger.

If he wanted me so badly, he would get all of me. Even the crazy part.

I would do it tonight. She'd said they would come tomorrow. Tonight was the only chance I had.

Two o'clock. Goran would be inside his tower, where he'd brewed his plan for who knows how long.

I put on my translucent teddy. Its sheer, soft lace kissed my skin as it flowed over my body. Then I shrugged on my robe. I buried the dagger in my sleeve. Close to me, for easy access when I embraced him.

He would finally know how my embrace felt, how my bosom felt against his cheek. And then he would pay dearly for it.

Sophie's snores filled the adjacent room. I opened the door, quickly rushed through it, and closed it softly behind me.

Everyone was sleeping. I wondered if Albert was resting tonight, given the information he'd received from Elena. *Does he sleep soundly?* I wondered bitterly. *Does he sleep like a baby?*

I pushed my husband to the back of my mind. Tonight I had to play a role I'd never played my entire life. I had to be convincing and I couldn't do it with Albert in the back of my thoughts.

I ducked through a hidden panel in one of the walls, taking a shortcut down toward the dungeons. I grabbed and lit a wall torch. I hated the dungeons. Why didn't Albert tear them down? It felt as if someone was watching from the deep corners, lurking in the shadows.

The torch in my hand only illuminated a few steps. After excruciatingly long minutes of creeping in the darkness, a faint light appeared ahead. I set my torch on the ground.

If my dagger slipped from my sleeve, I only had to reach his eyes to make him forget. Heck, I could daze him and maybe even paralyze him from the inside. I just needed to be convincing tonight. He had to believe he was the only one for me.

My mind lingered on Elena as I rushed through the passages. What would Albert have done if he'd caught them? Would she have revealed her identity to him? Would he have believed her?

My eyes caught on the steps that led to the east wing. Goran's tower was at the top where he brewed up the deadliest potions the realm had ever seen. Well, this time I had the deadly plan.

It would never happen. I didn't know exactly what would happen tomorrow night, but I refused to find out. I believed my daughter. Every fiber of my being trusted that what she had said was true. Thank heavens she had been brave enough to tell me.

I reached the bottom of the steps and rushed up as fast as I could. With every flight, my lungs burned. My calves seized as I reached the halfway point. After months in bed, I wasn't as fit as I used to be. This year of sulking over my baby, fretting over who would betray us, and aching for information hadn't done my body any good.

I rested for a few minutes, then pushed myself further

up the steps.

Gasping, I yanked the wooden door open, revealing the confined space in between the walls. A few short steps to another door and then I was inside the east wing.

Once in his tower, my roleplaying had to be flawless. *I want no one other than Goran McKenzie.*

I said that a few times over and over in my head. For my child who needed me. She was worth it.

A telltale light above revealed that Goran was working late as usual. I always wondered about the potions he brewed. Now I knew it wasn't a potion. It was an evil plan to destroy everything we loved, everything we'd built.

Wyverns, of all creatures. I remembered hearing Al's claims that dragon was dragon, that breed didn't matter. But Elena had left no room for questions: they couldn't be trusted. Something terrible involving a Wyvern had to have happened to her to make her distrust them so fiercely. My mind raged. Just thinking about scenarios almost drove me to insanity.

I finally reached his door. *You can do this, Catherine. You have no choice. It's either him or you.*

I took a huge breath. My face went numb. Tears glistened in my eyes. I needed to do this. My daughter belonged home.

I knocked on his door and waited.

When Goran opened it, his face lit up. He hadn't expected to see me. "Katie, is everything okay?"

My lower lip vibrated. I shook my head as I threw myself into his arms.

He hesitated, even though the desire to touch my body was evident in the stiffness of his posture.

"What is going on with you? Please, I need to know?"

I sniffed and pressed into his tower chamber. It was tidy, nothing out in the open. He was always such a secretive and organized man.

I took a huge breath and turned around.

"I should've never married him!" I cried. He wrapped his long arms around me. "Why didn't you fight harder for me?" I asked.

"Because you were in love with Albert. You made that perfectly clear."

I shook my head. "I didn't know better then."

"Katie," he crooned, leading me across the semi-dark room. He perched half on the table. I hovered a few inches from him. He wiped my tears away softly. Desire radiated from him. I moved in for the kiss, but he pulled away.

"We can't do this!" he said.

He feels guilty now? "I thought this was what you wanted." I pouted.

"It is." He grabbed my hand but closed his eyes so I couldn't use my gift on him. His lips touched my knuckles. He was so cunning. Albert must have told him what they'd said.

"Let's run away. Let's do it now."

"Katie." He smiled. "You don't know what you are saying. Just tell me what is bothering you, please." His eyes flitted open but never met mine. He spoke with his lips against my head.

"I'm so lost, Goran. Without Tanya…" I didn't know how to finish. I remembered a conversation between Al and Bob. The time Bob wanted answers, Al had to tell him something. Even if it was a lie. Anything to protect our daughter. "He told me to choose between him and Tanya. I *never* should've chosen him."

"He did what?"

A shock of regret sliced me in two; I'd only fueled his hatred for Albert. But I couldn't let him discover the existence of my little girl.

"I never thought he was the jealous type, but he never liked my dragon very much. She always said what was on her mind." I smiled, remembering my sister and how she'd used to be.

"How could he give you an ultimatum between Tanya and him? She was your Dent."

I shrugged. "She didn't like Bob. Said he was capable of betraying us. You know Al, such a goody two shoes. I used to love that about him, but now... Now I despise it." *Good one, Catherine.*

He brushed my cheek. It took all my self-control not to recoil from his touch. I laid it on thick. "Why didn't you fight more? Was Sarafine really everything to you?"

"I only took Sarafine to get over you," he admitted. It struck me how sad that was. But he'd send his followers to chase down my daughter like a dog. She would have no home because of him.

I inhaled deeply. *This is it.* His head bowed toward mine. Before our lips touched he veered off course and kissed me on my temple with his hand still on my cheek. My left hand covered his. The fingers of my right hand gripped my dagger inside my sleeve.

"If I could run away with you, I would. But now is not the right time." With a wistful sigh, he pulled away, out of my reach. "I promise you, if you want me, you have me. Just not tonight."

I looked at him. "Why not tonight?" I tried not to rouse his suspicion.

"I am working on something really important." His lie was smooth. "I think you just gave me the missing ingredient. Wait till tomorrow. I promise you everything will be sorted."

I blew out a breath. He wouldn't give me the opportunity tonight. He was a man of many talents and if I struck now, right this moment, he would know that our guests got to me. Surprise was my element. And it was not going to happen tonight. He was much too powerful for that. I nodded.

He walked me back to my chamber. We chatted about the good old days. He was my friend again. Goran, one of my best friends.

"Join us for breakfast tomorrow," he cajoled. "I've missed you around the castle."

I nodded and smiled. "See you tomorrow then, I guess."

We said goodnight. I had to carry on my part, so I gave him a kiss. It wasn't one that would allow me to grab my knife and swing away. No, it was a sweet, soft kiss. I went inside and shut the door behind me.

He wanted to attack. He still planned to do this. What *were* his plans with me, exactly? Elena was right; he was a psychopath if he believed I would select him after he killed my Albert.

There was no choice. I had to end this tomorrow before the attack.

I had to.

I struggled to fall asleep that night. Where was Elena now? Had Tanya at least ensured her happiness? By now Jako would know what she'd done. How was he treating her? He was a Copper-Horn. He'd been King Louie's dragon, so I doubted he would hurt Elena. He was wise, always had the perfect answer for anything. Even in the darkest scenarios, he saw the light. I prayed that he could see the light around her.

My mind drifted to the daughter I'd met tonight. What future did she inhabit? How was her life? Was she excited, disappointed? Would they come back and warn me again if I failed? How many times had they come back in time? I knew of two already—when I'd shot at them in battle, and this time.

I tossed under my sheet restlessly. My mind chugged like a steam train.

I missed my sister. She'd always been able to make me laugh. She could brew up one hell of a plan, could concoct crazy stories to get herself out of any situation. People called them lies. I called them creativity. She'd never lied to me. I could tell.

But she had promised she would stay, and she hadn't.

It hasn't happened yet, Katie. It's not going to happen. You have to make sure of it.

The sky outside my windows turned gray as the sun peeked out from the horizon in the east.

I hadn't even pulled the curtains closed last night.

I rose, feeling wired and useless. I went over to the sill and watched the sunrise. Today was a new day. Today might be the first of many happy days. I just had to do this. Pinks and oranges slid across the sky like wet paint. Surely the beautiful color wasn't an omen of bad luck.

Assassinating Goran in a private place hadn't been fruitful. I needed to find him wherever he was. Even if Al was around. He might throw me in the dungeon. Goran was highly ranked, set to take over the kingdom if anything happened to Al. I was just his queen, not a ruler.

I didn't care anymore. I had to do this for my child.

I took a long bath. Sophie came in to wash my back. "You are in a better mood this morning," she said.

"I've made up my mind to stop sulking and embrace today."

She gasped. Tears shone in her eyes. "There *was* hope after all," she said.

Those were Al's words.

I got dressed.

"Can I call up some breakfast, my queen?" Sophie asked.

I smiled. "No, I think it's time that I face everyone I've pushed away from me."

Her reply came in the form of a big grin.

I took the dagger from last night. The one I'd cut Elena with. Blood flaked off the blade. I felt so guilty staring at her blood. I could've killed my own daughter last night. I pushed my emotions away.

There was no time to clean it properly. If I wanted to do this, it had to be now. With this dagger. I put it into my sleeve again and went downstairs.

The dining hall was much fuller than I preferred.

Albert was reading the morning paper. Helmut and Emanual joked at the coffee station, each busy getting a cup. Bob sat close to Albert. Caleb and Yvonne were missing, which was a good sign. One fewer dragon and rider pair to worry about.

A few staff members would flee at my outburst, but

the three guards near the entrance worried me.

I made my appearance. Goran was the first to look up. My lips curved softly. So did his.

"Katie!" Albert's tone was shocked. He gave me that beautiful smile of his. The one that lit up his eyes, the one he used when he saw his favorite things in this world. Though it hurt, I ignored him. I had to in order to accomplish the mission for my daughter to come home. One thing my months of anguish had given me was the ability to focus on a single thing. I made my way to the coffee station past Goran.

The dagger was like a hot rod in my palm as I neared. I could see everything clear in my mind's eye. Time slowed.

I pulled the knife out. The brilliant blade sliced his neck. He dropped like a bag of rocks. I just needed to cut one of his main arteries and keep everyone away from him until he was beyond saving.

Everyone shouted at the same time. Thick crimson blood coated my hands.

Goran lay on the floor, gurgling, watching me with big round eyes.

I blasted Emanual and Helmut back with an incantation.

I hit Albert and Robert with my gift. Bob fell into a trance immediately. Al tried valiantly to fight it.

"What are you doing?" he grunted through gritted teeth. His fury at what I'd done made the words hard to spit out. But he couldn't get closer.

Goran clung to life, clutching his neck where my blade had made a gaping hole. His blood was splattered all over my cashmere sweater and had pooled on the floor.

I bent down. Emanual and Helmut couldn't get through my shield. All of them were trying to get to me.

"You would have burned me on my bed," I spat at him. "You never loved me. You don't know the first thing about love. Possession is not love. You are a scumbag and I could never love a man like you!" I shouted. I could see out of the corner of my eyes that Albert realized that the two extraordinary visitors had gotten through to me last night.

A pair of arms grabbed me from behind and pulled me up. Something other than blood oozed out of Goran. He started to turn to dust. Very slowly. He screamed. Pain—no, anguish—filled the horrible sound that reverberated in the dining room.

Helmut finally reached him. Grabbing what remained of his body, he let out an unbearable scream.

It turned into a sob. He knelt beside his brother, holding him tighter. Albert made his way over. I couldn't take my eyes off Goran. Whatever my blade had done to him worked its magic.

He was disintegrating. He had no more fingers. His legs were just two heaps of black dust.

"What did you do?" Helmut roared at me. He looked back down, staring with huge eyes at his brother.

I didn't know how to feel, but knowing a small fact was enough to not cry over this scum that used to be one of my favorite persons. My daughter could come home.

THIRTEEN

CATHERINE

I was tossed unceremoniously and immediately into the dungeons. Sophie came to see me.

"My queen!" Her tone was shocked. Grave danger lingered on her face when she took in my grim, barely lit cell.

"Have you got any news for me?" I asked.

Her eyes welled up. "They are forcing the king's hand. Goran was second-in-command. Why did you do that? I don't understand!"

I touched her wrinkled face with my hand through the bars of my cell. "The less you know, the better."

"My queen," she cried. "There is talk of executing you. King Helmut is demanding it."

I nodded. My heart beat like crazy. My daughter might not meet me, but at least I knew she would grow up inside Paegeia. She would have a home, have her father, know about dragons. It was enough to put a small smile on my face.

"It's fine. Please just tell Albert to come and see me. He must. Before nightfall."

She nodded and left.

I needed to tell him about the Wyverns' location. Goran's betrayal still loomed despite his death—maybe even more so in retribution.

I had asked Albert to come hours ago. Why didn't he come?

The sun still stood high in the sky. Slowly it sank and disappeared from the opening way above my head.

My dank cell turned cold. Huddled on the bare stone floor, I missed Tanya. My amazing Green-Vapor dragon would've broken through these walls to rescue me.

Finally, footsteps approached. It could be a dragon or Albert. I couldn't tell. Then Albert's face appeared.

He's eyes were rimmed red. His lips were thin. If he had been a dragon, he would've spit fire.

He succumbed as he saw me sitting in the cell. He rested his head against the beams. His body shook.

So many emotions rushed through me. I was heartbroken, enraged, and exultant all at once. "How is Helmut?"

"How is Helmut?" he spoke softly. "Katie, you murdered his twin. How do you think he is? They want your head."

Tears welled up in my eyes. Anger took over. "Want my head. My head!" I got up and walk toward him. "If you'd had the balls to do this, like you promised me you would when you discovered who was going to betray us, I wouldn't be in here."

He closed his eyes. "They got to you, didn't they?"

"Yes, because you refused to listen to them, Al." I was shouting now. "You promised me. You lied and then betrayed me."

"He would've never…"

I threw up my hands. "Stop saying that. A Wyvern militia waits on the north side of Etan. Waiting for who knows what. If I'm wrong, you can have my head. If not…kill every last one so that my daughter—our daughter—can come home."

Albert just looked at me. It was my turn to breathe imaginary fire. I couldn't remember the last time I'd been this angry at him.

He didn't say anything. He just grunted and stomped away with huge strides.

Energy drained from my limbs. Fighting with him did that to me. It always had. It was one of the reasons we never fought. It was too hard. Loving him was easier.

I sat down in the corner. I scraped my knee against the rough stone floor. Dark blood glinted on my filthy skin, but I failed to care. I could hear men being assembled. At least he still loved me enough to go and check it out. Or maybe he did this for his people.

I had done a lot of damage, I realized, in my months of pulling away from him. He thought me mad.

It didn't matter. I did this for my daughter.

The shadows deepened. Minutes felt like hours, hours like forever. What was taking so long?

To keep the anxiety at bay, I tried reasoning with myself. Long wasn't bad. It meant that there *was* an army waiting, just as adult Elena had predicted. But it was also not good; I might be husbandless and baby Elena might never know her father.

I paced for hours. When I tired of that, I attempted to

tune in my enhanced hearing for a clue as to what was happening out there. But it was too far. I could only hear faint murmurs of voices. Chaos reigned at the castle.

Maggie's voice filled my ears. She was doing her duty as queen. She was calming people down, but what was happening? Why were there so many people in the castle, and why were they in a state of panic? I listened harder for signs of war. But I couldn't make heads or tails of what little I heard.

I returned to my corner. I had no idea what time it was.

My mind couldn't stop focusing on the image of Goran's body turning into dust.

How could he have done this? What made him do it? Why did he hate Albert? Was it my fault? The depression I'd fallen into for such a long time, that... that what? Made him loathe Albert? It was hard to believe, but thinking about how close we used to be, it was the only explanation I could come up with.

I knew he loved me. But did he love me so much that he would kill my husband to free me from my darkness? What? It was driving me insane thinking about questions with answers that I would never get.

Tears, whether angry or sad, I didn't know, streamed down my face.

Why would he have done this? Why?

There was no way to know how long I cried, but it felt good. I hadn't cried like that for a long time.

I must have dozed off through it all. Hollow footsteps against unforgiving stone woke me up. Startled, I sat up and hastily wiped my mouth and eyes.

Light danced off the walls. I looked at the bars.

Bob appeared. He looked tired or shocked—or both.

I could never tell with him. He was so hard to read, and it was difficult to earn his trust.

I got up as keys rattled in the keyhole of my cell. "Is Al okay?" It was all I needed to know.

"Katie," he said in a low voice. He struggled to speak for a moment and cleared his throat. "How did you know what was going to happen?"

"Because the Rubicon and his rider told me." I closed my eyes in delicious relief. My head was going to stay on my shoulders for a little while longer. "Where there many?"

His stare remained unreadable. "I never knew there were so many Wyvern colonies...or that they could function together."

All of this just made it more real. "The Rogue, whoever he was, got the surprise of his life tonight."

"Is Albert okay? He needs to be okay."

"He has minor injuries, but he will live."

The tears just flowed again. I didn't know why I wept. Bob really struggled to find the right fucking key. He eventually found it and unlocked my gate. He pulled me into his arms and hugged me tight.

"You saved a lot of lives tonight, Katie, because you trusted a couple of strangers."

"They weren't strangers," I murmured.

"What?"

I shook my head. "Just take me to him. Please."

The lobby was full of people. Crammed in groups. Woman, children, the elderly, and the disabled.

They'd all come to the castle when the fighting must

have spread to the village. How many lives had been lost tonight? I grabbed blankets and started handing them out.

"Thank you, my queen," one old lady said as I handed her a blanket and a bottle of water.

I touched her shoulder and smiled. "You are safe here," I whispered.

I comforted the children. Guided the bigger ones to play a game to keep them occupied. Laughter soon filled the lobby. Adults started watching the kids play, which made everyone else's jobs easier.

My eyes found Maggie's red ones. She stood next to Isabel with blankets in her arms. She didn't look angry. She didn't even know about Elena. How was I going to tell her now that I had a one-year-old daughter? She was my best friend. We shared everything.

I pulled my gaze away and returned to my duty as queen.

I kept handing out supplies as needed. I gave out soothing words to expel fears. Many Swallow Annexes came, healing most of human injuries and then lifting spirits.

The doors opened and Caleb returned with Yvonne, both worse for the wear but alive. I could just imagine what it would be like if either one had died tonight. They had been a pair almost as long as Bob and Al.

Emanual came in next. Helmut was badly injured but breathing. Maggie and I rushed to his side. I backed away. He might not want my help or care to see my face.

He cussed and cried. Fury punctuated every syllable. At whom, I didn't know, but when he mentioned a "he" to Margerite, and how he'd always known, I realized he was speaking about his brother. Goran. He'd always been evil. We just hadn't seen it. We'd never wanted to see it. Poor Helmut. Of course this was hard to take.

The doctor rushed in. Maggie disappeared after him.

Isabel's arms hugged me from behind and rubbed fast on my back.

"Where is Blake?" Mother to mother. I had to know.

"He is safe with my mother. He and Samantha both."

Samantha was about Elena's age—just over a year old. She was the cutest Fire-Tail dragon I had ever laid eyes on, but seeing her, knowing my own daughter her age was far away, always reminded me of what life could be like. Unfairly, I had pushed her away because of that.

"I came the minute I heard. You are such a brave woman, Katie. Who knows how all of this could've turned out if they didn't know about that army?"

I didn't want to think about it. Elena had told me how it would've turned out. But I wasn't going to share that with Blake's mother.

"Constance said she is on her way." Lee's voice came from behind. "How are you holding up?"

"As best as I can. Thanks, General."

He sighed and shook his head.

"Don't," I said. "No need to say it." I smiled and he nodded and walked toward the room they'd dragged Helmut into.

"Katie." I heard Albert's voice coming from the stairs. I wasn't angry at him anymore. He was not himself. He'd gone through almost another war—one created by our best friend. He didn't need further punishment.

I ran to him and flung my arms around him. He flinched; one arm was in a sling.

I let go of him and he pulled me back in, wanting to

be close to me…and then he just cried. The disappointment of who was behind this hit him harder than the harrowing deed I'd committed this morning.

"I'm sorry I didn't listen," he said.

"I did," I replied. "It's over." My voice broke. "She can come home."

He sniffed. Tears rolled over his cheeks. I wiped them away, gazing at my husband.

Everyone around us had been attended to. Things had calmed down.

Their faces lit up as they realized Al was in the lobby. He spared a hug for Isabel and then was forced to make a speech. "This morning, our queen did something that I couldn't do. I wasn't brave enough, I didn't want to see the truth, but she had." He looked at me, took my hand gently in his, and for one moment, I felt like I used to feel before Elena left my arms. "She saved us from a great war, a destruction even. The past few hours, we fought many Wyverns, and we lost a good few dragons, brave Copper-Horns and Fin-Tails." He wiped a tear off his cheek. "I promise I will never be blind again. I will look after my people, and will never be misguided to do what is right for Paegeia. Darkness will come in many forms, but I promise, as long as I am king and my queen is next to me, we will protect each and every one of you with our lives. You have my word."

He set their fears aside with his words. It made me cry just thinking it was our best friend, his best friend, the man he'd trusted the most, who had betrayed all of us.

"You can stay as long as you need," he concluded. He spread his free arm toward me and gave me a side hug as we walked toward the library where Bob had assembled all our closest friends.

They were waiting for us. It was past time to tell them the reason for all the secrecy. The reason behind all the tears from the past year. They needed to know who was going to come home.

We entered and found everyone that we cared for. Maggie was there.

The vibe lingering around us was a sad one.

"Al, what is this about?" Bob asked, standing up from the chair he shared with Isabel.

Al jutted his chin toward a chair. "Catherine and I need to tell you something. Sit, please."

Bob took his seat again. I knew it was hard for him, too. Tanya hadn't wanted Al to tell Bob about Elena. She'd suspected even Bob might betray us.

Irene arrived, looking confused and on edge. I wondered what she'd seen of the future. Had she glimpsed the outcome Elena and Blake lived through—and had it just disappeared?

Al cleared his throat. "A year ago, when Katie and Tanya left on a quest..." His voice broke. I touched his shoulder and nodded, looking exhausted.

I mouthed *sorry* at Maggie. She just looked at me with equal parts compassion and fear.

"I didn't go on a quest," I blurted. "I gave birth to our baby girl." Gasps filled the air. Isabel cupped her mouth. Everyone stared at us with huge eyes.

Everything we'd put them through the last year was explained with that single admission.

Why I couldn't cope. Why my tears eventually turned into anger. Why I resented my husband.

"We couldn't tell anyone. And as you know, it was foretold that someone close to us would betray us. We needed to keep her safe so that one day she could claim the Rubicon."

Isabel started to cry. Bob stared at the ground. Betrayal was written over his own face. Al said nothing. What could he say that would make this all right?

"You want to tell me that Blake has a rider?" Isabel finally asked.

I nodded. Tears flowed over my cheeks. A smile sprawled across my face.

Isabel had always worried about Blake not having a true rider. We couldn't lose this Rubicon like William had with Quitto. Albert wouldn't have made it if he'd had to slay him one day.

Irene's prediction when his egg hatched was the only hope anyone had for him to be a good Rubicon, not evil like the previous one.

I went to her and hugged her tightly. Relief seemed to wash over her body; her knees wobbled.

"And now she can come home."

"You have a daughter?" Maggie finally asked.

I felt so small. So stupid, but I couldn't share it with anyone. "I'm sorry," I mouthed.

She just rushed over and hugged me tight. "No wonder no one could get through to you. Where is she?"

"Tanya gave her the Calypso potion. She went into Cara. They are on the other side."

"The Calypso potion?" Isabel sounded scared.

"It worked. She is fine." I tried to put her mind at ease.

Her expression was weirdly blank.

"One wouldn't make it, but two might." Irene spoke softly.

I rushed over to her and hunched in front of her. Those bright blue eyes of hers held my gaze. "Tanya had no idea what you could possibly mean by that when you gave it to her," I said. "But she said it made sense."

"Why? Was she sick?"

I nodded, tears forming in my eyes as I remembered that day. It was the worst day of my existence.

"Wait," Albert finally said. "How do you know it worked, Katie? How do you know she's fine?"

I froze. I'd just wanted to alleviate Isabel's fears. I didn't think about my actions. I closed my eyes.

"Katie, how do you know this? It was a long shot to begin with."

I opened my eyes. "Because your extraordinary visitors…were extremely extraordinary, Al."

"They saw them?"

I shook my head and moved toward him. Sat in front of him on my haunches and touched his face with the palm of my hand. A tear rolled over my cheek. "It was *them*."

Everyone gasped again. "What?" Maggie exclaimed. She looked worried.

"What is it, Maggie?" Both Al and I asked.

Her face blanched. "The Wyverns."

"What about them?" I went to her side.

"I spoke to Merica yesterday when I came with Lucian. He fascinated her. She told me that Wyverns were going to come and search for a truce." Her voice shook but her words rang with clarity from the memory of my daughter's words. "She said I should do everything in my power to not give in. That they can't be reasoned with, they can't be trusted. If not, I would lose loved ones."

"We won't trust them. Believe me, this attack made sure of it. We won't trust them." I cupped her face. Now I knew why Elena didn't trust them.

I kissed her temple and went back to Albert.

"What do you mean it was *them*?" Al asked. I could tell from everyone's faces that they wanted to know this just as much as he did.

Isabel sat down on the nearest chair, holding Bob's hand.

I ran my fingers through my hair. "Blake will receive a new ability when he is thirty. Like Al, I didn't believe them when they claimed Goran would betray us. But then she told me Blake can jump back in time, and they chose to come and warn us about what was going to happen. They had to use an enchantment to hide their true appearance because of their resemblance to us."

Albert gaped at me. Everyone stared at me with slack faces as if they thought me insane.

"She said she had word about Elena." I wrung my hands. "I almost killed her, Al. Then she told me you refused to listen. And if I did the same, I would be burned in my bed."

"What?" His voice was husky with emotion.

"I still didn't want to believe her. She told me Elena would grow up not knowing who she is as Tanya would break her promise and come back after my death. She would leave Elena. Jako would raise her alone."

"Jako found them?"

I nodded.

He swiped at his eyes.

"She won't even know that dragons exist, Al. I was adamant. I demanded to know how she knew all of this and she told me that it was her life, and that they are actually from the future. A future where I had been killed by Goran's hand. She begged me to kill him so that she could come home." A laugh escaped my lips. "To convince me, she removed the enchantment that changed their appearance."

"And?" his voice was gruff.

"Blake was the first to change." I looked at Robert and Isabel again. "He looks so much like you, Bob, but he has Isabel's peacock eyes."

Isabel gave a startled and pleased little laugh. She rested her head on her husband's shoulder.

"I was so mesmerized by him. He reminded me of the last time he saw me in the garden, giving him a scolding. He understood all our glares and warnings. And then she said my name." Goosebumps rose on my arms. "She called me Mom. It was her. It was the image I saw in the pond. She looks just like you." I hugged Albert close. He cried.

"We need to keep this new ability of the Rubicon a secret. They are going to be so powerful that…I have to be honest." I looked at Al. "It scares me to death."

Al chuckled through his tears. I laughed with him.

"Sweetheart, you were scared the minute you found out she was a girl."

Bob and Isabel laughed, too.

"They can read each other's minds. It's like nothing I've ever seen before."

"What?" Everyone burst out at the same time.

"It's not just old Dents anymore. She was twenty-six, and she could read his mind."

"They are that powerful?" Al asked.

I nodded and cupped his cheek. "You were right about everything. She is going to help him master his dark side and he'll remain good. I saw it."

He closed his eyes and smiled.

"Except about the Wyverns. You are wrong about

that. They can't be trusted. Please tell me that you will give that a rest."

He laughed. "I've had my fair share of Wyverns. If they say they can't be trusted, then that is where it will stay."

FOURTEEN

CATHERINE

The next morning Al announced to all of Paegeia that we had a baby girl on the other side of the Wall.

The press conference showed a happy Catherine for the first time in a year. I was going to be reunited with my child. The thing I wanted most.

She'd given me the opportunity to change the past and to raise her myself, with Al by my side. She would have a home. She wouldn't run anymore. Her old life would never come to pass.

We were finally going to be a family.

Al sent Robert and Theodore, a Moon-Bolt, to track them down. I gave Bob a letter for Tanya. Just like we'd agreed when the danger was over.

This entire week revolved around bringing our little princess home.

We received many calls from the other side. The news

reached everyone. People wanted to know if they could assist in any way in bringing her safely to us.

I couldn't sleep. Instead, I used my excited energy to help set up her nursery. The one she should've had a long time ago. Albert himself picked up the screwdriver and assembled her crib.

The walls were painted a soft pink. Angelic bears floated among puffy clouds. Crisp white curtains hung at the windows. The shelves were home to baby books and teddy bears of all colors and sizes. Drawers were stuffed with infant clothes, diapers, and hygiene products.

Al moved back into the west wing with me. He was finally out of the dog house. Elena's room was a few inches away from us.

He wanted to hire a nanny. "Over my dead body!" I said, half laughing. "She's my only child. I have so much catching up to do." I planned to smother my little girl with love.

I still worried about this Blake thing. When I saw the two of them together, they were so intense. A part of me loved to know she had such a strong connection, such a deep love. But it scared me. What would they be like growing up? Their bond would be so much stronger.

Bob and Al argued before he left. I was scared that he might ring my dragon's neck for making him out to be a villain. I was even more afraid he might refuse to come back. He was offended that we hadn't trusted him with our secret. I felt dreadful about it. I made a mental note that if I ever met the adult Elena from the other night again, I would drag her life story out of her. I wanted to know every aspect of what she'd gone through—what had happened to everyone in her timeline—if she came back.

We received word that they were on their way. Tomorrow was the big day.

I couldn't stop remembering how it felt to hold her little body in my arms—couldn't stop imagining how it would feel to do so again. It had been such a long time ago, but the memory...the memory was still there.

She had been so tiny back then. I'd dreamed of this day for so long. I wondered what she looked like. I knew it would be the female version of Al. She had his eyes, his hair, and almost nothing of me. I scowled wistfully at the thought, but my grin replaced it immediately; I couldn't be unhappy now.

"You coming to bed?" Al's voice filled her nursery. I was staring at the garden.

He padded in and hugged me from behind.

I shifted into his embrace. "I don't know if it is going to be possible to fall asleep."

His lips lingered on my head. "Try. The hours will go by faster."

I laughed.

"Okay." I turned to face him. He captured me with the same green-eyed stare he'd had the night we met, both hiding behind masks.

"I'm sorry that I was such a coward."

I lay a finger on his lips. "Don't, please. She didn't tell you who she was."

"Because I didn't give her time."

"Well, she got through to one of us. Just promise me that she will always get through to one of us," I said.

He pulled me close. "Finally, a way I can redeem myself."

I laughed in his shoulder. "Don't become one of those fathers who gives her everything. I don't want her to hate me."

"She will never hate you, Katie."

I gave him a half-joking, petulant pout. "Promise?"

"I promise."

I followed him to bed. We made love like young lovers, not the two-century-year-old people we were. It was the first time we were both really present in the act of love since we'd sent our baby away.

The next day I was up early, making sure that everything was ready for her. Maggie came in with a huge teddy bear with Lucian at her side.

He'd grown so much. I touched his face. "I missed him."

"He was busy. Believe me, he didn't even notice."

I gave her another hug. "How do you feel?"

"Excited. Scared. What if she doesn't want to come to me?"

"It's normal. She will get used to this."

I nodded.

Maggie's voice was soothing. "Just don't take it personally. Desi is at the stage where Helmut is everything. I doubt that I ever had her, and Lucian... Well, he will always be my boy."

I laughed. "So in short, she is going to be Al's baby."

"When she finds out what her mother did for her, he can't top that." She scrunched her nose. I laughed. Maggie always knew how to make me laugh. Though Tanya was my sister, Maggie was the one who could put everything back into perspective.

At ten we all gathered in the expansive gardens outside the castle to wait. Reporters buzzed like a hive of rumor-mongering bees. Albert answered most of their questions. I chirped a few comments like "over my dead body" here and there.

The papers weren't just filled with Paegeia's new princess and her story. The revelation that the Rubicon had a rider rocked the world. Hope sparked everywhere. Plastered in the papers and on the television.

The mood remained buoyant as my eyes stayed glued to the horizon for silhouettes of three or four dragons, depending on how Jako felt about all of this.

I knew Al dreaded it. To look another father in the eyes and know we had traded his daughter's life for ours. It was like murder. But we'd teach Elena about Cara, the special Thunderlight who had saved her life. We would always honor Cara.

The minutes ticked slowly. Impatient, I glanced at my wristwatch every five seconds.

"Relax, sweetheart. Bob is with them. He promised he would protect her with his life."

I nodded and gave him the ghost of a smile. But I would keep on worrying until they were in view.

Everyone gasped. My heart leapt as I saw them: four dragons on the horizon.

Camera flashes went off like mad. It overpowered everything.

The Green-Vapor clutched something small in her arms. My breath seized in my lungs.

"See? What did I tell you?" Al's lips brushed against my ears. Then he stiffened as his gaze fell on Jako, flying at the rear of the procession.

It was my turn. "It's going to be okay. Whatever he needs, Al."

He nodded.

They started to descend. I craned my neck, but couldn't see Elena. Irrational fear of something happening to her lay heavy on my gut. "Where *is* she?"

"Shh, calm down. Bob would've already said something if she wasn't with them."

Bob landed first. Then Tanya. Gosh, I'd missed her. Theodore hurtled in. Jako took his time.

My eyes locked onto my dragon; Tanya had shifted back into her human form and accepted a proffered robe from a servant. She pulled it over her perfectly shaped body as she made her way to me.

Where is my child? My eyes were wild. Hers weren't. She grabbed me around my neck and just hugged me tight, ignoring my concerns, my crazily thumping heart, my emotions that must have overpowered her.

"Katie! I missed you so much."

Flashes went off like mad.

"I missed you, too. But where the hell is my baby?"

She pushed me away so that our eyes could meet. She gave me her perfect, dashing smile. The one that made knees go weak. "That one only has eyes for the men."

"What?" I demanded. She merely pointed at Jako as he came to a lumbering landing.

His right paw was curled gently into a ball. When he changed, a small package was in his arms. He grabbed and donned a robe. He slung the baby sling over his neck, pushing one arm through the straps as he walked up to us.

Cameras flashed like crazy.

I felt paralyzed. She was here. She was finally home.

Al wrapped his arm around me. Tanya took my other side.

Theodore and Bob positioned themselves right behind us. Jako walked up the stairs and he stopped in front of me.

Tears blurred my vision. His eyes glistened, too.

"Jako?" Al sounded grave.

The Copper-Horn waved a hand. "Don't. No need."

I had eyes for one thing only: the sling. A tiny, chubby arm reached out. My heart stopped.

He pulled her softly out of her sling. Soft blonde curls clung to the nape of her neck. She was wearing the cutest yellow dress—and no shoes.

"Yeah, not so fond of shoes either," Tanya quipped. I couldn't help but laugh.

"Bear," Jako murmured. "I want you to meet your real mommy and daddy."

She finally looked at both of us. My lungs decided to start working again. I took a shaky breath. She had her father's beautiful green eyes.

I didn't know if I should hold out my arms to her or if I should give her space to get used to me for now.

"She won't bite," Tanya whispered. "She hasn't reached that phase yet."

I laughed through my tears and stepped forward. I reached out my arms, and to my surprise she came to me after the briefest hesitation.

She fit perfectly in my arms. As if they were created just for her. She just stared at me as my happy tears rolled over my cheeks.

"Hello, baby girl," I said.

She immediately went for my necklace as my lips

lingered on her head.

"Already intrigued with the expensive stuff," Al chirped. The media—whom I'd forgotten entirely— laughed as they snapped our pictures.

He bent over and kissed her head.

I was never going to let her out of my sight again.

Isabel walked over with Blake in dragon form. Elena needed to get used to him; she was going to be his rider one day.

I crouched on my haunches with her in my arms. Albert kneeled at my side.

Blake was not one of the most beautiful dragons out there. Already he was terrifyingly huge, and the dark purplish hue of his scales hinted at his dark side. He was still so young; he hadn't taken a human form yet. But I remembered the way he would eventually look. Why were they always so damn pretty? *To lure girls like mine into sin. She is one year old, Katie, not there yet.*

At first she didn't notice him. She only gazed at my necklace clutched in her tiny fist. Then he let out a baby growl, a growl of boredom. That got her attention.

Her entire body shook as she got a fright and started to cry.

I got up and walked away from him. I couldn't help the smile, and Isabel had to suppress hers as well.

"Not there yet?" I said. The reporters laughed. "That's my girl," I whispered in her ear.

FIFTEEN

Tanya and Jako stayed with us for the first six months.
The first night was the hardest. Baby Elena didn't
want Albert or me. She bawled for Tanya and Jako. That
was expected. But two months in, nothing seemed to
change.

Her rejection broke my heart.

This was what Margerite had warned me about, but
how did one handle it? Albert was really good. He gave
her time and space. But not me. I hated every minute of
her crying out for Jako or Tanya.

"It will get better, I promise." Tanya hugged me and
kissed me on my head. "She's just not accustomed to all
this. She will get used to it."

It carried on for about another two excruciating
months. I slowly came to terms with the fact that a year
was just too long for Elena. She'd forgotten about me,
but that was fine. She was so little. It wasn't personal.

Still, I spent all the time I could with her. Playing

peekaboo in the garden, hide-and-seek, all sorts of games Jako and Tanya had played with her.

Albert got his fair share of playing with her, too, and I respected Jako and Tanya for stepping aside when it was our family time.

One night, about four months after her return, she screamed again. I didn't go to her like I did in the beginning. Tanya rushed into my room.

I followed her to the nursery and stood by the door as Tanya picked her up and bounced her up and down to calm her.

Her little arms reached out for me. My heart fluttered like a girl who'd just fallen in love.

I took her from Tanya and held her close. She finally stopped crying. For the first time, I was the one she wanted.

Tanya smiled and said goodnight. She kissed Elena on the head and left.

After that, well, it was a downhill battle. She would fall asleep in her crib and wake up between Al and me.

She'd gotten really fond of her dad, but Jako was still the number one guy in her heart.

Around the six-month mark of her return, she called me Momma for the very first time. I lost my voice, and let out a silent scream of excitement. The feeling that I felt was one of pure happiness. My little girl acknowledged me as her mother, the woman who carried her for nine months, the one who had sent her away to be safe, the one who killed the man who was going to betray us, so she could come home. She knew I was her mother. I couldn't wait to hear her say that word again, 'Momma.'

Still, Jako and Tanya were always around. She loved

Jako dearly. I wondered if she could ever feel that way for her own father. Eventually she went to Albert instead of Jako, and we knew the transition was complete.

We could finally be her parents.

Jako would always be welcome at the castle. He was a big part of Elena's life. We named him and Tanya her godparents. Isabel and Blake also visited regularly.

If it were up to me, I wouldn't allow it. Not that I was mean…it was just that I would never forget how close they were that night. They were so in touch with one another, they could hear each other's thoughts. It scared me a lot.

She cried each and every time she saw Blake. He got annoyed with her and ended up in the garden playing with his cousin, Annie. This left Elena, Isabel, and me on our blanket of disliking the Rubicon.

Albert thought it was funny that I was never going to make peace with this. To him, Elena was Blake's, not the other way around.

I knew he only said it to drive me mad, but I always scolded him, rambling about how I'd carried her for nine months, I'd had to let her go, I'd protected her, and now I was her mother and she was mine.

Years ticked by fast. Before we knew it, Elena's third birthday was coming up.

She grew into a living doll as she shed her baby fat and became a smiley toddler. Her hair bounced on her shoulders and framed her cherubic face. She was gorgeous.

We spared no expense in her education, and by the

age of three, Latin was her strongest language. Perhaps because of her fluency in the language of magic, she got used to Samantha—Isabel's daughter and Blake's sister—fast. Sammy still hadn't taken her human form, but Elena didn't seem to mind. Sammy had the most beautiful face a dragon could ever have. Like all Fire-Tails, she was gentle. I suspected those two were going to be lifelong friends.

We planned an extravagant party for her, even though she was just turning three. Maggie went the extra mile. She was so good at planning events.

A reporter or two showed up, along with over two hundred family friends.

It was at her third party where Elena faced her fears and stood up to Blake for the first time.

Not that he was worth standing up to. In fact, he was a bit of a wuss. Annie always got the better of him. She already had her human form. Blake was still a dragon; it worried Bob and Isabel that he hadn't yet morphed into his human form. They were only a few months apart.

But this time when he pounced on his sister and she yelped for help, Elena was at her side, pushing him off with all the strength she had.

Isabel was dumbfounded, but started to laugh as she ran after him, after he hightailed it out of there.

Elena, as small as she was, helped Samantha up. Sir Robert kissed Sammy's booboos. Elena ran as fast as her little legs could carry her toward me.

"High five, pumpkin," I said and she jumped to hit my palm.

Al roared with laughter as I wrapped my arms around her.

After that Blake and Elena started to become friends.

It progressed way too fast for my taste.

Elena's Latin was better than her English at times. It was the only way she communicated with Samantha, and now it was the only way she communicated with Blake.

At least they couldn't hear each other's thoughts. Yet. *Thank heavens for that.*

Even though it was silly, I tried to make her dislike him just a little. At times I thought I had when he ended up hurting her, but the next time she saw him, all was forgiven and they just picked up where they'd left off in their games. In her eyes, the Rubicon could do no harm.

I knew it was innocent, but it wasn't going to stay innocent for long. Their bond was already growing. One day, it would be so strong that none of this would even matter.

I didn't think that I would ever be ready for that. I couldn't bear the thought of losing my baby girl all over again.

Time marched on. Elena was a precocious five-year-old and Blake was almost nine. He still hadn't shown his human form, and to call Sir Robert and Isabel "anxious" would have been the understatement of the year.

"Just take it easy," said Al one crisp fall afternoon as we lounged in the great hall by a crackling fire. "He will get his human form when he is ready." Al was trying to put Bob at ease.

Scientists had performed so many tests on him that he was terrified when his aunt forgot to take her doctor's coat off. He would run every time he saw a person with a doctor's coat.

Elena was a cheeky five-year-old. She tried to protect him from their visits, but it always ended up upsetting her more than it did Blake.

She cried every time they took Blake to yet another appointment. We couldn't handle it anymore. Each instance, we had to get Isabel and Bob to bring Blake after the test, so that Elena could see that he was fine.

She would make a nest for him on the floor. He would curl up next to her bed. They would speak in Latin and then fall asleep.

I didn't like it, not one bit. But Albert would always wrap me in his arms and say their bond was extra beautiful, extra special, and that I had to get used to it. Make peace with it.

She was only five years old. Not fifteen.

Only the night before, Albert had laughed at me when I voiced my worry. "It's not like that, woman. They are children. It's innocent."

"I know," I grumbled. "But it's so intense."

"No, it's not. *You* are making it intense."

I tried to make peace with it, but it was not as easy as he thought.

But now, as the fire light flickered and danced on the crystal vases on the mantle and the kids played together outside under the watchful eyes of Tanya, Al and I begged Bob and Issy to stop with the tests. He would get his human form when he was ready.

"What if…" Issy started.

"He will. I saw him, Issy. He will. Just be patient."

She nodded.

The door opened then and Elena ran in. Horror filled her eyes, making them as huge as orbs.

"Mommy, Mommy, come!" she screamed.

"What happened?" I shouted. As one, all four of us shot up from our chairs by the hearth and ran after Elena. The only thing I could figure was that something had happened with Blake.

This can't be. We'd just spoken about it.

Elena was really fast. Her pink scarf flapped behind her as her little legs pumped down the hall and out onto the lawn. We followed her toward the lake where they always played.

Sammy stood at the tree, apart from the commotion. Her red beanie hat was askew and her auburn hair a tangled mess. She got her human form a few months ago. Lucian and Arianna, Caleb's daughter, were hovering over someone on the ground, while Tanya spoke to him softly in Latin.

A naked boy lay there, trembling from the chill or shock, or both. When I saw him I froze. He had light brown skin and raven-dark hair.

"Issy, it happened," I said softly to her. She rushed to his side.

Bob took his mantle off his back and pulled it over Blake's shivering body.

He'd gotten his human form. The image of him as an adult flashed through my mind again. This boy would grow up into that handsome man.

Elena had no idea what was happening. She hadn't witnessed the transformation. She was scared, hugging my leg.

Good, I thought.

Albert hunched in front of her.

"Baby, don't be scared. Remember how Daddy told you that Blake would get his human form? That is him."

She shook her head fast. Blonde curls whipped her

cheeks.

I couldn't help it. A feeling of happiness rose inside me.

"It's going to be fine." He picked her up.

"No! Where is my dragon?" she yelled, full-on tantrum.

Her dragon?

Al and I shared a look. We'd never told the kids Elena would be Blake's rider.

"He's right there," Al said, quickly recovering from her statement.

Sure, it was plastered in tabloids time and time again, but it was doubtful that she could've discovered that at the age of five.

"No!" she yelled "It's not him. Where is Blake? I want Blake."

Blake's peacock eyes stared at Elena. He felt sorry for her as she buried her face in Albert's neck and cried her little heart out.

I could hear Isabel explaining to Blake in Latin why she was crying. And then he just had to act on it.

He morphed back into a dragon. We all stared at him with gaped mouths. No dragon had ever transformed so fast after receiving their human form.

"Elena," he called her in Latin. "I'm right here."

She tore herself out of Albert's arms and ran to him. She hugged him around his neck.

"Where were you?" she asked in Latin.

"I found my human form."

"That was really, truly, you?"

He nodded and that was it. She didn't argue, nothing.

I gaped at them and found Albert trying to suppress his laughter.

"It's not funny," I muttered to him. Impotent anger rushed through me. I was mad. Blake could tell her to jump in the river even if she couldn't swim and she would do it. She would drown for him.

Their bond was already intense, this connection they shared. And I was the only one who wasn't blind to it.

What was I going to do?

SIXTEEN

ELENA

"What do you mean you don't know?" I asked Blake. We lay inside my treehouse looking up at the wooden ceiling. It was the second treehouse I'd known. Blake had had the hiccups once before he'd gotten his human form when we were smaller...and burned the whole thing down. I'd taken the blame. Said it was a lantern accident.

"I don't know. It's just how I feel." He took a drag of his cigarette. His dad was so going to kill him if he found out.

"It's Arianna, Blake," I teased.

"So?" he asked.

"Seriously, how can this be such a surprise to you, you never saw how she looked at you, how she acted when you are around?" I persisted. "Blake and Arianna sitting in a tree, K-I-S-S-I-N-G!"

"Seriously," he grunted.

I was twelve, Blake was sixteen. He was like my big brother. He hadn't found anybody he liked. It was strange. My dad said it was because I was his rider. Eww.

Sure, the guy was cute. But I'd grown up with him.

He was going to start at Dragonia Academy a year earlier. I wouldn't see him as much. I sure was going to miss him a lot.

"It will happen when it happens, okay? Just don't spread the word around that Arianna likes me."

"You scared that you might like her back?" I goaded.

"NO!" He always seemed annoyed lately.

It was silent for a few minutes. I turned serious. "So, you feel it yet?"

Blake shifted on the floor. "Feel what?"

"You know, what everybody is talking about. The darkness."

"Sometimes."

I wanted to turn and look at him, but I left my gaze on the ceiling. "What do you mean, sometimes?"

"I don't know," he grumbled. "I don't feel it now. My mom thinks it's because of you."

"Me!" I laughed.

"Yes, you. A little annoying brat…" he teased.

I hit him as hard as I could on the chest and he pretended it hurt, which made both of us laugh.

When we subsided, I ordered, "Promise you will write."

"Your dad still hasn't gotten you a Cammy?"

"No." I sulked. I wanted one of those awesome phones that allowed face-to-face hologram calls. "It's my mother. I'm sure of it."

He shook his head. "Fine, I'll write."

"Awesome. Now, one poem about your day."

Blake scoffed. "Seriously?"

"What, you going to stop with them now?"

"I don't know. I haven't felt like a poet the last few weeks."

I couldn't help it. I rolled over to watch him. "Because of the darkness?"

His face went emotionless as he stared fixedly at the ceiling. "I don't know," he said. He released a huge breath. "It scares me."

"Then let me know when it becomes unbearable and I'll ask Dad to bring me. I'll help you feel normal again." So farfetched, but yeah, why not? They all said we were going to be the greatest dragon–rider team everyone had ever laid eyes on.

His lips curved at the corners.

I barreled on. "Just promise me one thing, okay?"

"Fine. Anything for you to stop talking." His annoyed tone was back.

"Don't stop playing, Blake. Your band is really good. I mean seriously good." He gave me a sideways look.

"Please don't tell me you played my song to anyone, Elena."

Guilt washed over my face. "It was just Phoebe."

"Phoebe? That girl is like a walking *Paegeian Times*," he huffed and got up.

"It's not that bad. Don't be such a baby."

"I'm not the one who is twelve years old, Elena." He jumped out of my tree house and walked toward the castle.

I sighed and cussed. Yes, twelve year olds did need to cuss sometimes.

He would get over it, just like he got over everything.

But he didn't get over it. He stayed mad. He fumed all the way up to the day he left for Dragonia. Today we said goodbye to Blake and Annie. They were headed to the school in the sky. Next year Lucian would go; his birthday was late in the year and Blake's was in the beginning. Lucian was the Prince of Tith and Blake's best friend. And the Master of Dragonia Academy thought it was best to enroll Blake now, hoping it would help with the darkness in him.

I couldn't wait to go there myself. Dad took me to Dragonia once. I couldn't fathom how an entire school could stay up in the air. He was the founder of the place. The minute he discovered that humans born with the mark of the riders could gain an ability at the age of seventeen, a process known as Ascending, he'd erected a school just for them.

He'd built it a long time ago with one of his best friends, Goran, who had died in an ambush. They never talked about that. Goran had been my parents' best friend and King Helmut's twin. All I knew was that the Wyvern King had wanted to kill my parents. Why? Because that was what Wyverns did. They couldn't be trusted. Not one bit.

We hardly spoke about Goran, but I knew he was one of the best Dragonians-slash-sorcerers this world had ever seen. Sometimes I secretly wished he was still alive.

My father and mother didn't like talking about him. I think they missed him too much.

Dragonia was huge, and seeing it made me even more confused about how it just hovered above, in between the clouds.

It was an awesome place. The dragon statues moved, and they had a lake where the students who didn't go home on a weekly basis could swim. A young, female doctor was on campus. And Chong Longwei was the headmaster.

Master Longwei was a Fin-Tail dragon, my favorite kind in the whole world. He was majestic, gold in color with fur around his paws. Annie, a Sun-Blast dragon, was his granddaughter and Blake's cousin. Isabel and Constance were twins. Constance, who was married to General Lee, Master Longwei's song, was the head of the Health Department and on my father's council. Okay, it wasn't really my father's council, but he was sort of running it as Paegeia was ours. King Helmut and King Caleb were just his helpers.

I saw all of them on a regular basis; the castle was never closed during the day with meetings upon meetings. So boring. Sometimes I felt sorry for my father.

I waved at Blake as he rested his head against the window of the carriage.

He looked away.

Seriously? It was just Phoebe, and she is not a walking newspaper! I yelled in my head.

"Don't worry. I'll speak to Plucky," Annie said. We both laughed at the nickname. He was so not going to get rid of that name.

"See you soon!" I shouted. My mother stood beside me, watching me like a hawk like always.

"See you," Annie said.

Sammy draped her arm around my neck. "What did you two fight about?" she asked. I gave her the eye; my mom was inches from us.

Mom heard and gave me a piercing stare. Nothing new. She had, like, this enhanced hearing, literally. Tanya, my godmother and her dragon, had given it to her.

"Nothing that can't be sorted out."

Mom squinted at me. I returned the look with interest.

I walked back to my room with Sammy on my heels.

"Don't get me wrong. I love my mother," I muttered. "But she makes my life miserable." She forbade me from going to sleepovers outside the castle. If I wanted to catch a movie with friends, she said no. It was the only answer she knew.

Even if I told her Blake was going to be there, she still refused. In fact, she acted like that piece of information made it final.

Sometimes I got the feeling she didn't like Blake very much. Well, not as much as my father did.

But there were times that I totally adored her, like when we went shopping. She was like my best friend then. The stores usually closed down when the two of us arrived. A spree straight out of heaven.

It was one of my mother's best features and I loved that about her. She was the best shopper out there. If there was an award for it, well, Mom would have won it, hands down.

When we reached my room, Sammy asked, "So seriously, what was the fight about?"

I fell down on my bed. *Why was he so angry at me? It was just a stupid song, and Phoebe…*

"Because I played his song to Phoebe."

Samantha gaped. "That was why he was growling the past few days."

"Lame, I know."

"It's his darkness. He seriously becomes a pain in the ass."

I laughed at the way she'd said it. Still, he didn't seem that dark around me. He was still the Blake I knew. The Blake I'd grown up with.

"Want to go to the mall?"

"You sure Mommy Dearest is going to say yes?"

"No, I'm sure she will want to come with." We both laughed.

"Okay, why not?"

We went to hunt my mother down. I found her in the library, playing the piano. We hovered outside uncertainly.

"You think it's the right time?" Sammy asked me softly.

"I don't know," I said. Mom never played the piano unless something seriously haunted her.

"It's fine," Mom's voice emerging from the library. Like I said, enhanced hearing "What is it?" She sounded friendly.

We both walked in and find her still sitting behind piano. "You up for a shopping spree?"

"Not today, sweetheart."

My face fell.

"But the two of you can go if you want."

My jaw almost fell on the floor, and when I looked at Sammy, hers was there, too.

"Alone?" I asked.

Mom looked confused. "Sure, why not?"

"Thanks, Mom." I kissed her on the cheek and moved to leave. She pulled my arm back.

"What was that for? Not that I didn't love that kiss."

"You said I could go to the mall…alone."

"Goodness, Elena. You always make me feel as if I am the witch in the family."

"I didn't mean it like that."

"Go." She shook her head and returned to play the piano again, smiling.

CATHERINE

Summer break was upon us. So was Elena's thirteenth birthday.

Blake's first year at Dragonia Academy was over.

They weren't like kids who swore to be pen pals and never followed through. They wrote to each other regularly. Sure it was sweet, but I kept feeling that their bond was just growing too strong too fast. I felt that it was up to me to help slow it down.

I read one of his poems It was just about his day. Elena had spread it open on her desk.

I sneaked in most nights to watch her sleeping. I thought back to the night they'd come to warn me. When I'd turned around and found a much older version of my girl. What was that Elena's life like? Was I ever going to meet her? Did a part of her even exist? I would always wonder about her.

The next day, I met Tanya and Maggie at the Ridgemont club.

"Why the long face?" Tanya asked me. Maggie hadn't arrived yet.

"Just give it to me, please."

"Blake is seventeen. She is thirteen. No seventeen-year-old would ever think a thirteen-year-old is awesome.

And I promise you when the time comes, I'll help you conjure up a great plan so they will never know we were behind it."

I laughed. I loved my sister. I gave her an awkward hug. She was right. I should stop worrying about the future.

Maggie showed up. We changed the subject.

We greeted her with two kisses on each cheek, and then we started planning Elena's thirteenth birthday.

ELENA

In one hour, guests would start arriving for my thirteenth birthday party. I hadn't seen Blake since he came back from Dragonia. Samantha had told me he'd changed a lot. It was the darkness in him. I'd never gotten that from reading the letters we exchanged by crow.

I loved how we sent post like in the old days.

If my mom knew about that, she would probably shoot down the crows and burn his letters.

Maybe I was just being paranoid. Mom wouldn't do that. But she was playing her piano for the first time in a long, long while. Something was bothering her.

I found Dad nibbling hors d'oeuvres from one of the platters. I slapped his hand. "It's for the guests, Dad."

"There is plenty where this came from, sweet pea."

I laughed and poured a glass of juice from the fridge.

I plunged onto the high chair of the oval island in the middle of our kitchen. Most of the servants were bustling in the great hall by now, but fragrant food smells lingered from all the party preparations.

Pluggs, the monkey Blake had bought me for

Christmas, jumped onto my shoulder. I kissed him softly.

"Where have you been, Mr. Pluggs?" I asked softly.

"Samuel found him in the garden eating berries again. He was not happy about that, Elena."

"Berries are his favorite. Samuel has the greenhouse if it's such a problem, Dad."

"There is no space."

Then add on, like you did with my tree house. I didn't say it aloud. "Besides, Pluggs is a monkey. Berries taste best when they are snatched from a grumpy old chef's bushes." I gave him a tiny piece of a sandwich that was on one of the platters and he took it in his nimble fingers.

"Elena!"

"What? He won't die. I've seen you feeding him plenty of crap before, and he lives."

He shook his head.

I jutted my chin in the direction of the library. "So, why is she playing the piano again?" Maybe I could get the truth if I caught him off guard.

"Not *she*, Elena. Your mother," my father corrected me. I rolled my eyes. "And I told you, your birthdays make her sad."

"Sad, Dad, seriously?"

"You're getting older, Elena. One of these days you will attend Dragonia and then she won't have anyone. The castle is going to be so quiet."

"It's still three years from now." I shook my head. "And I'm going to Dragonia, not the other side of the Wall."

"Still, your mother is a sentimental human being and we love her for that."

"Maybe you do," I joked.

He gave me a stern look. "She loves you more than

you will ever know. And one day when you are older, and wise enough to appreciate this story, I will tell you just what your mother did for you, Elena."

Whoa, this is new. I squinted. "What did she do?"

"One day. You are way too young for this story."

I scowled at him as he left the kitchen.

Still it made me curious, wanting to know what my mother had done. Would it explain how weird she was about some things? I had always known she was a kickass queen. She was the fifth person to make it out of the Secret Cavern, and the last. Not a lot of women had the guts to do that. I still didn't know why she'd done it. She'd given me the lame excuse of wanting to know what I was going to look like one day. Yeah, right.

She also fought in the great war. On both sides. First on my grandfather Louie's side as a man, because her father had been too sick to fight and her brother too small. She was, like, seventeen. They didn't make women like that anymore! Then she'd fought at my father's side; they had this insane fairytale story of how the two of them had met trying to free all the dragons and give them a voice. I treaded lightly with that side of them.

Their love story reminded me of a Mulan–Cinderella mashup. If it weren't for my parents, it would probably not be so gross to think about. I was intrigued to know just what my mother had done for me that was so great, and why my father thought I was too young to appreciate it.

I poured another glass of juice and headed to the library.

Heartrending music streamed out of the room. I opened the door.

She seemed surprised to see me, and even more surprised to see Pluggs. She took him from me as I neared. She kissed him on his head the way I had earlier.

"I thought you would love a glass of juice."

"Thanks, sweetheart, how kind," Mom said.

"Mom, why do you play?"

She sighed, smiled, and tapped on her stool as she shifted over.

I hadn't played with her in a long time. We started with Chopsticks. I wasn't as talented as she was, but it was a fun tune. Then it stopped.

She looked at me. "I love you so much." Tears—actual tears—glistened in her eyes.

I hugged her. "You're scaring me."

"I just don't want you to grow old. I want you to stay my baby forever," she murmured in the nape of my neck.

I could feel there was something more. "And?" I said.

She laughed, let me go, and wiped her tears away. "And the older you get, the more scared I am of your bond with Blake."

I sighed, exasperated. "Mom, we are *not* Cooper and Merica. I know the stories. I can't hear his freakin' thoughts."

"But you will."

"One day, but not now. Seriously, he's like my brother."

"You think he will always stay your brother?"

I laughed dismissively. "You are worried about *nothing*."

She smiled. I burst out laughing. This was so silly. "Eww," I said. "Please stop playing. I'm sure aunty Tanya will be here any minute now."

"She's already here," my mother said in that eerie

way she had when she heard something impossibly quiet. The door opened. Tanya spotted my mom behind the piano and made a face, which made me laugh.

I got up. "Honestly, he's like my brother," I said to Tanya. I was sure she and Mom talked about everything. Like, e-v-e-r-y-t-h-i-n-g.

"That is what I told her," my godmother said. She gave me a kiss as I passed. "Jako is in the kitchen."

"If he eats all my party food, I am going to kill him. Slowly."

I rushed toward the kitchen to go and stop my godfather from devouring my guests' food, leaving the two women chuckling in my wake.

I skidded to a stop. Blake and Jako stood in the kitchen together, picking at the platters.

I squealed and ran full-speed into Blake. He caught me. He almost never came home anymore. He said it was too much of a hassle, and that he preferred to stay at Dragonia over the weekends. I suspected it was more of a freedom thing than anything else.

"When did you arrive?" I asked.

"Just now. With Tanya and Jako." He looked at me. "You grew."

"Hello, mister," my Mom's voice said. Blake let go of me gently.

She smiled, and kissed him on the cheek. "How is Dragonia?"

"Busy. I am overpowered with girls who seriously…" He didn't finish, but my mother cackled.

Poor guy. What a shame. I felt sorry for him. Girls always wanted a piece of the Rubicon.

"You want to see the ballroom?" Mom frowned at my overexcited tone.

"Sure. Show me the over-the-top thirteenth birthday party decorations," he said in a playful tone. My mother slapped his arm with the back of her hand.

"Ow!"

"You always were a wuss," she joked.

Blake just laughed and followed me toward the ballroom. "She is friendly today."

"Ugh," I said, glancing back and hoping we were out of preternatural earshot. "You don't know what her problem is?"

"Oh please, do tell."

"Cooper and Merica."

Blake roared with laughter. "No."

"Yes, she thinks we are going to turn into them."

"Eww. You're like my sister."

"Exactly what I said."

We walked through the doors. Blake whistled. It made me laugh.

"It's not that over the top. I love it."

"Of course you would. You're a spoiled brat."

I punched him hard on the arm.

"What is it with you Malone women? Always hitting me."

We walked through the tables, each with spindly lanterns that were waiting to be lit and transform the place.

Right at the front was my present table, and my table for the surprise cake Samuel had worked on.

I couldn't wait to see what it was going to be this year.

Last year he'd made the Rubicon symbol. Blake had blushed crimson when he saw it. He carried it on his left shoulder, and the tail reached the middle of his arm. It was flaming hot. But that was where it stayed when it came to Blake. His sign was hotter than him.

Stiff and Revy were still busy setting the last tables.

"Welcome back, Blake," Revy said with her dashing smile. I suppressed mine as he greeted her, apparently oblivious to how much he'd made her heart beat faster.

We took one of the side doors outside.

"So how does it feel to be thirteen?"

"Still the same as when I was twelve."

Pluggs came out of nowhere and jumped on top of my head. "Mr. Pluggs," Blake called to him and held out his arms. The monkey ran across his arms and went to sit on his shoulder.

Blake petted him affectionately. Pluggs was just as fond of Blake as I was. It was why I loved that monkey so much.

"It's a miracle he is still alive."

I gave an exaggerated gasp of horror. "What is that supposed to mean?"

"C'mon, Elena, with the way you always feed junk food to Felix and Shauna." One was a Great Dane, the other a Persian cat.

"Haha." I rolled my eyes as we made our way to the treehouse. It was our sanctuary. Once up there, Blake took out a packet of smokes and lit one.

We spoke about how insane everyone was, thinking we would somehow fall in love. They were so wrong. Their expectations were way too high. I was sorry for the big disappointment that awaited them. But we talked regularly about the claiming. It was going to be the first Royal claiming Paegeia had ever seen; we were the first generation who had grown up with dragons. They were already making a fuss about it, and it was still three years away.

Blake and I chatted about that, imagining what it was going to be like.

Then the conversation took a different turn.

"You were about one when I met you for the first time," Blake said.

"One? How? Did they keep me hostage in my nursery?"

He laughed. "No, you lived with Tanya and Jako on the other side."

Disbelieving, I stared at him. My mind whirred. "On the other side? Other side of what, Blake?"

"The Wall, Elena."

Shock poured over my skin, rendering me motionless. "How?" Surprise filled my voice. "No human can go past the Wall."

"Well, you did."

"Why?"

"It was all hush-hush. Something Irene said. Then Tanya left. To be honest, none of us knew about your existence for an entire year."

"Are you serious?" It started bothering me.

"That's what I remember." I knew he was telling the truth. Dragons could remember everything. Even the temperature of what their eggs were when their mothers incubated them. Blake would've told me if he knew more.

What were my parents hiding from me? Were they really my parents to begin with?

I was no dragon, so they probably were my parents, but getting past the Wall made absolutely no sense to me. Humans couldn't go past the Wall. They just *couldn't*. They would be incinerated the minute they tried. Even if they used transformation spells to look like a dragon. The

Wall always knew.

"You should ask your mother, Elena. I don't know the entire story." He looked at me as if he could see how much this truly bothered me.

I shrugged uneasily. "I guess."

We went down to the party, which was now in full swing. It was amazing. I couldn't remember the last time I'd had all my friends under one roof. I hated the fact that Lucian was going to leave for Dragonia soon.

We'd grown up together. They were always at the castle with their parents whenever there was a meeting. Arianna, Princess of Areeth, was a year younger than Lucian and sort of the odd one out. She was fourteen and beautiful in a regal way, not a tomboy like me. She was more of a princess than I could ever hope to be.

Sammy was there. Lucian and the beautiful Desi, too. She was engaged now to a handsome guy who was about as normal as they could come. They'd gone to college together and at first, King Helmut hadn't liked it very much, but Queen Maggie was crazy about him.

Sammy and I were also crazy about him. We loved Desi. The times she'd babysat, which were many, she disguised us and took us to the theme park or to the movies.

She was funny as hell, too, and one of my favorite people in the world.

"*Thirteen*," she said. "Elena, where does the time go?"

I just laughed and gave her a hug. I indicated her fiancé. "He is hot."

She laughed. "Yeah, not too shabby."

I hadn't been at her extravagant engagement party. My mother had forced me to stay at home with my nanny. Not that she was really my nanny. Mom never liked nannies. She said she wanted me to know who her mother was, and not think that my mother was some old woman, like the way my father had been raised.

I'd never met my father's nanny, though I knew she was a dragon, twelve thousand years old, and had raised three kings. When she celebrated her twelve-thousandth birthday, Dad threw one heck of a party, and she'd died a week later.

Someone tinkled silverware against a crystal goblet. Time for my mother's speech—though these were always finished by Tanya since my mom always started crying.

Then Samuel revealed his birthday cake. We all gasped. It was in the image of the Sacred Cavern. One of my favorite places inside Paegeia.

He'd copied it rock for rock, step by step. He even did all the cracks in the steps.

The candle was the Keeper. Mom told me once about him. He was a hulking giant. He'd breathed the mark onto her wrist after she'd written her name inside the book with her blood. I loved all the stories about the place. Although I'd begged and begged her to tell me what was inside, she never would. She proclaimed that she would die if she ever told anyone what was inside that cave.

I guessed it was a high enough price to pay.

But she had told me about the pond inside. Everyone wanted to see the pond. It was the price everyone went for. It could show the past, future, or present. Anything a person wanted to know. And only five people had ever done it.

I always wondered what I wanted the pond to show

me, but I had everything I wanted. It was useless for me to want to go in there. Regardless, it fascinated me.

We finished my perfect thirteenth birthday cake up in my tree house: Blake, Lucian, Annie, Samantha, and me. Arianna was too much of a girly girl to want to climb the ladder, and she had a boyfriend now. The year away from Blake had done it.

Blake had a bottle of booze with him. Amid appreciative whoops, he passed it on to all of us.

I hated the smell and the taste. I took one sip and that was it.

A cigarette passed between him and Lucian. I almost choked when I saw Lucian taking a drag. "Your father is going to kill you!"

"My father won't. His own fire lingers around him like a wildfire's damage. So the only way he will know is if a little spoiled brat goes and tells him."

I narrowed my eyes at him. "I'm not a tattle-tale."

He laughed and puffed out the smoke from his lungs. It stank.

"I swear if you burn down my treehouse again, Blake Samuel Leaf, I am *not* going to take the blame again."

"I know how to smoke, Elena," he said in a nonchalant tone.

We spent the entire night talking about how amazing Dragonia Academy was. Lucian and Blake would share a room now that he was going to go to Dragonia. The awesome thing was that royalty, although not treated like royals, got perks of having the room of their choice, and Blake hated sharing a room with three others, so Lucian said he could share a room with him.

I was right about Blake feeling free at Dragonia. It was why he didn't come home over the weekends. They could basically do whatever they wanted. It sure did sound like freedom. I couldn't wait until Sammy and I could finally go. Just three more years.

The 'rents called. Time for everyone to go.

I hugged Blake. "See you soon."

"Yes, I will see you in the next few days."

"Promise."

"I promise. Now let go of me," he sulked. I let him go and kicked his ass as he walked towards his mom, who was already waiting in her Swallow Annex form.

Sammy was next. "Enjoyed your party."

I grinned. "Best party ever."

She laughed.

Blake took off his shirt, but stopped. "Oh hey, I forgot." He turned around with his bag still in his hand and took out a wrapped box.

My mother's one eyebrow rose but I pretended not to see it.

"Enjoy opening the present, Elena."

I grunted. I knew it was going to be boxes in boxes, at the end revealing a pebble or something he'd made.

Everyone laughed, except my mother. "Promise it's not a Cammy," Blake sang.

My mother finally laughed. "I will kill you if it is."

We waved at them as they morphed into dragons and lifted off.

My father whistled again. "He's really getting big, Elena."

"So? His dragon form never scared me before."

We went inside. I kept ruminating on what Blake had mentioned before my party.

"May I please speak to the two of you?"

Both my parents stopped and smiled.

"Sure, sweet pea. What is this about?"

I led them into the kitchen. All the serious conversations we had were held in the kitchen around the island.

"That serious?" my father joked. A smile broke out, but it wasn't a laugh.

"Sweetheart." My mother sounded grave. "What is it?"

They waited. I took a deep breath. *It will be okay if it turns out they are not your biological parents, Elena. Just ask them.*

"You know you can tell us anything, right?" my father asked, sounding worried.

"Is it Blake?" my mother asked.

"No, and yes." I sighed. "It was more of what he said tonight."

"What did he say, Elena?"

"Are you my real parents?"

SEVENTEEN

ELENA

Mom went from tranquil to hysterical in two seconds flat. "What?"

"Calm down," my father said to her. "Sweet pea, why on earth are you asking us this? Of course we are your parents."

Wordless, I toyed with the salt shaker. I was afraid to go on.

"Blake brought this up?"" my mother demanded.

"Mom!" She was suffocating me.

"Just calm down." My father seemed to be unaware of the fruitlessness of these words.

"We spoke about the past and he told me he could only remember me as a one-year-old. There wasn't anything before that, Mom. He said I used to live with Tanya and uncle Jako on the other side of the Wall. How is that even possible?" I was beginning to sound like my mother. Deranged.

Mom took a huge breath. "I will...that little..."

"It's not Blake's fault. Now tell me the truth. Did I live on the other side?"

"Yes, you did," my father said.

"Albert!" my mother yelled.

He shrugged. "She has the right to know."

"She isn't ready for this." Mom tossed her long, dark hair over her shoulder.

"Ready for *what*? What are you hiding from me?"

"It's not like that. Both of you just calm down. Elena just wants to know how it happened," my father said to my mother and looked back at me. "Right?"

I nodded, my jaw muscles pumping and my arms crossed.

"Then we tell her."

My mother shook her head. Her fury was scaring me.

"Before you were born, Irene had a vision of the future. Someone close to us was going to betray us."

"Who?" I asked.

"That is for another time, Elena." He used his stern, fatherly tone. "Then your mother got pregnant with you. We had no choice but to keep it a secret. We had no idea who was going to betray us. Only Tanya knew the truth about your mother and me. Before your mother's belly starting showing, she and Tanya went on a self-enhancing quest."

"Self-enhancing what?" I yelled. My mother could see perfectly and hear perfectly. She didn't need to enhance anything.

"Her hearing."

I narrowed my eyes.

"It was just a cover-up, but the Ancients granted her

wish. She and Tanya left and stayed away until you were born. We couldn't get you out of Paegeia. That wasn't the plan. The plan was that we would hire someone to look after you. Just until danger was over." He blew out a deep breath.

I looked at my mother for confirmation. The rage in her face had been replaced with tears.

"But then you showed signs that you weren't going to make it," my father carried on.

"I was dying?" I shrieked. My father nodded. His own eyes shone. "Tanya told us then what Irene had said about her egg when it hatched."

It.

"She," my mother said in a stern tone.

"Sorry, she." He looked at her. "She said that one wouldn't make it but two might. We never knew what that meant." He shook his head. "Until you got sick."

My volume dropped. "I don't understand."

"She gave you the Calypso potion, sweetheart, and you went..."

"What?" I was yelling again. I knew about the Calypso potion. Frank, my tutor, had told me about that. It was forbidden because of what it could do. Still, none of this was making any sense. I needed another human body for the Calypso potion, and it would've disintegrated me, too. "Who?"

"Tanya's daughter. Her name was Cara. She was a Thunderlight," my mother said. Her voice cracked.

I gasped. "A Thunderlight? They died out like two hundred years ago."

"She was the last of her kind, Elena. And she gave you her life..." my father's words continued but I stopped listening. I shook my head. My hands tangled in my hair. Tears formed in my own eyes. I'd killed my godparents' child. *Why did they do that? But then...*

"A Thunderlight sacrificed her life for me. Dad, she was a dragon. I would've become..." I couldn't think about it.

"She didn't have her human body yet, so the way Tanya explained it to us, was that her human form would turn into you."

My eyes jumped to his again.

"I am a dragon?"

"No, baby." A tear rolled down my mother's cheek. "Cara disappeared the minute you shifted into you."

"So one of the kindest and noblest dragons there ever was, died to save my life?"

Both my parents didn't say anything. How could they have kept this from me?

I jumped up and ran to my room.

"Elena!" my mother yelled after me. But I didn't stop. I opened my door and fell, sobbing, onto my bed. I'd killed a Thunderlight. The worst part was that I couldn't even tell Blake what they'd said. I didn't want to tell him this at all. I was a murderer.

CATHERINE

"Elena!" I yelled after her.

"Let her be. She needs to deal with it." Albert put his hands on my shoulders.

I gave him that look. The one that told him that he'd better keep his mouth shut; otherwise he was going to win himself the east wing again.

"Blake should know better. Why were they even

talking about it?"

"It's not Blake's fault. He's only seventeen, and nobody told him to keep it a secret, Katie. We should've told her. She was ready for this. Blake probably just mentioned it offhand. He doesn't know much."

"It doesn't matter. He told her that. She thought we weren't her real parents. The entire night she felt that, Albert. Not to mention what she must be feeling now. I'm going to phone Tanya. They need to come back."

"Katie, you're making this into something it's not."

"I'm not!" I shouted. I picked up my Cammy.

"Tanya Le Frey," I intoned. It beeped.

I was so mad, if I were a dragon I'd be breathing fire. I could always take that information from Elena's memory and just tell her myself. *Maybe I should do that.*

She picked up and a hologram of her popped out of the Cammy. "Hey babe, why..." Then she saw how angry I was. "What happened?"

I started to speak fast, yelling about what a little dirt-bag Blake was. I was really trying to make peace with their bond, the intensity of it. I told her everything.

"Calm down. Blake did what?"

"He told Elena that he'd only met her when she was one. She knows about Cara." I started crying.

"Okay, deep breaths. Calm down."

"She is not taking this well," I finally got out.

"We'll be there in ten minutes. Just don't do anything stupid like trying to erase this from her mind, Katie."

She knew me so well. Still it was an option that I wasn't going to eliminate yet.

We waited. I loathed the fact that I could hear Elena crying in her room.

I knew how this night was going to end. We were

going to have to go to get a certain dirt-bag to calm her down. It was days like this that I wanted to wring a certain dragon's neck. I didn't care how special he was.

BLAKE

It was late. I was lying in bed and was speaking to Tabitha on my Cammy. I didn't understand why she just couldn't leave me alone. We weren't like that. Sure, she was pretty, but she was also a Snow Dragon. *Do I need to say more?*

At least she was good for something: doing my homework on a daily basis.

I heard a commotion downstairs. Even if my room was soundproof, noise always made its way to my ears. I guessed it was how I was built; I always knew when danger was near.

"I have to go. Speak to you soon," I said and pressed the disconnect button. Her face disappeared instantly. I put down my Cammy and walked over to the door.

When I opened it, Tanya's voice filled the room. *What is she doing here?*

She was speaking about her daughter, Cara. I remembered her. I'd wondered after they came back what had happened to her, but I'd been too young. Then I heard Elena's name. Something about Elena finding out. *Found out what?*

I reached the stairs and found a sleepy-eyed Sammy already at the bottom. "Mom, is everything okay?" she asked as I skipped down the last few steps.

"Everything is fine, baby. Go back to sleep." Nothing in my mother's tone told me that it was okay.

Sammy shuffled past me back up the stairs to her

room. A natural Sleeping Beauty, that one.

"So she found out about the Calypso potion? She knows you sacrificed Cara to save her life?" my father asked.

Icy pressure, like my snow, pressed all the air out of my lungs. "You did what?" I asked.

"Elena was sick, Blake. We had no choice," Tanya said with tears lingering in her eyes.

"You gave her the Calypso potion." I couldn't believe this.

"It worked. Irene predicted that it would work."

"When?"

"When she was a few weeks old. We had no choice." Tanya sounded angry. "Why did you two even talk about the past?"

"Don't you dare try to pin this on me. You should have told her about Cara and what she did for her, a long time ago. Now I have to go sort this out!" I whirled to leave.

"Blake!" my father called.

I didn't stop. I was already out the front door, busy getting undressed and keeping all my clothes inside my hand. I lifted off, morphed into a dragon and made my way to the castle.

I could sense Tanya behind me, but she wasn't fast enough to keep up. When the castle came into view, I could hear King Albert, Jako and Queen Catherine arguing. Elena didn't want to see anyone from what I gathered.

She wouldn't, especially her godparents, because of the guilt over something she had no control over, over something they had done. Then I heard her sobs, though I couldn't pinpoint her location yet. I hated it when she cried. It was something she hardly did. She was always so happy. She was my happy place.

I came in hard, morphed two seconds after, and pulled on my jeans. Tanya landed behind me as I made my way to the door.

"Blake!" she yelled, still in dragon form. I ignored her and went in. I made my way into the lobby, rushing through the hallways, and down another flight of steps into the kitchen.

"How could you do that to her?" Queen Catherine yelled the minute she saw me. "Tell her that you only met her when she was one. Do you know what you put her through tonight?"

"What *I* put her through?" I scoffed. "You sacrificed Tanya's daughter to save her life and forgot to mention that to her. This isn't my doing; it's yours. And now she probably feels guilty that she took the last Thunderlight's life because of your mistake."

Queen Catherine gasped. King Albert and Jako looked guilty. "I didn't even…"

"You seriously didn't think about that?" I shook my head. "Then you don't know her that well."

"Blake!" King Albert yelled.

Okay, I was out of line, but come on.

I shook my head. "Where is she, so I can at least try to help her get through this?"

"Oh, you know her so well, why don't you find her?"

I threw the queen a filthy look. "Treehouse it is."

She grunted, which told me I was spot on. I stormed out.

The sobs grew louder the closer I got to the treehouse. The ladder was pulled up.

"Elena," I said.

"Go away!" she yelled.

"Just let down the stairs, okay? I don't want to ruin another treehouse. I actually like this one."

I could hear her trying to compose herself and suppress her tears. After a minute or so, she let down the ladder.

I climbed up and found her sitting with her head on her knees and her back against the wall. I climbed in and pulled up the ladder. She didn't even look at me. I moved over to her and just wrapped my arms around her.

She burst out crying. I held her tighter.

"It's going to be okay."

"It's not okay." She lifted her head. "I killed a Thunderlight, Blake. A freakin' Thunderlight."

"You didn't kill anyone, okay?" I wiped her tears away. "This is not on you, Elena. It's on them. And yes, a Thunderlight died in the process, but she died a Dragon's death. To die for royalty is the noblest death there is. She's a heroine because she saved your life. It's not your fault."

"I still don't even know how the hell it worked."

"I can give you my theories," I offered calmly, "but they are just that. Theories. Nothing else."

She waited.

"She didn't have her human form. Something tells me that they prayed you would become it."

Elena sniffed wetly. "We weren't compatible, Blake."

"Maybe not, it could be the reason she isn't here today. Because of it." I released her and settled in beside her. She sighed, an exhausted sound, and lay her head on my shoulder.

"What if she is still inside me?"

"Why, you feel something?"

She shook her head.

"Then it's best we don't wake her up, okay?"

She nodded and shifted closer, resting her arm on my chest. I stroked her back.

"I still can't believe a Thunderlight died for me. Do you remember her?"

"Yeah, sort of," I lied. I did remember her, but I had to be gentle. It was easy to go gentle on Elena. "She was about a year older than me when they disappeared." I didn't tell her what an amazing dragon she was. It would only make her feel guiltier for something she didn't even do.

"Why did they keep this from me?"

"I don't know. Maybe because of this. They didn't want to hurt you, Elena. I know for a fact that your mom and dad love you with all their hearts. It's something my mother's always said."

"Okay," she sniffed and wiped at her tears.

"But I doubt your mother will let me come visit soon."

"What did you do?" Her entire body tensed.

"I yelled at her."

She started to laugh…which made me laugh.

"At least I can still count on you."

"Always there when it gets too dark," I promised. "This is definitely one of those moments."

She laughed and lay on my chest again. "Thanks, Blake."

"You are welcome, Princess."

EIGHTEEN

ELENA

Summer break melted away. Blake was wrong about my mother not letting him come and visit. She felt guilty for keeping the truth from me. All of them did.

Jako told me everything he knew, how angry he was, but then I'd crawled into his heart and made the loss of Cara a tiny bit easier. He echoed the sentiment that she'd died a noble death and that he'd known since the moment they discovered she was a Thunderlight, something monumental was going to happen. Something sad but beautiful. Only something great could make her egg hatch.

He made me feel less shitty about killing his daughter.

Tanya couldn't handle my mother's sadness and because of Irene's words, she truly believed that it was what she'd meant. That Cara would save my life.

I was still paranoid. I demanded tests to find out if

there was a dragon inside me. Blake was at my side every single time I went to see someone. The results were always negative.

Still, their answers didn't put me at ease. My father brought in a Night Seeker. His face was ashen, and he had red lips with sharp teeth protruding slightly from his lips. They were blood drinkers. Some of them were blind because of the daylight thing, and some were just plain scary with their skeletal features. But they had an amazing ability. They had a gift of dealing with problems and situations like no shrink could. It was as if they could speed up the process.

He scared me, but he was gentle. His name was Leo, someone whom my father trusted with his life.

His pronouncement was that Cara had given her life to save mine. He said although there wasn't a dragon inside me, she would always watch over me like a guardian angel. She would be there in times of grave danger, until Blake could fulfill his dragon duties. So it was better to keep her asleep.

Just what Blake had said.

Blake spent almost every day with me when he wasn't recording songs with his band at the studio.

It was just like old times. All summer long, we swam in the lake and talked for hours up in the treehouse until it was time for him to go back home.

For once, my mother didn't object. "Whatever she needs." I heard my father say to her one night.

But the day came when Blake had to return to Dragonia Academy and I had to admit, it wasn't easy to say goodbye this time.

"Remember," I admonished as he prepared to go, "when the darkness gets too much, just let me know."

"Okay," he tapped me on my nose and gave me another hug. "See you at Christmas."

"Better make it a great present."

"Yeah, yeah. I'll go think hard about the Christmas present."

I laughed, but disliked every step he took away from me.

He morphed into his dragon form. He was getting gigantic. My father put his arm around me and pulled me into his chest. My mother smiled sweetly, said goodbye and wished him a good flight.

"Stay out of trouble, Elena," he said and lifted off.

"You stay out of trouble!" I yelled after him and watched until I couldn't see him anymore.

CATHERINE

I was preparing for bed. Worry clouded my thoughts.

"Love, if you rub your hands any more, they might fall off," Albert said from the bed, glancing up from the crossword in his hand.

"Did you see how she watched him leave?"

His shoulders hunched wearily. "Let it go." He opened his arms and I shifted closer to him.

I plopped on the bed and lay my head on his chest.

"What worries you about them so much, Katie? It can't be just the intensity of their bond."

I looked up at him, saying nothing.

"We always said it is a good thing that she'd have someone who will love her that deeply and will never hurt her. So what is it?"

"I don't know," I evaded. "She is only thirteen,

Albert."

"And next year she will be a little wiser, and a year older."

"That is my problem," I said. "She will get older and he isn't always going to see her as his little sister."

"And your problem with that is…? You forget we met around that same age, Katie."

"That was two hundred years ago, Al. Heck, women married at the age of fourteen back then. It's different now," I argued hotly. "Not the same."

He laughed. It was a laugh I hated, one that made me feel stupid and small. I got up in anger.

He pulled me down into another hug again and rested his lips on my temple. "I didn't mean it like that. It's just…you worry about things we have absolutely no control over. And if you push too hard, I'm scared she'll despise you. Give her some credit. Give her some rope and see what she does with it, love. It's been twelve years. You need to let this go."

I sighed. It was hard. So hard.

"So, give her some more space, more responsibility, and a rope to hang herself," I joked.

He laughed. This time it was the laugh I always loved. I joined in.

"She is not going to hang herself," he assured me. "And do you know why?"

"Oh, do tell me?"

"Because she has the most amazing mother a girl could ever ask for." He kissed me on the tip of my nose.

ELENA

Blake wrote almost every day in the first month and then fewer crows came—like twice a week. His letters grew shorter and less. He was having fun. It carried on like that until Christmas.

We spent every Christmas with the Leafs. One year it was with them, the next with us. This year we went to our summer house in Sovereign. Mom loved the summer house, the sprawling two stories and the waterfall in the backyard. Whenever we went there, we caught fish with our bare hands. Some part of me had always guessed that I was part dragon because I could do the things they could, except for flying of course.

My family descended on the house first, along with some staff members. Over the course of two days, we decorated the house with festive baubles and a massive Christmas tree. The dragon ornaments were my favorite. They were molded to look like family members who were going to join us. There was a Night Villain that represented Sir Robert, a Swallow Annex for Aunty Isabel, a Fire-Tail for Sammy, and on top of the tree was the present Blake had made me for my thirteenth birthday: a Rubicon that perched on a star.

I'd begged Mom to put it on top, just for this year.

"Please, Mom," I begged. "Please."

She sighed. "Okay, fine. Go get it."

I ran to my room, which I would be sharing with Sammy. I removed it from the black wooden box Blake had also made, and brought it back downstairs.

She just laughed as she looked at it and then climbed on the ladder and put it right at the top of the tree.

The tree was perfect.

On the Friday two days before Christmas, the Leafs showed up. I was thrilled to see their outlines in the sky.

"They're here!" I yelled from the kitchen to my parents, who were sitting on the porch. Without waiting to see if they followed, I ran and opened the front door just as they landed one by one. The backyard quickly became crowded with the hulking, glittering forms of dragons. They smoothly morphed into their human forms and took the robes the staff held out.

"Merry Christmas, Elena." Aunty Isabel wrapped her motherly arms around me.

"Merry Christmas," I said.

My father's dragon, Sir Robert, gave me a passing kiss.

Sammy hugged me with a huge smile. We both went to the same private school that non-gifted kids attended until age sixteen. Still, Mom insisted on a private tutor in the afternoons to introduce me to the subjects at Dragonia. He was old, and one of the professors who used to give classes at Dragonia, but because of his interest in dark potions—his fascination with their danger—they'd had no choice but to let him go. He believed I should know about all the objects, spells, and potions in Paegeia that were forbidden.

Blake was last. I hugged him tight. I hadn't seen him in six months. Either I was crazy, or he was taller and a lot more grown-up looking than before. His muscles were visible beneath the planes of his stiffly starched shirt.

His thoughts must have mirrored mine, because he said, "Seriously Elena, you should stop growing."

"You are way taller than me. No one grows that much

215

in six months."

He smiled. "Merry Christmas, wiseass."

"Merry Christmas."

We spent the cntire day up by the stream, catching fish. Being around Blake loosened me up. He was really funny and I could speak to him about anything.

"So, Elena, no boyfriend yet?" he asked.

"No," I said. "Eww."

He laughed. "Arianna had, like, two last year."

"I'm not Arianna."

"That you aren't," he chirped.

"Don't lie, Elena," Sammy goaded.

Blake gasped with raised eyes. A smile tugged at his lips.

"Who?" I yelled at her.

"Oh, Leeeee," she sang.

I shook my head in mock disgust.

"Who is Leeeee?" Blake wanted to know.

"Someone Elena is dying to have."

"I'm not." A fish slipped through my hands while I was distracted, and I scowled. "He's just a boy at my school. His father owns a big transportation company."

"Elena and Lee sitting in a tree."

I slapped him. "It's not like that. Sure, he's cute but he is a bit of a ladies' man. The girls are always clucking around him."

Blake struck a pose. "Something Lee and I have in common."

I laughed again. "Yeah, okay, whatever," I sang.

Lee wasn't mentioned again.

A while later, I rubbed my arms briskly. "Can we please go? It's freaking cold up here."

"It's refreshing. C'mon, a little cold never bothered

you before."

"Not *this* cold," I said. "There are literally ice cubes floating in the water."

"Okay, fine. Let's go before Elena's feet turn into popsicles."

I giggled. Sammy trudged out of the water with a wriggling fish in her hands.

The 'rents cooked the fish. Over dinner we listened to stories. Somehow these gatherings always ended up with us talking about Merica and Cooper. Blake loved those the most, but my mother always got so quiet, really weird, and my father usually cut them short. He switched over to a topic they almost never spoke about.

Uncle Goran.

The laughter vanished. His death was hard on all of them, especially my mother, even after all these years. I wondered for the hundredth time what Goran truly meant to her.

After Goran's name came up, all talkativeness dried up. Isabel sent us all to bed.

The next day we went skiing. We spent the entire day on the slopes. Blake did his own thing. The girls wouldn't leave him alone. We only saw him again around five, and the girls almost cried when he said goodbye. I thought it was as funny as hell and teased him about it the entire night. My mother also teased him. It was funny as hell.

Blake just grunted a lot, which made everyone laughed.

Finally, Christmas dawned cold and clear.

We opened presents around the fire. Blake gave me a stunning bracelet he'd made from his own skin.

I stared at the creation in horror-filled awe.

"Blake Samuel Leaf," his mother scolded.

He fluttered his lush black eyelashes innocently. "What? I heal fast."

"I need to speak to Master Longwei. It's all those weapons at Dragonia."

"Relax, Issy," my father said. "The boy said he heals fast."

"Oh, I would like to see the two of you if Elena carved out a piece of her skin to make him a bracelet."

They all laughed the way Aunt Issy said it, but I was *so* with her.

When I remained speechless, he mouthed, "What?"

I shook my head and give him a soft smile.

"Over my dead body," my mother burst out, pointing an accusatory finger at him. "Don't ever do that again."

"Yes, *Mom*," Blake joked. I couldn't help but join in their laughter. He always teased her; he knew that she worried her ass off about us becoming like Cooper and Merica.

"Thanks, Katie," Aunt Issy said in a playful manner.

"What are friends for?"

I presented Blake with a journal I'd made myself. A fierce dragon glowered from its cover. My tutor had helped me put a spell on it so only Blake could open it with his Pink Kiss—as he dubbed it. Lame, I knew. *But how freakin' cool is this journal?*

He adored it. Now he could write whatever he wanted with absolute privacy.

Samuel whipped up a delicious Christmas lunch. With full bellies, we all had a snowball fight in the backyard. Blake threw me over his shoulder and tossed me in a deep snow drift. I retaliated by tripping him and laughing as he fell on his ass. We made snow angels—

and snow dragons! —and the icy blue sky rang with our happy calls.

The 'rents went back inside when it got too cold, but we loitered. Blake went for a smoke break. When the sun started to set, it was time to go back into the house.

We had to say goodbye the next day.

"See you on your birthday." Blake hugged me tight. I inhaled his trademark musky scent, already missing him.

"See you. And be good."

"Oh, I will," he said.

I didn't stay to watch him leave like I had the last time. For some reason I didn't like watching him leave anymore.

It was one of my favorite Christmases. I hated that it had gone by so quickly.

Shortly after Christmas, my mother bought me my first pair of high heels. She wasn't kidding with those heels. I took a few wobbly steps in those strappy green stilettos and bam! I toppled down the stairs. I was lucky that I'd only broken an ankle—and not my neck. It took an entire two days before Constance came over to heal it.

Blake's second semester at Dragonia was the hardest. Why, I didn't know. Probably because I only received one crow a month. He'd never been this quiet before. But he wrote that he had the coolest journal and laughed each and every time someone tried to open it. It was like a party trick. They had parties. It was so freakin' unfair.

I couldn't wait. Two more years and I'd join them.

Still, it upset me when the once-a-month crow

dwindled to once every two months. It stung that he had all the fun and had forgotten about me.

I wanted a Cammy badly. But my mother refused. At least with a Cammy I could've phoned his ass.

One night, I sat on my bed.. Mom had loaned me her Cammy to speak with Sammy. Mom didn't even have Blake's number. I'd looked. I sighed, and then Sammy's hologram hovered over my dingy cast, wearing a sympathetic expression. She hadn't heard a thing from her brother either. I was making her crazy. After pestering her, I begged her not to tell him anything. I didn't want him to think that I was becoming like Arianna, who had annoyed him for an entire year.

Just thinking about it made me shiver. I wished he would just write. I had no idea what was going on in his life. We'd never been like that. We'd always known what was happening in each other's lives.

When I switched off Mom's Cammy, I heard a tapping at my window. It was a crow.

He perched on the sill.

This couldn't be.

I jumped up off the bed and ran to the window to the crow, and eventually took the letter from the pouch around his neck.

I eagerly tore the envelope open without giving the crow his treat. He pecked me hard. A crimson droplet of blood appeared.

"Ow! Patience. Don't they teach you that in flight school?" I stuck my finger in my mouth. It hurt like hell. *If Blake were here, he could heal that easily.*

I bent down my desk and grabbed a dried mouse. I hated keeping them, but crows were picky. If the treat wasn't good, then they wouldn't bring another letter.

He took the dried mouse meat and lifted off. *Greedy crow.*

I opened Blake's letter.

I met someone, he wrote. *Her name is Tabitha. Don't judge me, but she is a Snow Dragon. Haha. I guess one can't choose who they love.*

For some reason my heart sank lower and lower as I read a rambling page he'd written about a stupid Snow Dragon. Nothing about his day. Nothing about the past month. Just about her.

I chucked the letter into my drawer. Why was I so sad? He was like my freakin' brother. I should be happy that he'd met someone. But it hurt that someone else got so much of his time and I, the girl who was fated to be his rider...none.

What if she didn't like me? Would I see him less and less?

I already didn't like this girl, whatever her stupid name was.

She was going to make trouble for us. For sure.

CATHERINE

My happy daughter was turning into a not-so-happy daughter. I missed her cheeky comebacks. I missed her smiles. What if she ascended sooner than she should?

We were sitting around the dinner table one night. I broke apart a flaky, golden roll and was rewarded with the scent of fresh-baked bread. "Elena?"

"What, Mom?" It was barely a grunt.

"What is going on?" I asked.

Albert give me a raised eye. *What am I missing here?*

"Nothing," she whined. She got up without asking to be excused and left.

I turned on Albert. "Seriously, what is up with her?"

"Calm down. She's okay."

"She isn't okay, Albert." I smeared creamy yellow butter on half the roll. "What if she ascends soon? You think it's a sign? I need to phone Constance and find out." I dropped the uneaten bread and was already on my way to the phone.

"He met someone, Kate!" Albert yelled after me.

I paused. "What?"

"Blake met someone." His tone was gentler. Softer.

Oh. This was why she was sulking. "But he's like her brother. You said it yourself…"

"I think Elena is past that stage," He sounded annoyingly wise. "I think she just realized it after she got that letter. She hasn't even written him back yet."

I closed my eyes. They weren't even there yet, and he was already breaking her heart. I looked at Albert. "Why do you know about this and not me?"

"You really want me to answer that?"

I wanted to kick myself. She took her heart problems to her father and not me. *Screw that.* I got up.

"Don't push this, Katie."

"I'm not pushy," I said, even though I knew it was far from the truth.

I walked up to Elena's room and knocked on her door.

"Enter," she said and I opened it.

Her eyes rolled at me from the bed. I climbed onto her bed and took out one of her earphones. I lay down next to her and put it in my ear to hear what she was listening to.

His voice blared in my ear. It took everything in me

not to roll my eyes like my daughter just had. *Don't. Just don't,* I said to myself. It was the Shifters' brand-new album. Blake's band. They'd recorded it during summer break when all Elena had wanted was for him to be near.

He'd asked if she could come to one of the recordings, but I'd said no. She needed the space from him. They were constantly in each other's space that summer. The summer she discovered about Cara.

"It's his new song?"

"I don't care," she said. She yanked out the other earphone.

"Sweetheart." I sighed. "We both know that's not the truth. Daddy told me. He met someone?" *Seriously, you have a princess for a rider? How could you dare to choose someone else?*

She looked at me. "I thought you would be happy."

"I thought so, too, but to be honest, I'm not," I said. A tear welled up in her eyes. "What happened to 'Eww, he's like my brother, Mom?'" I mimicked her and she laughed.

"I don't know. I thought it was still *Eww.*"

"Absence makes the heart grow fonder." I tucked a strand of hair behind her ear.

She let out a frustrated groan and got off the bed.

"It's Blake, for crying out loud. The guy who always got me in trouble."

"Uh-huh, I always knew it was that little jackass," I said.

She laughed again, but it vanished really fast. "Why does this hurt so much, Mom?" She started to cry.

I pulled her in for a hug. "Because he's like your brother, but he isn't. We want only the best for them, and to be honest, nobody is going to be the best for them,

Elena. This was what I was so afraid of, and to be honest, now that I'm there, it was stupid to be afraid of it. It's breaking my heart. I never imagined that he would choose someone else."

"I told you before. We aren't Cooper and Merica, Mom."

I kissed her on her head. *If only that was true, sweetheart. If only.*

The months flew by and our relationship grew stronger. I helped her write a letter back to him, ecstatic about the news that he'd met a lame-ass Snow Dragon. But we pretended that we were really happy about it.

I even told her to put in that she was busy training in the art of fighting. It was a happy letter; it was a letter that sounded like the Elena he knew.

A few weeks later, he sent her another letter back. This time, the first person she called was me.

I opened it and read her the letter, peppering my own colorful commentary alongside it. "That's great that you're training. Don't get too good at fighting—I'm only one dragon!" *Yeah, right. More like ten dragons in one.*

"I'm on my way to fame. A record label wants to sign the Shifters." *So far so good.*

"My classes are getting a lot harder this semester." *What did you think? That Dragonia would be a walk in the park?*

She laughed at all my little comebacks.

And then I fell silent. Elena looked up at me with huge eyes. "What?" she asked.

"He's talking about the ice queen." I sighed. It was

the name we'd given Blake's new girlfriend.

"Just read it, Mom."

"Okay," I sighed. *It's your heart.*

"'Tabitha really wants to meet you, so I sort of invited her to your fourteenth birthday. I hope you don't mind. She is really not that lame for a Snow Dragon. You will like her.' Ugh," I spat. Elena just took a deep breath.

"You are not seriously going to consider it, are you?"

"What do you think?" she asked me. She never asked me for my opinion anymore. What I thought. I had my baby girl back. *Make it a good one, Catherine. One that won't bite you in the ass.*

"Honestly, if it were me, I wouldn't agree. But we need to sound like you," I said. She nodded. "So as hard as it's going to be, baby, just tell him it's okay. You can't wait to meet her, too."

"Okay, then let's do it." She jumped up.

I held up a finger. "I'm not done. There is a 'but' in this."

"But what?" she asked.

"He might really like this girl. He might kiss her. He might always be close to her. You might not spend a moment of your time with him."

She swallowed hard. I bent over and kissed her head. "You don't need to answer him right away. Remember, you are too busy to give a crap."

She laughed.

"Think about it first, sweetheart. Let him sweat a little."

NINETEEN

ELENA

I thought about what my mom said. I wrote Blake a letter saying he could bring her to my birthday party so that I could approve—and next to that in huge letters, I scrawled *HAHA JOKING*.

I hated the fact that my mother hadn't been worrying all these years for nothing. She'd always known. I was the idiot for not wanting to believe her.

I tried to prepare myself, thinking of worst-case scenarios. Them kissing, dancing, holding hands...everything. Mostly I wanted to puke just thinking about it. But I knew I was supposed to pretend to be happy for them.

He was obviously ecstatic over the news and sent me a crow back, saying:

You will love her. The two of you are so alike, except for the Snow Dragon part.

That angered me the most. How dare he compare me to a freakin' Snow Dragon? Seriously!

Everybody knew Snow Dragons were smart and probably owned one of the coolest gifts, but they were also cowards and ran away every chance they got. *Unless she is somehow extra special*. It was funny how that came out sarcastic inside my head.

I disliked her already just for liking him. He didn't belong to her. He was my dragon. The Princess of Paegeia's. It wasn't a freakin' secret, which told me that she wasn't a typical Snow Dragon material; she actually had a backbone. Yet that pissed me off even more.

As much as I wanted to hope she was ugly, I knew she wouldn't be. Dragons were known for their godlike beauty.

A huge sigh left my mouth. Blake was eighteen. He would never see a fourteen-year-old as his ideal girlfriend. To him I was probably still like his little sister. He saw himself as nothing more than my guardian who'd promised to be there when it got too dark.

Well, my world was dark. And he wasn't here.

One thing that didn't turn out to be a lie was my training. Mom hired martial arts instructors. It was becoming the highlight of my day. They taught me the basics of fighting. I learned how to judge opponents, how to throw a punch, how to aim a kick. I discovered that my weapons of choice were the bow and Frankish axes. I excelled in them.

The days crept closer to my birthday. Funny how no crows showed up again.

How was I going to pull this one off? Would I be able to handle seeing him with another girl?

I had no choice. Mom drilled it inside my head to pretend that my day was too hectic to even worry about what he was doing at Dragonia Academy or who he was with. She claimed to be positive that it wouldn't last, that he would be mine at the end. But I wasn't so sure anymore. Just because Cooper and Merica were a couple, it didn't mean that Blake and I would end up as a couple. We grew up together, and I wondered if Cooper and Merica had also grown up together.

I wondered where they even were.

It was said a long time ago that no two Rubicons could live at the same time, but somewhere inside Paegeia there was another Rubicon. So they were wrong about that, too. But wherever they were, they didn't want to be found. It was like they'd just vanished.

Thinking about that made me feel all sorts of emotions. I didn't know if I wanted that to be true. It still felt so weird thinking of him as my boyfriend, but at the same time I didn't want him with anybody else.

What did any of that even mean? That I wasn't ready for that yet? Then why was I so upset that he was with someone else?

Love was so complicated. It made my stomach churn and my palms get sweaty. It made me sad just thinking about it.

So, I tried to push it aside as I drew another picture of his dragon form. I loved drawing dragons. Mom said that I got my artistic talent from her dad.

He had died a long time ago before it was common knowledge that dragons could bequeath their essence to their riders. Dad and she had both gotten the essence from their dragons, which was why they were both two hundred and sixty-odd years old. I wondered if Blake would ever give me his essence. I wondered what it would be like to be semi-immortal.

The dragon came out great. I struggled with his face, though. It didn't look anything like Blake. *Well, practice makes perfect.* I tore off the page, rolled it into a ball, threw it into the trash can, and started over.

An hour later, Mom came in with a sandwich and a glass of juice.

"That is stunning, sweetheart." She leaned over my shoulder to look at it. "A real keeper." She kissed me on the head and left.

She was becoming my favorite person in the castle. Dad was still cool, but Mom had amazing ideas about how to cope with the latest developments. I just hoped that her tactic—pretending not to be bothered—wouldn't bite me in the ass one day.

At times I thought Blake was just doing this to see what sort of reaction he would get. I was scared, but then again, any eighteen-year-old doing that to find out what a fourteen-year-old would do, would be lame as hell. Nothing like Blake.

He just didn't fall in the lame category. And I doubted he ever would.

CATHERINE

The day was upon us. I didn't know who was more anxious, me or Elena.

What if Blake breaks her heart again?

I hated the fact that I'd suggested pretending that it

didn't bother her. It clearly did. I didn't know if she was strong enough to handle this. I was scared she would be humiliated. How was I going to fix that? Not to mention how unhealthy it was for me to teach my daughter that she had to set her feelings aside and hide them from men.

I had to admit I loved every moment that they were apart. Not in a bad way. There was going to be plenty of time for them to read each other's thoughts. I'd seen it. It would happen. But how could I tell a fourteen-year-old girl that the two characters from my past that she couldn't stop hearing about were, in fact, herself and her best friend?

She couldn't cope with that. That much I knew. She was still too young to carry that burden. We all vowed to keep the ability Blake would receive around age thirty a secret.

I wondered about that grown-up Elena a lot. Would she ever show herself? I wanted to meet her with all of my heart. To show her that I had given her a better life, that I had slayed the nightmares of her dreams and turned her life into a beautiful nightingale song. But my Elena never acted differently. She was always the same with consistent responses to whatever she was going through. She never spoke in tongues about stuff we didn't know. I watched fruitlessly for signs that she remembered her other life.

I hoped that one day she would know I loved her so much I'd killed my best friend, Goran—who had been to me like Blake was to Elena—without hesitation. Even though he'd betrayed us, I'd done it for her.

Because of how much I loved her.

He sometimes haunted my dreams. His eyes blazed with questions, with the realization that I knew what he was going to do, with sorrow. I believed that in the moment of his death, he felt remorse. The specter of him I saw was sorry. So, so sorry that he'd strayed. But what haunted me the most was the way his body had disintegrated. It was almost like I'd used the King of Lion sword and its magic on Goran. Albert's sword caused its victims to explode. My dagger had magically made its victim turn to dust. It was a slow process. And his screams left no doubt that it had been an extremely painful process as well. Sometimes I could still hear it echoing through the castle.

But that was a long time ago.

"Love, you ready?" Al appeared from behind me.

I shook myself to clear my maudlin thoughts. "For this birthday? Never," I said softly. "Is he here yet?"

"No, he got word to me that he is running late. I should pass it on to Elena."

"How is she?"

"In desperate need of help with what to wear."

My face fell. "Don't you miss the days when we used to dress her? No worries about anything."

"I do, my love. But they all grow up eventually."

I rested my head on his chest. "You ever wonder about her?" I asked.

He stoked my hair. "Whom are you referring to now?"

"The old Elena. Merica."

"I remember her as a redhead with freckles. I don't remember her the way you do."

I sighed. "She's starting to resemble her more and more each year."

He kissed me on the tip of my nose. "We will know when she makes herself known, Katie."

"How? What if we miss it?" I knew I wouldn't, but I was so scared that she would just shut up.

"I think she will love you with all of her heart."

I slapped him in mock anger. "She already loves me, thank you."

He laughed. "Go, help our fourteen-year-old get dressed and stop worrying about what-ifs. We won't miss it."

I smiled, kissed him, and headed to Elena's room.

ELENA

Mom came and helped me get dressed. I went with a pair of jeans, a shirt, a sweater and my black pumps. It looked like normal stuff I would wear. *Pretend that they aren't going to bother you.* I was going to fail miserably.

Pluggs was on my shoulder and I was waiting for my guests to arrive. Tanya and Jako had already arrived. A year ago, my birthday had ended with the discovery that they'd sacrificed their daughter, Cara, to save my life. I'd found out as much as I could about her since then, and in my eyes she was taller than the Rubicon. She was my heroine.

Sometimes I even pretended that she spoke to me from deep within me. Even though there wasn't a dragon inside me, I imagined that I could hear her voice guiding me through everything in my life. She always called Blake a rodent, as his choice in a girlfriend reflected a rat.

I just hoped she would guide me through tonight, too.

"So you ready?"

"Yes." I smiled at my godmother. I was sure she already knew everything. At times it even looked like they could read each other's thoughts. That was why my mother used to be so crazy.

The McKenzies showed up first. Lucian gave me a hug.

"Fourteen, huh?" he said, as if it was the lamest age ever.

I sighed. "Yep, and not as lame as you make it out to be."

He laughed and dropped my present off at my table. Everyone started to arrive. Sammy and her parents arrived with much fanfare and a flurry of hugs. My heart actually beat faster, but there was still no sign of Blake.

"He will be here," Sammy promised me. "He is just running horribly late."

"I really don't care that much, Samantha," I lied. I was dying to know if she had seen the Ice Queen yet, and what she thought about her. But it was dangerous to tell the sister of my dragon how I truly felt.

She gave me an appraising look. "This really doesn't bother you?"

"What?" I asked airily.

"That he is actually dating."

"Eww," I said. "He's like…"

"Yeah, I know." She rolled her eyes. "Your brother."

"I'm happy for him, Sam," I said.

"Yeah, I finally see it now. I told the 'rents they have absolutely nothing to worry about, but you know Mom."

"Your mother is sweet, but seriously. Gross." I went over to my mother. I couldn't speak too loudly; Sammy also had enhanced hearing. Thank heavens my mother wielded her shield.

"You okay? Where the hell is he?" she asked me. She reeled Tanya in with us.

"He's not going to make it, Mom. I can see it already."

She lay a hand on my shoulder. "Calm down and smile."

I did as she said.

"I will use a full dose on him and wipe that girl from his memory if he doesn't show tonight," my aunt threatened.

Her sudden venom made me throw my head back and laugh.

"You're doing great, honey. Just watch the heartbeat," Mom warned and lowered her shield.

I hated that she could hear my heartbeat's elevated tempo.

I spoke with Arianna and Desi for a bit. We'd all attended her wedding just after Christmas. Blake hadn't shown up then, either. Now I knew how it felt.

Desi was already expecting her firstborn.

She seemed happy. I wished I could just magically jump into the future to be her age and not worry about any of this. To be as happy as she was.

Sammy reached me again and we slipped out to my treehouse.

My father started to speak over the mic. The evening was going to begin, even if Blake wasn't here yet.

"Seriously?" she asked.

"It's okay, Sammy, really," I said as I desperately tried to push away the tears.

What is keeping him so long?

"It's not okay. Elena, he is a douchebag and if he doesn't show, I hope you never speak to him again."

"That's harsh."

"No it's not. I hate his girlfriend!" she yelled. It was

what I'd been waiting for the past few hours. "She is such a prima donna and a pain in my ass."

I couldn't help but laugh. *Pretend Elena, pretend.* "She can't be that bad."

"Oh, wait. You'll see. You are going to spin another story at the end of the night. She's behind all of this. She's insecure."

Is she beautiful? Please, Sammy, just answer that. But she didn't bring it up and I didn't ask directly. She just complained about what an evil cow she was.

"You're his rider, or you will be," she said. "You should forbid him from dating her."

It made me laugh again. I wondered if he would even obey if I did say it. Would he stop seeing her, even if he wasn't technically my dragon?

I took my seat next to my mom. Sir Robert was on his phone.

My mother's annoyance at Blake's absence was evident in the way she fidgeted. She crossed and uncrossed her legs and smoothed her silk blouse a hundred times.

It was not okay. But tonight I would pretend that it was.

Every birthday party of mine was the same. Important people got up and made speeches, because I was the princess. I didn't listen to any of them. I was so distracted by the fact that Blake wasn't here.

His father was angry, too. I made a mental note of never speaking to him again if he didn't show. My nonchalance became harder to maintain as my rage bubbled up.

But then, during my mother's speech, he finally arrived.

I saw the Ice Queen. Calling her beautiful would have been an understatement. White hair framed her long, oval face. Her light blue eyes sought mine immediately. I saw a challenge there—or did I imagine that? Their entrance made everyone gasp. My mother's words dried up. Oh crapity creek. She was going to be livid.

"Oh, look who finally decided to grace us with their presence. Welcome, Blake and plus one." Her tone dripped sarcasm.

"Sorry," Blake said in an overly friendly voice. He took a seat, not even his, at the table right at the back.

My mother caught my eye and winked.

"Like I was saying. Every year you get more beautiful, Elena. I just don't have the words anymore to tell you what I feel." Her eyes started to glisten. "Thank you for being such a wonderful teenager." I sucked in my lips and could see my father squinting slightly at her.

"You are growing into such a wonderful young lady. You're a great fighter, a sharp student, and will one day be an excellent queen. And you're a stunning young woman now. I'm honored to be your mother. To my *beautiful* daughter Elena. And may she have the best birthday ever." Everyone raised their glasses and cheered. Camera flashes went off as the assembled party raised crystal goblets in a toast.

I kept my face expressionless. She'd really put an emphasis on the word 'beautiful' tonight, even though I couldn't feel beautiful next to the Ice Queen.

Then chef brought out my cake. I had no idea what it was going to be this year. But when he revealed it, it was a beautiful shoe. A strappy green stiletto.

I laughed. Mom and Dad laughed even harder.

BLAKE

I didn't think we would be this late. I saw the missed calls from my father. He was going to be livid, which for some reason didn't bother me that much. Lately, I resided in seventh heaven. I finally knew what it felt like not to be a virgin anymore.

This wildcat next to me was more than just a lame-ass dragon. I just hoped Elena could love her as much as I did.

She had to.

I didn't want to make it all the way to where I usually sat. Too many people to squeeze past. I plunged down at the nearest table occupied by men from King Albert's court.

Elena's mother had sounded so sarcastic when we came in. She hated tardiness, but hated it more if someone interrupted her speeches. So this was expected. Her speech this year was a little different, though. She kept emphasizing how beautiful Elena had gotten. Elena was always beautiful, just like Sammy. The girl had soft green eyes. Big, soft, emerald eyes, which had the ability to make it impossible to tell her no when she really wanted something.

Fuck! It hit me. I hadn't gotten her a fucking birthday present. *Not cool, Blake. So not cool.* I needed to find some way to make it up to her.

"I feel underdressed," Tabitha whispered in my ear.

"Nonsense. You are gorgeous," I whispered back.

She took a huge breath and smiled. She was looking forward to finally meeting the royals. She'd always only seen them on TV, never in real life. This was like a dream come true to her.

I tried to see Elena, but Sir Laudy's gigantic body blocked my view.

The room was a low roar of way too many heartbeats to hear hers.

I hoped she was okay with me bringing a plus one. My mom had dreaded tonight and cautioned me not to bring Tabitha. But Elena had said she wanted to meet her to approve of her—with a big *HAHA JOKING* next to it.

She was like my sister, and I was like her big brother. I'd tear anyone apart if they ever hurt her.

"Look," I murmured to Tabitha. "Elena is a bit extravagant. Always runs into my arms when she sees me. Please don't throw a fit."

"A fit?" She raised one graceful eyebrow, but with a faint smile. "She is the freakin' princess. What she says goes."

I laughed. This earned me the baleful stares of the men at the table, but I didn't care. Tabitha sure knew how to make me laugh. She was one step away from perfect.

The speeches wrapped up and I excused Tabitha and myself. We made our way to my usual table. I swept over to Elena and bent down. "Sorry I'm so late," I said.

"It's okay," she shook her head, but she was different. She didn't act like herself. She was… growing up.

Queen Catherine glared at me. I pulled my face. "Your mom is so not happy with me."

Elena giggled. "You know how she feels about someone interrupting her speeches, Blake. She'll get over it."

"Okay, I hope so." I moved along to my seat, which wasn't far away from Queen Catherine's ubiquitous glare.

"Sorry," I said sheepishly.

King Albert chortled.

"You'd better be sorry," she sniped. Then she turned to chat with Tanya.

I rolled my eyes and shook my head while Elena tried desperately to suppress her smile.

The evening went great. We ate and then Chef brought out his cake.

I always loved his big reveals. This year, though, it was disappointing. It was a shoe.

King Albert, Queen Catherine, Elena, even the freakin' reporters laughed like it was the funniest thing they'd ever seen. I didn't see the humor in it.

What did I miss? Why is she getting a stupid shoe?

"Thank you, Chef. It's the best cake ever!" Elena said.

I struggled to decipher if she really meant it or not.

Then King Albert and Elena opened the dance floor with the dance. They did every single year. But tonight it was a new song. This year, they really upped their games. It was like a tango, with flamboyant moves in time to an upbeat tempo and warbling strings and horns from the live band.

"She is so cute!" Tabitha yelled.

Queen Catherine heard it. Tanya wielded her shield and I could see her lips moving as the queen's gaze locked on her dragon. But whatever she said, I couldn't hear. I saw Queen Catherine smiling and then the shield disappeared.

Okay, that was strange. Why did I get the feeling her mother didn't like my plus one very much—or that comment she'd just gave? Of all people, I had expected the queen to be thrilled that I had met someone. I always treaded lightly around Queen Catherine. One did not want to upset her in any way, especially when it came to

Elena.

When their father-daughter dance was over, our table cheered the loudest.

Servants cleared the dishes and tables were pushed off to the sides of the room. The night finally started.

Elena disappeared. She was just gone. I didn't know where she went.

It wasn't like her to just disappear.

I was really starting to worry about bringing a plus one to her birthday.

ELENA

I went to my bathroom and cried. It was the only room in my chamber that was soundproof.

Tabitha—no, the Ice Queen—was perfect. I would never beat that. It didn't matter how many times my mom emphasized the word "beautiful." And now, now I had red-rimmed eyes and couldn't show my face in public. He would know I wasn't okay. Under normal circumstances, somebody would have to be dead for me to cry like this. This was so lame.

There came a knock on my bathroom door.

Please don't let it be him. Please.

"Elena?" my mom's voice said.

I opened the door.

She looked at my tears and hugged me tightly. "The night is almost over. He's asked where you are a million times. I don't know what else to say anymore."

I gestured forlornly at my face. "I can't go out looking like this, Mom."

"This can be fixed with a small incantation,

sweetheart. I'm just scared you're going to give yourself away."

"I'll be fine. Take it away. I hate crying. Especially over this."

She was busy when my father made his way in. Even more humiliating.

"Get out. This is girl stuff!" my mom yelled at him. Without a word, Dad spun on his heel with his cocktail sloshing in his hand. His hurried obedience made me giggle wetly. Mom smiled. "She is nothing compared to you, sweetheart."

"She is everything to him, Mom. Didn't you see how he whispered to her the entire night and kissed her fingers? It's gross."

"It is, but just remember, he is your dragon. She, no doubt, feels more threatened by you than you do by her."

I never thought about it that way. "Okay, I'll remember that."

I looked at my eyes in the mirror. It didn't look like I'd cried at all. "So what is my excuse?" I said.

"Pappi phoned." Mom's eyes sparkled with mischief. "You know how long he can talk."

"He would know it's a lie, Mom. He knows Pappi never phones me on my actual birthday."

"You saw how confused he looked at that cake. He felt left out. He had no idea what that shoe represented. Things have changed. He's going to learn the hard way that if he doesn't pay attention, he's going to lose out on a lot."

I smiled. "Thanks, Mom."

"You're welcome. No more tears, okay?"

I nodded and went back to my party.

The night wasn't a total flop. He totally bought the

Pappi phoning tonight story; they'd had some malfunctions with signals lately. I gave him a hug, but not the deep way that I always hugged him. It was a quicker, cooler embrace. I met the Ice Queen. She was seriously so annoying. She wanted a tour of the castle and freaked out when she met my father, who pretended to be just as excited as her. He jumped up and down on the spot like a teenager.

I couldn't help but laugh at him. He was so clever. How did he manage to make his subject feel important, and make his daughter happy that he'd made fun of her?

I played tour guide and even showed her my treehouse. But out under the tree, Blake and Tabitha started making out. I felt like an intruder when they couldn't keep their hands off each other. I decided that I was going to fill up my glass.

I found Lucian, Arianna, and everyone else at the swimming pool. All the windows of the pool room were flung open to embrace the warm night air. I planted myself beside them and stayed there.

The two lovebirds finally made their way back and were surprised to find me sitting with my friends, and enjoying actual conversation.

"Here you are!" Blake said. "We were waiting for you to get back."

"Waiting?" I rolled my eyes. "That tree house got too small all of a sudden." I laughed, light and unconcerned.

Blake blushed and Tabitha flared her nostrils. Everyone laughed.

Lucian gave me a surprised look and took out a bottle of booze. "Are you insane?" I yelled at him. "Put it away, my mom will skin me alive."

"Oh c'mon, Elena. It hasn't stopped you before,"

Blake teased.

I stuck out my tongue at him. I knew it was too immature, but that was what he was used to. Besides, I was only fourteen. I wasn't going to act older than I was anymore. I didn't need to pretend anymore. It came naturally.

"Fine. Just don't get caught," I said and took the first shot.

The rest of the bottle made its way around. We played thirty seconds, a game where we had to describe words and people without uttering the actual words.

Blake and I used to win every time, but tonight he teamed up with his precious—as Sammy called her. I teamed up with Sammy.

She wasn't as good as Blake, but we still won. Tabitha, as smart as she was, didn't know what Blake was talking about half of the time. It gave me plenty of moments to jeer. They were so not compatible after all.

We swam for a while, under dancing electric lights that mimicked the stars outside. At eleven o'clock, Tabitha was horribly drunk. I had a suspicion that she'd shown up tipsy, because she hadn't had enough shots to get her that wasted.

My mom finally called it a night. I had to help Blake put Tabitha in the SUV my dad sent. Gerald was driving. He was one of the new guards who had started a few weeks ago.

"Sorry about this, dude," Blake said. "She is out like a stone."

"It's why they call it stone cold, Blake," I chirped.

He stood behind the door.

"Sorry we were late tonight."

"It's fine. My birthdays are huge affairs. You know

how it goes."

"I do." He looked guilty.

"What?" I said, dreading what was going to come out of his mouth.

"I was so busy this year, Elena. I know it isn't an excuse, but I will make it up. I promise."

"What are you talking about?"

"I forgot your present."

It was a shock, but I feigned nonchalance. "It's fine. Classes are super difficult at Dragonia. And you can be glad you are dating a smartass."

"Still, I feel like crap."

I admonished, "Better make Christmas a good one."

"Oh, you bet it will." He frowned. "I didn't understand this year's cake."

"It's stupid. The 'rents thought it would be funny."

He just looked at me. "I'm waiting."

"She should get to bed, Blake."

"C'mon, Elena. Just tell me."

"I broke my ankle this year, wearing that shoe, okay?" I said through a smile.

His face fell. "You broke your ankle? Why didn't you tell me?"

"You had other things on your mind, Blake." This wasn't a lie. "I'm not going to bother you with stupid things like breaking my ankle."

"Elena, it's not stupid. You broke your ankle. I'm sure it hurt like fucking hell."

"It did." Also not a lie. "After Constance came, she healed it fast, and it was over. So only a day, not much. Besides, like I said, you were busy." It sounded sadder than I wanted it to be.

We both sighed. "Come here," he said and he pulled

me in for a hug. The second hug he'd given me tonight. It felt so good. "I messed up this year. I'm sorry."

"You didn't mess up, okay? We both knew that this was going to happen eventually, Blake."

"Yeah, but I completely missed the punch line, and if you broke your ankle, it's cruel of them to laugh about it, Elena."

"They weren't cruel. It was funny as hell."

He forced an uncertain laugh. "I promise I will always be there. This," he pointed at Tabitha in the SUV, "will never change that, Elena. So next time you break something, send a fucking crow."

I smiled. He really cared about me. And then I didn't think. I kissed him.

He pulled away immediately, before my lips fully made impact on his. "Elena, what are you doing?"

"Sorry," I said. My cheeks burned. "I shouldn't have done that. Sorry." I turned and ran, holding back the tears.

"Elena!" he called after me, but I didn't stay. I kept it together until I was inside.

What the fuck did I just do? This was such a big mess.

TWENTY

CATHERINE

Blake just climbed into the SUV and left. Elena cried the entire night.

I was livid. Albert wasn't. I resented his cool-headedness in that moment.

I tried to comfort her, but she didn't want me to. Around two, I heard an annoying tap like something hard on glass.

I went to investigate and found a crow on Elena's sill, rapping against her window. She was so dead asleep, she didn't even hear it. I went to her drawer, got a dry mouse treat, opened the window, and took the envelope in its sachet as the treat went down the crow's greedy gullet.

I held onto the pouch so the bird couldn't fly away, and opened her letter.

It was from Blake of course, about tonight.

Why did you do that? I thought I was like your

brother. This changes everything. I don't feel what you feel, Elena, and I can't become the bad guy in this story. You are my rider. Why did you do that?

I am so mad at you. You've just ruined everything, and I mean everything.

I looked at the bird. If this was the sort of letter he was going to send her, then no more letters.

I used meta-compulsion on a fucking crow.

It was forbidden. Meta-compulsion was like a virus. The order would spread with every bird it would come in contact with.

Green Vapors were actually one of the deadliest dragons out there. Some of them had no idea of the depths of their power. Tanya had granted me her Green Vapor gift that allowed me to control minds.

I told the bird what he needed to do. Every time he made contact with another crow, my order would spread.

Starting tonight, crows would be compelled to deliver every one of Elena's letters to my window and not hers. And every letter she sent him, they would be forced to fly halfway to their destination, then return to me with that letter. The crow's eyes turned green and went back to black.

He would do as I said, spread it, until I reverse it. I let him go and he flew away.

He was going to break her heart. I'd break his fucking neck, whether he was Bob's child or not.

He had no idea how lucky he was.

ELENA

A month passed. I sent, like, four letters to Blake, apologizing in each one and I hadn't received one back.

Why wasn't he answering me?

I told him I was drunk, as stupid as it sounded. *Why did I kiss him?* It wasn't supposed to be like that. He'd said he would always be there. He'd made it sounded like he cared more for me than he did for her.

My mom tried. Heaven knew she tried to get me out of my sullen mood. But nothing worked. Nothing.

Was he really going to do this—punish me for something I did? How many times did I have to apologize? It wasn't fair; I wasn't the only one who had behaved badly that night.

I felt him slipping away. Things would never be the same as they were, and I didn't know how to deal with that. He had been the biggest part of my life.

I felt so humiliated. Blake had always been the best at comforting me. When we were younger and someone hurt me, he would humiliate the other person in front of others so spectacularly that they wouldn't show their face for weeks.

I never thought he would one day be the one humiliating me.

But I guess my mom was right. Things changed. People changed, and dragons changed, too.

CATHERINE

Elena sent four letters. Four letters apologizing. She wasn't the one who should apologize.

Still, the sleazeball sent six letters. Six letters wanting to know how long she would keep ignoring him.

Albert found out what I'd done with the third phone call on my Cammy. Blake wanted to speak to her, and I told him, "Elena is out, but I'll leave her a message."

I saved his name as someone completely different on my Cammy so that Elena wouldn't know that we paired cammies.

He grunted, "Don't bother."

I put down the Cammy. I glanced up to catch Albert standing in the doorway, his expression thoughtful. *Busted.* "You are seriously digging a grave for yourself, woman."

I ignored his disapproval, and he didn't interfere.

He scolded me even more the next time, when he found a letter in a box underneath a lose floorboard. "Katie, you have to stop this."

"I can't give them to her now. She would know that I read them. She would never trust me again," I pleaded with him.

"She has all the right to feel that way," he said reasonably. "You've broken her trust."

Tears welled up in my eyes.

His eyes grew softer. "Why did you withhold that other one from her, Katie?"

"Because it would have torn her heart out, Al. I couldn't let her go through that. You know how hard that night was for her."

"I saw the tears. I can just imagine."

"Why did she kiss him?" I whispered. *Why?*

Albert shrugged. "You know how Blake is with her. Charming as hell. He had no idea how Elena truly felt."

I scoffed. "For once, he doesn't know her that well."

"I agree, he slipped up. But what you are doing, Katie? It's not helping at all. She'll discover it sooner or later."

"Then I'll take full responsibility. They will end up together. I've seen it. But until then, a little distance can only do them good." I was adamant.

"She is going to end up hating him, and that will be on you." He turned around and walked away.

Heaven knew I didn't want her to end up hating him, but a little hate never hurt anyone that badly. They were going to be a Dent one day. A strong couple. Soulmates. I just needed her to be a teenager, a happy teenager, for now. Blake failed to make her happy at this moment. She should go shopping, check out other boys, and not just have eyes for one. It wasn't fair or healthy. She was going to end up having just that one.

I was doing them a favor. It felt right. A little distance and a little anger never hurt anyone, and in the end it would only make them stronger. I knew it in my bones.

Then why did I get a feeling this was going to bite me completely in the ass?

Five months passed. Elena recovered from her sulking mood—somewhat. Anger still stalked her daily. We couldn't mention Blake's name in this house.

He even showed up a few weeks ago. Thank heavens Elena wasn't home. One of the servants told him that they would give Elena the message. I watch from afar. I end up erasing another memory and didn't tell Elena about Blake's sudden visit.

They would end up together. They would.

And then another fear started.

She had her first boyfriend. Lee Evers. For weeks she couldn't stop talking about this boy.

I was extremely happy at first. After all, my meddling had always been about helping Elena have a normal childhood and not being obsessed with Blake her entire life, right? But then Lee was all she talked about. He was turning into her sun. I had to admit, I understood why Al didn't like it one bit.

With Blake, we knew what we were getting ourselves into. With this new one, we had no idea. Still, Al decided to invite him and his family over to the castle for dinner.

They showed up in evening wear. Al was the only one who wasn't underdressed. The three men wore dark suits, even Lee. His mother wore a ruched lilac gown.

Elena and I ducked out to change. In a hurry, I selected tasteful dresses for each of us—a gold silk dresses that contrasted well with my dark tresses for me, and a pale pink dress for Elena, which she fought me over because it was too babyish. I thought she looked like a perfect princess once her lady-in-waiting hastily pinned her blonde hair atop her head.

Al kept the guests busy with finger foods and champagne, chatting about Paegeian politics. Al loved small businesses; Lee's father, whom I'd only met through Elena's stories, knew the family business well. He owned a string of transportation companies.

We swept across the gleaming teak floor. Albert and our guests clustered around a spindly table that was overpowered by an extravagant vase with a spray of orange and red heliconia flowers.

"Lovely to meet you, my queen." His mother curtseyed to me. Al suppressed his laughter. He knew how much I hated it.

"Please, call me Catherine. No need for formality," I said.

She smiled. She was plain but had an honest face. I couldn't help but like her a little. "Jody. Jody Evers. This is my son, Lee."

I narrowed my eyes slightly. Everyone laughed.

"Sorry, Katie is a bit overprotective of our daughter. If you are going to mess with Elena, you will have a crazy person to deal with," my husband joked.

Good-natured laughs tinkled around the table. James, Jody's husband, added, "And she has authority, so Lee, my boy, you need to tread lightly." He was funny. Smart, but funny.

My eyes were on Lee and Elena the entire night. Their connection was almost as intense as the one she shared with Blake. But it was gentle. A bit more doable.

Jody was a nice, elegant woman. She was an artist, sculptor, and writer. I loved reading, and she said she would get her publisher to send me some of her novels.

The evening progressed without a hitch. At ten we said goodbye.

We all went back in when they drove off.

"So," Elena asked. "What do you think?"

My husband started, "Do you really like—"

I slapped Albert and he stopped mid-sentence.

"I like him." I gave my input.

Her eyes light up. "You do?"

I nodded.

She hugged me tight.

I added, "Just as long as he doesn't break your heart, sweetheart."

Christmas was upon us. Blake was due to come home.

Elena was just getting over him. Dating Lee helped. The boy was really nice. He stuck to my rules. He wasn't a jackass like that Rubicon who lately got himself into so much trouble.

Issy confessed that she was glad he would see Elena again. Apparently they'd gotten letters from Dragonia complaining about his attitude. His Chromatic nature—his darkness—threatened to take over. Issy truly believed Elena was the antidote.

Well, Blake should've treated her with respect and not broken her heart.

Elena wasn't the only one who was angry. Blake was livid. Crows still came bearing letter after furious letter. I knew what Issy didn't know. Blake wrote about everything he was doing. The bad and the ugly.

He lost his temper on a daily basis now. The school didn't want to let him participate in activities. In both attitude and size, he was ten dragons in one. More advanced.

The first few letters expressed his sadness. I almost told Al to take her to Dragonia. But I knew when she saw him, I would lose my daughter. Everything was too damn perfect to risk that. The next few crows were hurtful.

My anger at him returned, and I decided that he didn't deserve her good, kind heart or the calming effect she had over him. He didn't treat her like the light of his life.

Then a letter arrived detailing how much she'd disappointed him., *I never thought you'd be as stubborn as your mother,* he wrote.

What a douchebag.

Her letters stopped way before his. She said goodbye to him, and told him that she hoped he would be happy. That was it. Pride surged in my heart as I read it. My little girl was getting so mature.

No more letters. But she was still mad that he'd

ignored her for so long, punishing her so long.

It was really gnawing at me.

Tanya—whom I told everything—thought it was hilarious. But when the letter about Blake's darkness came, she sobered. "Katie, this isn't funny anymore," she said.

"He'll be fine," I insisted. "A little darkness hasn't done anyone any harm."

Tanya's eyebrows show up. "Oh really? What about Goran?"

I scowled, but even so, my subconscious sent out alarm bells. *What are you saying?* The old Katie would have been shocked at my blitheness.

Tanya rambled a couple of other things, but I shut her out. She was just as naïve as Al. I ignored her.

I was disappointed with myself. I didn't need my conscience to make me feel shittier. This web of lies I'd woven was going to destroy me one day. I knew it, yet I couldn't stop.

Blake and Elena were going to see each other on Christmas. Once they talked and realized their letters hadn't been delivered, everything would be over. I would be caught. I was still thinking of something brilliant to say. If only Al could see things my way. I could always try to persuade him. Ugh, I was turning into an evil mother. I hated that.

I played my piano almost every single day. It was haunting me, what I was doing to them. And my clever plan from five months ago didn't seem so great anymore.

A knock came at the door of the library. My fingers stilled on the ivory keys. Elena popped in her head.

"Hey, baby." I smiled, but I felt like shit.

"Can I ask you something?" she said.

I nodded, tapped on the stool.

She came in and sat where I'd indicated.

"Spit it out," I said as she took two deep breaths.

"Can I spend Christmas over at Lee's? His mom invited me. They're going to their winter spot. Please, Mom." Her voice was a husky whisper. She wasn't ready to see Blake either.

This wasn't just my escape plan; it was hers, too. "Not ready yet?"

She shook her head as her eyes welled up. What was going on in her mind?

"Okay, but Elena, I swear, if you…"

"Mom!" she gave me shocked look. "No," she shook her head with exaggerated vehemence.

I laughed. We'd had *the talk* a few times.

"Seriously." She laughed and gave me a hug. "Thanks. You're the best." Despite getting her way, she sounded so sad.

She left. I noticed the way she slouched. She didn't resemble the confident girl I'd raised. I started playing the piano again.

She would get over this. She would. Even though she'd grown up with him. She would.

Keep telling yourself that, Katie, maybe it will come true, the old Katie snapped, her tone sarcastic.

BLAKE

Five fucking months. How many times did I need to tell her I was sorry?

I'd sent how many fucking letters to her? She hadn't even answered one. She didn't care about the darkness.

She said she would come, and she didn't.

I even went to her, and still no reaction what so ever. Not to mention all the phone calls. So fuck that.

This Christmas I was going to give her a piece of my mind about how shallow she was. I packed my bags, stuffing clothes in with such force that one of the zippers broke.

Tabitha was going home. I knew now that Elena had never been okay with my relationship with Tabitha.

I zipped up my bags and stormed out.

I found my dad's SUV in the parking lot of Dragonia. Dad was behind the wheel and Mom was in shotgun. They both smiled at me, but at my dark expression, didn't say much. I gave Tabitha a brusque kiss and slammed the car door. We went home.

I brooded on the drive, barely aware of my parents' chatter. *I gave Elena a piece of my skin and she won't even come keep me sane when things get to be too much. She's abandoned me.*

I had to work through that, using Fire Caine to keep me stable. To keep the beast in me stable. Fire-fucking-Caine. My dad would rip off all my scales if he found out.

It was something the brat could never know either.

How long was she going to punish me? It was going to stop real soon. And I didn't care what her mother said. She was a spoiled brat, throwing tantrums because...what? I didn't share her feelings? What happened to "you're like my brother"? When did it all change?

The drive wasn't that long. I hated the elevators. They made me unbalanced for days. I said goodbye to my family at the port—they all stayed in the car—and flew home alone.

When I eventually reached the manor, they'd beaten me there. Sammy was glad to see me without Tabitha.

Christmas decorations were hanging everywhere. Christmas was at our place this year. The place was a veritable explosion of red, green, and silver.

"Where is the Ice Queen?" Sammy asked. She'd gotten bigger, and if I was not mistaken, a tad more beautiful.

"She went home. She has a family, too, Sammy," I snapped. I hated the way it came out, but I always felt so angry.

"Oh, I thought she didn't."

I rolled my eyes.

Everything was set up. Elena's stocking hung on the mantle and her ornament glinted on the tree.

Early on the twenty-third, King Albert's SUV pulled in.

I didn't see Elena. I didn't like this. *She better be here.*

Then again, her mother would never let her stay at the castle alone. She was here, somewhere. She had to be.

She must be sleeping in the back. *Yeah right. It's not even a ten-minute drive.*

I watched King Albert close his door. He walked past the passenger door, opened the trunk, and took out two suitcases. Queen Catherine emerged with her handbag.

My dad was happy to see them.

"Where's Elena?" Mom sounded worried.

"Don't even ask," King Albert joked. "Katie here's played the piano nonstop the past few days."

Where the hell is Elena?

I waited in my room until they were settled in before I made my way to the lounge.

"Hi, Blake." Queen Catherine got up. My lips curved as I saw her. She came over and gave me a hug. "What are they feeding you at Dragonia?"

"Junk food," I said, trying not to bark it out. I plopped down on the sofa.

Sammy was in her room. Maybe Elena was with her.

"So?" Mom asked, looking at the queen.

"He's okay," Catherine said, apparently continuing their conversation. "I told him if he ever thinks of laying so much as a finger on her, I would be his worst nightmare."

My father laughed the hardest. "Poor boy," he said.

Poor boy? I didn't like that.

"She's exaggerating like usual," King Albert said. "His father owns all the transportation companies that go to the other side of the Wall."

"That's him?" my mom asked.

"Yeah, really smart, too."

My head bounced back and forth as if I were watching a tennis match. I had no idea what they were talking about.

"So, you just let her go?" Mom asked.

"She promised me on her life she would be good. So, yes. She's spending Christmas with them. We speak every day and it sounds as if she is really enjoying herself."

She's not coming.

I could see how my next six months were going to be. More fucking Fire Caine.

ELENA

Christmas break was amazing. I never thought my mother would say yes. Maybe the way I'd asked her had done the trick. I guess she knew how I felt about Blake.

I wasn't ready to see him, not after what he'd done. I was so not ready to see the Ice Queen again, to see her gloating. No doubt the idiot had told her about that kiss. I was sure she would think me a poor baby.

No, I wasn't ready.

My mother saw that. Although she played the piano nonstop for the next few days, she still let me go.

Seriously, she thought I would sleep with Lee?

Sure, we went to second base a few nights, feeling each other up, but that was where it stayed. He knew where he stood with me. I wasn't in love with him. He was just a distraction. A really good distraction.

He'd been afraid of Blake in the beginning, but the more we'd talked about Blake, the less he'd feared him. That actually led to our first date.

On the second date, my parents met him and his family. They loved Lee. Of course they would. They saw the person he wanted them to see, not the bad boy...I sighed. The one who reminded me of my dragon—that side of him was reserved for only his close friends, and of course, me.

I started to listen to new music. I was tired of Blake's voice in my headphones. There were a few new songs that I felt were just written for me. And I told myself that it would pass. I would get over Blake. Everyone did eventually.

"Elena," Lee stopped kissing me. I opened my eyes.

He wasn't hard on the eyes. Even in the light of the

moon streaming in the window, I could appreciate that. He stared at me with his deep brown eyes and knitted eyebrows. His blond hair was tousled from our make-out session.

"What?" We were on his bed, riling each other up again.

If his mother found out I wasn't in my room, like all good princesses should be this hour, she was going to phone mine, and this would be the end. But I didn't care.

"Where are you?"

I felt confused. "Here."

"No, you are not," he said and rolled off me. We were still stuck on second base because I refused to sleep with him. I'd given him so many reasons why not. They all summed up to one truth: I wasn't there with Lee.

"Is it *him* again?"

"Who?" I pretended that I didn't know.

His voice was sullen. "That lame-ass fucking dragon of yours."

"No," I lied. "Seriously, I could've seen him this Christmas, but I'm here with you." I pushed myself from the bed. "I hate your insecurities, Lee."

"I'm sorry." He reached out for me.

"Just go to bed," I said. I shoved myself off his bed and tiptoed out of his room.

I had to lie. I loathed the lying, but Lee could never know the truth. If he knew I had no intention of ever sleeping with him, that I really was still stuck on Blake, he would break up with me. And he was such a great distraction.

BLAKE

School started again after our break. It was hard to pretend to be happy and jolly when all I wanted to do was rip out a little royal's heart for running away. So she had a fucking boyfriend now. It wasn't because of that fact that I was pissed off. She was still like my little sister, I told myself. No, it was just the fact that I was dark, and she didn't care because of one lame fucking kiss.

The next few months flew by. No crows came. Not even a birthday wish.

As her birthday neared, invitations started to reach everyone…except me. Lucian and Annie got their invitations for Elena's fifteenth birthday. I didn't.

I called my father and asked if I could go home with Tabitha. The darkness was growing stronger. Phil, her brother, had Fire Caine.

To my surprise my dad asked, "What about Elena's birthday?"

"I'm not going."

His hologram frowned. "Blake, what the hell is going on? You've never missed a birthday of hers."

"Yeah, there's always first time, Dad." I slammed down the Cammy.

The next day Lucian asked me if he was going to see me at Elena's party.

"Nope," I said. "I'm going to visit Tabitha for the summer."

He just looked at me. "And what do I tell Elena?"

"Believe me, she isn't expecting me," I said.

"Blake, what the hell happened?" Lucian asked. I'd told him some, but not all of what was going on between us. "The crows stopped coming, I get it. But I know you found another way to communicate with her."

I scowled. "She is a spoiled brat, Lucian. A spoiled brat who only cares about herself." I opened the door. "Enjoy your summer break."

ELENA

I sent him an invitation. By now he would've RSVP'd. Why was he doing this?

So he doesn't want me. I'd never taken him for such a fucking jerk.

I'd ruined everything with that kiss. The hardest part was that I didn't know how to take it back. I'd apologized. I'd sent him almost a dozen heartfelt letters. Things would never be the same.

It had been a year since I last saw him. Well, my birthday would mark a year.

My mom kept telling me that his dark side had started to rise. Aunt Issy fretted about that. She was disappointed, apparently, that I hadn't showed for Christmas. She believed my effect on him, as lame as it sounded, would have made the past six months a little easier.

"Then why doesn't he let me know, Mom? He might not like me that much, but at least I can take the dark away."

"Because he is Chromatic. Chromatics doesn't want good around them. You know that."

My brow puckered. "It doesn't make any sense. He promised."

"People sometimes break their promises, Elena, especially the ones who tend toward the dark side."

"It's not like him," I whined.

"Elena, what do you want me to say, huh? Lucian is going through the same thing with him. His mom told me that they are only roommates."

My mouth fell open. "They aren't friends anymore?"

"He's even pushing Lucian away. Even aunt Issy is worried about him. About the two of you. I don't know what to tell everyone. I'm trying to say the right words to you. I don't know, sweetheart."

I felt sorry for my mom. I knew she was trying really hard.

"Don't get your hopes up that he's going to come to this year's party. At least Lee and all your other friends will be here."

I scowled. "Lee isn't coming," I said.

"What, why?"

"He doesn't like Lucian, and told me if he Lucian came, he wouldn't."

"Lucian?"

"Yes. They were in the same grade until Lucian went to Dragonia, Mom."

She gave me a calculating look. "You okay with it?"

"It's Lee, or Lucian. Lucian is by far one of my best friends, Mom. So, sorry, Lee."

She shook her head and kissed me on my temple. "Already breaking hearts." She gave a satisfied sigh, which made me laugh.

My fifteenth birthday was in two days. Blake still hadn't RSVP'd. They'd brought nametags, and his wasn't even printed.

Tabitha could've come with. I would've acted as if

nothing had happened. I would've even ignored him. I just wanted him to be there.

Why was I even hoping?

The Shifters had a brand-new single out. It was a haunting song. A bit on the dark side. No message lingered in the lyrics. Nothing. He sounded so angry.

One song was about betrayal. It was how I felt. Had he written it from my point of view? It was as if he knew what he was doing to me, and he didn't know how to make it right. Because he was dark. Or maybe it was a song that made him and that cow of his laugh their heads off.

The song's title was "What If?" What if...what? What if I hadn't kissed him? More like "What if that Snow Dragon had kept her grabby paws off him?" He wasn't hers. She knew how it would end and still...

It angered me all over again.

A knock came at my door. Mom popped her head into my room. She didn't look happy. She had grave news.

"You don't have to say it, Mom."

"Okay." Her expression was sympathetic. "Sorry sweetheart."

"Let me guess, he didn't go home for the summer."

She shook her head. I nodded with a faint smile.

He was with his Ice Queen. She really was a pain in the ass. The wedge between us. Something I never thought anyone could do. Everyone had been wrong about our bond. I was right. We weren't destined to be like Cooper and Merica.

Still, I put on party clothes. I wore a sequined black miniskirt and cute boots, and pretended to have the best birthday ever.

We even ended up inside my treehouse—all of us,

even Arianna. The air between us felt dead without Blake.

Nobody mentioned him. Not Annie, Lucian, Sammy, or Arianna.

I had to disrupt the tenuous peace. "Are you guys not friends anymore?" I asked Lucian as he took a drag of his cigarette.

He shook his head and handed it to me.

"Why?" I asked. The cherry glowed red as I inhaled. But I lost my cool when I almost coughed up a lung. All of them laughed, happy for the levity.

Lucian's face got serious again as he took the cigarette back from me. "Because he's an asshole. He's fucking angry at everyone. The worst part is, he doesn't speak to anyone."

I knew the feeling.

"When was the last time you spoke to him?" Lucian asked.

"You really want to know?"

He nodded.

"A year ago."

All of them stared at me.

I studied them back. What was I missing?

"You haven't spoken to him for a year?"

"Yes," I said. "I wasn't here for Christmas, and the last I heard from him was my birthday. I tried. He never replied to my crows. So what am I supposed to do, Lucian?"

"See? He's a fucking asshole." Lucian glowered.

"He might have changed if you weren't dating fucknut Lee," Sammy said.

Lucian looked at me. "Who's Lee?"

I glared at Sammy.

"Where is he tonight anyway? You didn't break up, did you?"

The others gasped—except Arianna. "I'm with Sammy, Elena. He is a douchebag."

"So? He's my douchebag."

"Lee who?" Lucian repeated. My face said it all. "Lee Evers. You're fucking kidding me, right?"

I laughed. "What's the deal with you two, anyway?"

"He's an asshole, Elena." I'd never heard him so mad. "Believe me, punching him felt fucking awesome. The grounding after that, not so much, I'll admit. And what did his dad do? Bought him a fucking bike because he's a fucking man."

I giggled. "You guys were in a real fight?"

"He's an asshole. Break up with him."

"It's not like that, okay?"

"So why isn't he here?"

"Cause he gave me an ultimatum." I hesitated. "Um, involving you."

Lucian smiled and we high fived. "Seriously?" he said.

I nodded. "You're one of my best friends, Lucian. There wasn't even a doubt I'd pick you."

We went back to the party and danced like there was no tomorrow.

Overall, my fifteenth birthday sucked. My best friend was dark, didn't want anything to do with his friends, all thanks to a certain Snow Dragon with perfect tits and a perfect ass.

I told myself that was all she was to him. But he'd been with her for more than a year.

I didn't look forward to going to Dragonia Academy anymore. Just one more year before Sammy and I were going to join. Then I couldn't avoid him.

How did everything get so upside down?

The new school year started. It was my last year at Mastersons. The tutors at home increased, too.

I knew almost all the spells there were, all the subjects I was going to have, and all the potions, even the deadly ones, thanks to Frank's fascination.

My favorite subject was Art of War. I was now on my second trainer; the other one could only teach me what he knew. I'd surpassed his talent. Mom got a ninja. He had many dans and whatnot. His training was exceptionally hard, too, but I was giving it my all.

My body started changing. Mom didn't like that I was growing up.

Lee kept his toehold in my life. Part of me wished he would just move on, but I let him stay. He was a delicious distraction.

I hadn't been in the spotlight the past four months. I hated the cockroaches who called themselves the media. I hid underneath shapeless hoodies. Anytime they succeeded in getting a shot of me, it made front-page news. Lee made it into the photos a couple of times, too. He loved the limelight. The question was starting to get asked: why didn't they see me and Blake together anymore? After all, the fates of the Rubicon and the Princess of Paegeia affected the whole nation.

I tried not to be bothered by their headlines.

My mom scolded me once when they took a picture of Lee and me running from the cameras—I'd given them the middle finger. I was grounded for a month. That picture was on the cover of every magazine. My face wasn't visible. Just my rude gesture. I'd promised that it was the last incident like that. Now I hid from the cockroaches.

Other headlines made the front page, of course. Stuff about Blake, pictures of him and Tabitha at nightclubs. He was drunk, yeah, but so effing hot. How could I have ever thought of him as my brother? I missed him so much.

He was going dark. Even in photos I could see it. I always whizzed through the transcripts of his interviews to find the one question I needed answered. *Where is Elena, Blake? Why don't we see the two of you together anymore?*

He ignored this question every time. He never answered a thing. It was as if I didn't exist.

Still, I ignored it. They always published whatever they wanted to, anyway. No matter what I said, they twisted my words and made me sound more horrible than reality. Maybe they did the same to Blake. I eventually stopped reading magazines and newspapers.

My father made a speech about respect for the private lives of young people, when the cockroaches got to be too much.

Everything stopped after that. Life couldn't be better than it was, and I'd made peace with that.

BLAKE

I took another snort of Fire Caine. Usually the darkness would subside for a couple of days after I used.

I didn't hate Elena as much as I did when I came off

the Fire Caine.

I missed her face. I missed her laughter. I missed her irritating the living crap out of me. And yes, there were times that I wished I hadn't stopped her from kissing me that night and just gone with it. At least it would've been better than this.

This darkness.

She would always be my happy place. It was evident in the poems I wrote, evident in my music. I hated her for just giving up.

Was she even going to claim me one day? Now that was the big question.

When all was still fine, before that party that ruined everything between us, Lucian had asked me what I loved about Tabitha. I'd told him she was one step away from being perfect. She was beautiful. She made me yearn for her in a way I'd never wanted anything. She was funny as hell. She was kind. I couldn't help but fall in love with her. Her ice had a calming effect on my Pink Kiss.

Lucian had narrowed his eyes and asked me what the one missing step was.

It was that dash of trouble. She was too scared of just letting go, too scared of cutting class with me, too scared of taking that drag with me. What could I expect? It was how Snow Dragons were built. But other than that she was perfect.

He'd laughed and shaken his head as if he knew something I didn't. He left it there.

I stared at the white lines on the sideboard in front of me. Should I take another? Now I suddenly wondered what the fuck he knew. Why had he shaken his head like that?

I still saw Elena as my little sister, as my best friend. It hurt that she didn't want to see me. She held a grudge like nobody else I'd ever met. Hopefully, she would decide that it was enough. All I could do was hope. A part of me knew that in the morning, when I came down, I wasn't going to give a shit about any of this and I would hate her for not fighting harder.

I flicked on the television. A news story was on. I straightened. It was Elena's dad, asking for help.

I squinted to focus. A picture of Mr. Pluggs the monkey came on screen. He was missing.

It seemed like a great idea. To be the one to find him. Maybe I would be her hero again.

I started the search. But hours later, the Fire Caine clouded my thoughts and I ended up in a club, dancing and flirting with Sophie, a beautiful brunette. Tomorrow, Pluggs would be a distant memory.

Christmas came again

This time we were going away. My dad phoned and said that he'd booked a trip to China. The people there would make me feel like a god again. Just what I needed. The last time I'd seen them, I hadn't had my human form yet. They adored the Rubicon.

It was time to go back and let them meet the guy behind the Rubicon.

I hated the fact that Lucian was going to spend Christmas with Elena. They'd invited them this year.

I secured a seat on the flight to China for Tabitha. She was coming with; her parents had said it was okay. At least it wouldn't be boring.

ELENA

A scream shredded my throat and left my mouth. Tears poured over my cheeks.

My mother was the first to reach me. My father and Sir Robert dogged her heels. When she saw the blood on the walls of the porch, she grabbed me tight.

My horrified gaze, blurred with anguished tears, was riveted to a tiny body, a brutally slit neck. Pluggs. My Pluggs. My heart felt like it would burst.

"I told you they couldn't be trusted!" my mother roared at my father. "Why didn't you listen to me?" She dragged me into the house.

Pluggs had paid for his mistakes. He'd wandered off and been missing for a month. My father had held a press conference asking for help. The entire nation had searched for him. Nobody could find him.

And here he was, laying in a congealing pool of his own blood.

A message to my father, written in Wyvic, was scrawled across the white porch floor in monkey blood.

Why had he even had that meeting with them? Mom had insisted that they couldn't be trusted. Why?

Felix the Great Dane and Shauna the Persian cat stayed inside my room. I didn't let them out of my sight. It was two days before Christmas and I could do nothing but clutch my two remaining pets and sob.

I swore to kill the Wyvern who had done that to Mr. Pluggs. But my father, always diplomatic, didn't want us to make a fuss. It would create more chaos among our people.

I didn't understand Wyvic. Not even Dad did; he had to get a translator to come and tell him what it meant. He was scared afterward. He refused to tell anyone what it said. It was something bad, though. He doubled the guards around the castle.

I cried for two days. When the tears finally dried, I slept.

Christmas was upon us, but I wasn't in the mood for people.

Sir Robert left on a long-overdue trip to China. Something to do with them meeting Blake's adult form. I was too grief-stricken to care.

I'd broken my silence and sent him a crow about Pluggs. I'd thought he would at least send condolences. But who had I been kidding? He hadn't even bothered to find Pluggs after the press conference. No reply came. I didn't know why it even bothered me anymore.

He only had feelings for his Ice Queen now. She had turned him into an Ice King.

I hated him. I never thought it would ever be possible, but I did. I didn't want to start the new school year at Dragonia in a few short months.

I tried to get out of it, but my father put his foot down. Mom couldn't help this time.

A knock came at my door. Mom's voice called from the hall, "Elena, our guests are here."

"Fine, give me a minute," I grunted and she left.

I'd really missed Lucian. I figured I should make the best of his visit. After all, it was Christmas.

I combed my hair, which I'd cut into a scruffy bob. Mom even let me go a shade lighter, which really brought out my eyes. It was one of her attempts to lift my mood, but nothing could.

I was almost sixteen. She was getting seriously worried. The piano had been working overtime again lately.

She'd caught Lee in my room a few nights before Pluggs's murder. So humiliating. I was technically grounded. If only she knew what Lee really was to me, she wouldn't worry so much.

She wasn't ready for me to go to Dragonia Academy, and neither was I. Once there, I would have to pick the date of the claiming. I didn't even know if I wanted him as my dragon anymore.

I pulled on my jeans and a loose sweater, and went downstairs.

I found them in the lounge having eggnog. My father wore the horrible Christmas sweater he loved, the one with reindeer and elves all over it. His face lit up as I walked in. He was the very picture of Christmas cheer.

"Elena." Queen Margerite got up first to kiss me. I greeted all of them. Desi was pregnant with her second baby.

Her eyes grew when she saw me.

"I love that hair," she said, kissing me on each cheek.

"I'll give you the name of my hairstylist," I said.

"You'd better."

I said Merry Christmas to King Helmut and then found Lucian behind me.

He looked surprised to see me. "Whoa, is that really you?"

"Oh, c'mon! You saw me six months ago," I said and gave him a hug.

The way he hugged me back was awkward, almost…nah, surely not. What the hell was he doing? He was my best friend, for crying out loud, or one of them anyhow.

"You trained?"

"Yes, I have," I said. We ended up chatting about the Art of War the entire night. If there was one thing Lucian was good at, it was Art of War.

There was even a time that I thought he was flirting with me, which was awkward in the beginning, but I quickly got used to it. Real quick.

It turned into the best Christmas I'd had in a long time.

King Helmut started bragging about Lucian and how good he was at Art of War. Lucian blushed.

My father finished off another eggnog. "You want to put a wager on that, old friend?"

"Albert," my mother scolded.

"Against whom?" King Helmut laughed.

"Elena, of course."

"Stop this!" Mom sounded angry.

"I'm up for it if you are," I teased. I loved a challenge.

Lucian laughed. "I don't want to hurt you, Elena."

"Aww, scared I'm going to beat your ass?"

"Elena," my mom said. "Language."

"Fine, let's do this, big mouth," Lucian said with his face really close to mine. I thought he would kiss me. Instead, he blushed even harder, spun, and stalked to the table for another drink.

My mother just stared at him with huge eyes. Dad laughed.

I went to my room and dressed in slacks. I pulled on my vest. It was a stunner. The best technology money could buy. When I came back downstairs, everyone had gathered in my training room.

Lucian's eyes boggled at the sight of my vest. "What the hell is this?"

"Oh, impressive right? Dad pulled some strings. It's the newest on the market. People don't even know about it yet."

"What is it?"

"The Samurai 3000."

"Nice." He knocked on my vest and then looked at his own—top of the line from last year. "Where's mine?" Lucian asked his father, who was sitting on one of the benches that bordered my training room.

"Soon!" King Helmut cried.

We started to spar. We fought with shields and blunt weapons. I danced circles around Lucian. He was fast, but not as fast as me. Whenever he thought he had me in his grip, I easily wriggled out of it, throwing him on the floor and taunting him.

Nothing made him angry, though. He had a sloppy grin on his face the whole time.

The two queens put a stop to it after an hour. We were hardly out of breath.

Lucian hugged me. Awe was written on his face. "What the hell, Elena?"

"Told you," I said with a smirk.

"Okay, you two," my mother said. "Showers. And *not* the same one."

"Mom!" I yelled, but Lucian just laughed.

CATHERINE

It was getting late. The McKenzies planned on spending the night. Watching Elena and Lucian all night had awakened another fear, and not just with me, but with Maggie, too.

Albert and that stupid wager.

Elena had kicked Lucian's ass. She was so fast she scared me a little—and made me proud. I wondered if I would be able to take her on and win. She was getting so good at this.

The familiar way they spoke to one another, their jokes...I knew where this was leading. He wanted to touch her. What was he thinking? Was he really not afraid of what Blake might do?

She'd turned into a beaut, and Lucian only confirmed it tonight when he saw her. She'd become this young lady who lit up everyone's faces overnight. It was the haircut and the fact that she was allowed to wear makeup now. Still, I didn't think Lucian would actually make a move.

I was watching them swim in the indoor pool from behind the curtains like a peeping tom.

Albert's voice startled me. "First Lee, now Lucian. Woman, you are driving me insane."

"This isn't good, Albert," I said without taking my eyes off them.

"Well, if you hadn't kept those letters away from Blake and Elena, none of this would've happened."

I sighed. "Would you stop with that? You know how bad I feel."

"Let it go. They're old enough to sort out their own problems," Albert said in a sleepy tone.

"Go to bed and let me be," I snapped. In the pool, Lucian and Elena were drawing closer to one another.

Suddenly, Lucian pulled away. My jaw hung on the floor. Not even a peck on the lips. Well, I definitely didn't expect that! How much more rejection was this girl going to handle?

ELENA

"Forget about it. Don't worry, okay?" I pleaded. I'd misread the signs again and almost ruined it with Lucian, too. I'd just tried to kiss him. My cheeks burned with shame as I clambered out of the pool.

"Elena, wait!" He climbed out after me.

"Seriously, I'm fine." I still didn't look at him. "Really. It was stupid if I think about it."

His voice was gentle. "So you get why?"

No, I didn't get why. Was he gay?

"If you weren't Blake's rider, I would've gone for that. Totally." He hugged me, forcing me to face him.

I chuckled ruefully. He'd rejected me for Blake. Still, I didn't argue. I was tired of having fights because of Blake.

"He's not going to know what to do with himself when he sees you. You've turned into a fox, Elena."

"Don't stop," I joked.

He put his arm around my neck and we made our way to the castle. "Still that awesome sense of humor. Care for a nightcap in the treehouse?" He waggled his eyebrows.

I pursed my lips. "I haven't been up in the treehouse since my birthday. Sure, why not?" I sneaked down to the wine cellar for a bottle of liquor. When I returned, I found Lucian waiting in the treehouse.

We passed the bottle and started to talk. He told me about who he had in mind for claiming. It was this was Sun-Blast who had the uncanny ability to speak about himself in the third person. He was one of Blake's closest friends at Dragonia, or as close as one could get.

Lucian hadn't ascended yet, which was sad. He had been born with the mark, but it was hardly visible. He was starting to doubt that he would ever ascend. He would, though. He was just a late bloomer—something the two of us apparently had in common.

An awkward silence descended as we exhausted that subject. "So, um, why did you cry tonight? I mean before I got here."

I shifted. "What?"

"I saw the bloodshot eyes, Elena. No amount of makeup could hide that."

As if on cue, thoughts of Pluggs rose and my eyes filled up.

"Please don't tell me it's because of that ass." Blake, he meant.

I shook my head. "No, it's Pluggs. We found him a couple days ago." I wiped away my tears. "My father didn't want to make a fuss about it, but I think it's the reason he invited you over for Christmas—to speak to yours about it."

"What happened, Elena?"

"The Wyverns left my dad a message. They used...they used Pluggs as the ink."

His eyes bugged out. I took a huge pull from the bottle.

"*What?*"

"Pluggs is dead, Lucian. I found him, murdered, on the porch two days ago. Sir Robert almost canceled their trip to China. He was scared. But my father told him to go. I don't know what the message said. My dad refuses to tell anyone, and I can't read Wyvic. Tonight is the first night my father has been himself."

He pulled me in for a hug. "I'm so sorry, Elena."

"I'll be fine. I've lost two friends now." My voice cracked.

"He's an asshole," Lucian exclaimed fiercely. "He will eventually return to you. I mean, you are part of a Dent, Elena."

I huffed. "You ever wonder what the Dent is really about?"

"I know it's awesome."

"What if it isn't? Blake wants absolutely nothing to do with me," I said. "It's never going to change."

His arms tightened and then he released me. "Don't say that."

"What if it's a spell?"

"Not the Dent. It's much cooler than that."

I smiled without mirth. I wasn't so sure about that anymore.

"What happened between the two of you, anyway?"

I shook my head. "It's stupid. And my own fault."

"What, you kissed him?" I could tell it was a joke, but when I didn't deny it, Lucian gaped at me.

"When?"

"The night of my fourteenth birthday. Stupid, I know."

"Elena…"

I crossed my arms over my chest. "It's fine. He didn't share my affection. He ignored me after that."

"Because of a *kiss*?"

"Yes, lame. I didn't think that I would ever put Blake and lame in the same sentence, but he did. I sent him so many crows. He never replied. Not once."

Shock was written all over his face. "I never thought

he was that type of guy."

I shrugged. "It's in the past. We can't go back and change it. It was my mistake."

He touched my arm. "Sorry about that."

"It's okay. I got over it." I tried to sound flippant.

"He was your best friend, Elena. I don't know if I would ever be able to get over something like that."

"Okay, seriously, change the topic," I said. He laughed. We moved on to Desi and the new baby.

The conversation surprised me when it turned toward Arianna. Lucian didn't know if he wanted to be with her romantically. She'd kissed him a few days ago, and part of him liked it.

We laughed as I gave him a look. It was Arianna.

"What? She is royalty, and has been a great friend."

"Makes sense. So what, your theory is that all good friends end up together?"

He smiled. "Yeah, even the dark ass ones who want nothing to do with their riders."

BLAKE

Christmas was over.

I flew straight from China through the Wall to avoid the elevators. I wanted to land because of Tabitha; she wasn't used to the limelight. But when I saw so many camera flashes, my eyes zoomed in and I realized the royal family, the Malones, were nearby.

So I flew straight to Dragonia Academy.

A day later Tabitha caught up with me at Dragonia. She immediately chided me for my behavior. "You just left us there! You know how I feel about them."

"They don't bite," I said. "Well, not yet."

She laughed and climbed onto my bed. "She gave me such a hateful look. As if I'm the problem between you two."

Elena was there? "Who are you talking about?"

"Queen Catherine. She does not like me much. It's all because of her spoiled little brat who doesn't get what she wants."

I chuckled. "She was there?"

"No, why would she be?" Tabitha asked.

I spread my hands. "Just curious."

The door opened and Lucian sauntered in. "Welcome back. How was China?"

"An ego booster from hell."

Lucian laughed. "Tabitha," he said in greeting.

"Hi, Lucian." She smiled.

He put his bag on the bed. A huge grin was fixed on his face. Why was he always so happy? It pissed me off.

That night I sat in bed with my laptop. I surfed the net for Elena. Thousands of results popped up. Most of the images were kind of old, back when she was fourteen and younger. There were plenty of a figure hiding under her hoodie. I smiled at the one where she was flipping them off. I missed her spunk.

I could just imagine what she'd gone through with her mom and dad.

Many of the clippings covered how she was training heavily. They came from far and wide to instruct her. I couldn't find any recent pictures. What was she doing? Hiding, like usual.

"Why didn't you send her something?" Lucian asked.

I stopped, surprised; I had thought he was already asleep.

"What are you talking about?" I tried to sound nonchalant.

He sat up on his bed. "I saw her at Christmas, and *man...*"

I looked up. A huge grin was plastered on his face.

"Man, what?"

"She isn't the fourteen-year-old who kissed you that night."

I froze. "How do you know about that?"

"She told me, Blake. So she kissed you, just get over it. It's not the end of the fucking world. But to ignore her like that..."

"Ignore her like that?" It felt as if someone bowled me over. I started to laugh. This was fresh.

He didn't think it was funny. I still wanted to know what he meant with that "Man" comment.

"Blake, Mr. Pluggs died."

My entire heart shriveled. I knew how much she loved Mr. Pluggs. "What?"

"Two days before Christmas. They found him. She tried to cover up her blotchy eyes, but no amount of makeup could. She's had a really hard time. Your father didn't tell you?"

So that was why he was always on his phone.

I shook my head. "What happened?"

"Wyverns. They left a message for her father using Pluggs's blood. She found him on the porch."

"That's why my father wanted to cancel the trip," I spoke softly. I got up and grabbed a sheet of paper. I'd promised myself never to do this again. I had to, though.

Sorry about Mr. Pluggs. I know how much he meant to you. Just speak to me, please. I miss you.

I folded it up, put it in a pouch, and went to the window. I called the crow with a low, rumbling whistle. In a few minutes, he landed on the sill with a ruffle of his strong black wings.

I connected the pouch to the bird, stroked his bony head, and gave him a treat. He took off.

I looked at Lucian who just stared at me. "I never ignored her. If I told you how many crows I sent…I know it was just a kiss, Lucian. She was fourteen and probably felt that I was abandoning her," I trailed off.

"Then why aren't you guys talking?"

"Because she never answers any of my letters. I begged. I begged her to come when I turned dark." I waved my arms to take in the room, the castle, the school campus. "You see her here?" It was still a sore subject.

"No, Blake. She told me how many letters she sent you. She never got a reply."

Something didn't add up, but I was too tired to think about it anymore. "Just leave it, okay?" I put on my earphones. My tears welled up. Mr. Pluggs wasn't in her life anymore. He had been her twelfth birthday present from me, and now he was gone. I had no more connection to her.

How did things get so wrong? From a kiss, that was how.

CATHERINE

Another crow came. The first in a long time. Elena was busy training with one of her tutors. He was crazy fast and I watched how they trained. She loved Art of War; it was in her blood.

Albert saw the crow and stood, blocking the doorway.

"I'm begging you, Catherine, just give it to her," Albert said.

"I can't. How?"

He threw up his hands. "Just put it in her room and tell her the crow came when she was out."

"He said he misses her. They're going to talk."

"Then let them talk. Please. Don't let her think he didn't care about Pluggs." His face was hard now; his patience with me was slipping. "He loved that monkey as much as she did."

He gave me a pleading look and left for his three o'clock meeting.

How the hell was I going to do this? I knew my daughter. She was going to be livid.

Blake would be around again. I wasn't ready to love him yet. To forgive him for that night, the way he'd rejected her, for that letter that had started all of this. It was hurtful. He was the dragon who was never supposed to hurt her, ever.

But Mr. Pluggs was dear to us all.

I opened the box underneath the loose floorboard. I placed his last letter about Pluggs in the box and closed it. She was doing great. She almost never spoke about him. She was smiling again. Laughing.

Lee was a great distraction, although I hated his hormones.

My happy child was returning to me, and this time it wasn't because of a stupid bond. It was because of her normal human life. A dragon-free life.

Albert would hate my decision, but she wasn't ready for this yet.

They would speak when she started Dragonia, and then she would hate my guts. Six more months. That was all I wanted.

BLAKE

It had been two weeks, two weeks since I sent her that message. No crow showed. Lucian saw me send that message.

He walked into the room.

"The crow come?"

I looked at him. "Why would he? I told you, I wasn't the one ignoring her, Lucian."

He frowned.

"You want to know the real truth why we went to China?"

He nodded.

"I didn't get an invitation to her birthday and begged my father to go. It was a visit long overdue."

"What?" Lucian sat down at his desk. "No, Blake."

"She is not the person you think she is, Lucian. She's like her mother. Holds grudges like no man can."

He shook his head firmly. "No, I don't believe that. She didn't sound angry when you were mentioned. She wanted to know if we weren't really friends anymore."

"And..."

"I told her you're more like my roommate now. I told her how you pushed everyone away. I'm not going to lie to her." His blue eyes held a challenge.

I looked at the carpet. If only she were here. Then this darkness wouldn't have been so suffocating.

"Are you sure the crow didn't lose its way or something?" he asked.

I laughed. "They are trained birds, Lucian. They

always find the location they need to find. She didn't reply."

He ran his fingers through his cropped blonde hair. He was disappointed. In me or in her? I'd carried that look a million times myself.

She never even sent me a birthday card. It was the second year now. If that didn't spell out that she was still mad, I didn't know what would. Lucian even saw that.

He looked so confused.

School was different this year. Exams came earlier. They were harder. Lucian did a Moon spell that wowed the entire crowd. He was only in his second year. Arianna excelled, too. I didn't want to know what Elena would do next year.

But that wasn't what was rumbling inside my heart.

We'd spoken a lot about Elena lately. If there was any truth in what he said—that she'd sent me letters that had never gotten a reply—then that meant something had seriously going wrong. I didn't want to think this way, but Queen Catherine was very powerful and I always had this feeling that she never liked me much. What if her mom was behind this? I knew what her compulsion could do. I had experience with that lately myself. Especially on animals. It was a great party trick among friends.

But that wasn't it.

Lucian was one of the best fighters out there. If Elena wasn't born, I would've wanted to pair with him. He would've found a way to claim me.

He'd sparred against her during Christmas. Put on a

huge show for their 'rents.

She'd gotten fast and skilled. What could I expect with, like, six different Art of War tutors? It worried me. What was our claiming going to be like? Violent? Marred with hatred, anger, and darkness?

The way Lucian told it, I was going to meet my match. And he'd made it clear that she was my match in every way.

When I denied it, he scoffed. "C'mon Blake, seriously? What do you like about Tabitha?"

"I told you before why I like her. What is your point?"

"She is beautiful, get that. She is smart, get that. She makes you laugh, but belly laugh. And her ice calms the Pink Kiss. Well, that is utter bullshit. I know about the Fire Caine."

I clamped my jaws and glared at him. "How do you know?"

He rolled his eyes. "You're not very good at destroying evidence. Don't worry, I didn't tell anyone, but you need to be careful with that, Blake."

Acidic fury rose in me. "You know why I had to do that? Because of the darkness." *Asshole.* Still I didn't see where he was going with this.

"You said the only thing that was missing from making her perfection was that dash of trouble."

"So?" I snapped. I hated when he quoted me.

He shook his head, smiling. "You don't see it or hear it, do you?"

"What are you talking about?"

"You're describing Elena, Blake."

I groaned. "For the thousandth time, she's like my little sister. What don't you get?"

His eyebrows rose. "She is far from a little girl, Blake.

She's not that Elena anymore. When I saw her on Christmas, I couldn't believe my eyes. My heart was actually racing. She's still the same Elena, but at the same time, she isn't. She grew up, Blake."

I didn't like the sound of this. What was he trying to tell me?

"She turned into one hell of a fox," Lucian said. "And if you don't see her next to you in the near future, then you need to get used to the fact that plenty of guys are going to take your place. If you weren't my friend…"

"What did you do?" It came out jealous.

"Calm down, nothing." He sounded pissed off. "But she almost kissed me. I didn't see that little annoying brat anymore. It was so hard to not give into her."

It hit me. He rejected her because of me.

It didn't surprise me that she'd grown up. Sammy had grown up; she had womanly curves, even though that sounded sick coming from her brother's mouth. I was worried about Sammy joining the Academy soon because of what she looked like. Now Elena was all grown up, too. Of course she had. It was stupid that it hadn't occurred to me.

Lucian turned his back on me to do his homework. I grabbed my laptop and tried again to find pictures of her. I needed to see her before she attended next year. But nothing. No fucking picture.

This was starting to drive me nuts.

TWENTY-ONE

ELENA

My birthday was coming. Sixteen.

I found myself staring at a tattoo parlor. My mom would kill me, but once it was on, well, she'd have to deal with it.

I went in and hid underneath my hoody. Inside it was quiet, accept for a girl in her late teens, with dark hair tied up in high short ponytails against her head.

She was chewing bubblegum and had a goth vibe going on. Her arms were covered in ink.

She looked up from her magazine.

"Hi," she said, smiling. "Can I help you?"

I nodded as I walked toward the desk. "Can you keep a secret?"

I walked out with a tattoo. The artist, Kevin, and

receptionist, Tracy, said that they wouldn't tell a single soul. It wasn't as sore as I thought it would be. And I was still contemplating the design. I didn't do it for him. I did it for me. It was the sign of the Rubicon that was on Blake's arm. It was now inked on my shoulder blade.

A reminder of who I am, not who my dragon was.

I didn't know how I was going to hide this from him, but I knew for a fact that he would see it eventually.

In a few months Sammy and I would join the Academy. Reporters wanted an interview with me about Blake's claiming since my sixteenth birthday was coming up.

I wondered if he would reveal that I sent him an invitation. I was contemplating that, but I knew it would only show him how pathetic I was.

I sat with my mom, Aunty Tanya, and Queen Maggie around a table. It was an annual tradition when my birthday was coming up.

I stared at the list of names of who we were going to invite. I stared at the name Leaf. I sighed and closed my eyes.

"Are you going to invite him?" my mom asked.

I shook my head. "He isn't going to show, so what's the use?"

She rubbed my arm. "You know what?" She took the list. She placed her hand under my chin. "Look at me. I think it's time to choose your own type of party."

WHAT?

"Katie?" Tanya yelped. Queen Maggie looked at my mother as if someone had just told her Christmas was canceled.

"Are you for real?" I asked.

She laughed. "I'm sure I will regret it, but yes. I'm giving you the rope, Elena. Whatever you want, it's yours."

New excitement emerged from my core. "Arianna had hers on a yacht this year, even though I wasn't invited…"

"You know why she didn't invite you. She thought he would come."

"I know, and then he didn't. Can I have it on the yacht?"

"I'll make the arrangements," my mom said with a smile.

I flung my arms around her. "Thank you, Mom."

She laughed. "Now go. I'm sure Sammy is waiting for you somewhere.

The days flew by. Lucian, Annie, Sammy, and so many RSVP'd. I contemplated sending Blake that invitation for a while, but then I made up my mind. He was still my dragon. Even if he was a douchebag at the moment. He was my dragon. Not some Barbie Snow Dragon's.

I rolled up one of the invites and wrote on the back, *Please come. I really miss you. You can even bring your plus one. Just come.*

I contemplated "XO" at the bottom, but neither of us wanted to remember that kiss. Hearts signified love, too, and it wasn't like that. So I just put, *Elena.*

I whistled for the crow. They were stationed on the east wing's tower. He finally came with a ruffle of warm air and midnight feathers.

I put the invitation in his pouch. He gave me the same look he always gave me. *You're not getting the message,* those eyes said. *You are wasting your time and getting your hopes up for nothing.*

"Shut up," I said to him. He shook his feathers. "I have to try."

I tied the pouch around his leg and prayed that this time Blake would answer, or just come. Anything would be better than not having him there.

CATHERINE

I heard tapping on my window. When was Blake going to give up? Luckily for me, Albert wasn't in the room.

He'd found out about my keeping the letter about Pluggs from Elena. He was furious with me for a week. He warned me not to come to him when things fell apart. He would go out of his way and use the words I hated the most: *I told you so.*

I'd made this bed, and I would sleep in it. I'd take full responsibility when the time arrived.

I took the pouch from the crow. To my chagrin, the letter wasn't from him; it was from Elena. She hasn't sent him anything for a long time.

It was an invitation to her yacht party. I closed my eyes.

I was starting to contemplate this. But with Lee there, it was too risky. I shook my head and placed the invitation in the hidden box.

I felt like I was on a runaway train with no brakes. *Just a little longer, sweetheart. I promise.*

I wasn't going to be on that yacht, and neither was Albert. I'd seen the way Lucian reacted when he saw

Elena during Christmas. Blake would do the same. And he would lure her into sin. So no. Over my dead body.

The box was stuffed with letters now. Letters that drove a wedge between them.

All my doing because of one stupid, malicious letter. All because I couldn't bear to see her heartbroken. The letter that started all of this.

Sorry. Sweetheart. One day you will forgive me. I hoped that was true.

BLAKE

Lucian had already RSVP'd. I hadn't even received an invitation yet. Still, Lucian kept watching for the crow. He even went up to the tower with binoculars to have a look. He didn't believe me. Well, he was going to be pretty disappointed.

When school was out, we went on our summer break. I still hadn't received my invitation. Sammy had gotten hers.

"Just come with me. Fuck the invite."

"And do what, Samantha?" I got annoyed.

"Talk to her. Sort this shit out, Blake. She is your rider."

"No, to be honest, I already have plans tomorrow."

My sister stamped her foot. "Then cancel them."

"I said no, Sammy," I practically yelled. I pushed her out of my room and slammed the door.

My Cammy rang. It was Lucian.

"What do you want?" I barked.

"No invite?"

I gave a humorless laugh. "I told you I'm done with

kiddies' parties. I really don't give a crap."

He raised one eyebrow. "And I told you, she's not a kid. Come anyway. Be the bigger person and apologize."

"I have, so many times. She doesn't want to hear it. So just drop it, okay? Besides, I have a gig tomorrow night. I can't come."

Lucian was not amused. "Cancel the fucking gig, Blake."

"I can't."

"Fine, I'll tell her you say happy birthday."

"Whatever." I slammed down the phone.

I considered canceling on Isaac. This party only wanted three of us. He phoned like two days ago. "Blake," I answered. Of course he knew it was me; he saw my hologram.

"You up for a gig on Saturday? Fancy affair, only wanted three of us. They even said they would supply the instruments."

"Fucking perfect," I said, not wanting more details. It meant I wouldn't sulk Saturday for missing Elena's party again.

He'd understood immediately. "She didn't send you an invite again? Damn, chicks can hold grudges."

"So not a problem anymore." I waved him off. "What time?"

"Around five."

Perfect again. That was when Elena's party would be in full swing. "See you at three at Ernie's."

"Cool. *Ciao*."

I put down the Cammy. Gigs were flying in lately, and so were the record label offers. A pity we couldn't distribute behind the Wall. We were huge in Paegeia, or busy getting there.

One of our singles, "Stupid Damn Idiot," reached the top ten on last month's chart. Best damn feeling in the world.

I jammed my schedule in the next few weeks of summer with gigs and recording sessions. I'd just drown myself in my music.

Elena would be so far from my mind.

ELENA

The yacht was about to set sail. I was only waiting for Lucian now. He'd promised that he would be here, and at two o'clock on the dot, he showed.

He was out of breath.

"Sorry I'm late."

"You are just on time, actually," I said. He gave me a hug.

"Happy sweet sixteen, Elena."

I smiled. "Never thought I would reach this age."

"None of us did." He winked. Flirting again.

I lowered my voice. "Just a heads up, Lee is here."

"You seriously still with that ass?"

"No," I hedged. We broke up a few weeks ago because I found out about Clair. "But I invited him as he is a friend."

"Fine, whatever. I'll play nice. Besides, I feel sorry for anyone who is going to try fuck up this party."

I laughed.

The yacht pulled away as I looked at the horizon one last time. My eyes caught on Sammy. She stood nearby, her auburn hair whipping in the sea breeze, watching me with soft understanding eyes. I pretended to look at something else. We pulled out of the dock.

He didn't come. I couldn't believe he'd done it again. That crow had been so right. His stares had warned me that I was getting my hopes up for nothing.

CATHERINE

This was it. Al and Tanya spoke to me. They found Elena's invite and they were right. It was time.

I got the Cammy number for Isaac, Blake's band manager. I phoned him. He picked up immediately.

"Isaac," he said and when he saw my face he almost choked.

"Blake there?" I asked.

"No, not yet. I mean, no, Your Majesty. You want me to tell him you are looking for him?"

"No," I said too fast. "No." It was gentler. "How does one hire you guys, not all of you, just say, three of you?"

"Easy, what do you need, Majesty?"

I laughed. "Blake needs to be one of the three." I never thought that I would say it.

"Okay." He didn't sound so sure but he got a pen and paper.

"All the instruments will be there. Just show up."

"Where?" he asked.

"Half-past four at the docks. A speed boat will get you there. And don't be late. Don't tell him, please. He might not show, and he needs to be there."

"Okay, I won't tell him."

"What is your fee?"

"About five hundred pagoleons."

"Five hundred? You guys are popular, aren't you?"

"If you want the big guy," he joked. I could tell he

said that a lot.

I laughed. "Make her feel extra special and I'll pay a thousand."

His eyes widened. "Deal."

I said goodbye.

The day of her birthday finally arrived.

"Thanks for handing me the rope, Mom."

I gave her a hug. "Don't make me regret this, Elena."

"You won't."

"And I hope you are going to love your surprise."

A smile lit up her face. "What surprise?"

"You'll know when you see it."

"You got me a Cammy!"

"Wait and see," I said with a tone of playful mystery. "I'm not going to give anything away."

She hugged me again. "Thanks, Mom."

I played the piano after that farewell..

ELENA

We weren't many. About ten or so. Half of them were from my class, the other half were my best friends—Annie, Arianna, Lucian, and Sammy—and Lee. Lucian kept his word. He greeted Lee and Lee greeted him back. Civil.

I'd told Lee it was over. The night after my mom caught us in my room, he'd slept with Clair, who was also in my class.

Sammy didn't understand how I could still invite both

of them.

They'd RSVP'd and I'd never really been in love with Lee. Sure I was used to him, he was a decent friend, and although the news of him sleeping with Clair did hurt, I got over it in record time. Someone else had already torn my heart to pieces.

Lee was flirting with Clair and Sophie. Sophie was another girl from class. She was gorgeous with her dark hair and big blue eyes. Everyone was trying their luck with Soph, but she was picky as hell.

It didn't really bother me. I doubted Soph would fall for him. The rest was the guys I'd grown up with.

For some reason, my dad hadn't removed the podium on his yacht and the instruments. They had probably been left there from whatever event had been held last. Seeing the instruments gave me a twinge of grief. I missed Blake.

I loved this yacht. So many good memories on it. It was where all of us discovered Blake's love for music. He'd just picked up the guitar and started playing. His father hadn't even known he could play.

But that was then, and this was now. Nothing was going to ruin my sweet sixteen.

We ate finger foods, then Lucian made a funny speech. Sammy made a cute one filled with kind wishes.

I missed my mom, but this was her present to me, and whatever her surprise was.

I got on the mic and threatened to kill my friends if they touched my father's instruments. Two staff were on board: Mica, the captain, and David, who took care of the rest. Only they were allowed to touch the equipment.

Then we started to party.

Around half past two in the afternoon, the music

blared from the speakers. I was on my first wine cooler. I took a few drags of Lucian's cigarette as I lay baking in the sun on the roof of the yacht.

"Why were you almost late?" I asked him, handing him back his smoke. "Do you know how worried I was?"

"Why? Thought I wouldn't show?"

I grimaced. "I've been let down before."

He frowned. "Why didn't you send him an invitation, Elena?"

I stared at him. "You're shitting me, right?"

"No, I'm serious."

"I sent him one, Lucian." I wiped a bead of sweat from my brow.

"When?" He took another drag.

"A few days ago."

"So he would've been at the manor?" he asked, frowning. "I phoned him this morning, Elena. He said he didn't get one."

"Bullshit. He is my dragon whether I love him or hate him at the moment. He's always gotten an invite, Lucian."

"Bullshit, Elena." He threw my word back at me. "I know you Malones. You and your mom can hold grudges like no man."

"Seriously, is that what you think of me? That I've been holding a grudge for two years?"

"Elena, you didn't even answer him when he sent you that note about how sorry he was about Mr. Pluggs."

I froze. "He *knows* about Mr. Pluggs?"

"Of course he does. He loved that monkey as much as you did. I was asking him why he was such a douchebag and he told me to just let it go and I let it slip that the Wyverns killed Mr. Pluggs. He wrote you a really nice message. He was heartbroken. I saw the crow."

I felt dizzy. "I didn't get any message." I started to get upset. *If Lucian saw this, then why didn't I get a message?*

"Something doesn't add up, Elena. Either he's lying, or you are. And I saw the crow."

I pushed myself up. "I swear to you, I never got his message, Lucian." Tears welled up in my eyes. "I thought he hated my guts and that Mr. Pluggs meant nothing to him if he couldn't even put our differences aside and just send me something about how sorry he was. Do you know how hard it was for me to get over that?"

"Okay, calm down. None of this is making any sense. I'm going to phone him. I need to find out what the hell is going on."

He would do that for me? But then again, it was Blake. He knew Lucian was here. He wasn't going to answer. It would just end up disappointing me again. I started to pace as Lucian took his Cammy out.

"Sit down. You're making me nervous."

I was the nervous one. But I plunged down next to him, staring at his Cammy as if it might bite.

"You're telling the truth, aren't you?" he asked.

I nodded.

He brought the Cammy up to his mouth. "Blake Leaf," Lucian spoke. His Cammy rang slower than the beating of my heart.

BLAKE

It was that time again. I needed a fix before the gig.

Tabitha laughed in my ear as I wedged myself on top of her.

Then my Cammy rang. Probably Isaac to find out where the fuck I was. Why didn't he just tell me where the gig was?

It was Lucian. My face fell. I chucked the phone in my nightstand.

"Aren't you going to answer that?"

"Nope." I smiled again.

Her smile disappeared. "Who is it?"

Her insecurities came back. "It's Lucian, woman, probably wanting to know if he can shag Elena. Who knows what he wants?"

I thought it would make her laugh, smile, anything. But she just got angrier.

"And you are not answering?" Her expression turned to ice.

The ringing stopped.

"What are you implying?"

"You don't want anyone near her! That is what I'm implying, Blake. It's why you aren't answering your Cammy. Because you don't want to give him permission."

I grunted. "It was a *joke*, Tabitha." I got up from the bed and went into the bathroom. When I came back in, my Cammy rang again.

Lucian. What the fuck did he want? I didn't pick it up.

"Pick it up. Tell him he can do whatever he wants with Elena."

I gave her a scowl. *Nobody will ever tell me what to do, especially a pathetic Snow Dragon.* I hit the disconnect button.

"Problem solved. Now get out of my room. I have a

gig tonight."

ELENA

I should've known. "Hate to say this, but he knows you're at my party and…I told you so."

He saw the disappointment on my face. Why did I even hope for this?

"That fucking asshole. He's been lying to me all this time."

"Don't. Believe me, he's only going to give you restless nights worrying about all the shit he doesn't do. It's not worth it, Lucian."

I got up as the yacht stopped in the middle of the ocean. "I'm going to swim, since this is my party. So you can either sit here and sulk, or you can come and join us." I went back downstairs. Everyone cheered as I reached the bottom.

I was the first to jump overboard. I hurtled through the air, free for one millisecond. *This is what it's like to fly.* Then the water engulfed me.

When I resurfaced, everyone was cheering from the side of the yacht. Lucian backed up out of sight, ran and cannonballed into the water.

After our swim I went to the bathroom for a cry. I couldn't help it. I missed Blake so much. I wanted so badly for him to pick up that phone, but he hadn't.

Sammy found me in the bathroom. I let her in and she hugged me tight. "Why are you crying?" She let go of me and I covered my eyes.

"Is it about Lee?"

"Just drop it, Samantha."

"Elena, he's an asshole. I don't know what you saw in that guy." She was deadly serious. A laugh burbled up through my tears; she always misunderstood everything.

"You are right. Big asshole." I pretended that it was Lee. I would die if Sammy found out that I'd kissed her brother two years ago, and that I was still missing him like crazy.

"Big asshole. Let him take Clair."

I let her help me clean up and returned to the party. All the while I was plagued by a single thought: *What if Lucian was right and Blake never got the invite?*

BLAKE

I had time for one beer at Ernie's. Isaac didn't offer many details about the gig, just that it was intimate and it would only be Ty, Isaac, and me in attendance.

Lucian's phone call had upset me, not to mention Tabitha's jealous reaction. Why had he phoned?

By the time I'd finished my beer, Ty was surrounded by girls. He flirted like crazy and took down a couple Cammy numbers. Maybe I just needed to get laid. No, I needed Fire Caine. I felt like I was going to kill someone.

Isaac paid the bill and nodded for us to go.

I'd thought the gig was here, but we climbed into Isaac's Jeep and he drove to the docks.

"Dude, where the hell are we going?" Ty leaned in between the two front seats.

"Private party," Isaac said. He parked the Jeep and got

out.

I saw a small speed boat. A yacht. Arianna had had her last birthday on their yacht. I blew out breath. At least it wasn't the castle.

The only thing I was worried about was that phone call and Lucian. My phoned had beeped when I left the manor and I hadn't checked the message.

I took out my phone and read it as the boat was speeding to the party. It was from Lucian.

Elena said she sent you an invite. You should've fucking canceled the gig and just came.

"Dude," Ty said next to me. "You okay?"

I felt like throwing my Cammy in the ocean. "Yeah, I'm fine," I grunted.

We neared a yacht. It was one of *those* parties. As we slowed down, a couple of the heads looked over.

"It's The Shifters!" one girl shrieked.

I looked at Isaac, not impressed.

He shrugged. "The pay was really good."

"What?" I heard a familiar voice. *Arianna?*

Her head appeared from the railing as we pulled it. "You've got to be fucking shitting me!" she said. She ran to what was probably the stairs where the boat was pulling in.

"Whose party is this, Isaac?"

He didn't look at me, just smiled. "You need to sort out your shit, dude. The queen requested us."

Shock trickled down my scalp, leaking a horde of goosebumps in its wake. "You're fucking kidding me."

Ty laughed. "The princess's sweet sixteen, ouch!" I wanted to bash his head into the fucking yacht.

"You are here, with or without a fucking invitation. Suck it up," Isaac said as Ty climbed out first.

I could hear them greeting Lucian and Annie. Then I heard Arianna being overly fucking friendly as usual.

I wanted to fly away, but I knew Elena was onboard. Heaven knew I missed her, and heaven knew how Lucian's words had been bothering me. I needed a fix. I wondered if the effect she had on me still worked.

I was nervous as hell.

Isaac and Ty were already onboard as I was contemplating this.

"Come on, you big baby. She doesn't have fangs." Arianna beckoned from the stairs and I decided…what the hell. She reached out her hand. I ignored the friendly gesture and jumped onto the steps.

The minute I reached the top, I felt dizzy. My mood was fading. It still worked. It was because of her. She was near. She always had this effect on me. Where the fuck was she when I couldn't hold on?

Arianna wrapped her arms around me as someone spat out their drink. "You made it," she said softly into my chest. She'd tried to get me to join her party, but I hadn't.

Lucian just shook his head when he saw me. "Glad you're fucking here. She is going to pee herself."

My lips curved at the way he'd said it. Arianna let go of my waist.

I slap-shook Lucian's hand, which we hadn't done in a long time. I was usually so pissed off. But tonight I would feel like myself again. I really missed that feeling.

I walked out onto the yacht and looked around. There was no sign of the brat.

Isaac and Ty had already made themselves comfortable on the soft pillows that were packed all around the edge of the yacht.

"So, where is the birthday brat?"

Lucian winced at my word choice. He looked around. "Where's Elena?"

"I think she's with Sammy and Olivia somewhere," one of her friends answered. When she locked her gaze on me, she spat out her drink. I just shook my head.

The guy who sat across from her looked over his shoulder and gave me a challenging stare. I tried to ignore it. I didn't know the ass from anywhere. He was probably pissed off that we'd just ruined the eighty percent chance of him getting laid tonight.

"What the hell is *he* doing here?" he asked. I ignored it.

Where Elena had gotten all these friends was beyond me.

My eyes locked with Sophie. *Fuck.* I felt like a jackass. I didn't even look at her again. *Pretend that I don't know her? Yeah right. You fucking know every inch of her body.*

Annie jumped straight into my arms. "You came!"

"I'm with the band, jelly bean. I had no choice."

She gave me that look, the one that begged me to tell her how the hell I pulled this off.

"I don't know how Isaac did it," I said dismissively.

"I didn't," Isaac chirped. "The queen phoned me, ass."

I squinted. "That's a first."

Annie laughed, climbing off me.

"So the 'rents here?"

"Nope, just us. Her mom said she could do whatever she wanted tonight."

"What?" I said, shocked. Her mom *never* gave her a fucking break. What was she planning? She despised me.

It's a trap.

"Chill. Relax. I'll get you a beer."

I went over to Isaac and Ty in the corner with Lucian. Arianna and one of the other girls came over. In less than five minutes, foxes in bikinis surrounded us. I hated to love it. I considered who would be the lucky one tonight. I was just getting it on with Tabitha when we'd had that fight. I needed release.

Lucian lit a cigarette and handed it to me. I cupped my hand over the cherry to protect it from the incessant sea breeze.

Annie couldn't stop smiling.

One of the girls was already flirting, but when she saw she wasn't getting any attention from me—just monosyllabic answers—she flirted with Ty. I'd already decided she wasn't the one.

Some of these girls were hot. But Sophie was by far the most beautiful. She reminded me of Irene with her dark hair and big blue eyes. Maybe we could make up. She was sitting with the guy on the opposite side.

My eyes then caught on Sammy exiting behind one of her friends on the deck. I was still waiting for Elena to come out.

They went over to the bar and I leaned past Annie to look at the girl whose back faced all of us.

She had a light shade of blonde hair cropped in a messy bob. One of the rich kids. She wore a knitted dress that barely concealed a tan bikini. She was built like a fox and had an ass like a racehorse. I glimpsed the tattoo on her shoulder: the Rubicon symbol. And we have a lucky winner! Just my type of girl.

Still, Elena didn't show. Where the hell was she?

The girls downed a shot. Sammy laughed and downed

another one.

I'd seen plenty of gorgeous backs and then they'd turned out to be dog ugly. I just wished this mystery girl would turn around.

Annie turned to see what I was staring at. She smiled even wider. "Plucky, stop staring," she whispered.

"What? I can stare if I want. They're my eyes, not yours."

She laughed again and I saw the same guy who'd given me that look, walking over to them, leaning over the blonde.

"Can we talk?" he said.

The girl didn't answer, but they left together. A challenge. Even better. I smiled and wiggled my eyebrows at Annie.

She grinned and closed her eyes, shaking her head as if she knew exactly what had formed inside my head.

"Damn some of these girls are foxes," I said to Lucian and he laughed.

He looked at me. "There's plenty to go around, dude." He smiled at one of the redheads. "It's why I'm glad I received an invitation."

We laughed.

"You guys are disgusting," Annie said.

We both shrugged with innocent expressions on our faces that said, "What?" We were teasing the living crap out of her.

"I know you, Blake Samuel Leaf, and thank heavens I'm your cousin."

We laughed again.

"Someone caught your eye?" Lucian said as I kept staring at the door, waiting for Elena to exit.

"Oh," Annie answered in a singsong voice on my

behalf. "The one who just left with Lee."

Lucian looked over at Sammy, who was still standing at the bar. She looked pissed off as she sipped her beer. "He did *what*?"

"Relax, Lucian. That girl can take care of herself," Annie said with a sly smile. "She is, after all, going to tame the mighty Rubicon in a few months."

I spit out my beer and coughed.

Both of them laughed.

"Dude, you okay?" Lucian asked and tapped me hard on my back.

I kept blubbering for a second, in pure shock. "That was...Elena?" *She has a fucking tattoo. She's hot.*

"Yes, Plucky, you perved over Elena," Annie laughed.

"Told you she'd grown up," Lucian chirped. "But dude, that Lee." He had that laugh he usually reserved for when he was extremely irritated with someone. "Promise me you'll make him disappear. Devour him or something."

I laughed. I couldn't help it. "I'm not a cannibal."

That was Elena? Man...

They both laughed again, probably at the doofus expression on my face. "You're fucking with me, right?"

"I hate to say it, Blake, but..." Lucian gave a dramatic pause. "I told you so."

I wiped my hands—which were now sticky from my spilled beer—on my jeans. "Who the fuck is Lee?"

All of them burst out laughing. This wasn't funny, not one bit.

"Warned you about that, too."

I didn't like the way he said it. The fucknut had been flirting with that other girl. I'd fucking kill him if he was going to break her heart. *I'll kill him just for the fun of it.* She wasn't his to start with. *Calm down, Blake. Just calm down.* I took a huge breath. Then I remembered that Christmas. She'd had a boyfriend. It couldn't be the same guy, could it?

Sammy finally discovered we were here. She was just as excited as Arianna when she saw me. She wanted to go get Elena, but Annie just told her to give them some time. I hated my cousin at times. She loved pushing my buttons.

They were gone for a long time. I was already on my second beer.

"I fucking hate Lee," Sammy said.

"So do I." She gave that knowing smile.

"What are you getting at?" Sammy squinted.

"Maybe she will work in a training session, kick the living crap out of an ass."

Sammy laughed. She sounded like a pack of hyenas. All of us joined in. I couldn't remember the last time I'd laughed this much. It felt good. Better than Fire Caine. Elena always was my happy place. Yes, in my head she wasn't the girl I'd secretly marked to take down tonight as if she was prey. She was still that fourteen-year-old kid who'd broken my heart. I tried to tune in but there were soundproof walls. I didn't like this.

Annie kept me occupied. Every time I found her eyes on me, she knew exactly what I was doing.

"Soundproof walls. Bummer."

"Yeah, yeah." I gave her a lopsided smile. She was enjoying every moment of this. "Would you shut the hell up?"

She laughed. "I've been waiting for the day when you finally realized Elena isn't a little girl anymore. It's so much fun finally seeing it."

I wanted to kick her. She was so cruel. But I laughed instead.

Then Isaac clapped his hands. "Guess we should sing a bit. It's why we are here."

"How much did she pay for tonight?" I said.

Isaac gestured with his hands wide apart like a fisherman demonstrating his legendary catch.

They went over and got the pair of hand drums and two guitars. One electric and another acoustic. He handed me the electric one.

"What about some cover songs? You guys up for one or two?"

The party attendees all shouted their agreement. A staff member—he looked familiar...David maybe? — turned down the music that was blaring over the speakers and switched on the mics and everything.

Isaac started singing the first song.

ELENA

"I don't care, Lee. Honestly." I laughed.

"Don't say that. I made a mistake, Elena. Clair means nothing."

"We were never serious," I insisted. "I told you."

The background music went softer and then someone changed the music. It played over the speakers of all the cabins. I just wanted to get back to my party and get away from this idiot who was now professing his undying love for me after he fucked up. The worst part was that I didn't even care.

It was a slow, haunting song I knew, though something was off about it. The lyrics had once meant something to me. I'd felt like a freak. That was why Blake didn't like me, ignored me. He didn't see what my mother and I were seeing. The artist had a deep, soulful voice. It wasn't the band that performed it originally, though. It almost sounded like Blake, but it wasn't him. I knew all his recordings and they'd never covered this song.

I listened more closely. I could've sworn I'd heard this guy before.

"What is it?" Lee finally asked.

"Who is this?" I pointed with my thumb at the speakers.

"It's a fucking song. Who cares?"

"You're being an asshole. I'm going."

"No, wait. Please," he begged. I heaved a giant sigh and sat down on the bed.

"It's because of Blake, isn't it?"

I looked at Lee. Tears were welling up in my eyes. Why did he have to mention his name? Where the hell was this coming from? "You are an asshole," I said and went to leave again. I made it as far as the door, opening it, before he pushed the door closed.

He clasped his two hands against the door with me in front of him. The air in the room was suddenly suffocating.

Count to ten, Elena. You'll put this guy in the hospital.

The main electric guitar started to play. Cheering sounds came over the speaker. Was this a live version? I shook it off.

"Elena, look at you. Why do you even care about him?"

My face hardened. "It's got nothing to do with you."

"Yes, it does, because I love you."

I thought my eyes would roll out of my head. "You don't know the first thing about love."

"He's always going to hurt you," Lee said, petulant. "You know that."

"Then that's my life. I can't fucking turn around and run. I'm the only one who can claim him. You knew it the minute you laid eyes on me."

"Don't do this, please."

"What do you want from me, Lee? You fucked this up, not me." I laughed. *I know the guy singing. Who is that?* I stared at the speaker.

Lee pushed my chin to look at him. "I know. I'm sorry."

"I don't care. You can be with Clair if you want. Why don't you get that? I want you to be happy. No hard feelings." This was true. If I had been heartbroken, I wouldn't have invited him.

He set his jaw, which sported a pathetic dusting of whiskers that weren't enough to call a beard. "I want to be with you."

I sighed. "I told you not to fall for me. We were just having fun. I'm not…"

I didn't want to think about it. His name had been mentioned way too many times today. Tears welled up in my eyes just thinking how fucked up the situation was. I still secretly believed I belonged to Blake.

I stared at Lee for a long time. My mind was set. It was over. I felt trapped. He was still blocking the way out.

Lee bent his neck, facing the floor.

Don't cry. Please don't.

He faced me again. No tears. *Thank heavens*. "Please don't do this. I'm begging you." The music stopped. *If they fuck up my father's yacht, I'm going to kill them.* I wanted to get out there.

"I need to get back, Lee," I begged.

The next song started to play. I cocked my head. It was also one of my favorites. I used to listen to this song and think I should be more patient when I was older, like the lyrics admonished. How was I supposed to know he would ignore me forever? Lucian should've never fucking phoned him today. He was going to dwell in the shadows of my mind for the next four days.

I was so over this shit.

"I love you, Elena."

I squinted at him, brought back to the moment. Why was he doing this? He'd been fine the past few hours. He'd sat and flirted with Clair and Soph right in front of me. Why was he so crazy again?

The vocals started. I froze.

"Elena." Lee frowned.

It wasn't the original artist singing this. I realized it was Isaac singing the previous song. My mother had gotten The Shifters. This was her surprise.

I hope you are going to enjoy your surprise. She didn't want to give it away.

This was Blake's voice.

My stomach dropped to the floor.

"He doesn't care about you!" Lee yelled. He could tell that I had figured out who was singing.

I ignored Lee and shoved him away. I opened the door.

Blake's voice blared over the speakers. My heart was beating like crazy. I just needed to get upstairs. How long had he been here? Fuck. Lee. He'd known. That was why he'd dragged me down here. Why hadn't I seen him?

I slipped and fell on the stairs, slick with sea spray. I pushed myself up and ran the rest of the way.

He was here.

I opened the door that went to the deck. The podium was empty. The entire party was grouped in the corner. Everyone was swaying to the rhythm. I walked toward them slowly. Ty beat on a djembe between his legs with his palms. Isaac had a box guitar in his lap, playing. His long hair was loose. He caught my eye, smiled, and winked. He was singing backup to Blake.

My eyes fell on Blake. Damn, he was more gorgeous than ever. Blake was singing his heart out with his eyes closed, his raven hair flinging across his chiseled face as he moved with the music. He strummed an electric guitar. He sang the song, his voice dripping with emotion. *The words I used to say and feel. One day. Just be patient.*

Then he played the guitar again like there was no tomorrow.

I just stood there like an idiot and drank in the sight of him. Someone else had written a song I felt was made just for me. For us. And he'd chosen it to play.

Blake belted out the chorus, eyes still closed. Strumming the strings fast. Really getting into the song. Isaac and Ty helped with backups. Goosebumps cascaded down my arms, my entire body. Only his music could do that to me. He was so freakin' good.

Then suddenly he opened his eyes as they reached the bridge and the song slowed down. He glanced at Isaac, who raised his eyes and jutted his chin toward me. Blake turned his head and looked at me.

He finally looked at me.

Those shimmering peacock eyes took me captive. I sucked on my lips. Tears sprang up in my eyes. He just stared at me, not taking his eyes off me. He didn't miss a beat. But the words really were for me now. Or was I imagining it?

I loved seeing him play. He kept singing, kept staring. My heart was beating like crazy. I even pinched myself softly.

It was real. He was here.

I broke the gaze, scared he could peer into my soul. My heart pounded as fast as the song. When I looked again, a slow, delicious smile formed on his lips. I couldn't help but smile back. He sang and let out a whoop. His gaze finally broke as he looked at Isaac and they played together. Everyone cheered.

A laugh escaped my lips just looking at them, enjoying playing on their instruments.

Then the whole party sang along. Annie lifted up her arms like an idiot, swaying to the left and right. A couple of girls undulated their bodies, Soph included. Damn, why had I invited her?

He sang it better than the original artist.

Then the chorus came again. I couldn't help but sing along with him under my breath.

How many times had I sang these words?

Everyone cheered. Fucking the song up. All of them gave it everything they could.

It didn't matter anymore. He was here. I pinched myself softly. Still hurt. He was really here.

The song finally stopped. Everyone applauded. Blake bowed, putting down the guitar and getting up. He walked past the group. Straight for me.

I felt like crying. Two fucking years of not seeing him. My feet finally found a way to move forward and I ran towards him as fast as I could. My body collided with his. I was in his arms and held on tight.

He was hugging me back, which was a good thing. He turned in a slow circle, as if we were dancing.

"You came! You actually came." I hadn't felt this happy for ages.

Vaguely, I heard girls' voices saying, "Aww!" They didn't matter. Nothing mattered but this.

He smelled amazing, like musk and something sweet. I never wanted to smell anything else ever again.

"Well, maybe if you'd actually sent me invitations, Elena, I would've come sooner," he spoke into my neck, all serious.

I lifted up my head and looked at him. "I sent you plenty of invites. Why is everyone saying that I haven't sent you invites? You never answered any of my crows." I disentangled myself from him.

"Have you smoked something? I sent you a gazillion crows, Elena." His tone was still playful.

I shook my head. "I didn't get any. Not even when Pluggs fucking died." I had tears in my eyes again.

"Come here." He grabbed me again, and just held me tight once more. I shut my eyes and forced myself not to hold on too tight. I didn't want to stay in his arms too long. I pushed away.

"Wow, look at you." I changed the subject. "I just asked Sammy earlier what the hell they're feeding you guys at Dragonia. You are huge, Plucky."

The whole party chuckled, which made me remember they were present. Annie laughed the hardest.

"Why is she laughing?"

"No idea." Blake looked at her.

"Isaac," I said as I saw him. "Congrats on the album." I hugged him. I'd missed all of them. Even though my mother never wanted me to go and see them record their albums, they were Blake's friends, and the times I had met them they'd been all protective of me, just like Blake.

"I'm not the songwriter, Elena."

"Hey, Elena," Ty said and got up. He was a bad boy, just like Blake. Girls were crazy about him. He had no filter from his mind to his tongue, either, and said exactly what was on his mind. He looked at me in a way that made me uncomfortable.

He took my hand in his and lifted it slightly up.

"You want me to twirl next?" I sounded sarcastic and everyone laughed.

He'd gotten buff these past two years. Isaac had gotten taller but was still lean.

"Look at you. Ow!" he exclaimed. I blushed. He pulled me in for a hug.

"I hope the two of you are finally going to sort out your shit tonight," he whispered in my ears.

"Ty!" Blake cried.

"Tune fucking out if you don't want to hear what I'm saying." He shot a challenging glance at Blake.

Everyone laughed.

My eyes caught on Lee standing at the bar. The bastard. I was so angry. He'd known Blake was here. He didn't love me. He just wanted to possess me. I shook my head.

Ty squinted at Lee and back at me. "We need to take him out, Elena?"

"No, I can actually take care of myself, Ty, but thanks for the gesture."

"Okay, just don't say I didn't warn you."

I narrowed my eyes. What was he talking about?

Blake reached us again. "Enough. Just sit here before I end up with one less band member," Blake joked. He pushed me gently down onto the seat next to Lucian, who was barely suppressing a chortle.

I didn't want to imagine what the joke was, but I laughed. Probably about me. I didn't care. I was just happy that he was finally here.

"Didn't you hear what Elena said? She can take care of herself, Blake," Ty said.

"What-fucking-ever," he chirped.

Sammy handed me a beer. "Good surprise?" she asked, squirming herself in between Lucian and me.

"You knew?"

"Heck no," she said. "I don't even think *he* knew."

I smiled as Blake joked with Ty.

"So what, I'm only going to get to hear two songs?" I said.

"Not even close, Princess," Isaac answered. "Which one next?"

"Any," Blake said. He took the electric guitar as they sang another cover.

The next hour went like that. We listened to the three of them singing their hearts out, drinking in between. We all cheered and the next song would play.

"How about we sing Elena one of the new songs?"

"Ooh!" I clapped my hands.

"Which one?" Blake sounded confused.

"You know. 'Home.'" Isaac muttered as he tuned the acoustic guitar. They were brilliant at getting guitar sounds out of anything that looked remotely like one.

"Okay," Blake said after he just gave Lee a stern look. Lee didn't seem to notice. Blake had a huge grin on his face. "But we take this one on a faster tune. Just follow me."

He started to play. Ty laughed the hardest. Isaac smiled and followed Blake.

Then Blake sang. Fast was an understatement. I couldn't hear a single word. It was either too fast or way unclear. Just the chorus which was *Home, I didn't care if it was the East of Paegeia or the North, I just wanted to go home.* And then he just spun out into *la-la-las.* Isaac laughed again. Blake stopped. "What?" He was serious.

"Nothing, dude," Isaac said. Ty laughed so hard that he couldn't play anymore.

"What was that?" I asked. "I hardly heard the words."

Blake shook his head while Isaac and Ty recuperated. What was with them? I didn't get the joke at all. Annie sure did, she was cracking herself up.

"Because I still haven't figured out the words yet, it's still a work in progress," he said, very solemn.

"Did your band smoke something? Because I want some of that."

"They're assholes, Elena." He strummed the guitar again.

Annie snorted and hid her face.

Blake just shook his head. He didn't look very impressed.

"Okay, next song," he said. They started playing another cover. I still wanted to know what the joke was about "Home."

My eyes caught Lee, who sulked in the corner. At

least Clair and Soph kept him company.

After the song, which gave me goosebumps again, they took a break and went to the bar with Lucian. I wished I had enhanced hearing as I looked at them. Annie was listening and I nodded at her.

She looked at me with a raised eyebrow, started to laugh and shook her head.

"What?" I demanded. I wanted to wield my shield, but she didn't let me.

Later, she mouthed, as her hand caught mine.

"Fine, then why the hell did you laugh with 'Home'? What the hell is so funny?"

Later, she mouthed again. So there was something attached to this song.

Lucian laughed hard at something. I saw Blake looking appraisingly at someone.

Don't look, Elena. Don't you dare look at who is catching his eye now. I didn't need to. It was Soph. She was so damn beautiful.

They all came back, timing their strides with the gentle rock of the yacht on the rolling waves. Blake came to stand in front of Annie. I saw the way Annie stared up at her cousin through the corner of my eye.

"Stop staring at me like I stole your fucking scales," he said.

"It's so sweet, though."

"What is?" I said. Blake frowned at Annie. He picked her up, and then threw her overboard.

"Nothing," he answered. She yelped before she hit the water. A loud splash and then surprised shrieks came from the water. The whole party careened to the side, cackling.

Blake pulled off his shirt. I gaped at his chest. He was

built too last. What the hell? Sammy laughed at me as Blake jumped overboard. "I saw that," she said.

"Oh, shut up. When did he get so big?"

"Last two years," she said. "It's good to see him smile again, Elena."

"I'm just glad he came." I ignored that last statement. I decided I wasn't going to misunderstand anything tonight and just let him have fun.

The night progressed way too fast. I didn't want it to stop. After our swim, we put on dry clothes again as the sun teetered to the west. I put on a low-cut red dress I'd been saving for this party.

We played thirty seconds. Sammy and I partnered up. We got more or less everything we said.

Blake, wearing tight, knee-length trousers, a clingy black shirt, and a button-down shirt rolled to his elbows, watched us intently. He and Isaac were ahead by a few points.

Arianna flirted with Ty. Why was everyone flirting with fucking Ty? We all laughed so hard at some of the things they tried to explain without saying the forbidden words. Especially when Ty tried to explain a word with *cock* in it.

As the sun's rays lengthened, The Shifters played a few songs again. Sammy started drinking like there was no tomorrow. She threw back so many shots, I wondered if she knew what was in it.

But nevertheless, we drank right along with her.

"Break time!" Blake announced. He got up, went to the bar, and got himself another beer. A cigarette dangled between his lips. I stayed behind. I wasn't going to interfere with anything tonight.

"Elena!" he yelled.

"What!" I shouted back playfully.

"Step into my office." The way he said it made everyone laugh.

"Yes, go sort your shit out," Isaac said and all our closest friends clapped their hands.

"Ass," Blake grunted.

He was already walking up the stairs to the roof where Lucian and I had been sitting a few hours before, speaking about the devil.

I followed him as my eyes caught on Sophie. He probably just wanted to know what her name was.

I found him lying on his back, gazing at the sunset.

I sat next to him. This was a gorgeous evening.

"Her name is Sophie, she is in my classes, and yes, she is a really nice girl," I said.

Blake laughed. "For your information, I already know Sophie."

"You do?" I asked. Of course he did.

"Yeah, don't want to go there," he said and pushed himself up, hugging his knees, looking at me. "So," Blake said. "You didn't get any of my crows?"

Oh shit, he really wants to talk. "I told you I haven't. Not one."

"I didn't either, Elena."

"I sent you like a million fucking letters, Blake." I sighed.

"I did, too. I can promise you Lucian saw me when I sent the one after Mr. Pluggs died." He fell quiet and looked at his hands. "I loved that monkey as much as you did. Since the first day I first saw him."

Tears welled up in my eyes again just thinking about Mr. Pluggs.

"I wasn't that big of a douchebag, okay?" he said and pulled me in for a hug.

"I missed you," I said. "I really thought you were pissed off with me."

"C'mon, you were fourteen years old. You didn't even get the crow I sent that night?"

I shook my head. He'd sent me a crow that night? To say what?

He scowled.

"What is it?"

I could see him weighing whether to say the words on his chest. "You wonder…who may be behind this?"

I blinked. "No. Why? You think it's someone, like, sabotaging us?"

"Elena." He laughed morosely. "Crows are trained to deliver. Unless someone shot them down each and every time over the course of two long years."

He had a point. "What are you saying, Blake?"

He didn't answer, just sighed. Then he said it. "Your mother is a powerful woman."

I tensed. "Why would my mother have anything to do with this? She's the one who phoned you guys for tonight's party."

"Yeah, that does count a lot."

I laughed the way his nose wrinkled. It was always one of my favorite quirks about him.

The reddening sky glowed on his skin. "I just don't understand this."

I sighed. "It doesn't matter anymore, okay? It's in the past."

"Just like that?"

"Yes, ever since I've been training, I've learned a lot about forgive-and-forget."

He laughed and shook his head.

As the sun sank on the ocean, the sky went up in flames and the ocean turned the color of wine. Words spilled out of us, a floodgate opened. We talked about his darkness, how pissed off he was when he had to take other measures, measures he didn't want to speak about, because I hadn't gone to him. We always had this connection. I used to calm him down.

It was so far-fetched, but here he was at my side, being normal as always. No hint of darkness. Not one.

We talked about Lee. He teased me about him good-naturedly…like a brother. Not a good sign, but at least I knew where I stood with him.

He's still not there. Just be patient, Elena.

I told him what Lee had done because I didn't want to have sex, how he went after Clair who had put out. It didn't even bother me.

Blake just shook his head.

"What? It doesn't!"

He cocked a disbelieving eyebrow at me.

I just shrugged. "I made peace with how things are. I just try to have fun."

He roared again. "So breaking boys' hearts is what you call fun?"

"Oh, shut up. Speaking of boys…what is the—what does Sammy call her? —Ice Queen doing?"

Blake laughed. "She's good. Still doing the ice thing."

"Oh, good," I said and finished my drink. So they were still together. "Then where the hell does Soph come in?"

He laughed again and shook his head. "If I told you,

I'd have to kill you."

I laughed. "Then you won't get claimed, so it's a bit of a situation." But despite how lighthearted I was, I wanted to know exactly how he knew her.

My eyes caught on Lee lurking in the stairwell. *What the fuck does he want?* Blake grinned at my irritation.

"Sammy's throwing up in the bathroom."

"Ugh." I looked up. "Your Fire-Tail sister can so not handle her drinks."

Blake laughed.

"I need to go and see if she's okay." I got up.

I reached the stairs and looked back at Blake. "No hard feelings?"

"What hard feelings?" he said.

Smiling, I went downstairs in the gathering gloom to the bathroom.

Sammy was hurling violently. I held her hair out of her face. I tried not to breathe in the horrible smell of vomit. When she was finally done, I handed her a bottle of water, washed her face, and helped her to go back upstairs. We struggled to get up the stairs. She was all legs and no stability, and every rock of the boat sent her tumbling.

"I shouldn't have had that last shot," she whined.

"Babes, you shouldn't have had those last *ten* shots," I corrected her. She laughed.

She needed fresh air.

I opened the door of the deck and caught Blake speaking to Soph. He had his shield over them. I sighed. *Anything he wants, Elena. Anything he wants.* It wasn't worth losing him again.

Lee came over and helped me settle Sammy on a seat. She immediately lay down.

"Okay, so fresh air isn't good after all," I amended. "She needs to go lay down in the cabin," I said.

"I'll help," Lee offered.

I glanced over my shoulder and saw Blake hugging Sophie. His shield was still over them.

Anything. I kept telling myself, but in reality I wasn't ready for this.

"You never fucking listen." Lee gave me his two-cent comment.

"You're a fucking asshole. You knew he was here. That was why you wanted to talk so desperately."

"I meant every word I said."

"Like hell you did." I felt so angry. I lifted Sammy up. Her head and limbs flopped like a doll's. Her dead weight was crazy heavy. Lee helped me get her onto her feet.

She moaned.

If I didn't need his help, I would've told him to fuck off. To my surprise, I saw Blake hurrying toward us.

"I've got this," he said to Lee with a smile and lifted Sammy over his shoulder as if she weighed nothing.

"I'll show you the way," I said and led him to the cabin where she could go and sleep it off. I was so happy that he was helping and not the ass. Her head smacked against the wall three times. I scolded him to be more careful. We reached the cabin at the end of the yacht and opened the door. I switched on the light and heard Sammy's head smack against another wall.

"Blake!" I said. "Be careful." I started to laugh when he did.

"She's a big girl, Elena. Should teach her not to drink this much."

He laid her gently on the bed. I covered her with a blanket I found in the cupboard.

I tucked her hair out of her face and went down on my haunches and just smiled at her. She was by far my best friend.

"You think she needs a bucket?" I looked up at Blake.

"You worry way too much. Let her sleep it off."

I tapped her nose. She was seriously a stunner.

"You sure about Lee, Elena?"

I got up from my haunches. "Yes, why? He say something?" Lee was so possessive.

"There were words, but nothing I can't handle." He had a huge grin on his face. He was teasing me about something I felt was going to be my biggest fucking mistake.

I closed my eyes. *Lee, you fucking idiot.* I opened them. Blake couldn't contain his glee.

"What did he say?" I was all serious. Blake just laughed.

"Nothing for you to worry about."

"What did he say?"

He cuffed my shoulder with a playful fist. "I think it's really sweet."

"I don't care if it's sweet. I need to know what he said to you." I was getting angry.

"Okay, chill. What happened to forgive-and-forget?"

"Not that fast," I chirped. I was ready to go kick Lee's ass.

"Just that there isn't really any room for me in your life."

I gasped. Was he out of his freakin' mind? Blake

laughed as I marched to the door. "Relax, Elena. It's not as bad as you think. The guy just cares about you."

"You're my dragon, Blake." I groaned inwardly, walking fast toward the end of the hallway. Lee was more than just possessive; he was insane. Then again, everyone had warned me about that. I hadn't listened. No, I'd just wanted some fun. I wanted to kick my own ass.

Then one of the cabins opened. Nobody came out. Blake grabbed my arm and pulled me in. He wasn't going to calm me down. I didn't care what he said.

But what happened next…I didn't expect at all.

TWENTY-TWO

BLAKE

Elena disappeared down the stairs. So, if Lee had come and tried to take her away to help Sammy, then why was the idiot still standing on the stairs?

He seriously isn't going to do this, is he?

I met his stare and squared my shoulders. They were a hell of a lot broader than his.

"What are you doing here?" Lee had a smirk on his face. "She's done great without you the past two years. Do us a favor and fuck off."

I smiled. *He didn't just say that. Easy, Blake. You don't want to hurt this guy.*

"There's no room for you in her life."

"Yeah?" I scoffed. "Then why's she spending tonight with me and not you?"

He didn't have anything to say back. I chuckled. He had balls; I had to give him that.

I walked past him and went downstairs.

Sophie caught my eye. I had to speak to the girl. To tell her I was sorry for my fucking dog-like actions. I wielded my shield around us. She listened and made me feel extra shitty by being so understanding.

"She really makes you normal, doesn't she?"

"Yes," I said honestly. "As fucked up as that sounds. She's always had that effect on me." I smiled.

She smiled kindly.

"No hard feelings," I said.

"You serious? None." She gave me a hug. It lasted a bit longer than I wanted to, but when I saw Elena struggling with my sister, who'd clearly just passed out, I told her I had to go. She smiled as she saw the messy situation. I lowered my shield and went to help.

"I've got this," I told the ass and lifted Sammy over my shoulder without any effort. Something he couldn't even do. Wuss.

Sammy's head was bumping against every corner we took. Elena scolded me and I just laughed.

She'd been driving me insane the entire night. That song, fuck, the guys had forced me to sing the song which was all about my happy place, about *her*. I had to think of something. Now that I thought about it, it had been fucking hilarious, but I'd been so annoyed with them a few hours ago. However, Elena had totally bought it.

I had to find out where she stood with fucknut. Not that it would have changed anything; I would've just upped my game then. But she'd made a mistake, told me that. She'd said she felt nothing for him. And in my experience, girls only admitted they were wrong if they really didn't want to be in that sort of situation. I should know. I'd heard that so many fucking times whenever a girl was hitting on me and I'd say, "But isn't that your boyfriend?" Not that I cared, I just wanted to make them feel shitty for what it was they were about to do.

Elena, well…she was a completely different story.

I kept staring at her tattoo. Why had she gotten my mark? I would love to know the story behind it.

We finally got to a cabin and she opened the door. Sammy's head smacked against the door. *Oops.* Elena scolded me to be careful but laughed.

I laid my sister down on the bed. Elena was so gentle with her. She made sure there was water on her nightstand and considered bringing her a bucket.

I'd missed her so fucking much.

Lucian was right. That fourteen-year-old girl was gone. Heck, that five-year-old was gone. I had no idea who this person was, but I wanted to know her so badly.

"She'll be fine. Just let her sleep it off," I said and she tapped Sammy's nose.

I told her about Lee. She got really pissed off. It was sort of funny. *I mean, I'm the Rubicon. I could kill him with a stroke of my hand.*

"I don't care if it's sweet!" She insisted on hearing what he said.

Wow, she was feisty.

I laughed again. She had no idea what she was doing to me. So I told her. She gasped in horrified rage. Then she gave me what I wanted. She said the words I had been aching to hear.

"You're my dragon, Blake."

Peace descended on my soul for the first time in twenty-four excruciating months. It was what I needed.

"Elena, just relax."

Fuming, she marched to the door with huge strides.

I kept staring at her tattoo. I wonder what her mother had said about that.

I sighed. Lucian was always right. Elena had that dash of trouble. An entire bucket.

I couldn't hold my facade anymore. I opened a door with my telekinesis. Startled, she shuddered to a halt. I pulled her into the dark room.

I shut the door and pushed her against the wall hard. I kissed her.

Her heart almost skipped a few beats and then it was beating like crazy.

At first, the kiss was normal, like other girls. She didn't even kiss me back at first, she was so surprised. But then she did. And this sensation I'd only felt when I snorted Fire Caine flowed through me. It was like I was getting high. She was my fucking fix, too.

My hands cupped her firm ass and pulled her close. The kiss became faster, deeper. I just couldn't get enough. She was driving me insane. She kissed me back, her hot breath flowing into me, her tongue vibrating with a barely audible moan.

My teeth scraped her lips. Animalistic sounds of wanting more escaped my core.

What the hell was this? I couldn't stop.

My hands finally touched her the way I'd wanted to since the minute I'd secretly marked her tonight. What had started out as a game had become something much more. Something terrifyingly powerful and totally addictive.

I pressed her harder against the wall. My fingers scrabbled at the spaghetti straps of that crimson dress of hers.

She smelled so fucking amazing, like vanilla and sunshine. She tasted sweet on my tongue. Everything was just right. Zero steps away from perfect. Just... perfect.

My lips left hers. She was out of breath. I grabbed her leg and pushed her even harder into me. A small whimpering sound left her as I sucked on her neck softly. A million goosebumps coursed over her skin.

My own hormones were skyrocketing.

"What are you doing?" A husky whisper.

She was not going to get out of this so fast. She whimpered again.

"Blake," she said a bit louder. I stopped and looked at her. "What are you doing?" she asked again with her eyes closed.

"Are you shitting me, Elena?" I asked and her lips broke out into a smile. A good sign. Then she laughed.

"I know *what* this is. I just want to know *why*." She opened those striking emerald eyes of hers.

I smiled. "You've been driving me insane since the fucking minute I saw you." I spoke the truth. I couldn't lie to her. Even if I tried. I didn't want to.

She squinted. "I don't understand."

She didn't see herself as the gorgeous being she was.

"Just shut up," I said. My lips found hers again.

ELENA

I had no idea where any of this came from, but all I knew was that kissing him was the best thing I'd ever experienced. My hormones were everywhere, like a pinball going for the high score. My skin sizzled at his touch.

I didn't want to stop him anymore. I'd speak to him later. *Just enjoy this*. I wanted this. I'd deal with the consequences later.

His hands got grabbier. He lifted my other leg off the floor and placed it around his waist.

The kissing got easier now that I was a head taller than him, my hands cupping his face. He walked me over to the bed and threw me down.

I yelped and burst out in laughter. Two seconds later, he was on me again.

"You yelling for help?" he said in a seductive, playful voice. Standing over me like a panther, ready for the kill. Taunting me with his eyes that even shimmered in the darkness of this room.

"Something tells me I'll only end up with you coming to my rescue."

He smiled. "Well, I'm here to serve and protect, Princess."

"Oh, is that what you're calling this now?"

He bent down and nestled himself between my legs, kissing me like there was no tomorrow. I thought I'd fall into his kiss forever. I was certain my mother hadn't been expecting this when she'd phoned them. *What did she think would happen?* Wait, I was *so* not thinking about my mother right now.

I tugged off his button-down shirt, leaving him with that black T-shirt that hugged his body tightly and shorts. Could he be more perfect?

"You sure you want to do this, Elena?" he asked as he pushed himself off me. It was as if he could already read my mind, knowing what I was thinking. He pushed himself onto his knees, scanning me like a prize he'd won.

"Just shut up," I breathed. I pushed myself up, grabbing his shirt and pulling him back down.

He took off his shirt and kissed me again.

It was fast, vigorous. Everything I'd dreamt his kiss would be. My body was on fire. His hands roved over my body. It felt so fucking amazing.

His hand slipped into my bikini bottom and I gasped. That was that. I was a goner.

We did it. Blake was my first and hopefully my only, too. It wasn't that wonderful, the actual intercourse part. I understood why all the girls who had done it said the first time wasn't as awesome as it appeared in the movies. But he'd been gentle and made it amazing on so many other levels. He did this thing with his tongue that literally made me squeal and squirm with a pillow over my head, trying to dampen sounds I didn't even know I could make.

I felt possessed. He was the only one who could calm me down or drive me insane with a mere touch of his hand.

When it was over, I rolled halfway onto his chest and was surprised to discover he was shivering.

"Are you okay?" I said, out of breath. He was warm like always. *Is something wrong? Did I do it wrong?*

His hand shook as he touched my head.

"Shh." He chuckled. "I'll be fine. Just need to get control over my body."

Control over his body? Oh man. When he was inside me and growling like some kind of beast, I had joked,

"Try not to shift." But maybe that was a real risk.

"Um, you're freaking me out. This always happens to you?"

He shook his head and grinned. He brushed his lips against my arm. A tiny electric shock marked the spot. "Actually, I think this is a Dent thing that wants to happen but can't, since you haven't claimed me yet."

He took a deep, shuddering breath and held it in for a good twenty seconds, then blew it out.

I grinned. "You serious?"

"I think so, yes. I've never felt this before."

Pure happiness shone in my soul at those words. I started to laugh softly. I lay with my head on his shoulder. When I woke up this morning, we hadn't been speaking. Now this. How the hell had this happened? How had I ended up here?

He kissed my forehead. Another little shock.

"Please," I said suddenly. "Don't let this be awkward. I don't know if I can handle you ignoring me again."

He laughed, his lips still against my skin. "Sweetheart," he said and I bit my lower lip. I loved hearing that. "I never ignored you. Besides, you're mine."

What, already? I squinted at him and he saw that.

"I didn't put my mark on you, you did."

Oh fuck, he saw my tattoo. Shit.

"Does mommy dearest know about it?"

I laughed. "No, she'd kill me. But it's not the reason you think."

"Oh no?" His fingers played in my hair. "Then why?"

"I had to remind myself who I am."

He smiled. "It's still the same. I'm your dragon, which means you're mine."

I laughed the way he made it sound so possessive. "And make sure Lee knows. It seems he's forgotten what is lurking inside of me."

"I was scared a few minutes ago that you'd forgotten yourself, and that the Chromatic nature was going to come out any minute. Just think about that."

We both laughed. "I can control the beast, Elena." He kissed the tip of my nose.

I sighed. "No regrets?" I asked.

"Not a single one."

Blake got dressed. I watched him putting layers back on his body.

Then he bent down. "Go take a shower. You smell like me."

Heat rose in my cheeks. He kissed me on my lips softly. "Just don't take too long."

He got up and walked out.

I sighed. *Please don't let this turn out to be the biggest mistake of my life.* I was terrified that this was the Sun-Blast in him. Annie had a thing for virgins; she was obsessed with them, and when she got what she wanted, well, she tossed them aside. I loved that dragon to bits, but she was wilder and more out of control than I was.

I freshened up in the bathroom and put on my clothes again. I checked to ensure my makeup wasn't smudged and dried my hair.

I went back up to the deck.

Blake was already up there. He speaking to everyone with a beer in his hand.

Our eyes met. But then someone grabbed me and

turned me around. I was facing Lee.

He hissed through clenched teeth, "Elena, where the hell were you?"

"I was…it's got nothing to do with you, Lee." I wielded my shield. He liked that.

"I'm not your possession. Stop treating me like an object!" I yelled.

"Where were you?" Lee was raging drunk.

"Go sleep it off, Lee," I said and let my shield down. Everyone was staring at us, especially Blake. He wasn't smiling anymore.

"No," Lee slurred. He pulled me back and kissed me. I'd had enough. I slammed my knee into his groin and hit him with my head at the same time. The movement was so fast, in a split second he was on the floor, writhing in pain.

Oh fuck. I saw the blood from his nose.

"Whoa!" Annie's voice yelled. "Ass zero, Dragonian one."

I kneeled down. "Stay away from me."

"Okay, calm down, sport." Blake was at my side.

"Get off." He pushed Blake away. "You broke my fucking nose, Elena."

"Sorry, but you deserved it."

"We are so through."

My laugh was cold. "Honey, we were never something to start with."

"Bitch," he said. I wanted to kick him, but Blake beat me to it. He lifted up his elbow and knocked him unconscious.

"Sorry, my elbow does that sometimes," he said, real cool, as I just gaped at him.

The whole party cheered. Then he grudgingly healed

Lee.

I stared at Lee's face as the blood stopped and his face returned to its normal color. The redness of his nose vanished.

I was in awe of Blake and what he could do. Completely in awe and crazy in love.

He dumped Lee on one of the side benches to sleep it off.

The party carried on. It was late now. I told everyone that Sammy had been a handful and I'd had to sit with her, and that I didn't know where the hell Blake had gotten off to.

"It's got fuck-all to do with you, or you, or you." He pointed at Ty, Isaac, and Lucian.

Then Ty got up. "Guess it's my time to tame the jaguar," he said. We all laughed as he strutted over to Sophie and started to chat with her. I guess his band knew him better than I did.

Blake just shook his head and took another pull from his beer.

"Elena," Lucian said. "That was a record time, knocking Lee down."

I struck a pose. "He is such a pushover."

"That was hot," Isaac said appreciatively.

We all laughed as Blake stared at him without any expression.

"Not like that," Isaac backpedaled. "I'm just saying a girl who can defend herself is hot. It means I don't have to do it."

I flexed my bicep to general applause.

"You're just scared, Blake," Lucian cajoled. "You know in the next few months it will be you facing this." He cocked his head at me and Blake started to laugh.

Yeah we've already faced each other… a few minutes ago.

"Little ninja." Blake touched my arm.

"You didn't fucking spar against her for an hour. I've never seen my ass so many times," Lucian said, remembering the day when they visited for Christmas. "How did you even do that?"

"Do what?" I asked.

He lit a cigarette and blew a stream of gray smoke into the night air. "You want me to tell him your moves?"

"Oh, hell no." I winked. "I've had, like, six instructors now."

"Six?" Blake raised his eyebrows. "Elena, I'm one fucking dragon, not ten."

Ty and Olivia laughed.

"You want to rephrase that?" I said, knowing that he was ten morphed into one.

"Okay, fine." He smiled. "Still, I only have one form."

We finally docked. I was glad that Blake was still speaking to me. We all said goodbye as we disembarked my father's yacht.

Lee woke up and Clair took him home. I said goodbye to Isaac and Ty, then it was Blake's turn. He took me aside and his shield went up.

"I'll see you tomorrow, okay?" He hugged me tight.

"Still no regrets?"

"Elena, none. You are not an insecure person, so stop that. Just do me a favor."

"What?" I whispered in his ear.

"Take a proper shower when you get home. Before your mother sees you. She has a nose like a dragon. She will know, and I really don't want her to hate me anymore."

"Still?"

He just laughed. I felt like a fish in a tank with everyone trying not to look our way, but they did anyway. "Everyone is looking."

He kissed me on my head and said goodbye. The shield vanished. Ty launched into teasing Blake.

He slapped the back of his head. "What? She can't hear us," he spoke loudly as they climbed into the Jeep.

Lucian took Sammy and me home. Lucian and Sammy had arranged to spend the night in my castle tonight, with my parents' permission.

Arianna slept over at a friend's house. They were still going clubbing.

I was dead beat. Tired and slightly sore. I couldn't get the images of him out of my head.

Once we were in the car, and Sammy was safely snoozing in the back seat, Lucian asked me, "Seriously, though, where were you?"

"Fine, Blake and I had a talk, okay? Everyone kept interrupting us and we had a lot of catching up to do."

"That was it?" he asked. "Just talk?"

"Yes, what else?" I lied.

He shook his head. "Nothing."

"Don't say 'nothing' like that. What?"

"He really checked you out this afternoon. He almost spat out his beer when we told him it was you."

My cheeks burned again. "He checked me out? When?"

"Before Lee took you downstairs."

I soured. "He's an asshole."

"He didn't like it, Elena."

"I get that much. Lee is extremely possessive, biggest fucking mistake I've ever made. I know, I know, you warned me."

Lucian laughed. "I wasn't talking about Lee. I was talking about Blake."

I gasped. "What did he say?"

"He was, like, crazy. Thought if you heard Isaac's voice you would come and investigate, but you didn't show. He kept staring at that fucking door. Annie thought it was hilarious."

Bad on you, Annie. I smiled. I'd misread all the signs tonight.

"And then he just said fuck that, got up, grabbed his guitar, and started playing that song. He was positive it would work. That the minute you heard his voice, you would come back."

I laughed.

"It did the trick. Lee still wanted to talk. Asshole."

Lucian laughed. "We all figured, because there were a few seconds when he was still waiting and then a huge smile appeared on his face. It's amazing what you do to him, Elena. He was so grumpy when he was still on the speedboat, but the minute he stepped onto the yacht, it was like he melted. He became the old Blake. The one who used to be my best friend. I've missed him."

Not as much as I did. "How did you know he was grumpy on the boat?"

"Oh, Isaac told me."

I laughed.

"But your shit is sorted out now?"

"Yes, it is. He thinks my mom's behind this." I

frowned. I still didn't know how I felt about that. "I told him she wouldn't even have phoned him if she was."

He kept quiet for a while. I knew exactly what he was thinking.

"Not you, too? She would never."

"Elena, c'mon. He has a point. Your mother was always so scared of this connection you two have. She wasn't one of his biggest fans to begin with."

"She would never do that, Lucian. You're wrong."

"Okay, but you need to find out who is behind this. I saw him send you a crow when Pluggs died. He even whispered sweet words to the crow."

I laughed as he said it. *Then why didn't I get that letter?*

It started to worry me. Was my mother really behind this?

TWENTY-THREE

ELENA

I did what Blake suggested and took a long shower—
at least double the length of time I usually took to bathe.
Tim, my shower's name, finally announced the final
rinse. I got out and toweled off. I'd never felt so clean
before. There was no way Blake's sent was still on me.

I pulled on my pajamas. As soon as I did, a soft knock
came on my door. I decided to leave the questions for
later.

My mom came in and she smiled. I ran to her and
flung my arms around her.

"He came," she sang.

"He came. We sorted everything out. He's finally
talking to me, Mom," I said.

She studied me.

"Thank you for calling Isaac."

Her smile crinkled her eyes. "Sweetheart, I couldn't

handle knowing that you were going to have a crappy birthday again. I'm just glad that he showed."

"Me too."

"So what did he say?" she asked.

"Something weird happened," I said, "because he swore he wrote."

"He did?" She sounded just as surprised as I was and that was my answer. She wasn't behind this.

"He never got my letters, either. So all my invitations, birthday wishes, and letters…he never got them. He thought I hated him. He said he had to take other measures when he got dark. He didn't even say what. I felt so sorry for him, Mom."

Something strange crossed my mother's face. Was it guilt? No, it must have been pity. "It's all over now, sweetheart. And soon we will have the biggest claiming Paegeia has ever seen."

I smiled.

"Thank you, Mom. It was the best birthday ever."

She kissed me on my head. "I bet Lee wasn't too happy."

I huffed. "He's an ass. I didn't even tell you what the shit did."

My mother's eyes rose. "What did he do?"

She closed my door and we sat on my bed. I told her about the thing with Claire. She was stumped. "You still invited him?"

"Yes, I had a soft spot for him, but not anymore. Can you actually believe that he cornered Blake?"

My mother threw her head back and laughed. "Oh my word, Elena. Seriously? He does know who Blake is, right?"

"Oh, he knows."

"He has a pair. That I can give you. Little shit. I hope Blake roughed him up a bit."

"There was an incident but it didn't come from Blake, I'm afraid. I broke his nose." I cringed as I said it.

"You go, girl." My mother held out her hand for a high five and I hit her palm. "I hope you didn't show all your moves to the mighty Rubicon."

"No, I didn't, but I think he's actually a bit scared."

She laughed. "As he should be. The Malones are not a family you mess with." She got up. "I'm glad the two of you are friends again. Isabel was so worried about him."

"He seems fine, Mom."

"It's only because of the effect you have on him, sweetheart. That still scares the living hell out of me."

"Relax." I fluffed one of my pillows idly. "I don't think he's there yet."

"He's still with the Snow Dragon?"

Oh fuck. I hadn't thought about that. I nodded. I had to lie in case my mother really was the one...No, she wasn't. She wouldn't have phoned him.

"Idiot. You're a better woman than she is in every way. He'll come around. You'll see."

"Thanks, Mom." I yawned hugely. "I'm beat. I'm going to sleep."

"Sleep tight. Have good dreams. I guess that saying, 'absence makes the heart grow fonder,' is true. I should send your dad away for a year."

I laughed.

She left. *Shit, was my mother behind this?* I didn't like her last statement.

CATHERINE

I practically floated back into my quarters. So happy. She didn't even suspect me. This shit was sorted without me seeing my ass. I was humming as I went inside the outer room and shut the door behind me.

"You sound happy," Albert's voice came from the bed.

I shut the door and tidied up a bit before joining him in the inner chamber. I didn't switch on the light and disturb him. Just my bedside lamp. "Everything is sorted."

My husband gazed at me with sleepy astonishment. "I still can't believe you phoned Isaac. What do you mean it's sorted?"

"I told you I know how to get myself out of a tight spot. My daughter doesn't hate me, and she and Blake are friends again." I was so happy.

"Really?" Albert sounded surprised.

"I'm the Queen of Paegeia, mister. I know how to handle sticky situations."

"Yes, sticky situations you caused. So unfair," he grunted playfully.

I was so proud of myself. "Can you believe that Blake still sees Elena as his little sister?"

"Thank the heavens for miracles."

I frowned at him, half in shadow with planes of light from my lamp across his face. "What is that supposed to mean?"

"If Elena had come home and told you that they were together, you wouldn't be in here bragging about your talents, sweetheart," Al observed. "You would've composed an entire new song that would put Bach to shame."

I laughed. "I wouldn't."

"Yes, you would."

"Go back to sleep," I grumbled. He smiled and rolled over. I went to the bathroom to get ready for bed.

He was fast asleep when I climbed in bed a while later. He'd been worried for nothing. And I...I was the happiest mom out there. I had the best teenager a queen could ever ask for. She hated the limelight and was transforming into this beautiful woman in front of our eyes.

Why Blake couldn't see it, was beyond me. Soon.

He would see it soon. *They will end up together, you didn't jeopardize that.*

ELENA

The next morning, we all had breakfast. Sammy had a hangover. My father teased her without mercy. She took it with good humor. She would rather have him than Sir Robert climbing down her throat.

Lucian left after breakfast. Dad called me into his office as Sammy went to her room to sleep more. I knocked on his door and went inside.

He looked so at home among the red velvet cushions and dark wood paneling of his office. He was so good-natured, sometimes it was easy to forget he was a king. But in this setting, he was downright regal. "So you enjoyed your birthday, sweet pea?"

"It was the best, Dad. You have something to do with getting Blake's band on board?"

He laughed. "No, that was your mother's doing."

I smiled.

"But here's our present. Happy sixteenth." He handed me a box and I opened it.

It was my very first Cammy. "For real?" I said and he nodded. I ran over to hug him and then ran out of his office to find my mother.

Her eyes widened as she saw me. "Thanks, Mom." I flung my arms around her. "You finally got me a Cammy."

"Oh, sweetheart, you're leaving for Dragonia soon. Of course I had to get you one." She helped me open the box.

It was the latest model—compact and shiny. She paired her phone with mine.

My father's was next, then Sammy's. I would get Lucian's later.

Sammy took a bath as I packed some clothes. We were going to a barbeque over at the mansion. I hadn't seen Isabel in a long time. And I was going to see Blake again. I hoped it wasn't going to be awkward.

My mom still sounded excited when I asked her, and told me to enjoy it.

She wasn't behind this. She couldn't be.

I threw my bag into Sammy's Mini Cooper parked in our garage and we went to the manor.

My heart hammered in my chest. I hoped Blake was here and hadn't crashed at Isaac's or Ty's last night.

Sammy opened the door. We found Isabel and Sir Robert around the table having a late breakfast. "Elena." Her eyes lit up. She came over and gave me a hug. "Look at you," she said. "I haven't seen you in ages. Crap sorted?"

"He's not here?" I pouted.

"Yes, he came in late last night. He's sleeping it off."

"Oh, good."

Sir Robert gave me a hug. "Happy birthday, darling."

"Thank you." My father's dragon felt like my second dad. He was always around, one of the two constant Leafs in my life.

"I need coffee," Sammy grunted. She got up to pour herself some.

"You enjoy your party?"

"Loved it! When Isaac and the others showed, it turned into the best one ever."

"I'm glad to hear that."

We heard someone skipping down the stairs and my heart beat slightly.

"Good morning. When did you get here?" Isabel asked and I turned around. It felt as if my heart had fallen into my stomach. It was Tabitha. *What the hell was she doing here?*

"Early this morning. I hope you don't mind." She didn't even look at me.

"Of course not," Isabel said. "Is he awake?"

"Sort of. The gig last night took everything out of him."

She caught my eyes. I forced a smile despite the bile that rose in my throat at the very sight of her.

She gasped. "Elena, is that you?"

"Guilty."

She gave me her dashing smile. "What are you doing here?"

"She's visiting me," Sammy barked at her, and Isabel just give her the eye.

"Look who got out on the wrong side of the bed,"

Tabitha joked. Isabel seemed to think it was funny. "Let me go get that cup of coffee. Nice seeing you again."

"You too," I lied. So she didn't even feel a tinge of threat. This sucked.

"I told you to be nice to her," Isabel admonished Sammy. "She's not so bad."

"She's a pain in the ass. You do know what's going to happen up there, right?"

I froze but shook myself from it real fast.

Isabel's mouth formed a thin line of disapproval. "She won't."

"Oh please, Mom, it's Elena. She's going to freak out on him," Sammy said as she got up and walked back to the table. "And she's fucking rude," she said.

"Language!" both her parents said.

"Seriously, what the hell is she doing here?"

"Don't. You are the teenager I don't fight with. I don't want that to change," Isabel pleaded.

Sammy smiled and I forced a skeletal smile, too.

He hadn't broken it off with her. Was he even going to?

BLAKE

Tabitha slammed the cup of coffee down on my nightstand. What the fuck was she even doing here?

"Elena," she started. "When did the two of you even talk, Blake?"

"I don't have time for this," I rolled over and pulled the pillow over my head.

"Tell me," she grabbed the pillow and stared at me.

"Why are you here?" I asked her in my grouchiest voice.

"Because I felt bad about how we left things yesterday."

"Tabitha, I don't have time for this shit. The gig was Elena's party. Yes, we talked last night and everything is sorted. I just got her back. Don't make this into a problem."

"Just got her back?" Her pale face twisted with suspicion. "Blake."

"Don't," I said a bit too loud. "I mean it."

"Fine. She isn't a little girl anymore either."

"Don't go there. It's still too early," I said, getting up. Moving past her, I opened my closet. I stepped into a pair of shorts and pulled a shirt over my head. I froze.

"Wait, how the hell do you know about Elena anyway?"

"She's downstairs."

Fuck. Fuck, fuckity fuck.

ELENA

We went out by the swimming pool. Sammy and I each took a chair. "So he's really still with Tabitha?"

Sammy turned her head over to me as if it hurt to move—which probably did.

"Yes," she said.

I was wearing a one-piece, one that hid my tattoo. Sir Robert would freak, not to mention the Snow Dragon, if she saw what it was.

"She's a pain in the ass."

"What did you mean by she was going to give it to him?"

"Oh please, Elena. I hope you didn't buy that 'Elena it's so nice to see you' bullshit," she mimicked Tabitha.

"She hates your guts because she knows what you are to him and that she can't beat that."

It made me feel a tinge better. I was something to him. She was…my smile vanished. Still with him. What was last night then? A one-night stand. I should've waited. I was so stupid.

Images of last night popped into my head.

"I can't wait till my brother Dents. She'll be so out of this picture."

"*If* he Dents," I whispered.

"He will." Samantha always heard my whispers, which was annoying sometimes.

Act, Elena. Act. She doesn't know how you truly feel about all of this or what happened last night.

I put on my shades to hide my angry tears. I could cry so easily when it came to Blake. Lee was right, he was only going to end up hurting me.

I shouldn't have come.

The two lovebirds finally came down.

I didn't even look at him. He went to his father by the grill and offered to help. His dad smiled at him and handed him the tongs.

Tabitha took the two deck chairs farthest away from us. I just glared at Blake from underneath my shades. He didn't even look at me.

Ass.

Sammy must have dozed off; she grunted when she saw Tabitha. "I'm going to be stuck with her the whole fucking day." Tabitha flipped her off after Sir Robert walked into the house.

"I'll show you what you can do with that finger of yours," Sammy said softly so only the two of them could hear it.

Tabitha got up, went over to Blake, and kissed him in his neck. I closed my eyes. I heard their voices, but I didn't hear what he said.

I shouldn't be here. I got up, took off my shirt, and dived in the turquoise water.

Sammy followed suit. We leaned on the edge of the swimming pool.

Fuck them. Fuck Blake and fuck Tabitha. If he wants her, then so be it. Still, I felt nothing but fucking regret for last night. I shouldn't have given myself to him like that. I was just a game to him, one he'd won. I hated that.

Annie walked out onto the patio. "Good afternoon, bitches!" she yelled. She took the chair right next to mine.

"Why am I not surprised to see you here?" she said and looked at Blake with narrowed eyes. He didn't look at her, pretending to be busy with the barbeque. She mumbled something Tabitha didn't like and dove in.

Constance arrived just as Annie pulled me underneath the water.

When I got up, I wiped the water out of my face.

"Elena!" She sounded just like Isabel, looked like her, too. They were twins, after all. She hugged Blake, and then Tabitha. She took one of the chairs. She put all her stuff down. "I never thought I would ever see you here," she said to me. "Look at you, all grown up."

I flipped my wet hair. "That happens in a blink of an eye, or so my mother keeps telling me."

She laughed and bent over to give me a hug. I kicked against the wall and pulled her in.

When she appeared again, she gasped for air, and splashed me with water. General Lee, her husband, walked out and laughed with Sir Robert. "Still as naughty as ever," Constance said and climbed out.

"That was the opportunity of a lifetime!" I yelled. Everyone laughed. Blake also had a smile on his face.

Fuck him. Fucking asshole.

I climbed out and enjoyed the conversation with Annie and Sammy. It wasn't such a crappy day, and I refused to feel belittled by Blake. Around five I got up and put my clothes on.

"Can I borrow the Cooper?" I asked Sammy.

"You leaving already?"

"Yes," I said, louder than necessary. "I still have some packing to do."

I didn't want to go to the Elps anymore, but I was glad for an excuse. *Running away again, Elena? Always running away.*

"You going somewhere?" Blake asked me the first question of the day.

Don't ignore him, Elena. Don't smile either. Okay, smile a little. "Yes, didn't I tell you?" I met his eyes with unwavering intensity.

He shook his head.

"I'm going to the Elps for the rest of the summer," I said. "Pappi wants to teach me something awesome."

"More tutors? You're scaring me just a bit now." He was serious, almost angry. Why was he angry? *I'm not the one with the girlfriend.* I took a steadying breath. *Calm down, Elena.*

I squeezed out a laugh. "Good. You should be very scared," I said it as a joke, but made sure he got the underlining message. He didn't laugh. The others thought it was funny, but he knew exactly what I meant.

Blake Leaf was going to discover that I wasn't just a fucking one-night stand.

I got up and started saying goodbye to everyone. Blake gave me a kiss on the cheek as he walked passed me. *Asshole.* He hadn't kissed me like that last night.

I said goodbye to Isabel in the kitchen. "You not staying for dessert?" she asked.

"I can't. I still have to pack for the Elps."

"Ooh, I'm with Blake. You are scaring me."

I laughed.

"Please don't kill him."

"Just a little, until he yields."

She laughed and kissed me goodbye. "You taking the Cooper?"

"Yes, I'll have Raymond drop it off tomorrow."

"Okay, have an amazing time in the Elps, Elena. I heard it's gorgeous up there."

"I will," I said and left.

I reached Sammy's Cooper and put the keys into the door. It ripped out of my hand and slammed just after I opened it. The idiot was here. Only he could do this. I turned around. He was inches from me. He gathered me in his arms and I struggled, incensed.

"What, now I'm good enough?" I hissed. "I'm not one of your toys, Blake. Go back to the Ice Queen." I tried to push him off me.

He just pushed me harder against the door. His shield was around us.

Easy, Elena, you don't want to fight with him in this courtyard. Big claiming...not a front-yard one.

"I don't know what she is doing here!"

I laughed. "Don't you dare give me that crap, Blake. You like having your bread buttered on both sides, don't you?"

"You are my Dent, Elena. I still have to hide the

shaking." He showed me his hand vibrating softly. "I feel like fucking crap that she's here," he said. "I want you, okay?"

I sneered. "It's just a pity you don't *tell her that*."

"Because we have a fucking barbeque with a shit lot of people. I need to tell her this in private. Please. Don't be like this." He rested his temple against mine. "I don't regret last night. I can't stop thinking about it. Why didn't you tell me you were leaving?"

I considered what he said. I decided to believe him. He'd break it off with Tabitha as soon as there weren't people around. "Because I didn't want to spoil everything, okay?" I spoke softly.

"So what, I'm only going to see you at Dragonia?"

I nodded.

"That sucks."

"I've got a Cammy." I took it out of my back pocket.

"Awesome," he said and took out his. He grabbed mine, opened it, and spoke his name in a seductive voice.

He made me laugh. Just like that.

As he lay his Cammy on mine, holding them in one of his hands, he pulled me into him and kissed me.

It wasn't a long kiss, but it was a flaming hot one, scraping my lower lip slightly and making my hormones fly everywhere like that pinball again. When the beep from the phone came, announcing that the pairing was done, we broke the kiss. My breathing was hard. I had to clear my mind so I didn't cause an accident.

He opened the door for me. "I'll tell her tonight, I promise."

"Okay," I said. I climbed into the Cooper.

He put his head through my window and gave me another kiss. "I'll see you tonight. Just answer your

Cammy later, okay?"

"Okay," I whispered and left.

BLAKE

I went back into the house. This could've gone terribly wrong. I needed to tell Tabitha tonight that it had been fun, but this was my reality. She'd always known it.

A voice cleared in the kitchen. *Fuck.*

I turned around and found my mother staring at me. "You spying on me?"

"So you *just talked*?" I'd never seen a more disapproving look on her face, and I had earned a lot of disapproval form her over the years.

"Mom, don't. You know what she does to me. Yes, okay, I don't see her as my little sister anymore. I thought this was what you wanted."

"What we wanted? Blake, Tabitha is outside." She pointed angrily toward the pool. "This isn't how I raised you."

"I didn't get the time to tell her yet, okay?"

She pinned me to the wall with her stare. "Oh, so now it matters how you deal with this?"

"Yes, I'm not that angry little shit anymore. I'm normal again."

She pointed that finger at me and shook it. "Do the right thing, Blake. I like Tabitha, but that's Elena."

"Mom, you think I want to hurt Elena? Jeez." Shaking my head, I walked back outside.

My mother watched me like a hawk the rest of the night. She wielded her shield as she spoke to Constance.

"Okay, what is up with you?" I heard Constance

whisper. If she knew that I could penetrate shields, Mom would rethink what she said in this house sometimes. "What did Blake do that you are giving him the evil eye? I mean, you're not even blinking. Did Tabitha lay an egg or something?"

Seriously? I thought.

"No," my mother said. She laid her head back on the chair.

I had my shades on, lying next to Tabitha and watching my mother closely.

"He's going to break up with Tabitha."

Constance gasped. "It's a good thing, right?"

"He kissed Elena," Mom said. My cheeks reddened; I hadn't been sure if she'd seen us. "And not just any kiss. I didn't even know you can kiss someone like that."

Constance laughed. The snorting kind. This was so embarrassing. "When?" she asked.

"Just now, when she left. The little fuck didn't go to the bathroom. He waited for her outside. I'm scared."

Constance made a thoughtful humming sound. "C'mon. About what? What Kate said?"

"Yes! She said it was so intense. I fucking saw that. With Tabitha it was one thing. They could do whatever they wanted just as long as it wasn't in their dragon form, but with Elena…"

Mom!

"I'm not kidding. Remember Cooper and Merica?"

Constance's gaze landed on me. "You know, I get the feeling he can hear every single word we are saying."

It took everything out of me not to smile.

"C'mon, he's not that good."

I tuned out and pretended to not care about their stupid conversation. I didn't want to give any of my talents away.

The shield finally vanished. My mother got up from her chair and walked to my father, who was chatting to General Lee. My dad picked up on it and asked what was up with her.

She just shook her head.

My Cammy was burning a hole in my pants. I wanted to speak to her so badly. The hours ticked off extra slowly. Around nine I told Tabitha that she needed to say goodbye, and that we were going to leave.

I hated that she was so friendly. Well, she needed to make it a good one as it was going to be her last goodbye.

My mom hugged her last. *Don't you dare give this away.*

"Drive safely," my mother scolded me. I narrowed my eyes.

We climbed into my Mustang and I pulled away from the manor.

"I'm still so fucking upset with you," Tabitha said, surprising me.

"About what?" I growled.

"You could've phoned me last night and said that it was Elena's sixteenth birthday party."

"And then what, Tabitha? Were you going to fly over?"

She got upset and stared out the window.

I sighed. "You knew who I was from the start, Tabitha."

"So?" she carried on.

"You knew this day was coming."

Her eyes narrowed. "What day?"

"This has to end."

"What has to end?"

"Us," I burst out, exasperated with how dense she was being. "You are one of the smartest girls I know. I can't do this anymore. Elena is starting Dragonia Academy soon."

"She understands, Blake." She started to change her tone. Guilt tugged at my heart. "She always has. She isn't that person you think she is."

"I don't want her to understand, okay?" I said in a stern tone.

Her eyes stayed on me, filling with tears. I kept one eye on the road and one on her. I saw it dawning on her. She crossed her legs and looked out the window. "Something happened last night, didn't it?"

I nodded.

"She's fucking sixteen."

"Don't give me that crap. We were sixteen, too."

"You don't mean that. Please. I love you, Blake."

I squeezed the steering wheel harder than strictly necessary. "It's over, Tabitha. It was never going to work. I told you that from day one."

"You're a fucking asshole. Just stop the car."

I glanced at her to see if she was serious. "Don't be like that."

"I mean it, stop the car. I can find my own way home."

"Fine." I skidded the car to a stop. She got out.

I watched in the rear view mirror as she pulled off her clothes and morphed.

Racked with guilt and more than a little anger, I drove back home. Everyone was surprised when I entered the front door.

"Everything okay?" my mother asked.

"Peaches and cream, Mom."

CATHERINE

Elena came back around five o'clock. This girl didn't give me any heartaches, none. "Party not interesting?"

"No, it was fine. I just felt like coming home," she said.

The three of us had dinner and watched some television together. Then Elena's Cammy beeped. She didn't look at it.

"I'm going to crawl in. See you tomorrow."

"Tomorrow is your last day!" I cried animatedly.

She smiled. "About that, do I have to go?"

Where was this coming from? "You don't want to go anymore, Elena? You would be the best of the best if the Elps guards trained you."

"He's just a dragon, Mom." So self-assured.

I muted the television. "No, he isn't. He's the Rubicon. I will kill him if he hurts you."

She ran a hand through her short hair. "It's going to happen, him hurting me. Whether you are going to kill him or not. It's a claim. That's what happens in claims."

I sighed. "I know."

"I'm ready with what I have. Please let me stay."

"Elena," Albert said. "It's the Elps' guards. Pappi is looking forward to your visit."

She swallowed as if taking a spoonful of ill-tasting medicine. "Okay, I'll go. I was just starting to wonder if I needed extra training. That's all."

I kissed her head. "He is the Rubicon. You do."

She smiled. "Okay, then I'll go." She went up to her room.

I turned to Albert and threw up a shield. "She's

worrying me. She was looking forward to this."

Albert smiled. "Don't do this, Katie. We both know what is making Elena want to stay."

I hated Albert's silly comments. He forced me to worry for the both of us. The chilled, laid-back attitude he'd carried with him all these years when it came to Blake and Elena was driving me insane. That led me do insane stuff.

I sighed and unmuted the television. I needed to clear my mind. I wanted to go and play the piano...but no, it wasn't that bad yet.

ELENA

It was a message from Blake. I closed my door and opened my Cammy. I had like a gazillion from Annie and Sammy. Both wanted to know why I'd left so early. I wasn't leaving until the day after tomorrow. I went with *I was tired*.

I opened Blake's message.

It's done. It's over. She's not happy, but she knew from the beginning. What are you doing?

I grinned. He'd broken up with Tabitha. Yes!

I wrote back, *I'm in my room. Tried to cancel the Elps. You are, after all, only one dragon. No luck.*

Beep. *We just made peace and now you're leaving again.*

I tapped out, *It sucks. I know*.

My phone beeped again. *Am I going to see you tonight?????*

I smiled. *You know you are. Where?*

His message was immediate. *Still a naughty little shit.*

I laughed.

Your treehouse, after the 'rents go to bed? He sent.
Okay. See you later.

My phone beeped again. *You bet your sweet ass you will.*

I laughed and put my Cammy inside my drawer.

I went to take a long bath. I shaved my legs and whatnot. The treehouse. *Oh my freakin' word.*

Images of the previous night popped into my head. I didn't know if this was going to happen again as I was still a bit sore from last night. But there would definitely be a spike in my hormones. My mother would have a fucking heart attack if she knew that I'd lied about Blake not being ready yet.

But for now, she didn't need to know.

I went to their room and said goodnight. My mother smiled over the pages of a book in her hand. My father blew me a kiss as he walked to the bed from the bathroom. He was seriously built for an old man. He looked at me. "What are you looking at?"

"You sure you're two hundred and seventy?" I asked and he laughed.

"He's your father, sweetheart." My mother laughed.

"So what? He looks good. I can't give him compliments?"

She laughed as my father did a little dance in front of my mother.

"Okay, that I didn't have to see. Goodnight," I said and left.

I could hear their laughter as I closed the door and went to my own room.

I waited for them to fall asleep and then I pulled on my slacks, rolled some of my towels up thick and placed them in my bed with one of my blonde wigs sticking out.

Just in case Mom checked up on me.

I pulled on a shirt and slacks and grabbed my sleeping bag and a lantern. I tiptoed along the hallway and down the stairs. Felix was snoozing in my father's room, so I closed the door. I went through one of the side doors and made a run for the treehouse a few yards away from the castle.

I climbed the ladder. Disappointment hit me; he wasn't here yet. I pulled out my Cammy.

Where are you?

He didn't answer. He was probably flying.

I waited for what felt like forever. The lantern was a globe one because of what had happened when I was five years old. It was before he'd gotten his human form. It wasn't my fault and it wasn't Blake's either. He'd had the hiccups. We couldn't get the fire out. I took the blame said it was the lantern, but my mother was furious.

I heard a rumble, not enough that it would wake my mother. Then I heard him climbing the ladder.

He only wore shorts. His shirt was balled in his fist along with his shoes. He hadn't bothered dressing fully after shifting. *Oh man.*

I lay in my sleeping bag already. He tossed his bag in the corner. His muscles bunched as he hoisted up the ladder.

He threw it into the corner and crawled over to me, and our lips met. I kissed him back. In two seconds I was on my back. He was climbing into my sleeping bag and carried on kissing me.

"You miss me?" he said.

"Not that much. I was pissed off with you for almost the entire day."

"Sorry about that. I felt really crappy. She just showed

up unannounced. I had no idea what to do. Sorry."

"Is it over?" I was stern.

"Yes, I told you it's over." He nestled himself in between my legs. Our lips found each other.

I flinched.

"You okay?" he asked.

"It's still tender." Heat rose in my cheeks; I felt embarrassed that he noticed.

"Well, I can fix that," he said in a seductive way and his head disappeared under the sleeping bag.

He pulled off my slacks and I had to suppress my laughter as he really struggled doing all of this in the confined space of my sleeping bag.

Then he did the tongue thing again and I was gasping for air.

CATHERINE

The phone rang. Who the hell was phoning us at eleven o'clock at night?

I picked up the phone. It was an unknown number. No hologram showed.

I heard a girl crying. "Who is this?" I asked.

"Your little princess is not as innocent as you think. She can't keep her hands off other people's property." The phone disconnected.

I squinted. Dragons were more likely to refer to "property" than humans. I froze. The Snow Dragon. No, Elena said that Blake didn't see her in that way, unless... she wouldn't.

She'd lied.

I went to her room, knocked, and peeked in. There she was, asleep in her bed. She was innocent. I closed the door and went to my chambers.

"Who was that?" Albert asked, his voice thick with sleep.

"Nobody, a spoiled brat. Go back to sleep."

"A spoiled brat?" Albert asked.

"Yes," I grunted. "Go back to sleep," I said.

He did, but I couldn't. Was she and Blake hiding their relationship from me? I didn't like that thought one bit. I tossed and turned and eventually got up and went to Elena's room. She could sleep late tomorrow. I had to know.

"Elena," I said but she didn't mumble or anything. "Sweetheart." I touched her. It wasn't a body. I flipped on the light and found towels in her bed as I pulled back her covers.

That little... She'd lied to me.

I fumed. Where the hell was she? I thought about to waking Al up. Then her treehouse jumped into my mind. I changed course and went to the treehouse.

A cold finger rushed up my side as I heard soft moans. *No, no, no. She is just a baby.* I rushed faster and wanted to explode.

She would be grounded forever. She would never go to Dragonia. Ever. "Elena Malone, you get your ass down here."

She went super quiet. I knew the little fuck had wielded his shield. I couldn't get up there; the staircase was rolled up. I left. I'd never been this livid in my entire life. I went and woke Al up.

He took one look at my face and scrambled out of bed. "What is going on?"

"She fucking did it."

He blinked owlishly. "Did what? Who are you talking

about?"

"I caught them in her treehouse. Her and that…" I took a deep breath.

Al squinted. "Lee?"

"No," I screamed, pacing frantically.

"Just get your ass downstairs or I will kill them both."

ELENA

"She's going to kill you!" I yelled at Blake. This was mortifying. How did she know?

"Elena, calm down." Blake smiled. "It's not the end of the world."

"I want to die," I cried.

"Just calm down, okay? I'm not going anywhere." He pulled on his shorts and shirt and leaped through the hole with the ladder.

I got dressed. His scent was all over me again. *My father.* I cringed. I followed him to the castle. This was the queen and she was crazy.

Blake smiled.

"It's *not* funny. My mom almost walked in on us," I whispered.

Blake's tone was light. "She can actually hear what we are saying right now, Elena."

That made my blood run cold. "She's fuming, isn't she?"

He grinned again and nodded.

"This is not funny. She's going to ground me forever."

His eyes were filled with mischief. "I'm not going anywhere."

The kitchen light was on. The side door next to it was

open. I walked through that door. My father and mother were both waiting for us. "You lied to me!" my mother shrieked as I entered the kitchen. If she'd been a dragon she would've breathed chlorine gas.

"You gave me no choice, okay?" I yelled back "You would just play your piano again."

Blake's smiled vanished. My father stared at him. "Don't look at him like that, Dad. It's not only him."

"Oh, you threw yourself at him, Elena?" Mom was apoplectic. "He knows better. He should've just told you no."

Blake raised his eyebrows at my mother.

"Don't you dare give me that look. I knew the minute you were back shit was going to happen. You are such a bad influence on her."

"Stop." I slammed my hands on the table. A teacup rattled in its saucer. "I messed up, okay. I'm not your fucking ideal daughter. Seriously, Mom. You've said it so many times."

"Don't you dare bring Cooper and Merica into this, Elena. You are sixteen years old. Blake is almost twenty. You know how bad this can get if it gets out."

I scowled. "Well, the way you are screaming, I'm sure it will, Mom."

"Don't." She pointed her finger at me. "You're grounded. You will leave for the Elps, you won't see Blake tomorrow, and I'm taking your Cammy away. I'll think of how I can tutor you here, as you can forget going to Dragonia Academy."

Shock hit like a wall. I didn't expect that. "Mom!" Tears sprang to my eyes at the mere thought of such a fate.

My father finally broke his silence. "Katie…".

"Don't you dare."

"Seriously, withholding Dragonia Academy?" Blake opened his mouth. "Tell me something, Your Majesty. How did the crows disappear?"

"Don't you dare use that tone with me!" Her rage kicked up a notched just because he was the one talking.

"Answer me." His fury almost matched hers.

My mother gave him a scathing look. "I don't know. Maybe there were no crows to begin with, Blake."

Though he was wound as tight as a piano wire, he kept his voice low as a counterpoint to Mom's hysterics. "I wrote to her every week for an entire year. There were crows. How?"

Every week?

"I warned you…"

"I know you can compel animals. It's not that hard to use meta-compulsion on them. I do it all the time. Best party trick ever."

My mother's nostrils flared.

The horror of this possibility descended on me. "What?!" I yelled.

My father closed his eyes and sighed as if all he had to do was wait for a grand spectacle to unfold.

I faced my mother and searched her eyes for any sign of guilt. "It was you?"

She sputtered. "Elena, I'm not on trial."

"Mom, he was dark. He *needed* me and—" I couldn't finish. I just couldn't.

"Why did you call my band if you hated me that much?"

"I wish I never had," she spat.

"I hate you!" I screamed at her. "You had no right. You lied to me." I started to cry. "You made my life a living hell for two years! How do you expect me to be honest with you if you lie to me?"

"Elena," my father said. His tone was quiet and pained.

"No, Dad," I cried. I rounded on Mom. "It's your fault. Absence made the heart grow fonder, Mom. If you'd just let me have his letters, none of this would've happened!" I yelled and ran to my room.

I could still hear Blake and my mother speaking. His voice disappeared.

My father tried to speak to me later that night. It turned into a fight about how disappointed they were. I didn't care about any of them at the moment. They'd tried to keep us apart.

She took my Cammy and I couldn't even speak to him.

The phone rang in the early hours. My mom was fighting with someone and from the yelling I knew it was Isabel. She would be furious to discover my mother had toyed with his struggle with darkness. I would be, too. He had teetered on the edge and she had withheld the one antidote. It was just a game to her.

It was morning before I finally fell asleep.

The next day I didn't want to see any of them. I took a long bath. I cried a lot. I only heard someone entering and exiting. When I got out, there was a box on my bed. I opened it.

It was letters. Our letters. There were so many. Two fucking years' worth.

I read all the ones he'd sent me. He had hated me after a while. Even the one he sent after Pluggs died. It made me cry. He missed me so much and just wanted to see me so badly.

She'd been here, lying to my face.

I threw the letters on the floor with the box and cried inside my pillow as hard as I could. The anger didn't dispel.

Felix slept in my room that night.

My animals were the only honest creatures I had in my life. I put Blake into that category, too. He'd never actually lied to me.

I struggled to sleep that day. I spent the entire day in my room. Staff entered to bring me my meals. I returned it untouched.

This was insane. She wasn't going to send me to Dragonia Academy. How was that even possible?

When I woke up, I prepared for my departure to the Elps. This was going to be three fucking long weeks. When the carriage arrived, I picked up my bag and went downstairs. Sir Robert was standing outside with my father and mother.

I didn't want to greet any of them, just went over the carriage and threw my bag onto the seat.

"Elena," my father said.

"Don't, just don't," I said.

"Let's just talk, okay? For a minute."

"I have nothing to say to you two!" I yelled at them both.

My mother didn't even flinch. She was a psychopath.

My father walked toward me. Gravel crunched under his feet. "What you did—"

"Don't, Dad."

"Let me finish," he said in his kingly voice. "I'm disappointed, Elena." He had tears in his eyes. Mine welled up, too. My father had never said that to me before. "But you are human, you are still my daughter.

Maybe I wasn't hard enough on you and Blake. Your mother felt that she had to do it for both of us."

I shot my mother a dirty look. "It doesn't justify what she did."

"I know we disappointed you, too. I'm sorry, sweet pea." He pulled me close and kissed my head.

I felt him put something inside my pocket. My curiosity sparked immediately but I kept my cool.

"We'll talk about the other things when you get back, okay?"

I nodded. He looked over to my mom. I wasn't going to speak to her. I didn't care how much I'd disappointed her. The steely gray sky above reflected my emptiness.

She just looked at me with her judgmental eyes.

Sir Robert's gaze was soft. All of them knew. It was so embarrassing.

I turned around and opened the carriage door, when I heard a screech. I turned around. We all did, except my dad.

It was Blake, flying in fast from the sky.

I looked at my father.

"Albert!" my mother yelled.

"You need to make peace with this, Katie. This is enough," he said.

"I can't believe you," she said through gritted teeth.

"Don't start," Sir Robert said to my mother. He was also angry at her, but I didn't care. Blake was here. He came in hard. The earth rumbled and then he shifted. A servant rushed out with a robe and he shrugged it on in a hurry. Nudity just reminded everyone of what had happened. I ran to him and collided with his body. He hugged me tight.

"Shh, it's going to be okay," he said.

"It's never going to be okay. She's ruining my life." I cried again.

"I'm not going anywhere, Elena," he said and I looked at him. His peacock blue eyes shone. He wiped mine with his thumb. "I love you," he said. "I always have; I just didn't know that until now. Sorry."

It made me more furious about what my mother had done. She'd kept us apart for two years. I'd missed two years of his life.

"I'm sorry. I should've hunted your ass down. Then none of this would've mattered."

He chuckled. "You should go. Go learn some more tricks that will scare the living crap out of me."

I laughed. I kissed him. I didn't give a shit if my mom was going to have a heart attack. Maybe then all my problems would be solved. I walked over to the carriage.

Thanks, Dad. I mouthed and climbed in.

The carriage took off as I put my hand into my pocket to see what my father had put in. I pulled out my Cammy. I burst into tears.

TWENTY-FOUR

CATHERINE

It had been a week. Elena hadn't phoned any of us. I wasn't speaking to Albert because of that stunt he pulled. He'd completely undermined my authority.

Now, I was looking for tutors. I wasn't going to see my daughter pregnant at seventeen. They could forget about it. She would get her lessons right underneath my nose. She already knew half of her classes.

A knock came on the door and Albert entered. He glanced over at the table and looked at the names and CVs on the table. "You're kidding me, right?"

I glared at him and dialed one of the numbers.

Albert shoved everything off the table. Papers floated in a mess to the thick carpet. "Enough, Katie. What don't you understand by enough?"

"Don't you dare…"

"No, you don't!" he yelled. I hadn't seen this Al in a

long time. "I told you this was going to happen when she found out. I wasn't even the one doing it, but she hates my guts, too. If we lose her it will be your fault, not mine."

"And what, Al? I should just hand her a pack of condoms and tell her to enjoy?"

He huffed. "Whatever works for you, Katie."

"Over my dead body!" I yelled.

"Remember what you said," he tried a different tactic. "When we waited for her to come back. To promise one another that one of us would always listen."

I remembered that day vividly.

"You weren't listening, not one bit. She doesn't give a damn that she disappointed us, because we hurt her more. We, her parents, tore her heart out and trampled on it. The two people she needs to feel the safest with. Who do you think she will go to when she has problems? It won't be us. It'll be him. You drove her into his arms. You made it worse."

Tears welled up in my eyes.

He barreled ahead. "I know you saw them, Katie. Heaven knows I wish it had been me, but I made peace with this a long time ago. You didn't." He had tears in his eyes.

"Blake turned dark without her. We know what she is to him and you withheld that from him. I know you felt bad, but he had to fucking use Fire Caine just to control himself. It's why we sent her away in the beginning, so that if anything happened to us, at least he would get claimed and we wouldn't lose him. We almost did, because of you."

I closed my eyes, thinking about what I had done.

"This is bigger than a mother's jealous love for her

daughter," he said bitterly. "You lost sight of the fate of the nation. You're supposed to be a queen. I don't know who you are anymore. You're losing yourself. This is tearing you apart, changing you into something you're not."

The truth in his words stung. I started to shake with sobs. Al wrapped his arms around me.

"When she comes back, she goes to Dragonia Academy." He paused and met my eyes to see if I was listening. "And fuck what everyone says. If she gets pregnant, we'll deal with it. But no more. I'm a king but I'm a father, too, and I don't want to lose my only daughter."

I gasped. *He doesn't care.*

"I need to know that you are at my side. Apologize to Isabel and Robert. Swallow your pride. You were wrong, Katie. I should've never let it go this far."

I nodded. He'd used Fire Caine. *What have I done?*

He hugged me again.

Who the hell had I become? This wasn't how I'd dreamt of raising her at all.

ELENA

It was time to go home from the Elps. The first day of Dragonia Academy's new year had just passed. Not that I was going. Mom had made that very clear. I would probably have an entire school building all to myself. This was so unfair. I still couldn't forgive her for that.

Pappi tried giving me some wisdom. Why she had done it. I didn't care why she'd done it.

My father tried to phone me, but I couldn't deal with

them. I was just so mad at all of them.

I called Blake a lot. I missed him. The first two weeks were great. We talked so much, but then I could see him fading again. He was grumpy, spoke about dark things. Why should we do this if I wasn't going to go to Dragonia?

I cried a lot. Especially when he didn't pick up his phone. He was going dark again without me there. I hadn't spoken to him in the past five days. I was worried that he was giving up on us. It would totally be my mother's fault.

Pappi hugged me as I went to leave. "Thanks for letting me stay, Pappi."

"Always, he said. "As long as you learned how to keep your heart calm and to slow down everything, you will dance circles around him. Go get your dragon, Elena."

I climbed into the carriage. Training with Pappi and the Elps guards had taken longer than expected. They were an elite group of guards. Only the best of the best were chosen to become one of the Elps guards.

I still had to choose a date, and if it was up to me, I would make it tomorrow. But I knew my father was going to want to make it a huge national event, as it was the first claiming in the Malone royalty line. Maybe we would see each other for the publicity he wanted to capitalize on.

It was going to be big. I should deprive them of it out of spite, but I couldn't.

So for the next few days I went through a lot of training, to refresh everything I'd learned the past two years.

I was still so upset. It made me feel sick at times. I

didn't want to live with this, or like this.

When the carriage stopped at the castle, my father and Sir Robert welcomed me home. My dad hugged me. "Go give your dirty clothes to Maria."

I shot him a puzzled glance. I wasn't going to unpack right this second. "I can do it tomorrow, Dad. There is no rush."

"Oh, really?" he said and squinted. "You need to go to Dragonia Academy, sweet pea. Classes have already started." My father had a confusing look on his face.

I stared at him. "But Mom said that…"

He smiled. "I sorted that out."

"I'm going to Dragonia?" My voice turned shrill at the end.

"That is what happens when you turn sixteen."

I shrieked and jumped up and down on the spot. "Thank you, Daddy!"

"Don't make me regret it, Elena."

"Never," I said and ran into the house. "Maria!" I yelled.

I still hated my mother, but she'd apologized tearfully. She hadn't given me an explanation of why she'd done it. Just some nonsense that she wanted us to have a break because of how intense our relationship would be. Then she retreated into her chambers.

That night my father discussed Blake's claiming date with me and Sir Robert. I hadn't ascended yet, but everyone believed I would if I faced him. I knew what would happen if I ascended. It was something my father looked forward to as I would see him. He would guide me through the entire claim so indirectly it wouldn't just be me who was going to claim him, but both of us, and we always referred to 'we' when we spoke about my claiming Blake.

Sir Robert had a huge grin on his face just listening to all of this.

"Dad, two weeks for marketing?"

My father laughed. "Okay, then when, Elena?" He was giving me everything I needed.

"Next week. Please. He's getting dark again. And fast."

"Okay, next week. I will arrange some tutors for this week to keep your mind fresh."

"And no Blake, Elena. He can't be present when you train," Sir Robert warned. "He's really fast at picking up moves. He will use it against you."

My father blew a gust of breath from his lips. "You sure about that?"

We all laughed. "Yes, he is the Rubicon. It's not in his nature to yield. It will be a claiming we won't want to miss."

They were looking forward to it. So was I. At least he'd stop shaking.

I could only imagine what this claiming was going to be like. It was going to be big. Something I'd only dreamt off for the last two years.

I tried to phone Blake, again no answer. I hated that so much. *Why doesn't he want to speak to me?*

He was driving me insane again. Making me worry for nothing. I sighed.

I tried Lucian, but he didn't pick up either. Where the hell was everyone? Sammy's Cammy went over to voicemail, too.

Dammit. One more night, Elena. Just one more night.

I left early the next day. Like, really early.

My father hugged me tight. My mother had a package in her hands. "Just in case," she said and I frowned.

"Fine," I said goodbye without giving her a kiss and climbed into the carriage.

"Enjoy your first year," my father said. I waved at him. He was in my corner, controlling my mother for once.

I couldn't wait to get to Dragonia.

I opened the package and flinched. It was a box full of condoms. How embarrassing. I put it in my bag.

I took an elevator to Elm and another carriage waited for me at the port.

It was amazing to dodge the reporters. My dad said they'd been at the Academy yesterday. Suckers. They'd be upset that they'd missed the photo op of the princess leaving for Dragonia.

Everything happens for a reason, like Jako always said.

I landed at six-thirty and was greeted by Master Longwei. He took me up to the girls' dormitories. I just wanted to go and say hi to Blake. He and Lucian were sharing a room on the seventh floor.

I would find it easily because he'd described Dragonia in detail to me during our first week of telephone conversations. His logic had been that if I sneaked off at night, at least I would knock on the right door. Of course back then, we hadn't known for sure that I would go.

It made me smile.

My room was way up in the tower. On the top floor. It was quite high looking down. It was the biggest. I could understand why none of the other royals wanted this view. But I loved it. I'd always loved the sky. I was made for the sky.

It made me think about Cara again. She hadn't awoken, not once. But she was still with me. I knew it, deep down inside my heart. The Thunderlight who'd given her life for a princess.

"Can I have a roommate?" I said.

Master Longwei smiled. "As long as it's not the Rubicon, Princess, yes."

I laughed. "No, his sister."

He nodded. "I'll make the arrangements."

"Thank you, Master."

"Welcome to Dragonia Academy, Elena."

I smiled.

I waited until he left and went to the boys' dormitories. It was still early and I couldn't wait to see Blake. I knocked on his door. My heart thundered inside my chest.

Lucian opened, and his eyebrows shot up to the sky.

"Surprise!" I cried and hugged him.

"I thought you were…"

"My dad overruled her. Where is he?" I spotted a girl's leg sticking out from a bed.

I raised my eyebrow at Lucian, but he didn't look embarrassed. He looked guilty. "Elena, he's really gotten dark."

I got what he was saying. I shoved him out of the way and stormed over to the bed. Snow white hair.

"Where is he?" I demanded. She was alone in the bed.

She woke up and saw me. If looks could kill, we both would've been dead.

Lucian pointed at the bathroom. *Fucking bastard.* I went in. I didn't even knock. I saw him leaning on his hand inside the shower. Water pouring over him.

"Seriously!" I yelled. "That was why you didn't fucking answer any of my phone calls?"

"Elena?" He sounded confused.

"Don't you dare fucking Elena me!" I yelled. I started to cry. I swallowed it as he got out and reached out to hug me.

"Don't!" I shrieked.

"Elena, please, let me explain."

"You are pathetic, Blake. Pathetic. I fucking hate you." I ran out of the bathroom and past Lucian.

"Elena, please."

"Just don't, Blake, fucking don't. You two deserve each other."

"No, please," he begged as he ran after me with only a towel over his waist. "It's not what you think. Please." He grabbed my arm.

"Get your fucking paw off me!" I yelled. "Or so help me, Blake…"

He let go as if he'd been burned. I just hurtled down the steps as Lucian reached us.

I somehow found my room though blinded by tears. I thought my heart would burst. I collapsed onto my bed and cried like I'd never cried before.

BLAKE

Classes resumed. I didn't know if I was going to see Elena or not. The darkness surged. I'd done so much fucking shit that didn't feel wrong at all, but I knew it was.

I ignored some of her calls because of it. I was busy fucking up big time. She wasn't here yesterday and I knew her mother had gotten her tutors.

I got out of bed and tapped Tabitha next to me. How the fuck did this happen? Fire Caine, that was how.

I was so out of it.

I went to the bathroom. I hated the low from the drug, but it still kept the beast inside of me drained. I felt slightly normal and opened the taps. I should phone Elena today and explain everything. She was going to find out about this, and I needed to tell her before that happened. "Fuck!" I yelled as the water ran over my head.

I'd seriously fucked up. I hoped and prayed that she would forgive me.

It was the drugs, and even though I desperately tried to hide it from her, I knew I wouldn't be able to. Not this time. She had to believe me that the darkness had taken over. I didn't want to imagine what a complete takeover would've looked like. How bad would I have been if my happy place didn't exist? If she didn't exist.

It was hard. I couldn't.

Two seconds before the door opened, I felt a strange lightness suddenly break through my mood.

"Seriously!" a voice yelled. "That was why you didn't fucking answer any of my phone calls?"

"Elena?" I said. *Oh, no, fuck. Please not this.* I opened the door and saw her standing there. She had tears in her eyes.

"Don't you dare fucking Elena me!" she yelled again and started to cry. She took a huge breath and stopped. I went over to hug her. What was she doing here?

"Don't." She sounded deranged.

"Elena please, let me explain," I begged.

"You are pathetic, Blake. Pathetic. I fucking hate you," she said and fled.

FUCK! I pulled the towel off and wrapped it around my waist. I followed her.

"Blake," Lucian said softly. I didn't care and followed her down the stairs. Plenty of eyes were on us.

"Elena, please."

"Just don't, Blake, fucking don't." She spun around. I hated this look on her. "You two deserve each other."

"No, please," I begged again as she just kept walking, and fast. "It's not what you think, please." I grabbed her arm. She needed to listen to me.

"Get your fucking paw off me!" She yelled, "Or so help me, Blake…"

She'd never used that tone with me. A foreign emotion entered me: betrayal, heartbreak. I let go of her arm as Lucian reached us.

"Blake," he said. He knew I'd fucked up last night. Tried to warn me.

A tear rolled over my cheek. She was never going to forgive me. Ever.

Everyone talked about our fight. It floated through the air like twittering birds.

Whenever I walked into a class or the cafeteria, everyone inside stopped talking.

So fucking what? I tried not to feel guilty, but I couldn't. Elena was here now, keeping me normal. Her proximity lessened the darkness. I felt better, and it wasn't the Fire Caine that had drained the beast.

The darkness wasn't going to come. I'd fucked up and it was killing me. I kept seeing that look on Elena's face.

She wasn't sitting at Sammy's table. She wasn't going to listen to me. I knew her; she was just as stubborn as her mother.

Every blonde who walked into the room made my heart beat faster. Not that I could hear it, but I felt the elevation through my entire body. But it was never her. She was hiding from me.

Rumors swirled the entire day around the school. The Parthenon dome was closed. Elena was training.

She was making me nervous. Especially now with what happened. But I was glad that she was still going to claim me.

During class a royal messenger came. Everyone looked up and Professor Gregory smiled. "Blake," he said. The messenger bowed out. I knew what that was. It was my date, the date that she was going to claim me. I got up and moved forward.

"Mind sharing?" Professor Gregory asked.

I tore the envelope open and took out a claim date. This was the way they'd done it hundreds of years ago. Her father was making a huge thing about this.

The date was next week.

"Next week Wednesday," I said and everyone cheered, except Tabitha.

That fast? She wants to claim me that fast? I needed to speak to her.

I put the parchment into my backpack. It was going to get framed.

I tried to speak to her during class, and I even went to

the Parthenon dome which was highly guarded. I could hear a sparring session in progress.

I would love to see her in action, but the guard told me to go back where I came from. I hated that. So what, I couldn't see her moves?

During lunch I sat at a table outside, picking at my food. I could feel Lucian watching me like a hawk.

I knew it was pity. I had gotten caught in the act, horribly, and nothing I could say would ever make this feel right. Nothing.

ELENA

I saw him at lunchtime. Our eyes met for a few seconds. *How could you do this to me?*

I felt his eyes on me the entire period. It got so bad that I got up and went to sit inside, where I could eat in peace. The whole school was talking about me catching him. How upset I was. None of them understood it as the papers were still carrying the narrative that we still hated one another.

I finished my lunch, pushed back my tears, and went back to the Parthenon dome. I had a lot of training to do.

Four tutors came today, another four would come tomorrow, and another four the day after that. He'd received his invitation today. My dad had gone all out to make this as memorable as possible. Now I didn't want anything to do with him. He made me sick.

Even with my head swimming with all of this, my trainers fell. All of them. I'd never felt this ready for anything in my life. Now I didn't care anymore. I should just put the poor dog out of its misery. I really didn't care anymore about anything. The snow bitch would always be there.

Murphy's Law. I walked past her up to my room.

She didn't even look at me, just glided past me.

I loathed her. I wished she would just roll over and die. It was because of her that all this shit happened. She'd started it. She was supposed to keep her grubby paws off him.

It took everything out of me not to bash her head against the railing.

And the fact that I was tired and needed a nap and a shower.

BLAKE

I didn't see her at dinner. I wanted to speak to her, but she wasn't there. I went back to my room. Tabitha desperately wanted to talk to me but I avoided her. I was so tired of her.

I couldn't get that disappointment on Elena's face out of my head.

The door opened and Lucian walked in. "You okay?"

"Yeah, I'm fine." I didn't growl. She had been here for one day and I'd already started to feel like myself.

Lucian spoke quietly. "You want to talk about this morning?"

I shook my head.

"Okay, I'm here if you do, Blake."

I knew he was. Always near, ready to talk if I needed him. "You spoke to her?" I had to know.

"Nope, she sees me as one of your pack dogs, Blake."

The next day, I just missed her. I caught her walking out of the back door heading toward the Parthenon dome. She was never going to forgive me.

She had training again today.

Reporters showed up. They were going to interview her.

Why did they always make such a fuss over a claiming?

Note to self. Stay inside your room.

I spoke to Tabitha in class.

"You didn't see her, the way she looked at me, Blake," Tabitha said as the bell rang.

"I'm sure it couldn't have been as bad as the one she gave me. Just stay away from her, you are good at that."

She followed me. "She was supposed to keep her paws off you. You were mine, not hers."

"We've been through this a million times," I said to her as we reached the lockers. "I'm not yours, Tabitha."

Everyone was staring again.

"You sure about that? That's not what you said the other night." She touched my face. I closed my eyes. I just wanted to fucking die.

"Stop touching me." I opened my eyes and looked at her. She knew what that had been, it was the Caine talking.

"To be safe, stay away. She's not like that, but don't push her, Tabitha."

She nodded as we made our way to our lockers.

I was walking behind her. I could feel Elena close by but where, I didn't know.

Tabitha smiled at me. "I didn't regret the other night."

I did, but I didn't say it out loud. It was cruel, and I wasn't cruel when I was normal.

She turned back around to look in front of her, when a locker opened all by itself. She smacked right into it.

My mind immediately went to Elena. I had to suppress a laugh. Okay, so it wasn't nice, but it was funny. "Let me see."

"You sure about that statement?"

"C'mon, you see her here anywhere?" I asked.

I looked at her face. She was going to end up with one hell of a shiner.

Something on the roof caught my eye. It was a blue jacket with some sort of symbol on it. I looked back at Tabitha for two seconds and when I looked up again, he was gone. Lucian? Would he do that for Elena to get back into her good graces? If so, what did that mean?

I decided to sit inside the cafeteria the entire evening.

I was going to speak to her tonight no matter how hard she tried to avoid me. We needed to sort this shit out.

Around seven, Sammy and Elena walked in. She was wearing a blue jacket with a symbol on it.

She can already do elevation spells?

It scared me even more. Sammy went over to the table while Elena went straight to the buffet. She'd been training hard. I could see it in her face.

I got up and walked slowly toward her.

Sort this out, Blake. Just sort it out.

ELENA

I knew I should feel bad for what I'd done this afternoon, but it was Tabitha. Her perfect face would heal eventually.

Thank heavens nobody saw me.

"Hey, Princess," a big man with a round belly and red beard greeted me.

"Good evening," I said, reaching out my hand. He kissed it softly, which made me smile. "And it's Elena."

"You love riddles?"

"I suck at riddles, always have," I joked.

He chuckled. "Bummer."

All the hair on my arms rose.

I looked around and saw Blake standing right next to me. I was still so fucking mad at him. I stared at the ground. My heart was beating like crazy. What was he doing here? I'd told him I didn't want to see him.

"Blake," Chef said.

"Chef," he spoke. It was silent as I heaped way too much potato salad onto my plate. *Stop, Elena. Stop.*

"Elena," he said.

I looked at him. "I told you to leave me alone. Go to your Snow Dragon."

"It's not like that. Can I just explain, please?" His shield was already around us.

"I don't care, Blake," I said even though it was far from the truth. It was the only thing I'd thought about the past two days.

"You don't mean it." He sighed. "I got dark, Elena. Really dark. It happened so quickly. And with your mother saying that you weren't going to come to Dragonia, I lost hope, okay? I was weak. That happens. So I had to take other measures again."

"Oh what, screwing someone, is that it?" Sarcasm dripped from my words.

"No." He took a deep breath. "I fucked up. I was

going to phone you and tell you that. I can't fucking lie to you, Elena."

"What measures, Blake?" I yelled at him.

He didn't want to say.

I wasn't going to listen if he wasn't going to be honest. Too many people were dishonest with me and I was fed up.

I turned around to walk away.

"Fire Caine."

I halted, shocked. *Fire Caine.*

I gaped at him.

"Yeah, not so fucking nice is it? It's the only thing that keeps him at bay, Elena. Except you. I fucked up on the high. You are the furthest thing from my mind on a high."

That was so not what I wanted to hear. I shook my head. "Fire Caine. Blake you could've phoned me. Pappi would've found a way to get me here. But you decided to take the other path, the dark path. Indirectly, you chose darkness above me." Tears rolled over my cheeks. I was uncomfortably aware that even though people couldn't hear us, they could see the scene we were making. What a great first impression at Dragonia. "Do you know how much that fucking hurts?"

"I do."

"No, you don't!" I cried. "I don't even want to claim you anymore."

He flinched.

"But I don't have a fucking choice. So I'll decide what to do with you afterwards. All I can think of is setting you free."

Horror spread over his face. "You don't mean that."

"Oh yes, I do." I reached him again. "Whatever this

was, it's over. It's all you ever do. Break my heart. You're really good at that. No more," I said.

I couldn't believe how honest I was being with him. Too honest.

His face hardened and he huffed. It was as if he was finally free of whatever hold I had on him. He didn't have to pretend anymore. He shook his head. "You're just like your mother. You never listen to what I'm trying to tell you."

"Well, she raised me," I snapped at him.

"I really thought you'd grown up, but I see you're just the spoiled little brat you've always been. I know it was you with the lockers. And yes, I actually regret that night." He turned around, his shield disappeared, and he walked away.

I should've just agreed with what a stupid idea that night had been. But I didn't. Hearing him say that only angered me more. My eyes caught on the stack of plates.

The movement was so fast. It started inside my head. I saw how I picked a plate up and threw it at Blake.

It shattered against his back. He tripped but landed on all fours.

"You're a fucking asshole!" I yelled after him. Everybody's eyes were on us. They were like statues, just staring at us.

Blake grunted and I saw how he started to tremble slightly.

"Go get Master Longwei!" Chef yelled from behind the buffet.

I couldn't keep my eyes off Blake. I watched how his body shook. He groaned.

Whether it was to tame the beast inside of him or tame his anger, I didn't know.

But it didn't last and he morphed into his dragon form.

I backed away. He was huge, much bigger than the last time I'd seen him. *Impossible. That was only a couple weeks ago!*

A shrill screech left his mouth. Spit spattered my skin.

My heart hammered like crazy, but I wasn't scared. Even if he'd gotten big, I'd never feared his dragon form, not like other people. This was a different type of emotion. It was as if I thrived on this. Pure adrenaline was my drug.

Unfazed, I screamed right back at him. The plates in the stack zipped through the air and smashed into his face.

A force blew me backward. I didn't even see it, just felt myself get shoved over the buffet line, and crash behind it.

Screams filled the cafeteria. Feet stomped on the tiles. Everyone stampeded toward the doors. Then it all went silent.

TWENTY-FIVE

ELENA

My father's laughter filled my ears. I opened my eyes. I still lay between the ovens behind the buffet area. "Sweet pea, what the hell did you do?" he asked.

I lifted my head. "What are you doing here?" His corporeal form stood in the cafeteria with me. Time stood still. It was our special moment. I'd expected this...next week.

"What happened to the big claiming in Etan? This wasn't supposed to be it."

I realized what he said. "No." I closed my eyes.

He laughed again. "You can't back down now. You have to claim him."

"He made me so furious, Dad."

"About what now?"

I shook my head. I couldn't tell my father. A tear rolled over my face. "I'm ascending?"

He smiled. "Look for yourself."

I got up. I stared at Blake's ugly mug. How had he gotten so big? The last people had just made it out of the cafeteria. But time was frozen in this moment. Nothing moved. No one blinked. I closed my eyes and thought of my mother. "She's going to kill me."

It was supposed to be a huge claiming. Inside the Colosseum of Etan where they held all the famous claimings, with cameras and thousands of spectators. Paegeia had waited for this for years. And I couldn't control my temper. I was so disappointed.

"Maybe not that much," my father said.

"What?"

"Your mother begged me to use this time to speak to you about everything and explain why she did this."

"It doesn't matter anymore, Dad."

"Yes, it does, Elena. Please, just listen.

I nodded.

"It started with the letter where he said he didn't feel the same way about you."

I'd read that letter. It still hurt me reading those words.

"She didn't have the heart to give it to you."

He was going to go with this crap?

"But you need to know why she did it, Elena."

"I know why, Dad. She has this stupid thing stuck in her mind that we would turn into Cooper and Merica one day." And she was right, but I didn't say that out loud.

"You done? Can I tell you now what she did for you?"

"What she did?" I'd always wanted to know what she'd done for me, ever since my dad had told me that day in the kitchen. He'd said I was too young to appreciate it.

I nodded.

He started with Goran. A tale my mom had never told me. He was like her Blake. But her heart belonged to my father. I knew the story of how they'd met; she was a commoner, he was a prince. What I hadn't known was that his parents never approved of my mom. They didn't want him to marry her because she was a commoner. However, on my grandfather's deathbed, he told him that he could choose who he wanted to marry. Goran had asked my mother to marry him, too, but she loved my father, and couldn't. It broke him, but he accepted it and they all stayed friends for a while.

My father's voice wavered. It was hard for him to tell me this story. I didn't know what it had to do with me. It was evident who my father was. I looked like him, not like King Helmut.

"You know that he died in the ambush set up by the person who was going to betray us."

I nodded. Irene's prophecy had been that someone close to them would betray them. Goran—Mom's Blake—died in the process.

He was like my father's brother.

"Three days before the ambush, Merica and Cooper came to us. We knew what they were, he was a Rubicon, like Blake, but he wasn't a threat. She was his rider."

"I know their story, Dad."

"We never knew who was going to betray us or when. Merica and Cooper did, and I didn't want to listen."

Why didn't he want to listen?

"It was Goran, sweet pea."

"What was Goran?" I asked.

"Goran was the one who betrayed us."

My mind whirred a mile a minute. "He couldn't. King

Helmut was his twin. You just said he was like your brother, and Mom…" Goran was her Blake.

"Hence the reason I didn't want to hear Merica and Cooper out."

He carried on. How they'd gone to my mother. She didn't want to listen either, especially when Merica told her that I would've had a different life if she didn't do it. I would have never known that Paegeia existed, never known Dragons existed. Jako would've raised me alone. I would have never known my mother. I tried to imagine that. I couldn't. She was a pain in my ass, but not knowing her, not knowing my home existed…

Goran would've tortured my father. They didn't know much since my mom didn't get all the details. My father had been hunting them. He wanted to throw them into the dungeons for treason.

"Ever imagine a life where you didn't grow up with Blake?"

I didn't want to. I shook my head, trying to suppress my tears.

"Your mother killed him. For you. You want to know why she believed Cooper and Merica?"

I gazed around the room for something to anchor me amidst the revelation. *My mother killed Goran. She killed her Blake!*

I shook my head. She'd trusted them with everything she had.

My father leaned against the glass partition of the buffet. "Because Merica told her if she wasn't going to do it." He had tears in his eyes again. "It would be her life."

I squinted. "I don't understand, Dad."

"Blake will gain an ability at the age of thirty, Elena.

He will be able to jump back into time, not just space. You, ten years from now, jumped back to warn us of a darker future. Your mother gave you a different life. So it wasn't Cooper and Merica scaring her into what you and Blake would become. It was *you and Blake* showing her how strong your bond *will* be one day."

I frowned. "You know how strange that sounds, right?"

"I do, but your mother isn't the lying type. Well, not before the past sixteen years."

A part of me was held onto my anger with her, but a part of me finally understood why she'd withheld my letters. Why she was always so crazy.

"She always knew the two of you would end up together, Elena. She just wanted to slow it down a bit. But she realizes now how stupid that was. The measures Blake had to take to stay in control."

"He told me."

My father closed his eyes. "That couldn't have been easy, telling you that."

I nodded. I knew it hadn't been.

"So the best I see it is take all your anger, and claim your dragon. Let all of this stop, Elena. You only have this one chance."

I nodded wiped away my tears. Cooper and Merica were us. It's why my family never tried to find them, why they weren't worried about the spare Rubicon. Because it was us from the future.

What was my life like? I didn't want to imagine it. I couldn't. And I knew that whatever Blake did, I would forgive him. He didn't know better.

I crawled over to my father and hugged him.

"He is actually a good boy, Elena. He never meant to

hurt you. We all saw it, what you guys will become. He adored you."

I sniffed again.

"So screw the big claiming, and just claim your dragon. Now."

I nodded.

My father vanished.

"Dad!" I said.

"I'm here, sweet pea. I won't leave. Ever."

Everything started to move again. Time sped up.

"Elena!" Blake roared. I jumped out and pelted him with pots and pans.

He didn't back away. He unleashed his first ability on me.

"Lightning," my father said. "Good, Elena. Own it."

It rippled through me first. It hurt like hell, but it started to feel like nothing. Then I took control of it and released it in his face.

He staggered back, his tail hitting the wall and the entire cafeteria rumbled.

Cracks ran up the wall like a deadly spiderweb.

"Take cover, Elena!" my father yelled. I scurried for one of the tables, slid underneath it, and covered my body to protect myself from the pieces of ceiling that were starting to come down.

I saw the Pink Kiss dancing off the walls. Blake was disintegrating them as they fell.

When the ceiling didn't fall anymore, I rolled out from underneath the table. He breathed fire on me. I screamed and from the searing heat.

"You are immune, own it, Elena."

The pain vanished. I took control of the Pink Kiss. I threw it back into his face. Every time a ball of fire left my hand, a new one appeared.

My lips curved. This was so freakin' awesome. Fire and lightning balls pelted him, left, right, and center.

He tried to gas me to get me to stop and it worked, but only for a few seconds. Next he spewed acid spit to burn me.

He didn't once back off or take it easy on me. He gave it his all. He refused to yield. Maybe he couldn't. This beast was so different from his human form. Part of me had always known that this was the real Blake. The human was just his mask.

My father cheered in my head as I ducked and slid between his legs, trying to get the upper hand.

I found my opportunity as I jumped on his tail. I was on his back in two seconds.

"Slow down, Elena. Don't kill him," my father cautioned.

I needed to bring his ass down. The entire cafeteria was ruined. I concentrated on the earth's gravity. Felt how it rippled through me. Felt how his hulking figure fought against the forces of nature.

"Yield!" I commanded him.

"Never!" he roared.

I concentrated harder. I used the gravity—all of his abilities—to overpower him as he convulsed beneath my feet.

"Careful, Elena!" my father yelled.

Blake shuddered to his knees. I tumbled off his body, hitting my head hard against a rock.

My eyes zoomed out. I could see his massive figure collapsing. He didn't get up.

"Whoa!" my father yelled. "We did it, sweet pea. We did it. You got your dragon."

My father's voice faded. I felt a force fill my entire being. Something massive, strong, and fierce expanded in my soul. It grew so big, too big. It wanted to tear me apart. I screamed a long, anguished howl. It felt like I'd broken in two. Everything went dark.

TWENTY-SIX

FUTURE MEETS PRESENT.

ELENA

Life came back to me. It was light, beyond my eyelids, but I kept my eyes closed.

Something was wrong. I was missing Blake's voice in my head. The last thing I remembered was the Beam. I had been flying on Blake's back.

I couldn't remember anything else, or the reason I was lying on a bed. We'd just told my mom what she had to do. She needed to kill Goran; otherwise she would die. My eyes fluttered open at once.

I found myself looking at a fan spinning really fast. I knew that fan all too well. I'd spent so much time waking up staring at it. What was I doing in Dragonia's infirmary?

"Good, you're awake." I heard my father's voice and I found him on a chair next to my bed, reading the newspaper. He set the newspaper on the nightstand and smiled at me.

I looked to my other side. There was no sign of my mother. A horrible feeling flashed over me. *No, please, no. She believed me. I know she did.*

My lip started to vibrate as my father stared at me with soft eyes.

"I know it wasn't what you planned, sweet pea. I was shocked, too, but…"

The floodgates of memory opened. I had been so sure that she would've done it. Killed the son of a bitch and been here.

"Elena," my father's tone changed to worry. "You're scaring me. What is it?"

"We failed, didn't we?"

He frowned. "No, we claimed Blake, Elena."

I looked up. "What?" I hadn't expected that answer.

"You claimed Blake, you were out for about three days." He smiled. "We didn't fail." He touched my cheek. And then I saw it. His face was burn-free. Not even a trace of that ugly scar on my father's neck and side of his face remained. He smiled. "You have tamed your dragon. I didn't think it was possible on the first try, but you did it. You do have Master Longwei to worry about."

Oh crap. What happened?

"But," my father carried on, "the cafeteria is back in place, so you don't need to worry about that. Just so you know, the cockroaches aren't happy that they didn't get their coverage of what was going to be the biggest claiming ever."

Biggest claiming ever? I frowned. "What are you talking about?"

My father looked concerned. "It's okay. You are a bit disoriented after receiving all your abilities. Well, that must have been a hard knock."

"Disoriented?" I spoke softly to myself.

"Elena?" My father sounded worried.

My hand clutched my hair. It was cut short. But I didn't worry about that now. It would grow back. "We failed, Dad!" I yelled. *I didn't save her.* I'd tried so hard. "What happened?"

"Baby, calm down. You're starting to frighten me."

"I really thought she would be here," I cried. "I failed…"

"Oh, look who is awake," a woman's voice came from the door. I froze. "The cafeteria. Seriously. What happened to the big event, Elena?"

Goosebumps rippled over my skin. My heart skipped a few beats as I slowly turned my head to the door. She had dark brown hair and big grey doe eyes. I gasped. Tears streamed down my face.

"Why are you crying?" my mother asked. She carried a coffee cup in her hand and the pair of shades she'd just taken off in the other.

"I think she's a bit disoriented," my father said softly.

I staggered off the bed and ran to my mother. I didn't care about the coffee in her hands. I flung my arms around her. She had to step back to keep her balance. I started to cry.

"Elena, what is going on?"

"Thank you, thank you, thank you," I kept saying.

"Sweetheart," she said.

"You did it, Mom. You killed that son of a bitch," I whispered.

My mom gasped and pushed me away. "Elena?"

"Who else would it be?" I laughed through snot and tears.

She hugged me tighter. "You're back?"

"Back?" My father asked sounding confused.

"Oh, shush, you'd never get this anyway," my mother chirped. I laughed at them backbiting one another. She'd done it. I didn't know how yet, but she'd done it.

"Okay, what is going on here?" my dad asked.

I didn't care. I just hugged her again. Scared that she was going to disappear in a puff of smoke.

"Oh thank heavens you showed up at the right time."

My father laughed. "You've got to be shitting me. I see what is happening! Welcome back, Elena, and good luck." He tapped me on the shoulder, planting a kiss on my head as he exited the room.

"Shut up," my mom said.

I pulled back suddenly. "Blake. Where is Blake?"

"Hold on, young lady," my mother said. I could hear my father's laughter coming from the porch.

"What?"

"You're not twenty-six anymore."

My face fell. "I'm not?" I asked.

"You don't remember a thing?"

I looked passed her. "No, the last thing I remember was telling you about Goran, and then we left through the Beam."

"The Beam?" She sounded worried.

"Yeah, it's what we named it. That bright light we use to time jump. I can't see it, but Blake can. I saw it through his mind and..."

"Don't do this to me." My mother looked up at the ceiling. She took a deep breath. "You just claimed Blake, Elena."

I hesitated. "What do you mean by *just*?"

My mother laughed uncomfortably. "You claimed him three days ago. You're sixteen. Sorry, sweetheart."

I grunt. "I'm a teenager again?!"

"And your mother is going to become your worst nightmare," my father chirped again.

"Will you shut up?" she yelled to him outside.

I laughed as I understood her fears. She had always been scared about this Dent thing from the moment she discovered that I was a girl and not a boy. "Mom, I'm not stupid. I still only remember *my* past. I promise to be the best teenager I can be, okay?" I put a stray hair that fell out of place behind her ear and I laughed.

She hugged me again. "Music to my ears."

"I still need to know where he is, though."

"He woke up yesterday and came in to check on you. He felt terrible and left."

"Wait, he felt bad?" That was new.

"Yes, why?"

"The twenty-year-old Blake I remember hated my guts. I only claimed him, I think, around my eighteenth birthday."

"What? Why couldn't I have that time?"

"Because you weren't in that past, Mom. Hence the reason we had to come back and save your ass."

She rolled her eyes at me.

I gasped. "A queen never rolls her eyes."

"Look who is giving me royal advice now." We both laughed. The ground rumbled as a dragon landed nearby.

It was him. He wasn't as big as he had been in my twenty-six-year-old memory from a few minutes ago, but it was him. He changed back, pulled on his robe, and greeted my father outside on the infirmary's porch.

"Elena, please. I don't want restless nights. I'm too old for this crap."

I laughed.

"I'll be as delicate as possible," I said and went over to him.

He saw me, and his eyes widened slightly.

Before he said anything, I jumped into his arms and my legs curled around his waist. My father roared with laughter.

"Look at you," he touched my short hair.

"Do you remember anything?" I asked.

"No. The last thing I remember is going through the Beam and then I woke up in my bed in the old manor. Tell me…"

"Hey mister," my mother scolded him. He froze as he turned around to look at her.

A broad grin appeared on his face. He put me down, and he ran to her, pulling her into his arms and twirling her around. Then he laughed. "I want details. Everything." He put her down.

She just shook her head. "First of all, you are not thirty years-old. You are twenty, and I know how twenty-year-old men think."

He squinted. "Isn't this supposed to be King Albert's lecture?" He laughed.

"He's a pushover."

"I'm not," my father chimed in. He went over to Blake. "Whenever you remember what happened, I was always on your side," he said through a huge grin. I squinted.

My mother slapped him. "Would you stop that?"

Blake and I laughed. Oh my word, what did she do? I didn't care. I had my real mom. Hopefully the memories would come back eventually and I would discover what she'd done, and I would decide if it was bad or not. But nothing she did could ever make me hate her. I remembered all too well how life was without her.

I had the chance now to know what she was like, to discover who she was. She laughed, the throw-her-head-back kind of laugh, and spoke to Blake. I couldn't stop watching her.

A happy tear rolled over my cheek. I knew life was going to be good.

Her eyes caught mine and she walked over and hugged me again. "Thank you, sweetheart," she said.

"For what?"

"For giving me the chance to be your mother." She looked at me and pushed a stray hair behind my ear. "I have to say it wasn't always easy, but…"

I smiled knowingly. "I gave you restless nights, eh?"

"That you did. And hours of playing the piano."

I gasped. "You play the piano?"

She squinted and hugged me again. "You do, too. We make a mean team playing chopsticks."

I bit my lip. I'd never played the piano. I didn't even know how. My life was so different. I couldn't wait for the memories to come back; I hoped that one day they would.

I gasped as I remembered everyone else. I pushed her away from me. "The Wyverns! Please tell me you remembered." I didn't give her a chance to speak. "Are the McKenzies still alive?" My mother's face fell into shock. "Are Lucian and Desi still alive, Mom?"

"The Wyverns killed them?"

I shook my head. "Not all of them, but…" I missed Blake's voice in my head.

"Calm down, Elena," he finally spoke aloud and walked over to me. "Why don't we just go and find out?"

My mother still looked shaken. I smiled at her. "Sorry," I mouthed and she smiled lovingly and shook her head.

"Just stay. Don't go anywhere." I sounded stern as Blake pulled me toward the castle.

He put his arm around me and pulled me into a side hug. He kissed me atop my head. "You happy?"

"So, so happy to see her." I couldn't stop thinking about it.

"I know. We did it."

"We did it."

In the lobby, everything still looked the same.

"Blake, Elena," Master Longwei said. He didn't sound happy.

"Master Longwei." Blake smiled.

I shook my head at him and raised my eyebrows. His smile disappeared. *I'll handle this*, I thought. But the minute it left, I knew he couldn't hear my voice.

"Sorry about the cafeteria," I said.

"The cafeteria?" Blake said.

I raised my eyes at him again. He needed to stop talking.

Master Longwei just stared at us.

"Luckily your father helped put it back up. But yes, we are very disappointed that we didn't get to see a royal claiming, Elena."

I arranged my features into what I hoped was a penitent expression. "I'm sure nobody could be as disappointed as I am, Master Longwei."

Blake stared at me and then a huge grin sprawled over his face. We walked away.

"You claimed me in the cafeteria?"

I nodded. "I don't know details, just what my dad told me. Nobody is happy about it."

"I couldn't care less," he said as we walked up to the boys' dorms to see if Lucian was here.

I gasped when I saw Brian skipping down the stairs. He hardly saw me coming. I flung myself onto him and hugged him. He froze.

"Princess, Brian certainly doesn't have a death wish."

Blake roared with laughter. He slapped Brian on the shoulder. "Blake won't go ape on Brian's ass."

He blew out some air and just looked between us. "Brian is happy that the two of you sorted out your shit. Really happy." And he walked further down the steps.

"Party tonight in my room," Blake said. "Brian needs to be there."

"If there is a party, Brian will be there."

I couldn't stop laughing as he walked out the main door. "I missed him so much. Nobody could speak the way he did."

"Yeah, he was a master," Blake said. "Sorry, *is* a master at speaking in third person."

We kept climbing the steps and Blake went quiet.

"Don't do this," I begged.

"It's Lucian, Elena."

"Yeah. And he doesn't know, Blake. He has a different life, one in which we never dated. I can bet my life on that. I just want him to be alive."

He sighed. "Okay." We stopped in front of their old room. Blake opened the door with his key.

"You're back." Lucian's voice filled the room and I closed my eyes.

He was alive. He was here.

I pushed passed Blake and entered his room. I gasped as I saw him. My first love, my perished love. Gazing at me with a slight frown furrowing his forehead. He looked the same. Exactly the same as I remembered him.

He started to smile at me, and then he looked at Blake. I ran and jumped into his arms. He hadn't expected that, but he caught me. I wanted to kiss him, but I refrained. This Lucian was just a friend.

I could feel him moving one of his arms and Blake laughed.

"She woke up a bit sentimental. So just go with it."

"Thank heavens the two of you sorted out your shit," He said and hugged me tighter.

I looked at him. "Our shit?"

He stared at me with squinted eyes. "Okay, what is going on?" He put me down. "I've got the feeling that I just stepped into the *Twilight Zone*."

Blake laughed. "Something like that." He came over and hugged Lucian. "I missed you, bud."

"Okay, this is getting freaky now."

We both laughed and he joined us. "You forgave him?" he asked.

Forgive, Blake?

"Yeah, we sorted out our shit," Blake said and I frowned.

"You are so fucking lucky." Lucian had a stern tone in his voice.

"Real lucky," Blake agreed.

"I need to run. We'll talk later. I want to know how you got yourself out of this one."

I squinted at Blake as Lucian left.

"What the hell happened?"

"No idea," Blake whispered and came over to give me a kiss. He sighed. "I never thought I would see my old room again. Or my roommate."

"Me neither."

I kissed his lips again. Life couldn't be more perfect. We'd grown up together, all of us had, that much was obvious. "See, I told you. He doesn't remember any history between us."

Blake's lips thinned. "The way he smiled when he saw you…"

"Not what you think. There must be an explanation for that. We'll untangle it all soon enough. Oh hey, you want to go see if Tabitha is fine?"

With a chuckle, he wrapped his arms around me and pulled me closer. "No need. I'm sure she is." He kissed me on the tip of my nose.

"I need to go find Sammy and Becky. I can't wait to see the old Sammy! And I have to get some sort of a down-low on why I claimed you in the damn cafeteria."

"Please do. I'm dying to know why you couldn't wait."

I laughed and left his room. I skipped down the boys' stairs and made it up to the girls'.

I found Becky coming down with another girl I never seen before.

"Becky," I yelled. She looked up. Her hair was cut in a funky style. She stared at me, confusion on her face. Then I got it. She didn't know me yet. We'd never become friends.

Oh, hell no. She wasn't going to be the price I needed to pay. Silho was.

I stepped up to her. She just stared at me. This was not her. She was always so filled with confidence, not this sullen Goth chick.

"I am going away for a few days, but when I get back, there will be a party in my room. You're invited," I said and ran up the stairs.

"Okay," she said.

"That was weird," her friend said. "How do you know her?"

"I don't. I didn't even know she knew my name."

I smiled. *You don't know me yet, but you will. You will.*

Sammy and I weren't going to make it without Becky's two-cent quips. She'd always been the strong one in our friendship. I would stalk her ass until we became friends.

I went to my room and found other girls there.

"Oh, hi, Elena. You're awake." A strange girl looked surprised.

"Um." I felt disoriented. "Where's my room?" Okay that didn't come out right.

The girl laughed.

"Way at the top."

"Thanks," I said and rushed up way to the top. I was extremely fit, leaner and stronger than I ever had been. I loved this version of me.

I opened my door and found Sammy. She gasped, got up, and rushed to me.

Thank heavens. We are friends.

"You woke up." She hugged me tight. Then she looked at me.

"You seriously couldn't wait? Why didn't you just walk the other way, Elena?"

Walk the other way? I shook it off. I didn't care about any of that right now. I was just happy that she was her old self again. Not some shadow of a girl throwing herself into her work, burying her guilt with the League.

"Speak," she said.

I laughed. "I don't know." It was the truth.

"I knew there was going to be shit the minute I saw him walking toward you," she said. None of this sounded right. We didn't like one another? Did my mom keep us apart? Was this the shit my father was referring to?

"What did he say when he wielded his shield? I only saw the two of you fighting. What happened?"

"He just made me so mad," I said, thought it sound correct. I hugged her again.

"You should've just ignored that and waited for the day. Do you know how disappointed Paegeia is?"

I laughed. I couldn't help it.

"It's not funny, Elena," she fussed. But then she laughed. "I have to admit, it was so you."

She hugged me again. I just drew in her scent. I'd missed her so much.

I remembered Becky. "I'm going away with my mom for a few days." Her eyebrow rose. "But when I come back, we are going to have a huge party. Becky is invited." I went over to my cupboard, pulled out my leather bag, and started packing my clothes.

"Becky?" Sammy repeated.

I nodded. "Rebecca Johnson."

She squinted. "The Goth chick?"

"Yes, the Goth Chick," I zipped up my bag.

"Okay," Sammy said, not sounding sure about that one.

"I promise, you'll love her, Sammy. Got to go. See you in a few." I kissed her cheek and then hurried for the door. I skipped down the steps rushed up Blake's room again and knocked on his door.

He opened up. George, Dean, and Lucian's voices emerged from within.

"He's here?" I asked, referring to Dean.

"He's here," he said and closed the door behind him. "Where are you going?"

"You need to ask?"

"No." He grinned. "Enjoy, Elena."

"See you soon." I hugged him and kissed him on the lips. It was tender and loving—and chaste. "Thanks, babe," I murmured against his lips. "For risking everything for me."

"You are so welcome." He winked and let me go.

I ran down the stairs again. "Phone me tonight and fill me in please."

"Oh you bet your sweet ass I will."

I remembered Becky. *Shit*. I ran back up. He smiled again. "Hey, try to be as friendly as you can with Becky. She isn't my friend."

"What?" his face fell.

"But not overly nice, she's Goth now."

He shook his head. "Goth?"

I started to laugh. "She's not the price, Blake. Her Dent is in there. The two of you are still friends. So…" I crossed my fingers.

"Okay, I promise."

"Thanks, babe."

He laughed. I skipped down the rest of the stairs.

I found Becky again in the lobby and saw her raising her eyes at her friends.

You did not just raise your eyes at me, miss-know-it-all. I know way too much about you.

"So remember, there's going to be a party," I said as I walked past her.

"Okay." She sounded sarcastic.

I gave her a pointed look. "It's going to be frawsome!"

Her head snapped back at me as I walked backward, still watching her. "Frawsome?"

"Freaking awesome."

She frowned. "Hey, that's *my* thing."

"I don't mind sharing if you don't." I grinned.

She finally laughed.

"Bye," I sang and she said goodbye.

I found my mother and father still waiting at the main gate. They were in a discussion with Master Longwei as I rushed up to them.

I hugged my mother from behind and she touched my face softly.

"So you're leaving again?" Master Longwei raised his eyebrows.

"You know I don't really need their classes, right? It's just for a few days."

He nodded solemnly. "Fine, see you soon, Elena."

"Bye, Master Longwei," I sang.

418

The elevator trip to Etan was filled with cockroaches, all asking why I'd claimed Blake in the cafeteria.

"I simply couldn't wait any longer," I said and my father laughed.

"Queen Catherine, how does this make you feel?"

It was a question I thought I would never hear in any of my interviews ever.

"Glad that it is over," she said confidently.

"Don't lie. Your worst fear just began," my father quipped. Everyone laughed, including me.

"Elena is a responsible young lady, no fears here," she said. We bid the cockroaches farewell.

We took the elevator to Etan. It was fast. My mom shrieked, throwing her hands up in the air, and I mimicked her. It was like we were riding a crazy rollercoaster ride for the first time.

I laughed at her hair when we stopped. She patted it straight with her hands, and laughed.

Music to my ears.

A stretch limo waited for us outside with guards I'd never met. My mom whispered their names in my ear so I could thank them by name as they congratulated me on my recent claiming of the Rubicon.

The drive wasn't a long one, but the scenery sure was different. There were no memorial statues, just houses and more houses. My mother saw the look on my face and clutched my hand. The gates to the castle finally came into view.

The building behind them towered high into the sky. It looked different than the one I used to call home. It was the same one I'd seen yesterday. The west wing was bigger than I expected.

"Welcome home," my mother said. I walked into the front door.

I was home. This was my home.

She took me to my chamber in the west wing. "I'll give you a minute. We'll be downstairs in the kitchen. Scream as loud as you can if you get lost."

"I remember this, sort of, Mom. Technically, we were here yesterday."

She laughed. "Okay." She closed the door.

My room was huge. A king-sized bed with a bright blue duvet dominated the room. Pillows were arranged on my bed. The curtains were blue, too.

Pictures of guys were hung on my wall. No Blake. I couldn't help but notice Blake was much better looking than all of them.

I walked over to the desk in front of a hulking window and just touched each object there.

A dragon letter opener was in the drawer. A snow globe on the desk. There was a box with letters next to my table. There were letters between Blake and me. I flipped through them. We'd grown up together, so why was there so much anger here? What happened?

My bracelet Blake had made for me from his skin was rested atop my dresser. I picked it up. It was the same one. He'd still made me one.

I set it down and checked out my closet. It was almost as big as my room. Rows and rows of shoes were stacked on the shelves. Dozens of handbags on another. And enough clothes for a small nation. I was a spoiled brat.

The thought made me chuckle ruefully. I'd never get to spoil Silho like this. Then it hit me. Silho was only going to exist in our memories, but she was never going to destroy our world. I would see her again after this life.

There was a cupboard inside my closet. Upon opening it, I discovered books filled with photographs. Of me and Blake, Lucian, Sammy, even Arianna. I touched one of Annie and me as little girls. I wept.

No darkness came, everyone was happy. There was even one of a monkey, sitting on a thirteen-, maybe fourteen-year-old Elena's shoulder. On the photo was written Mr. Pluggs. I had loved that monkey; that much was clear.

Blake was in every single photo. Most of them were at parties. Everyone had a different number and I couldn't find the fifteen- or sixteen-year pictures.

From the box of angry letters and the cryptic comments about "sorting our shit," I had a bad feeling something terrible had happened to us during that time.

I closed the door and searched for what to wear. I found a pair of jeans, a pair of flip-flops, and a t-shirt.

I was used to this. I went to my bathroom. It was pure white with a towel rack that held, like, fifteen towels. The floor was a soft pear wood color. The minute I took off my shoes, the spot I stood on was warm.

It made me laugh. I sure wasn't used to this. It was way too much. I stepped into the shower and got the fright of my life when it started speaking to me in a robotic voice.

"Welcome home, Elena," it said.

"Okay," I said, glad I hadn't fallen on my ass. "This is just plain freaky."

"Your normal shower?"

"Yeah, I guess." The shower started automatically. It carried on and on. How long was this stupid shower?

"Enough!" I yelled as it wanted to do another sort of wash and it stopped.

I got out real fast as if it might capture me if I didn't escape. I dried myself with a fluffy towel.

All my scars were gone. I hadn't gotten Blake's essence. He would have to go through all of that again, poor baby.

I looked at my wrist. The scar the Keeper had made was gone. I'd never gone into the sacred cavern. That just sucked. But my mom was alive and it didn't matter anymore.

I pulled on my clothes and went into the kitchen.

Everything looked so different from yesterday. The furniture was more modern. The spaces were open. Something told me my mother loved to rearrange everything. It was homier.

The carpets were still royal blue and not the cherry wood color my father had put in after the renovation. The Creepers had never come.

A great, heavy emotion overwhelmed me. It was a mixture of contentedness, happiness, and perfection. Everything was as it should be. I'd grown up in Paegeia. Though I didn't remember my life yet, I was sure I would remember it soon.

I found the lounge followed voices to the kitchen. A huge black Great Dane ran toward me. He jumped on me and I fell with his hulking figure pinning me down on the floor as I shrieked.

"Felix!" my mother yelled.

I giggled as the mutt licked my face. My father came to take him by the leash. "A Great Dane?" I asked.

"Oh you love everything that is abnormally large, Elena."

I laughed. It was good. I didn't cower away from big things. My mother gave me a hand and lifted me up. "Sorry about him. He's always so happy to see you."

"It's okay," I said. He barked. My dad took him outside and closed the side door.

I followed my mom into the kitchen. I gasped as Tanya looked up at me from her seat at the island. She was *alive*. "Hello, Elena."

The figure next to her made my eyes glisten. He looked up from the newspaper he was reading and smiled.

It was my dad. My other dad, that was. The man who raised me. Jako.

"Come here," he said and got up from his chair opening his arms.

I jumped into them and just started to sob.

"It's okay, bear. Welcome back, I guess."

I looked at him funny.

"Your mom told us that you finally merged with the other Elena."

I laughed. "She told you about me?"

"Of course she did." Tanya dangled her arm from my shoulders, burying her face in my neck. Jako put me down. This was so weird. Tanya still had her hand on my back.

"I should apologize, Elena."

"Mom," I started, my real mother, Catherine, gasped. "Sorry, I…"

"No need, sweetheart," my mom said.

I smiled at her, and looked at Tanya. "We had this conversation before and sure, back then I didn't want to hear about it but now, everything is different."

"That fast? You sure are different than the other Elena."

I squinted. "Well, what would you expect? I am an only child," I looked at my mom. "Right?"

"Only child," my mother confirmed.

"I think I rest my case."

They all laughed.

"All that matters is that you are alive." I hugged her again.

They all gasped again.

"I died?" Tanya wanted to know.

"Yeah. Many did."

She stroked my face and hugged me again. "We're all here, baby."

"Did I die, too?" My real dad, King Albert, wanted to know. I went over to him where he leaned his elbows on the table. I touched his arm.

"Nope, you I actually had the chance to meet. For the past eight years of my life, we actually became real close."

"That explains the lack of attention."

We laughed again.

"Aww, are we feeling left out? Now you know how it feels, Albert," my mother said.

I gave him a peck on the cheek. "I am a daddy's girl, aren't I?"

"Yep," he said. "So I'm certainly not used to this."

"Yeah, I figured that one out real fast."

"No, but seriously, Elena, you need to know what your mother did."

"Albert," my mother scolded again.

"I'm sure I will remember soon, Dad." He really liked joking around with my mom. "But to be honest, I really don't care."

"So unfair," he whined.

"That's my girl," my mother said.

That night I lay in bed. I spoke to Blake. I fretted about those pictures. Where were the fifteenth and sixteenth birthday ones? I knew we'd grown up together, my mother and Tanya had told me today. The stories.

Apparently, I had been a naughty little shit. Burned down my treehouse. Hid stuff in the maze and watched staff struggle to find their way out. I'd been a menace and at my side the entire time, filling my head with the hows was Blake.

"You don't remember anything?" I asked.

"Something tells me when you do, I will. It will come soon, Elena. Just be patient."

"Okay. Love you, babe."

"Love you more."

"I doubt that."

We said goodbye as a knock came from my door.

It was my mother with two cups of cocoa. She handed me one. She came to sit on my bed and we just stared at one another.

I accepted the cup and let it warm my fingers through the ceramic. "So tell me what you did, Mom."

She pulled her face. "You actually know. You hated me for what I did."

"Not possible." I lay it on thick.

She laughed. "Okay, you and Blake that night, it scared me Elena. The way you were so connected to one another. I mean you could hear his thoughts. It was so intense." She sounded worried.

"Okay, so what did you do?"

She sucked in her lips.

"I'm going to remember soon, and if you tell me now it won't be so bad."

"Okay," she sighed. "I never told you that you were Cooper and Merica but you knew about them. You knew what they could do and although you were sure it would not be you and Blake, I knew someday it would be.

"You always said that he was like your brother. He was always here. That boy could do no wrong in your eyes. I didn't know at this stage who was the influencer and who was the victim. It was an equal dash of naughty."

We both took a sip of cocoa.

"Over time he stopped being your brother figure."

I could see where she was going with this.

"Before your fourteenth birthday you got a crow."

"A crow?"

"Yes, I didn't want to get you a Cammy so you guys sent each other posts by crow."

So romantic.

"He told you about a girl he'd met."

I frowned. No, it couldn't be. "Was her name…Tabitha?"

"You know her?"

"Of course I do," I said. "He ended up with her in my timeline, too."

She squinted.

"Okay go on."

"He wanted to bring her to your fourteenth birthday party and that was when you didn't see him as a brother figure anymore."

"I see. Was I disappointed?"

"You were heartbroken," she said kindly. "But I gave you some motherly advice. We took the bull by the horns and wrote him back, saying that you had to meet her."

"We did?"

"Of course. I hated Blake so much then. He was a little shit for the way he'd treated you."

I laughed. She was on my side. Maybe a little too much so.

"The night went smoothly. You handled it well, and then Tabitha got drunk and you helped him put her into the SUV. He started to ask you about the cake."

My mother filled me in about my birthday cakes. Apparently by the end of the night, I misread the signs and kissed him. He didn't feel the same way.

I cringed.

"You never cried as much as you did that day," she said.

"It was when I fell for him," I said softly.

"Yes." She sighed. "You slept like a rock and that night I was woken up by the tapping of the crow on your window. He'd sent a crow. I read the letter. I know that I shouldn't have but I couldn't help it."

I took another sip. "What did it say?"

"It's in the box. I gave it to you when you found out."

"How did I find out?"

She told me about my sixteenth birthday and a boy named Lee and the whole birthday party incident and ensuing fiasco.

"What happened?"

"I caught you guys the night after your birthday in your treehouse."

My eyes rose. "Doing what?"

Her expression was disapproving. "Doing...*it*. You want me to explain further?"

I caught her meaning and felt heat rise in my cheeks. "How embarrassing."

"I blamed him. He was such a bad influence, Elena."

I laughed again. It wasn't like our lives. Nothing had worked out the same. It was amazing.

"It was the day you found out about the letters. You two worked out that your crows hadn't reached one another. He suspected that I had used meta-compulsion because he sometimes compelled animals for party tricks."

"You compelled the crow?"

"Just one, but whichever he came into contact with, well, it spread like a disease."

"I have persuasion, too, Mom. I know how it works. I just didn't think it worked on animals."

"Oh, it does, and really well."

She sighed. And finished catching me up on the letters. "I know it was wrong. I didn't think at first. Then after a while I was so deep in it, I didn't know how to get out of it. But Blake made me so angry."

I touched her hand. It didn't seem malicious, the way she described it at all.

"I felt so bad. Especially when the darkness got too much. He was so angry at you for not being there like you'd promised."

"What do you mean not being there?"

"Oh, you and Blake had this thing. He could really get dark at times, but when he was with you, it was like it just disappeared."

"Seriously?" I was in awe, then I remember how I had tamed the beast during that time I became a dragon myself. In this timeline it was just stronger.

She smiled. "Now you know why I was so worried, Elena."

"I totally get that. And it's quite funny if you think about it."

"Really, you are not mad?"

"Oh, I think the other Elena would still be livid with you. It's the Rubicon we are talking about here, Mom."

She laughed.

"But I'm here now, too, so I would just remind her how it was without you, and whisper some wisdom in her ear when we meet."

My mother laughed.

"So tell me everything please. Don't leave anything out. I've been wondering about this for such a long time. What was your life like without me?"

"You really want to know?"

"Oh it's not about want anymore, sweetheart. I need to know."

I laughed and sighed.

"Where do I even begin?"

"Easy. Start with what your life was like on the other side."

ABOUT THE AUTHOR

Adrienne Woods has been writing the past seven years.
Her debut novel, *Firebolt*, became an international bestselling
novel. Followed by *Thunderlight*, *Frostbite*, *Moonbreeze*, and
Starlight. *Moonbeam* is the first in the *Beam* Series, a spin-off
series from *The Dragonian Series*.
She has another series called *Dream Casters*.
She dabbles in many other genres under different pen names.
To find out more about Adrienne Woods, visit her at
www.authoradriennewoods.com